AWOKEN FOREST

ASHES OF THE INJAI - BOOK ONE

First printed in 2024.
Second Edition.

Map: Wesley Croft via inkarnate.com

ISBN - E-book: 978-1-7637631-0-4
ISBN - Paperback: 978-1-7637631-2-8

For my darling James
&
For a Novel Idea - The Word Appreciation Society - James S,
Wei Ying, Tina & Roxy

May this be worthy of seven waffles.

The Rahsu Lands

PROLOGUE

Eighty-one years ago ...

Glymm stepped away from the feast, her stomach brimming with wine and muk meat—a delicacy that merchants from the far-off Granite Hills had delivered. It had been a victorious day. Wherever she looked, the village pulsed with life; people were dancing and chatting loudly, and the town square heaved with a rowdy energy. Mirth and merriment spread across carefree faces as they ate and celebrated.

A joyful grin split Glymm's face as she saw her efforts bearing fruit, and her heart swelled with relief and optimism for the days ahead; the future was secured.

Today's Manna Rites had been the grandest in memory, and not only that: it had been announced that a new heir to the bloodline was blossoming in the womb of the Prime One's consort. Glymm cast a look up at the high banquet table where the Prime One roared with laughter, his cherubic face flushed with warmth. His wife and their two young children joined in the laughter, the children pointing at their father as wine dribbled down his tunic.

Glymm wandered away from the bursting rows of wooden tables, each brimming with the bounty of the local farms and rivers. A few townspeople raised their wooden cups to her as she passed—they would be toasting and blessing the Spirits well into the evening.

A large stone archway led to a path that wound down the grassy hill towards the boardwalk where the Flow's sluggish waters emptied into the Great Lake. The wide river shimmered like glass at this hour as a feeble mist filled the night's air.

As Glymm wandered down the path, a song erupted in the square behind her, sung by the villagers in between excessive gulps of wine and ale. The cacophonous singing that wafted down the banks was like sandpaper to her ears, yet people still

cheered, and the musicians carried on. It was a song Glymm knew all too well, having heard it a thousand times. It was a story about a girl born beneath an eclipse whose parents gifted her all the joys and beautiful wonders of the world, a song about the good things one finds on Arbonar, the world gifted to the people of the Rahsu. Though the villagers' voices grated at Glymm, the tune of the song itself danced merrily in her ears and professed how special and nurturing the world was despite being nestled in an ocean of darkness. Arbonar was a bastion. It protected and provided for its people. Fond memories of times long since passed washed over her, and thoughts of old friends and loved ones manifested as a solemn smile on Glymm's weary face.

Lamps and laughter both dimmed as she reached the ghostly docks. The river water's soft lapping against wooden pylons and the hulls of modest fishing barges tied beside the boardwalk replaced the song's raucous chorus.

Arbonar's two moons had long since sunk below the horizon, seemingly plunging into the depths of the Great Lake as if they were stones dropped from above. Without the light of the moons, the barges appeared as if they hovered in the darkness, the reflection of stars forming a myriad of shimmers and twinkles upon the surface. Ripples in the water danced with the wooden hulls and formed a song that reverberated in the swell and creaks of lumber against lumber.

Glymm gazed into the water, contented that the Prime bloodline was healthy again after what seemed like a lifetime. Her efforts would protect Arbonar for generations, although no one would know her role.

The mirror of sparkling stars entranced Glymm. She focused on one blazing sparkle that captured her attention—it shone brighter than the others and appeared to roll away from the barge hull, riding the ripples against the tide. The star's reflection continued to move across the Flow's surface. Glymm shot her head skyward and scanned the night for the source of the reflection, straining her eyes in the dark.

Glymm knew this wasn't a shooting star, which usually streaked across the sky in brief flashes before vanishing forever. She harboured a growing fear it may be something entirely different. Her eyes tracked the star, its trajectory unyielding as it dwindled toward the horizon. Silently, it disappeared over the waters of the Great Lake. A star was falling from the sky above her.

Glymm's heart tightened. She strained her eyes to look at the space where the celestial body had disappeared. With dread in her heart, Glymm blinked furiously. Had her eyes deceived her? How much wine had she downed? She turned and peered up the darkened grassy hill she had previously descended. The small town, with its steeply slanted thatched rooftops, sat high above the banks of the Flow. The village produced its warm, glowing light that radiated from the square where the feast ensued. A knot grew in her throat. Glymm knew no one in the village would comprehend the fear that circulated through her body—eternal apprehension that lingered like a blade above her head.

Glymm's mind wandered, anxiety seizing her. Such a small twinkle in the heavens, yet it gripped her every fibre. What could all this mean, and how was it possible after all this time? Though she knew the answers to these questions, hundreds more formed a tangled web in her mind.

Then, high above her, another faint light unmistakably crossed the night sky. Glymm was frozen in fear. Laughter erupted from the town behind her, pulling her attention back to the village. Those sweet fools, she told herself. The townspeople were carefree revellers, unaware of the dangers surrounding them nor what was at stake.

Glymm knew what she must do. She regretfully turned from the village; she'd find no answers there. Instead, she raced towards one of the fishing barges. She could have more answers in mere days if she left now. In her heart, Glymm knew her fears would prove correct, but she did not know to what extent.

7

It took seconds for her to jump onto the wooden dock and commandeer a barge. She unravelled the rope securing the barge to its port and, with the vessel's long guiding stick, she manoeuvred the vessel across the still waters.

The river splashed over the sides of the deck as she raced across, the glints of stars dispersing in its wake. As Glymm's muscular arms propelled the barge, a smooth, straight path carved into the dark waters before it crashed against the sands on the far bank. The force of the collision sent boxes of fishing tackle and empty barrels across the deck.

Glymm stumbled but adjusted to the inertia. She leapt off the barge onto the soft, wet sand. Wiping sweat from her brow, she glanced back at the town she was fleeing. Though the town's fires tried to illuminate the sky above, the thick smoke the fires gave off dampened the light and left the village in a dull glow. She imagined the dancing children and the feasting people lost in the stupor of the Manna Rites. In the daylight, would anyone wonder where she had gone? People she had known their whole lives would never see Glymm again. For a moment, she felt the pang of loss growing in her heart before she darted into the dense grain fields that lined the southern banks of the Flow.

Glymm sprinted into the night, her shoes filled with squelching wet sand. Yet she paid it no mind. She alone held the power to save the Rahsu from what was coming. Fleeing into the darkness, Glymm vanished into obscurity, never to be seen again.

1

LIRAN

Liran roused to thunderous ringing that shattered her deep sleep and tore from it with a spasmodic jolt. She shot from the chair she'd fallen asleep in, straining to understand the commotion that forced her to wake violently. Somewhere in Xylona one of the villagers was tolling the bells in the gardens.

Liran groaned, her annoyance barely audible over the cacophonous disruption. She strode across the room and slammed her window closed. The effort failed to block the ringing bells.

'Today of all days,' Liran lamented as her paint-stained fingers grasped for a goblet in her line of sight. She took a deep swig. Though it contained wine, as she had expected, it was mixed with paint from the maps she was restoring. She spat it out towards the wall before it had a chance to travel down her throat. She cursed, turning to the window to violently open it. The bells still resonated.

'Yes, we hear you!' she yelled, then slammed the window shut again. Liran sat and took a moment. *Why today?* she thought. Her mind battled with her body's reluctance to move and ready herself to attend the Manna Rites. She did not want to face the world today, let alone sing and chant with the rest of the town.

Liran surveyed her studio. It reflected a woman in perfect harmony with her art. Maps lay scattered across the floor, strewn by the breeze that had wafted through the open window the previous night. These maps constituted her latest undertaking—an endeavour that had become all-consuming, yet a lifeline to her sanity. She found solace in painting and immersing herself in her work. It was a refuge from the world.

Sinking further into the chair, Liran contemplated whether she could escape attending the Rites without facing

punishment. If the sick were excused, perhaps then the townspeople would sympathise with her absence. Wishful thinking. Her friends, she suspected, would encourage her to attend, claiming it was good for her to move forward and not dwell on the past.

Today, all over Arbonar, people would come together and pay homage to the creators. Then, once the eclipse passed and the garjee fruit was offered, the feasts and parties would begin. There were eight Manna Rites in a year, and she couldn't remember one in the last year she'd felt thankful to the Spirits. Liran held up and flipped over an empty wine jug and watched a solitary drop splash onto the stone. Maybe she'd thank the Spirits for the apris wine she planned to smuggle back to her studio tonight.

The clanging bells changed tempo from a melodious multi-tone dance to a single bell that resonated deep calls. Liran's eardrums vibrated. Three bells. Three hours to the eclipse and the moment the garjee fruit would be offered at the altar.

As Liran stood, her faculties returned, and she could now hear the telltale murmurs of people moving in the cloisters outside. Liran haphazardly gathered parchment strewn across the stones of her workroom and fastened them back on the table under the weight of a book.

The book had seen better days. Tears and smudges riddled the bindings and apris wine had been spilled over the title, *The Moving Stars*. Liran stared at the dark orange hues of apris on the leather cover. One year ago, she had written this book. One year ago, the book was beautiful, smelling of freshly pressed paper. This had been the last book she'd written before her world had changed. How could she face the hubbub of Xylona today?

The stone room was lined with old wooden bookcases and cabinets. They housed a collection of books and a wealth of paraphernalia and trinkets, some of them hidden away from eyes that may wish them destroyed. Liran opened one of the cupboards. Inside was a jumble of spare paints, fresh parchment, brushes, and charcoal pieces for sketching when she travelled. Liran pushed the contents aside as she searched the cabinet. Her eyes darted as she rifled, moving parchment and paints until she grabbed the prize she sought. It was a small black pouch made from the rugged leather of a granite muk, a hardy dromedary of the Granite Hills.

Liran untied the strings that fastened the satchel and walked back to the table, swiping away the book and parchment to create space on the desk. She tipped out the contents of the bag—three dark and sinewy roots. The black and furry bulbs rolled across the wood until they found a spot on the desk to settle.

She reached for a hefty book and strained under the weight of *Histories of the Primes, Protectors of Rahsu by G Jursaine*, slamming it down on the roots with a thud. Liran lifted and dropped the book three more times and then leapt onto the desk to sit on the tome. Using her weight to help crush the bulbs, she bounced. She snatched the goblet and tossed the remaining contents out the window before searching for water.

A fountain was outside in the cloister, but she knew it was likely surrounded by a gaggle of townspeople. She eyed a vase of flowers on the windowsill by the door and discarded the now wilted blooms to the floor, emptying the water into her cup.

Liran lifted the bulky book. The roots were now flattened into a black paste. She tossed the book aside. There was a time that she had cared about keeping her collection pristine, but now material things hardly mattered. Dropping the paste into the cup, Liran stirred the roots into the water with the end of a paintbrush. The roots leeched into the vortex, turning the dirty vase water a deep purple. Liran brought the goblet to her lips, the pungent aroma making her eyes weep; the stench was barely preferable to the scent of yar manure. With a hefty swig, she downed the foul concoction and sat back on the chair, allowing the liquids to go to her stomach. Soon, she would be in a tranquil state.

❁

****

The bells tolled again. Another scurry of villagers outside Liran's doors pounded like a thunderstorm. Her eyelids weighed heavy, as if magnets kept them shut. They opened with effort. A blur of colours formed into recognisable shapes, but her focus had not returned. Her neck was weak, and she struggled to hold up her head. It lolled, resting against the back of the chair.

Liran's eyes were transfixed by the textured cracks and brush marks on the ceiling. Her brush marks. The fresco above her had been her first task to cover the barren stone when she was appointed Xylonan Maven. She had quickly got to work and had painted the ceiling with one of her favourite sketches she had found in an old warehouse on a pier in Hydoran. It was a simple painting of a small girl standing in a meadow of white flowers. In the distance, sheer waterfall-lined cliffs sprayed mist into the air. Nowhere on Arbonar was there a place like this. The girl held a flower, and a sad smile adorned her face. Now, the girl watched over Liran in her self-imposed haven.

A thumping sound stirred her again. Muffled sounds accompanied another barrage of pounding. In her dazed state, she pieced together what was happening.

'Maven are you in there?' a shrill voice shouted, accompanied by another banging of fists on wood.

Liran crossed the room with parchment sticking to the cold sweat on the bottom of her bare feet. Lifting the door's latch, she paused. She inhaled deeply to oxygenate her body, hoping the zirge roots would wear off. She did not need judgment today.

'What could anyone possibly need today?' Liran said, cracking open the door. Though she sounded sober, her head pounded from the roots in her system. Sunlight filtered into the studio. Liran's eyes watered and blurred.

'A thousand apologies, Maven. The Prime One sent me. She requests you early.' She recognised the rushed voice that called her by her title. It was her assistant Euyan, a sageling of the archives. *Assistant* was not the best word for him; her *appointed sycophantic shadow* was a better description.

'This early?' Liran squinted at the blur of the figure before her. 'The tolls have marked three hours before the Rites. A little early to begin gathering at the altar, right?' Her eyes focused on Euyan's dark, glistening skin and his sweat-soaked underarms. The sunlight dimmed behind a wisp of cloud, giving her vision a reprieve. 'Did you run here, Euyan, or do I need to get you out of the archives more?' Liran said, adding a smile to appear less callous.

'I ran with haste. The Prime One said to fetch the Maven. It is of the utmost importance—'

'Euyan,' Liran cut in, rolling her eyes, 'Claudya thinks a crease in a tablecloth is of utmost importance. I don't believe fetching me this early before the Rites was that important. I have not even started the Prime One's address.' Liran remembered she had jotted down some key points for the Prime One's Manna Rites speech. Although Liran did this every cycle, Claudya would often disregard her passages and ad-lib, reading the mood of the masses gathered at the altar.

Euyan looked a little taken aback by Liran's cavalier attitude. His eyes darted around him, hoping no one in the street had overheard their conversation. 'Maven, please! Let's take this inside. And then can we depart for the Prime House?' Euyan said in a tone and volume meant only for the two of them.

Liran resisted the urge to roll her eyes again. She moved out of the way, gesturing for Euyan to follow her into the studio.

Euyan did not try to hide the fact that he scanned the room. He tentatively paused at the strewn papers and paint stains on the stones and peered at the liquid that was spattered on the wall near the desk as it trickled to the stone floor to form rivers in the grout.

Liran followed Euyan's curious gaze across the squalor and laughed. 'Apris wine and paint did not agree with my palate', Liran said.

Euyan's face was expressionless; he scrutinised her sincerely. 'Maven, are you alright? You look under the weather.'

Liran stood up straight and smoothed out a crease in her dress. She felt her assistant's judgemental eyes on her. The zirge coursed through her system, and her head throbbed from dehydration. Liran walked over to a copper bowl and picked it up to observe her face in the reflection.

A forty-two-year-old woman wearing a paint- and wine-stained cloak stared back at her through dark and heavy brown eyes. Her usually straight, shoulder-length brown hair was knotted and caked in paint. *Amusing*, she pondered.

'Would you allow me to freshen myself up before we rush off? Perhaps you could do me a favour and fetch water from the fountains,' Liran said.

Euyan said nothing, grabbing a bowl on the bench by the side door before heading outside. Liran ducked into an adjoining room where she kept a few personal items for evenings at the studio, which was most nights. She threw on an old shirt—one she found on the back of the door—and found a washcloth and a hairbrush. What could the Prime One need so early?

Euyan knocked on the door, and Liran cracked it open. She grabbed the bowl of water. 'Thanks. I won't be long,' she said, closing the door.

Liran soaked the cloth and washed her face, feeling an instant surge of relief.

'Did Claudya say what the matter of utmost importance was?' she asked.

❧

'The Prime One said it had to do with the Prime Scion,' Euyan's muffled reply came from the other side of the door, ignoring Liran's use of the Prime One's first name.

'Anything else about Ayon?'

Euyan hesitated, then said, 'When the Prime One asked for you, Reeva was agitated.'

'Reeva is back in Xylona? I thought she was travelling through the Granite Hills,' Liran said.

Euyan said nothing. She knew Reeva, the Scion's appointed guardian, was constantly agitated. Whether it was townspeople late to the Manna Rites or that Ayon was not in any rush to begin his tour of the Rahsu lands as Prime in waiting, Reeva approached everything with scorn. Liran ran the wet cloth through her hair, removing the paint before working out the knots.

'Reeva is too hard on the poor boy,' Liran said.

'She is concerned the Manna Rites will be at risk if the Scion does not take his position seriously,' Euyan said.

'Concern is one thing,' Liran replied, 'I've been in meetings about the boy before; Reeva's position as guardian should be reconsidered. The pressure put on him will only make him feel anxious and alone. He will be a nervous wreck when he eventually does tour the Rahsu. To which there is no rush. Despite what Reeva and Thessus say.'

She liked Ayon; he was an intelligent boy and had shown a keen interest in art techniques when she'd painted the altar's fresco. But maps were his favourite. He'd stare at them for hours and ask what the places were like.

'He is twenty years old next manna cycle, Maven. Time is running out. He has shown no interest in siring the next line of Primes.' Euyan allowed a moment of rebuttal, but Liran held her tongue. 'Maven, he is the only Scion, the only one who can perform the Rites when the current Prime One passes. We have not faced a crisis like this since the times of the Granite Hills dynasty two hundred years ago.'

Liran was impressed with Euyan's knowledge of the Prime lines but furrowed her brow. His attitude was soaked with a piousness she detested.

'It has happened before, Euyan; the blood is always found, and the lines continue. The world is not going to end. Have you touched the fruit at all, Euyan?'

'Absolutely not! It is forbidden!' Euyan exclaimed.

'Imagine that: Prime Euyan. Spirits protect us,' she muttered.

'Pardon, Maven?'

'Nothing. But catch my meaning? You could have the blood. You could be the next Prime without knowing it. So, stop fretting. If the Spirits of Arbonar deem it necessary, the blood will resurface. If not in Xylona, then in another village.'

Liran opened the door that led back to the studio. Euyan nodded. She interpreted it as approval that she was adequately dressed for the public's gaze.

They had been at odds before about the bloodline

Liran scanned her studio. Euyan had been tidying the space as she freshened up. Her paints had been organised, and the parchment pieces that littered the floor were back on the desk and weighed down by the empty vase.

Liran sighed and walked over to Euyan, placing a hand on his shoulder. She knew Euyan's concerns were valid and were discussed and debated among many in the town. To lose the bloodline put Xylona's grip on power in jeopardy. But more than that, the Manna Rites were at risk, and the Spirits of the planet would rain down untold horrors upon them. Appeasing the Spirits meant continued prosperity. Xylona was on edge.

'I apologise, Euyan. I am not myself today. Honestly, if I had a choice, this would be a Manna Rites I would rather forget.' Liran's words drifted off as she removed her hands from Euyan's shoulders and walked over to the window. She felt his gaze on her.

'It has been one year today, Euyan.' Her voice croaked.

'Maven,' Euyan's voice was soft. 'I forget myself—I had not realised the significance of today.' It was now Euyan who offered a hand for her shoulder.

'It is alright, and life goes on, nay?' Liran's voice broke, but her face was resolute. Today would be hard. To face the eyes of Xylona would be like one thousand cuts; eyes unseeing that behind her stoic face was a voice screaming out for the loss of the only child she would ever know.

2

OLBI

Olbi was being watched. An eerie tingle ran across his skin. It was not the first time he felt he was being followed within these woods. It was as if the forest knew him as an intruder and had not granted him consent to enter. His gaze swept across the trees; they concealed mysteries within their broad trunks. He wasn't supposed to be here. Perhaps this time, he had gone too far.

Despite the nagging feeling of eyes on his back, Olbi returned his concentration to the stream below his perch on a large boulder. When he looked down, dark beady eyes stared back at him from beneath the water. It took but a split second before his airborne spear impaled the animal's glistening scales. The spear pierced the fish's gills as it fed in the shallow river grasses.

Olbi only needed one more prized river jack before heading back into Xylona. The townspeople respected his commitment to finding the best fish, but they would be swift to scorn him if anyone knew he was in the sacred garjee.

This far-flung river was teeming with his quarry, but he had been foolhardy today and missed multiple opportunities to harpoon the brown and gold-spotted fish. Olbi was often careless when his mind wandered. Focusing on anything today was going to be difficult. The town would gather in the square tonight, and hungry mouths would gape at him once he emerged from the garjee forests.

Olbi launched himself off the lichen-splattered granite boulder he was balancing upon, feeling the rush of being airborne before landing barefooted onto the soft grass below. The grass grew lush here despite the darkness of the forest.

He stepped to the stream's edge, dipping his toes into the chilled water before wading deeper, feeling them sink into the soft, fine sand beneath. In the rippling water he saw shimmers of his face; his bronze-tinted eyes peaked from beneath hair the colour of the rusted brown tree trunks behind him. Olbi cursed the searing sun earlier that day; his cheeks were blasted crimson, forever blemished and scabbed from a life among the elements.

This stream was the lifeblood of Xylona—it ran through the forest like a serpent. Its bends and pools were the best spots for a fisherman to secure a meal. He had found this spot a few years ago when he had been curious about finding the river's source.

Olbi was young compared to the other fishermen in Xylona, but he had been building his skills for more than ten of his nineteen years. Others sat exclusively on the stream's banks as it flowed into Xylona, but Olbi knew the fish near the town were small and anxious about the open water. The game here was less cunning.

He waded through the shallows, the hair on his legs raising from the coolness of the water. The fish lay motionless, pinned by his spear and anchored in the soft sands.

'I got you good!' Olbi said, triumphantly yanking his spear from the sand. He gazed into the eyes of the pinned prize. His victory vanished. The eyes that had scanned the river moments ago stared back motionless and vacant. Pangs of regret lodged in his throat as he slipped the day's last catch off the spearhead and placed it into his sturdy netted bag to join seven other river jacks.

Shivers prickled the hair on his neck, the forest felt charged, heavy and foreboding. He cast his eyes on the trees, listening for movement and searching for the cause of his unease. Nothing revealed itself. He heard only birdsong.

The sack threatened to snap its threading, bulging and tightening under the weight of his catch. It was the last thing he needed—to stumble now and have hours of effort lost to the currents. He placed the bag on the bank and collected his tattered shoes and leather pouch from the base of the granite boulder he had used as his lookout. Sand scraped his skin as he coerced his wet feet into the shoes.

Only a few nuts and a handful of dried berries were in his leather pouch as Olbi had overlooked breakfast this morning when he sneaked out of the Stonehall—he had wanted to avoid waking the other patrons of the inn. Every room of the Stonehall, Xylona's inn, had been filled with farmers, travellers and traders who had swarmed into Xylona for the Manna Rites. Normally, he wouldn't bother fussing over the noise he made in the kitchens preparing breakfast, but today of all days, he knew it best not to ruffle any feathers. He also hated confrontation... He nibbled on a few nuts as the babbling stream danced through the forest.

His gaze wandered upward, seeking glimpses of the sun's rays. Amidst the twisting branches above, infrequent openings in the canopy allowed slender sunlight shafts to penetrate. However, the deeper one ventured into the forest, the denser the garjee trees grew, allowing minimal illumination. Their oval leaves, as large as wagon wheels at the loftiest branches, formed a dense barrier. Each garjee tree stood as a sentry of the forest, with formidable trunks and expansive limbs asserting dominance. This was unquestionably their realm. The garjee forest exuded an eerie ambience, making the passage of time feel inconsequential.

It was time to leave this sanctuary, this stream, and head back to Xylona. Olbi grimaced under the weight of his bag. Sweat built up on his forehead, which caused his dirtied brown hair to mat against his skin. No tracks carved their way through the trees, so Olbi followed the stream along the wide valley. People did not venture into the forest depths.

The forests induced reverence and apprehension into the Rahsu. The garjee were prominent in rituals as their fruits were offered to the Spirits in exchange for protection and, because of this, no garjee was ever used to construct homes or as fuel for fires and furnaces. The trees were sacred and protected.

Olbi stepped through grasses and over large boulders of granite. His feet twisted, and he found his footing hard as he climbed his way out of the valley and out of the trees. He envied the animals darting with ease through the dimly lit forests—a family of grey rabbits in a clearing nibbled at the ground, unaware of his approach. He barely had time to wonder if he could spear one at such a distance before the echoing squawks of two golden cockatoos frightened the rabbits—their tails bobbing through the grasses—back to their burrows. Olbi reluctantly moved up the granite ridge to the valley's top.

The ridgeline soon gave way to rolling hills where garjee grew sporadically, allowing more sunlight to kiss the verdant carpet of undergrowth. Birds twittered in trees, and subtle winds shimmered the grass. Olbi bathed in the comforts here, knowing he was getting nearer to Xylona.

He saw the green swirling sphere dominating the sky. The orb was one of the celestial bodies that would form the eclipse later that afternoon, plunging Arbonar into premature night. It was another world between the sun and their home—that's what he had been taught. The sun had not travelled as high as he thought. He would not be late, unlike last time.

'Plenty of time to spare. I don't know what I was worried about,' he mused out loud, frightening a small sparrow in a shrub.

He found a mossy granite boulder to rest upon for the sake of his shoulder. The thick rope of his bag strap dug into his skin and pressed hard against his shoulder blade. He rubbed the sore muscles liberated from beneath the strap. The pain would be rewarded, these fish would be genuinely welcomed at the feast tonight.

Others would be bringing food to the dinner, too: bakers would bring various breads and cakes; farmers would harvest fruits from orchards around Xylona; and traders would bring fare not grown or bred around this part of the country.

21

The garjee fruits, on the other hand, were never for eating. The tough stone surface of the yellow skin offered no sustenance and would induce stomach cramps if consumed. The fruit was strictly for the Manna Rites ceremony as the offering for their rituals. Town Monitors harvested them in the lead-up to each Manna Rites. They ensured the rites ran smoothly and performed other duties that supported the town between each cycle. Olbi hoped to be a Monitor one day— they were highly regarded and respected in Xylona, but the positions were challenging to obtain. He gazed up into the canopy—the treetops were speckled with growing fruits, each pulsating with a dull light like a heartbeat. A chest of these fruits would await today's ritual in the Prime House.

Olbi slipped off his shoes and found a flat boulder to sit upon and catch his breath. He emptied his shoes of the sand filling them, dug his toes into the dirt and wiggled them around, feeling the cool soil. After the lengthy walk up the ridge, it felt rejuvenating, like the soil was massaging his aches. Slivers of sunlight warmed his face as he shut his eyes; he enjoyed moments of respite, letting the breeze caress and flutter across his face.

Lost in thought, Olbi was caught in a gust of wind. With it, the sweet aroma of wildflowers growing nearby wafted into his nose. A few moments later, he opened his eyes to the sun shining directly into his pupils, dazzling him. With it came a flash of blue blinding light.

Through the afterimages left in his vision, Olbi spied someone, or something, lurking beneath a garjee tree around where he had just passed. He rubbed his eyes and blocked out the sun with his hand. There was no one by the tree.

The forests were known to cloud the mind. The aura of confinement within the gloom was suffocating. Olbi had before heard complaints from Monitors returning from the garjee harvests of headaches and profuse vomiting. In extreme cases, the Monitors had long-term spells of sickness. There were other forests on Arbonar, but only garjee forests seemingly induced visceral reactions. Because of these anecdotes, the garjee forests were avoided and remained a place the Rahsu never willingly ventured.

Olbi thought it odd that a revered fruit would grow from a feared tree. A tree that caused pain and yet bore a treasure that the Spirits demanded of the Rahsu. What was it about these inedible fruits that the Spirits yearned for? The scriptures said the fruit proved the resilience and faith of the Rahsu.

Despite the odd apparition, Olbi cherished his time beneath this shady umbrella of trees; it was somewhere he was assured to be alone, away from the townspeople he felt uncomfortable around.

Again, he saw a blue murk in the corner of his eye. He spun and saw nothing. Was he succumbing to the sickness? It wasn't the first time Olbi thought he had seen something in these forests. However, they were occurring more frequently in the last half dozen manna cycles. The energy Olbi felt in the forests built like an approaching storm before the first thunder. Lately, many things unfamiliar to Xylonans had been happening.

Just yesterday, a trading party from Hydoran—a fishing village—had arrived in town ahead of the Rites. Unlike Xylonans, the people of the Great Lake shared similar interests to Olbi. He would seek out their wares as they crafted the finest fishing supplies.

Olbi had bought a new pot for trapping the ebony crustaceans that lurked in muddy patches of the stream. The trader was an older woman with wiry grey hair and skin stretched like cured leather. She often shared stories about life in Hydoran, and yesterday, she spoke of losing her barge oar to a rogue tide in the middle of the lake. She laughed off how foolish she felt and how she had spent a long night alone on the barge assembling a new paddle out of a wooden box on her deck. She'd described flashes she had seen in the twilight and counted more dancing stars than anyone had ever witnessed.

'Twenty-three dancing stars in one night, can you believe it?' she'd said, passing him a roll of fishing twine. It was dawn by the time she'd paddled to shore with her makeshift oar. No one in town believed she had seen so many dancing stars.

Olbi liked the woman and her stories, so he had generously given her the meatiest rabbit he had in return for the items she'd traded. *Twenty-three* dancing stars. It was challenging to see two or three, but never more.

The trees that were spread around Xylona obstructed most of the sky. Only at the Manna Altar or the town square would people be able to see the splendour of the stars.

'Ok, my fishy friends, let's get you prepared for the feast!' Olbi said, picking up the bag of fish and slinging it over the opposite shoulder to the one that hurt. The crest of a hill allowed glimpses of grain fields and farmland on the horizon. Olbi turned, examining the gully tumbling towards the river.

Blue light flared in his vision.

Olbi froze, his heart jumping. A floating face materialised within the shadows of two twisting garjee he had passed. The contours of the apparition were blurred and gleamed vividly. Its piercing white eyes locked onto Olbi. He stared back, transfixed, grasping his spear tightly. He juggled whether to run or yell at it. He was paralysed, his feet shackled with indecision. The spectral face watched intently, making no sound or intent known. Olbi held his breath until the face withdrew into the shadows. It vanished into the depths of the tangled branches. Staring at the spot, he struggled to comprehend what he had witnessed. One certainty gnawed at him: the face did not belong to any animal of the forests.

3

OLBI

The bells tolled three times, their resonating clangs reaching Olbi as he emerged from the forest's final clutches. Before him stood Xylona's Great Mill, with its towering alabaster stone that overlooked neatly aligned rows of waist-high grain. Beyond that, Xylona itself peeked through the tangles of branches, its network of squares and gardens visible even at this distance.

Following hours in the dim forests, Olbi found the sun's warmth was welcoming and nurturing to his skin. However, he knew this warmth would not last. He looked up at the two soft white spheres of Arbonar's two moons, Orgus and Shoora and the mighty green world in the sky, Oaga, all three drifting closer to the sun. Three hours remained until the warmth of the day would dwindle.

As he reached the end of the field, it transitioned into a green sea of masticated and knotted grasses. The remaining blades danced in the breeze among piles of scat and ravenous insects, while dandelion spores swirled above. The pasture was a detour in his journey, one he always took. Olbi scanned the meadow and noticed the herd of yar rising over a hill in the distance, their lumbering figures silhouetted against the blue sky beyond. The thud of hooves and the clamorous clangs of a bell that approached ever faster pushed him to smile. One of the yar had separated from the herd and was making its way towards him as he clambered over a dilapidated wooden fence. The approaching yar was youthful and sprung into an uncoordinated gallop when it locked eyes with him. The yar calf collided with Olbi, briefly forcing the air from his lungs. The calf was getting bigger daily and did not yet have the grace to compensate for its growing size.

'Careful, boy! You almost knocked me clean over.'

He laughed as the yar bounced up and down on its four legs. Its scruffy face nuzzled at Olbi's side, using him as a scratching post. Olbi squirmed as it tickled him and quickly dug out his small leather pouch to free the berries he hadn't eaten. The yar licked at his hands with zealousness and let out a delighted snuff. Once done with the berries, he nudged Olbi's hand: the yar wanted something else.

'I knew you'd want some scratches today, Boji,' Olbi said as he reached behind the animal's ears. Olbi scratched vigorously, feeling the thick tufts of yar wool swallow his fingers like quicksand.

Boji was alone, set apart from the rest of the herd as he often was, which reminded Olbi of himself—never feeling comfortable in the pack. Olbi sat in the grass as Boji rested his head on Olbi's knee, looking up at him with large, soulful eyes that probed for more affection.

Olbi scratched absentmindedly as he thought about the apparition in the forest. Had it been his imagination? No, he saw something. That face amongst the thick trunks of the garjee had been watching him, and whatever it was, it had been watching him every time he ventured into the trees. A shiver ran up his spine. Boji lifted his head and locked eyes with him as his muscles tensed. Behind where Olbi sat, the crunch of approaching footsteps unnerved him.

'What in the world are *you* doing here at this hour?' a voice boomed.

Olbi's chest jolted as Boji, eyes wide, hastily rose from his lap and darted towards the safety of an apris tree. Olbi watched as he jumped over the tree's roots, escaping the unknown voice.

Olbi spun, ready to scold whoever had terrified Boji, but his voice withdrew when he saw who had spoken. It was the Prime Scion—Ayon, the son of the Prime One. The young heir stood above him, his slender figure blocking the sun. Olbi smelt the sweet fragrance of the Scion's perfumes wafting over the scent of yar manure. The Scion held two hefty jugs, one in each of his hands, his fingers firmly grasping the handles. The jugs must have been heavy, as Olbi could see Ayon's muscles straining beneath his olive skin.

'Why did you do that? You scared Boji, you moron!' Olbi spoke with much more bravado and bitterness to the heir of the Manna Altar than he meant to. He swallowed, then said, 'I am sorry, my Scion. Please forgive my words.' He waited for Ayon to reprimand him, as was his right.

Ayon instead beamed and cast a glance towards Boji. The yar appeared to have forgotten the ordeal and made his way to Olbi's belongings, which had been left on the grass. Boji's sniffs located the remainder of the berries in the pouch.

'Did I scare your best friend, or did I scare you?' Ayon said, putting the jugs down and reaching out a hand to Olbi—a small gesture of peace.

Olbi gazed at Ayon's hand. He hadn't been alone with the Scion in over four years and his heart thudded. Being the only heir to the Manna Altar, Ayon would be his leader one day. He took Ayon's soft, smooth hands hesitantly—hands that did not know manual labour, hands of those born to rule. They were unlike his: hard and calloused by a life of outside endeavours.

'Not used to hard labour, I see. Your hands look like they need a few days on the farm, Scion.' Olbi paused briefly, looking around for Ayon's guardian who shadowed him everywhere. Ayon appeared to be alone. 'Why are you here? Shouldn't you be getting ready for the rituals?' Olbi asked.

This would be the last place someone integral to the Manna Rites would be before the ceremony. Ayon looked down and gestured to the jugs placed at his feet. Olbi cocked his eyebrow.

'You planned on making cheese from yar milk and chose today to learn how?' Olbi quipped.

'Your humour astounds; is that why friends and admirers surround you?' Ayon was mocking him.

Olbi wondered if, behind the Prime House walls, Ayon had heard rumours about him preferring to be alone. But then why would the Scion know who he was? Surely, he didn't register as a person of interest within the sanctum of Primes.

'Well?' Olbi pressed before Ayon could get another dig in.

Ayon shooed a bug from his forehead—tussling his fringe—before responding. 'According to my grandfather, the yar milk in the Prime House is curdled. He sent me to retrieve more. He just wanted me out of the house so he could sneak to the kitchens to check what the hands were baking.' Ayon smiled with only one corner of his mouth.

Olbi's heart pounded as memories of the Prime House kitchens flooded his mind.

****

When times were tough, sneaking into the Prime House was a rite of passage for the youth in Xylona. Despite being a strict Prime One, Claudya Lyfera was, at heart, a kind woman who often paid no heed to thieving youths who hadn't seen a meal in a few days. Four years ago, Olbi had exhausted the food in his father's small residence. It was more of a storage room for his father's wares.

His father, who rarely stayed in Xylona, had been on a trading mission with the far-flung villages in the north, and his return was long overdue. Olbi had been fishing that day but had returned with an empty bag and an even emptier stomach. It had also been his fifteenth birthday, so he'd thought if he did get caught pillaging the Prime House kitchens, perhaps pity would be taken on him.

On that particular run, he had inadvertently caught Ayon there. Olbi had only seen the Prime Scion during the Manna Rites, but this had been the first time he had met the future leader. Xylona was not a big town, but Ayon did not wander the streets; instead, he would stick to the cloisters and gardens lining the Prime House.

Olbi had waited until nightfall, when the last candles had been snuffed, before entering the old cellar door. The cellar, with its cobwebbed cornices and broken furniture, had never been guarded, and even the passageway that led from the cellar to the kitchens had been unlit and effortless to sneak through.

When Olbi had reached the kitchen, locating a few old pieces of bread and hard cheese in a basket had not taken long. The basket had been placed on a bench by the entrance to the cellar. In hindsight, Olbi realised the food was left intentionally for people snooping for a meal. Olbi had sidled up to the basket to swipe its contents when he had heard someone clearing their throat from the shadows. Instinctively frozen to the spot, he had been mortified.

The figure had moved out of the darkness, and Ayon's gaze had regarded Olbi with mild curiosity. Ayon did not wear a shirt that night, allowing Olbi to spy the garjee necklace against the Scion's taut chest.

His eyes had darted from Ayon to the cellar passageway. How far would he have been able to flee before Ayon raised the alarm?

Instead, the Scion had been kind, much like his mother, the Prime One. Ayon had seemed interested in Olbi, asking him about his life and why he kept visiting. Olbi had guessed he and the Scion were similar in age, yet Ayon's sheltered life meant they would have never run in the same circles.

Olbi had explained that his father was a trader and had been gone for almost ten days and that no food was left in their house. They had talked in shallow voices that night, getting to know one another despite how awkward Olbi had felt talking with a Prime. When Olbi had said it was his birthday, the young heir had darted off, leaving Olbi to fidget with his fingernails.

Returning with a slice of honey cake from the cool chambers, Ayon's generosity had unsettled Olbi who had initially protested. Ayon, however, had silenced him with a gentle touch, a sensation Olbi had never experienced before.

Ayon had broken off a piece of the cake and had encouraged Olbi to open his mouth. The taste was an exquisite sweetness Olbi had never known, and his joy had shone through in a beaming smile. Laughter had filled the room as they shared the cake, though their merriment had been interrupted by approaching footsteps.

Olbi had bolted for the cellar passageway. He had turned just in time to see Ayon staring at him, a cheeky smirk adorning his face. With a wink, the Scion had darted down another hall. As Olbi had raced into the night, his heart fluttered, adrenaline coursing through his veins.

****

Memories of that night swam in Olbi's head. Ayon had been a boy then, but now a man stood by Olbi in the field. Though he had grown a foot taller, his slender physique remained. His dark brown hair, like his mother's, matched his eyes. Olbi felt his chest tightening and face warming as Ayon smirked at him.

'What job do you have for today? I can't imagine it involves talking to yar in the field?' Ayon said. Boji had wandered back towards them as if sensing the cause for alarm had passed. Olbi knelt and held out his hand for Boji. The yar affectionately nudged him.

'I always bring fish for the feast.' Olbi continued to stroke the yar's thick coat. Boji was chewing at a tuft of grass, decapitating the small yellow flowers nestled amongst the blades. 'The streams in the forest have the meatiest fish, and few people delve there.'

'That's because you aren't allowed—it is forbidden.'

'No, it's not advised. There is a difference. Besides, I doubt anyone will mind; I speared eight river jacks today.'

Olbi smirked, proud of his achievement. Ayon cast his eyes on the netted bag, weighing Olbi's claims.

'How can you stand hunting in the garjee forests? The harvesters say they cannot be among the trees for more than a

30

few minutes without succumbing to headaches; no doubt you are in there for much longer than that,' Ayon inquired. Garjee trees were well known to induce headaches, and in some rare cases, people returned with bloody noses and feverish symptoms. Therefore, the harvesters of the fruits rotated every cycle to mitigate the risks of sickness.

'I don't suffer sickness or headaches when I'm among the trees,' Olbi said, 'but sometimes I see—' Olbi paused. Perhaps he shouldn't suggest that he had seen things. The Primes were stubborn in the face of criticism and rumours surrounding sickness because of exposure to the forests, and their reverence for the fruits was apparent during the Manna Rites. The fruit protected the Rahsu. True believers of the Primes believed the sickness was inflicted upon those with weak constitutions and was a reminder that the Primes descended from the Spirits.

'Sometimes you see what?' Ayon asked, fussing with one of his buttons.

Should I share this with someone? Olbi thought. Perhaps he wasn't the only one who had seen odd things, maybe the harvesters had seen something too.

'Sometimes I think I see colours, flashes of blue lights maybe.'

Ayon narrowed his eyes slightly. 'Weird,' the scion replied.

The sound of bells on the winds pierced the silence. 'Damnation!' Olbi exclaimed, running to retrieve his bag. 'Two hours before the Rites start. I'm running late.'

Ayon moved with haste as he hustled to pick up the jugs. 'Where are you heading?' he asked Olbi as milk sloshed and dribbled down the sides of the jugs.

'Stonehall kitchens to prepare the fish. I must leave now; it will take me twenty minutes to hike there,' Olbi said. Alvar would reprimand him for crowding the kitchens for sure this time.

'The Prime House is closer; you can use the kitchens there. I am sure the hands won't mind. Unless you slip fish scales in their cakes.'

Ayon's offer was enticing and, not wanting to disappoint Alvar by stinking up the Stonehall kitchens with fish, Olbi nodded in agreement. Boji nudged at his leg as he swung the heavy bag of fish onto his shoulders.

'Don't worry, boy. I will be back tomorrow; we can spend the whole day together. I will even bring you the leftovers from the feast.' Olbi gave the young yar one last pat on his nose. Boji licked his fingers.

'Do you think he understands you?' Ayon asked. Olbi investigated Boji's eyes. Boji always understood him more than anyone else he knew.

****

They dashed through fields with hands full of yar milk and fish. Vaulting over posts and stone fences, they finally arrived at the ancient city walls, which had become overtaken by a tangle of weeds, moss and tree saplings that infiltrated crevasses and pried stones apart while establishing their roots. It wouldn't be long before the walls disappeared entirely from memory under the cloak of an emerging forest.

Townspeople near the edge of town were hurrying about excitedly, each going about tasks vital for the Manna Rites. Some gathered food and jugs like Olbi and Ayon, while others fretted over rolling barrels to a cart.

Olbi walked by parents who ensured their children wore their finest garments. One mother was chasing a tiny boy with little shoes in her hand. The boy laughed and climbed a tree barefoot, his mother pleading with him to come down.

'This way,' Ayon said, ducking quickly between the traders' hall and the hitching yard that was packed with yars belonging to merchants and travellers. Ayon led the way through a narrow back street lined with doors leading to traders' homes. Olbi strained under the weight of his bag and fell behind.

'I can't keep this pace, Prime Scion—' Olbi started to pant between breaths.

'Do not call me that,' Ayon snapped. Olbi felt his gut twist. Ayon glimpsed back at him; his eyes boring into Olbi.

'That is your title, is it not?'

'Yes, however, it is not my name and—' Ayon paused. Olbi stood motionless. The last thing he wanted was an argument with his future leader.

Ayon tilted his head downwards and sighed. He glanced back at Olbi through his fringe. The annoyance in his eyes had vanished. 'I'm sorry I snapped. That was inconsiderate,' Ayon said, maintaining eye contact with Olbi.

Despite feeling flustered and surprised by Ayon's sudden mood swing, Olbi nodded.

'Just around this corner, we can pass through the Western Cloister,' Ayon called, beckoning Olbi along. The two travelled in silence. Ayon had slowed his pace considerably—whether to allow Olbi to keep pace or because something was upsetting him, Olbi didn't know.

Olbi noticed the lingering stares of townspeople running last-minute errands. Ayon paid them no mind; however, Olbi felt their gazes following his every move. A few older citizens glanced and gabbed amongst themselves. Olbi overheard their chatter. They were concerned about the Prime Scion strolling the streets escorted by a dishevelled fisherman. Olbi looked down at his clothes. He was filthy, sweat running down his forehead. It was warranted gossip. Olbi shuffled quickly, avoiding their gazes and feeling the flush of shame wash over him. He never felt this uncomfortable in the forests.

In the Western Cloister gardens, kitchen hands picked herbs for the feast, raising their heads at the flustered men darting by. Some gave polite nods to Ayon as he hurried along. Olbi looked ahead to see the rising white stone of the Prime

House's western wall, which stood smooth and weatherworn under the shade of graceful trees.

Slim windows dotted the three-story building, filtering natural light into the house. Ayon lived in this wing of the house with his family. He took the lead through the gardens. Reaching the far side, they descended stone steps to wooden doors that appeared diminutive against the sheer stone facade. Ayon turned, pressed his back to the door, and pushed.

The smell of fresh bread drifted into Olbi's nostrils. So, this was the main entrance to the kitchen. Olbi followed Ayon into the large room. It bustled with the calamity of a dozen kitchen hands who were frantically preparing a banquet.

'You can use that wash area for your fish,' Ayon said, pointing to a stone surface in the corner. Ayon placed the now half-full jugs of yar milk on a nearby stone bench.

Olbi walked over to the spot Ayon pointed to and threw down the bag of fish. He rubbed his shoulders where the strap had aggravated his skin.

He then peered around the chaotic kitchen for a knife. How was he to fillet fish without his favourite blade? The cacophony of clanging pans and banging pots blasted his eardrums. Ayon was engaged with a kitchen hand and pointing to Olbi. The hand glared his way and gave him a look reserved for a rodent that had crawled into the kitchen. Olbi turned away, embarrassed. What was he doing here? Even if Alvar smelt the fish, Olbi was more comfortable in the Stonehall.

'Here you go. Do you need anything else?'

Olbi spun. Ayon had returned with a cutting board and three knives of different lengths. Olbi smiled.

'Perfect, but maybe I should go. I don't think I belong here.'

Ayon turned around and scanned the kitchen. Sure enough, the kitchen hands examined them with wide eyes ranging from disgust to curiosity. Ayon smiled and sidled next to Olbi at the sink. Olbi was conscious of his shoulder rubbing against Ayon's.

'Your hair is standing on end, are you cold?' Ayon said, looking at Olbi's arms that had immediately been overcome by goosebumps. Olbi rubbed his arm. The kitchen was a furnace with all the ovens and fires around them.

'Shouldn't you be getting ready for the ceremony?' Olbi said, deflecting the conversation. Ayon said nothing and instead removed a river jack from Olbi's bag. He grasped the fish in one hand and, with the other, ran a finger down its scales. Olbi observed as Ayon's fingertip circled the point where his spear had dealt the mortal blow.

'You are a fair shot. Even better than Reeva, I would wager,' Ayon said. Olbi felt his cheeks flush at the compliment. Ayon plopped the fish before Olbi. Despair flashed on the Prime Scion's face.

'Is something the matter?' Olbi asked. Olbi did not consider him a friend, but Ayon seemed genuinely friendly today. Even so, today's events were odd. Why had the Scion been in the fields the same day as the Manna Rites and so close to the ritual? Ayon had made no attempts to prepare; he wasn't in his Prime robes, and after a day in the field, running through towns and now sweating in the kitchen, he would certainly require a bath. Whether Ayon did not hear him or was intentionally avoiding the question, Olbi got no response.

'Ayon is everything o—'

The wooden doors they had entered through violently opened, cutting Olbi off.

At the entrance stood an imposing woman, her sharp hawkish features accentuated by a stern expression. Her lustrous grey hair, slicked back with precision, was immaculate. She wore the ornate uniform of those entrusted with protecting the Primes, both at the ceremony and whenever they ventured beyond the confines of Xylona. Olbi Instantly recognised the woman, his heart sinking.

'Scion, I have been searching for you for two tolls; I insist you leave immediately and prepare for the Manna Rites.' The

woman was forthright and her tone firm, more than anyone had any right to be when speaking to a Prime.

'Reeva, I need you to leave me alone. That is an order!' Ayon spat back, curling his usually handsome lips into a distorted snarl. The kitchen lapsed into silence. The only sound that remained was the mild clanging of a copper lid on a pot being jounced by boiling water within.

Reeva did not shift as she scanned the kitchen with an air of authority that made Olbi feel even more jumpy than he was. He felt small, even though he was often the tallest in the room. She towered over everyone in the kitchen, her nostrils looking down on every eye cast upon her.

'I do not take orders from you, Scion.' Reeva's response was steady and composed as she stared at the kitchen hands who shuffled back to work to evade her stare. 'I will only ask once more. Depart for your chambers and prepare for the Rites.'

The request was an ultimatum. Ayon nervously glanced at Olbi, their arms brushing once more. Olbi felt Ayon's warm skin trembling against his.

'Olbi, please stay and feel free to use the kitchens to prepare your fish; they will be the boast of the festivities,' Ayon said, staring into Reeva's malevolent eyes as if the statement was directed at her rather than Olbi. Olbi wasn't sure what to say, so he awkwardly returned to scaling his fish, grabbing the one that Ayon had removed from the bag. Reeva walked across the room to one of the corridors. Olbi surmised it was the way to the dining hall and the rest of the house.
Ayon stood unmoving, glued to the spot. Reeva glared and subtly shifted her hands to the hilt of a silver sword that hung at her side. Olbi had not seen it when she blasted through the doors. Ayon reluctantly began to drag his feet, shooting a dispirited glance towards Olbi as he shuffled past.

Before he realised what he was doing, Olbi clasped Ayon's shoulder, giving him a subtle squeeze. Ayon's eyes flashed to the spot where Olbi's hand was; his face was blank, but they locked stares as his eyes returned. Olbi quickly moved his hand, though Ayon continued to gaze into his now guilt-ridden eyes. Ayon broke his glance and, lowering his head, paced to the archway where Reeva stood.

'After you,' Reeva gestured to Ayon and the two vanished down the hallway. Olbi quickly spun around, clearly aware of the eyes that were now on him. He did not want to linger here—Ayon's blessings or not—with all these gazes steadily multiplying and boring a hole into his back. He would scale the fish and pray that a hand took them to the feast. He still needed to change out of these dirty clothes and into the clean garments he had stashed under the pillow on his bunk.

A loud bell rang from somewhere close: The final hour was being tolled before the Manna Rites were to begin.

4

LIRAN

The sun's warmth withdrew as if it could sense the approaching eclipse would extinguish its power. Liran rubbed her bare arms as the chilled air seeped into her skin. Hastily, she strode towards the Prime House with Euyan in tow, passing market stalls where vendors—hoping to offload their wares before the festivities—yelled at passers-by. The stalls' canvas tops fluttered slightly in the breeze, and fabrics, tchotchkes, and vegetables that hung from chains also swayed. Some stall owners were packing away wares as Liran hurried down the primary thoroughfare that led to the centre of Xylona.

'Maven, I've been pondering,' Euyan said, struggling to keep pace with Liran's inherently longer strides. 'Do you think the Scion's grandfather should lecture the boy on his responsibility?'

Liran mulled on the question. What business was it of Euyan's to propose such a notion and what had Thessus been feeding her assistant?

Thessus, Claudya's father, was continually concerned with strengthening the bloodline. With Ayon's father deceased, Thessus exuded a faux grandeur despite not possessing the blood himself. Few knew the true nature of Thessus, but Liran did. He was becoming senile and a conniving sleaze. She knew Thessus to be unnervingly liberal with his lecherous hands towards women in Xylona. She hoped that Ayon did not adopt his grandfather's practices.

'Euyan, there are vermin crawling in the Stonehall sewers that I would approach to offer lectures in responsibility before that man,' Liran said.

Euyan's silence indicated that he was inclined to drop the subject.

❖

Liran peered up at the pale outlines of the moons and Oaga—they had begun to unite. A divine embrace, each drawing closer to the sun.

If the bloodlines did run dry, would that be such a loss? Sure, the altar would remain dormant, and a worldwide search would commence. Liran expected a Consanguine Court would be proclaimed and Rahsu from across Arbonar would descend on Xylona to test their mettle. The world was vast. The bloodline may yet linger in some lost lineage.

Even if it didn't, would the Spirits punish the Rahsu if the fruits were not offered at every eclipse? What then? Would the scriptures that foretold the cataclysmic collapse of Arbonar become a reality? Would the rivers parch, and the forests burn? Would the air they breathe instead stifle all living things? Liran had more faith in the soil and trees around her than a belief that educating the masses would provoke anarchy and descend the Rahsu into chaos. Knowledge of the scriptures was the permit of Primes, Mavens and sagelings such as Euyan.

The southern cloister's archway loomed ahead. The cloister wrapped around a dense square that was filled with vibrant green.

Liran and Euyan kicked up sand along the dusty path as they passed through the lavish gardens. This was one of Liran's favourite places in town. It boasted an enviable display of flowers and plant life from across the Rahsu lands—too many varieties to count—and all were meticulously cared for by Monitors skilled in botany. It was a popular gathering place for Xylonans, but the birds outnumbered villagers today.

Liran felt a twinge in her chest. In her haste, she had passed through the garden she had been avoiding. This had been the last place she had seen him. Despite new plants and the ebbs and flows of life, the garden appeared the same as it had last year. Her stomach churned and her legs seized up. The smell of sweet flowers engulfed her. *His* favourites.

Euyan stopped beside her. They stood near a stone statue of a woman holding a garjee fruit in outstretched hands. His mouth jerked as if to speak. Liran cut him off. 'Sorry. It has been a while since I walked this fast. I need a moment,' Liran said. She held her hips and exhaled, bending forward. 'I'll be right behind you. Let the Prime One know I am moments away.'

Liran watched Euyan trot towards the Prime House. Glad to be alone, she locked eyes with the statue. Her vision began to mist over, and she felt lightheaded. Taking the zirge root had sapped her mental energy.

A group of villagers passed by and offered their greetings. They wore thick garbs of brightly coloured yar wool that smelt of incense. Robes that had seen many Manna Rites. Liran returned no smile or gestures; instead, she stared blankly into the gardens.

The garden was frigid as a shadow loomed; she cast her gaze up to see the three celestial bodies encroaching upon the sun. The eclipse had begun. Within thirty minutes, darkness would blanket Arbonar, and the Manna Rites would begin.

A bitter wind lashed her arms as the temperature plummeted. Liran swore under her breath: she had forgotten her shawl.

Two town Monitors scuttled by her with torches as they moved to light sconces that lined the walkways to the plaza ahead. The sconces bathed the surrounding buildings in faint light as the sky dimmed. Liran made her way to the arches at the end of the gardens and into the plaza of the Prime House.

Grand steps of white stone led to a columned balcony that wrapped around the curvature of the Prime House facade. Leafy green and orange vines crept up the first two storeys, strangling the tops of the columns. They resembled trees with stone trunks. The Prime House was an imposing presence, towering over the cloistered buildings and gardens surrounding the district.

❀

40

Liran climbed the stairs and stepped towards open doors. A warm glow beckoned her in. The great hearth in the welcoming hall was ablaze, flickering shadows onto the lofty ceiling. She could feel its warm tendrils reach her. At first glance, the entrance hall appeared empty—just the crackling of firewood. But soon Euyan's figure materialised: he rose from a bench by the blaze. He was waiting for her.

'Euyan,' Liran called as she strode across the hall to the flames. 'Have you seen Claudya? Does she know I am here?'

Euyan looked up. His gaze met the air above Liran's shoulder. She spun so quickly that the zirge still in her system made her dizzy. Claudya stood at the base of a broad staircase.

The Prime One was swathed in a plunging garnet dress, and her usually wavy auburn hair was intricately styled into a lavish lace braid that twisted and sat atop her head like a crown.

'Liran, thank you for coming; Reeva will join us in the Sanctum,' Claudya said in her distinctive, husky voice. She stepped down the last step and gestured towards a triangular hall behind the hearth.

'The Sanctum, Claudya?' Liran said, surprised. 'Pardon me, Prime; may I ask why this warrants meeting there?'

Claudya's arm fell to her side as she strode across the hall. 'Because as we speak, people are coming in and out of the residence readying for the ceremony. I have a proposition that requires discretion.'

Something about Claudya's tone bothered Liran as the Prime One clasped her hands together in frustration. Laugh lines around her eyes had been replaced with a furrowed brow. Her lips were tight, and a slight quiver in her chin told Liran their discussion was grave.

'After you, please, Liran. This will not take long, then you can head upstairs and dress for the ceremony. You will not have time to return to your house.'

Claudya turned to Euyan, who was warming his rump against the fire.

'Euyan, while we discuss matters, please see that one of the Monitors lays out a suitable robe for the Maven.' Claudya glanced at Liran with a quick smile and said, 'And perhaps a shawl; it will be chilly tonight.'

Euyan nodded, but Liran watched her assistant's stare linger on the Sanctum's corridor.

Few had seen the inside of the Sanctum. It was sacred, a place where guests would attend momentous rituals or intimate meetings with the Primes. Euyan would relish that privilege.

Liran strolled with Claudya through to the triangular hallway that lay in the core of the Prime House.

Liran had been there only once before, at the birth of Claudya's youngest child—Baylon. The boy had not lived, his heart failing moments after his birth. There was nothing anyone could do to save the child. He had been born many cycles too soon.

Claudya had summoned her that day to whisk away ten-year-old Ayon to spare him any grief. Liran had taken him to the gardens, where Ayon had spent the day drawing animals in the dirt.

Liran followed Claudya to a stone doorway at the end of the passage. The stone door was intricately engraved with images of earlier Primes gifting the garjee fruits. Each fruit emitted carved lines portraying the bright light they created when they were placed on the altar. On this door, the garjee fruit added an ethereal and eternal quality, one that would grace only those privileged to see it.

The door to the outer sanctum was often left open as the hefty door required several men to push it shut. It was only closed during ferocious storms that swept through Xylona in the warmer months. Liran crossed the threshold first. Claudya followed, the back of her dress sweeping the floor.
'Euyan mentioned we are to discuss the Scion. Is that true?' Liran inquired as they stepped into the outer sanctum.

The Sanctum calmed and fascinated Liran. The sweeping, circular room—dimly lit and cast in the subtle light of candles—was filled with books and historical relics from when the world was young. Liran scanned the shelves and marvelled at worn stones inscribed with scripture passages, books with deteriorating bindings, and intricately painted vases that were decorated with precious stones from across the Rahsu lands. Claudya's voice refocused Liran's attention.

'Yes, Euyan speaks true, but there is also another matter we must discuss,' Claudya said reluctantly. The Prime One seemed cagey—she had never been tensed like this before.

Liran continued to follow, treading upon a line of colourful woven yar wool rugs that guided them towards an ornately painted door at the back of the room.

Usually, two sentries stood abreast of the carved, golden door, each with a halberd in hand to defend the inner sanctum, though no such sentries were present today.

Claudya and Liran strode into the dimly lit room beyond. Unlike the outer sanctum, the inner room was smaller, barren, and much less lavish. The walls were stark and unadorned, made of a single domed stone—the smoothest Liran had ever seen. She wanted to run her fingers along the sleek walls. It bewildered her; the craftsmanship was flawless. Two worn and splintered wooden benches sat upon an aging, moss-green rug with muted yellow circles scattered around the trim. The orbs resembled ripe garjee fruits and, despite the rug's deterioration, they appeared to emit soft light.

The benches faced a square stone pedestal, atop which candles glimmered on either side of an ornate chest. Liran knew this box well. The whole town did: it was the vessel in which the fruit was delivered to the Manna Rites.
Liran flinched as a towering figure standing at the room's rear moved into the candlelight. It was Reeva.

She had her hands linked behind her back. She'd been waiting for them. Before Claudya could speak, Reeva had begun addressing them.

❖

43

'Prime One, I confirm the Scion has been found. He is in his chamber, supervised by a Monitor, and is now preparing for the rituals. The Monitor will inform us if he is to run again.'

'*Found?*' Liran blurted. Reeva's grey eyes pierced Liran, undoubtedly annoyed at the interruption.

'Yes, I am afraid we quarrelled with Ayon today,' Claudya said. 'He is upset with a proposal that Reeva suggested, which, truthfully, I see no choice but to heed … as much as it pains me.'

Liran's eyes darted between Claudya and Reeva. What would provoke the Scion into fleeing on the day of the Manna Rites? No doubt Reeva, as the Prime's guardian, had proposed something harsh.

Reeva had no status of authority on what the boy did, but Liran had noticed that the Guardian would find ways to persuade Claudya as no one else could.

'What is this proposal?' Liran asked Reeva, who was still scowling at her. Claudya must have called Liran to rebut the Guardian.

'The Prime Scion is no longer a boy, though many appear to overlook this.' Reeva began addressing Liran, placing her hands on the stone dais. 'He is of age to sire and replenish the bloodline. However, I have unfortunately learned that Ayon does not intend to honour his sole responsibility. Therefore, in the Rahsu's best interests, I see no choice but to dispatch the Scion to Hydoran or Kanowna to live with the heirs of the remnant bloodlines.' Reeva continued to glare at Liran as if challenging her to disagree.

Liran ignored the Guardian, sighing and returning to face Claudya. The Prime One's head was tilted down. Liran felt rage boiling in her stomach as Reeva broke the silence.

'My preference is Hydoran. The dormant line of the Prime's in that town has more females than the Remnants of the Granite Hills. He will leave tomorrow after the Manna Rites, and with the Spirits to guide him, soon we will hear welcoming news that the bloodlines will live.' Reeva stood up straight, her face unmoving. It was clear she had given this much thought.

Claudya sat on one of the benches that rocked unevenly on the rug. She looked tired, her face betraying her usually calm demeanour.

How could she agree to this? Liran found her voice. 'You sound as though Xylona is a lost cause for the Scion. Are you prepared to hand over power so willingly to Hydoran or Kanowna? He is twenty years old, and at twenty, he wants to explore the world. No wonder he is fighting you on this. If he feels backed into a corner, he will run. If Ayon does not wish to sire children, then we cannot force it upon him. The blood may yet exist somewhere on Arbonar, if we call a Consanguine Court we would know.' She grew annoyed. The zirge roots had dissipated, leaving numbness in her limbs and a growing headache.

'We did call a Consanguine,' Claudya's voice was barely audible as she lifted her head. Liran's gape widened.

'When? I don't recall a gathering of dignitaries recently?' Liran's annoyance laced her remarks. When did the Prime One announce a Consanguine Court? Why when the current Prime was healthy and of sound mind with a mature heir alive?

The last Consanguine had been called eighty years ago when the Prime One and his lineage had fallen ill. All three heirs had been taken by sickness that had spread through the Rahsu lands. Despite Hydoran objections and declarations of treason, it had been then that Xylona retook the mantle as the Prime seat. Claudya's grandfather had demonstrated his possession of the blood by activating the Manna Altar in Hydoran. There had been little celebration as the man was in his late fifties and held no successor. He had quickly withered away, but in his dying days, he had managed to sire Claudya's mother and her younger sister, only Claudya's mother had proven to possess the blood.

Reeva pursed her lips before responding to Liran. 'I called a Court in Hydoran and Kanowna last cycle. I travelled with garjee fruit and ensured those with remnant bloodlines were summoned to the tests. I affirm that dozens performed the tests, and no trace of the bloodlines emerged. Only Ayon remains. He *must* breed for the Rahsu's sake. This goes beyond who controls the Manna Altar now.' Reeva shifted her glare to Claudya. Liran sensed agitation and piety there.

'Perhaps you took an unripe garjee fruit,' Liran offered nonchalantly. Reeva looked disgusted.

'Mind your tongue, Liran,' Reeva spat. 'You do not understand the perils we face if the bloodline is extinguished from Arbonar.' Liran could not stop her eyes from rolling this time.

'Yes, yes; flames will devour the forests and lakes. Rivers will evaporate, and the air we breathe will destroy us all. It might surprise you, but I have read the scriptures, Reeva.'

'You mock the Spirits, Maven? Here in the presence of the Prime One, and in the Sanctum no less?' Reeva said.

'Consanguine is for all to test their mettle, not just a select few. Why was one conducted at *your* whim, Reeva? Consanguine Courts, by law, are public affairs, or haven't you read the history of the Primes? I'm sure there is a copy around here somewhere. If not, I have one in my studio if you would like.' Reeva's complexion flushed, her chin shaking.

'Enough of this, Maven! Know your place,' Reeva spat. 'I'm sure you would not wish a raid on your studio. Xylonans would look harshly upon a Maven with forbidden texts.'

Reeva stepped forward and leaned down to look Liran in the eye. 'I know more than you—or any of the Maven's before you—might think. I have seen the bloodlines struggle, and the Spirits will not—'

'Reeva, please,' Claudya cut in. The Prime One stood up, her eyes pleading. Reeva turned her head to Claudya, her face distorted with anger.

'Reeva, I agree with you that Ayon will leave. We can merely pray that he sees reason, while doing what we can to encourage him. If he does not sire children, it may be the will of the Spirits; this may all be a test to see if we are worthy of forging the future of Arbonar.'

Claudya held up her hand as Reeva began to stutter, beckoning her to halt. Reeva complied as Claudya turned to Liran.

'Now, on to the second reason I summoned you, Liran. You have documented the dancing stars, and we need to discuss a theory.'

'A theory?' Liran sat down, perplexed. 'You called me here for a theory … mere moments before the Manna Rites? I have yet to write you a speech,' Liran said, rubbing her brow. 'I know my findings are an issue for the Primes. I acknowledge the consensus of the majority that the stars are the eyes of Spirits guiding us through the darkness. If you recall, my research refuting this was condemned across Arbonar.' Reeva nodded at that. Liran hadn't forgotten Reeva was one of the first to decry her work.

Claudya linked her fingers together. 'Do not worry about the speech, this is currently more time-sensitive,' Claudya said, likely seeing the puzzled look in Liran's eyes. 'Yes, people see the dancing stars as guiding lights, and their presence in our skies *is* comforting. However, I have recently met with Tarak, a trader who returned from Aldrowen with an interesting tale this morning.'

'What sort of tale?' Reeva asked, her eyes boring into Claudya's; her expression was severe. Liran noted that Claudya had not informed Reeva ahead of the meeting.

'He was travelling down the Minor Flow at dusk. His trading party pulled the barge to the riverbank to establish a camp for the night when a light flashed, illuminating them and the surrounding forest. Tarak claims a thunderous star fell from the sky,' Claudya paused for Reeva or Liran to speak; Liran answered first.

'A star *fell* from the sky. One of the dancing stars?' Liran asked, looking at Claudya inquisitively.

Claudya continued. 'Tarak said he could not be certain as the section of the river was sheltered by garjee trees. However, the traders claim they saw the flash and heard the rumbles of thunder.'

Liran pictured the scenario in her mind. She would speak with Tarak. Undoubtedly, the man was in town tonight for the feast, and she could steal him away for a moment.

'Preposterous!' Reeva exclaimed. 'A drunken fool confused by the aura of the garjee forests. I would not take any stock in anything Tarak says. Or his son, for that matter.' Claudya furrowed her brow before Reeva added, 'That was who the Scion was with when I found him in the kitchens.'

'Do you mean Olbi?' Claudya inquired. Liran, too, scrutinised Reeva.

'Yes, I do. Olbi was far too familiar with the Scion. The boy was dressed in rags and showing him how to gut and scale a fish, most unbecoming for the bloodline.' Reeva seemed plainly outraged.

Claudya giggled like a child.

'Reeva, in my youth, I wove yar wool to sell at markets. Knowing how to gut fish and work in the kitchens is scarcely a vice,' Claudya said.

'I wonder if it fell to the ground,' Liran thought out loud, unconcerned with another of Reeva's lectures.

'I beg your pardon?' Reeva said, clearly puzzled by the change of topic.

Liran was still pondering the star. She'd heard a story of a falling star before from a traveller of the Great Lake.

'The star—I wonder if it fell to Arbonar. It may be out there, waiting to be found,' Liran said more for herself than the other women in the room.

Reeva laughed—a cold and haunted laugh. 'Sure, find a fallen star … In the forests. On the way, take the Scion to Hydoran, would you?' Reeva was amused at her own suggestion. Claudya's brow creased.

'The reason I've told you this, Liran,' Claudya started as Reeva recovered her composure, 'is that Tarak alluded to people in Hydoran whispering similar stories. A star tumbled from the sky, and even some whispered that as it fell, it shattered into several sparks that rained down over the eastern forests of Hydoran.' Claudya examined Liran's eyes. 'Liran, I need you to travel with Ayon to Hydoran at daybreak and deliver him to the Prime Remnants. Then, find out what you can about this phenomenon. I need to know if this has something to do with the Spirits.' Claudya finished by laying her hand softly on Liran's shoulder.

'Of course, my Prime,' Liran responded automatically. 'After the feast, I will pack my things. If you are sure …?'

Claudya nodded but avoided Liran's questioning gaze.

Liran pondered the request as the Prime One seemed to start for the door, but she spun in a graceful sway to face the other women again. 'I do not think that it will come as a shock that I am not happy with this decision,' Claudya said. Her eyes met Reeva before continuing, 'Soon, the people of Arbonar will be asking questions, and I don't want to shy away from doing what must be done for the sake of our people. We face challenging times, and I would abhor being the last Prime One in a line spanning over a thousand years.' Claudya's eyes welled as she turned back to the door and left the inner sanctum. As she did, the bells tolled. Xylonans were being called to the Altar.

5

LIRAN

Liran spotted Euyan still sitting by the hearth as she followed the Prime One out of the triangular hall. A neatly folded robe was draped over his arm: the standard dress for a Maven during the ceremony. At this distance, the garment's high quality was undeniable.

'One of the Monitors has set aside a room for you upstairs,' Euyan said, handing over the robe. Liran felt him searching her eyes for hints about the meeting.

'In time, Euyan, and thank you,' Liran said softly as Claudya left them and disappeared upstairs.

'You will be taking on extra duties while I travel to Hydoran.' Euyan's excited eyes betrayed his calm and unchanged demeanour. 'We can discuss it at the feast tonight,' Liran offered as she started for the staircase.

Euyan, ever the helpful presence, called after her, 'First door on the left,' before he departed through the main door.

The second floor was hushed as Liran entered the first guest room. She closed the door behind her and leaned against it, taking a deep breath. The room was simple with a single bed beside a slit window that proffered dim light.

Liran noticed items had been laid out on the room's small table for her: a hairbrush, a copper mirror, various soaps, and a bowl of water.

She slipped out of her clothes and into the soft white robes. She smoothed out creases in the arms, feeling the delicate embroidery on the sleeve cuffs. The tailor had stitched a series of broad leaves that wrapped around the wrists. The robe must have belonged to one of the past Primes. She wondered how old it was. Likely over one hundred years and woven by hands that were now a distant memory.

She regarded herself in the copper mirror. Claudya's request played in her mind while she brushed her hair. It was not Reeva's right to push the Prime One to relinquish the happiness of her only son. Liran felt a twinge of guilt for being the one to take him away from his home. She hoped that Ayon would understand that she was not condoning the assignment given to her. Claudya needed to know you cannot control your children, no matter how hard you try.

****

Liran crossed the deserted plaza alone, following lit sconces that dotted a path from the Prime House to the Manna Altar. Liran soon joined the throngs of moving bodies, all wrapped in ceremonial robes, ready for another ritual.

Claudya was right. It was a frigid afternoon, and the huddled bodies moved quickly through the gardens and archways of the cloisters.

The Altar stood in the centre of a large amphitheatre that plunged like a bowl into the ground and gave everyone an unabridged view of the Altar. It was a remarkable structure. One in which all Xylona could witness the fruits being bestowed upon the Spirits.

Liran watched the masses descend into the depression. As part of the ceremony, Liran would need to stand inside the covered altar. Beneath the domed covering and at its base sat the offering bowl, while above the dome, a smooth stone pillar shot towards the sky like a naked tree trunk. Had it not been built at the bottom of the hollow; it would tower over all of Xylona.

Surrounding the altar were numerous rows of stone benches that formed concentric circles around it. The benches were smooth and worn down from a thousand ceremonies. Liran often tried to comprehend how the first Rahsu could craft such an impressive feat of engineering. The amphitheatre could seat all the people of Xylona with enough room to seat half the town again. Having three thousand people sitting in the amphitheatre—all focused on the central altar, their songs and chants bouncing and amplifying into a cacophony of chaotic sound—was a true spectacle. It was no wonder many felt so connected to the Spirits during this day's ceremony.

Liran followed a path down past the benches. She envied the townspeople, all of whom would be seated during the ceremony. Couldn't the ceremony be altered slightly to allow her a chair near the altar? Nevertheless, she was required to stand among the elite, so there she would stand.

Excited chatter filled the amphitheatre as people laid down cushions and lit incense sticks to place at their feet. Wisps of smoke and scents wafted, exuding sweet vanilla and scented wood aromas. As the smoke's tendrils tickled her nose, Liran sneezed, scaring a small girl seated next to the path.

Farther down, great flames licked at the air and competed with the wafting incense clouds for what oxygen was available. The flames danced in a ring of iron braziers around the altar, the light illuminating the faces of those under the dome. Liran welcomed the fire, afraid of the chilblain that threatened her extremities.

Reeva stood under the dome and was flanked by two guards. Liran lifted the hem of her robe, climbed the small step, and joined the Guardian.

Liran straightened, assumed her position, and looked out at the filling seats. She saw the Prime's grandfather, Thessus, limping towards them, his thick brown coat unfastened, allowing people to see he was sporting evening garments underneath. Reeva's eyes locked with Liran's, though they held no affection, only a stark nothingness.

Liran averted her gaze to face the waning sun, its lustre diminished as three spheres encroached upon its dominance. It was a matter of moments before the remaining sunshine would be extinguished sinking Xylona into a lonely darkness. Feeling the chill in the air, Liran deftly adjusted her robes to cover more of her skin against the dropping temperature.

❖

As Xylonans and visitors descended into the arena and settled into their seats, unseen sonorous drums beat, filling the amphitheatre. The crowd's energetic atmosphere quietened to a murmur as townspeople craned their necks towards the back row that led towards the Prime House.

Four drummers appeared at the lip and descended towards the altar in rhythm with their beats. Their thumps became long and hollow. Liran's heart throbbed as the drumming vibrated in her chest; the people around her were motionless under the hypnotic reverberations.

Claudya followed the drummers in her deep garnet dress. The flames from the braziers cast dancing lights on the Prime One as she pursued the drums' percussion. Claudya looked straight ahead as she sauntered down, her gaze not deviating from the altar she was destined for.

In tow, two guards marched, dressed in the blood-red robes of the Prime family. Their towering figures contrasted Claudya's petite frame. They each grasped a halberd in one hand, while the other firmly gripped opposite handles of the offering chest wherein the harvested garjee fruits were secured.

Liran ran the process of the ceremony through her mind and wondered what would happen to the fruits if the bloodline was gone forever.

The gathering masses continued their rapturous stares, watching the procession descend towards the altar.

Ayon appeared at the theatre's canopy, not far behind the guards. His eyes scanned the crowd, and in return, the crowd's gaze shifted to him. His face was flushed; Liran wondered if he had been crying.

She spied Reeva appearing pleased beside her, her lips curved upwards and obviously content in her success of ensuring the Scion partook in the ceremony.

Ayon wore robes of white, much like Liran's; however, the Scion's robes had deep red trimmings, and on his chest, he wore an ornate brass pin of a garjee fruit. He shadowed the guards and walked in unison with the beating drums; his eyes flickering before becoming set like stone. The flames that danced behind him cast a golden glow over him as he descended the passageway.

The drums' tempo quickened as trumpeters announced their arrival—with bursts of brassy touting—behind the Scion. Liran shuddered; the horns hit her ears wrong, their shrill screech bouncing around the arena. Her headache threatened to return.

Liran recalled when she was one of the spectators in those rows watching the altar and questioning her mother about what was happening and why they were gathered. Her mother would smile and tell her that the offerings ensured her safety and that nothing could harm her.

Liran's mother had been patient, teaching her the hymns and the cues to stand and chant. They would often rehearse on the morning of the Manna Rites: her mother would use an apple and, together, they would pretend to present it at the altar for the Spirits. Liran had never imagined that she would be standing here as a Maven. Those memories of her mother were bittersweet as she reflected on watching her mother teach the same things to her grandson when Liran's son was a mere boy.

Claudya and her procession reached the altar—the drums and trumpets still singing in unison, transitioning into long rumbles of rhythmic baritones that drew the focus of the gathering.

Liran licked her lips and swallowed, readying her vocal cords for the hymn of the Rahsu that initiated the Manna Rites, which was sung as the three converging celestial bodies completely vanquished the sun's light.

Standing upon an elevated stone dais, Claudya surveyed the vast sea of faces illuminated by the flickering braziers. Above them, Arbonar's two moons and Oaga finished converging and smothered the sun and the devilish constellation representing the demons of the Rahsu.

Darkness had prevailed and blotted away the light. With a resonant and guttural hum, Claudya incited the primal bass of the hymn, and gradually, the assembled masses joined in the sacred song.

Oh, Spirits of the Rahsu
Hear our voice
Your children live now
Feel them rejoice

In the dark o' the spheres
See our might
Your elders pass on now
Feel their light

In the flames of creation
Feel our love
Our blood is your blood
Beneath and above

The world you gift us
Taste our fare
Now, your people grow
The life you share.

Rahsu, born of the soil
Blaze and glow
Oh, Spirits of Arbonar
With love, we show.

Though the hymn ended, the partitioners continued to hum in unison as the drums rumbled again. Dusk now enveloped the sky.

Liran focused on the chanters in the dim light. They all swayed with their eyes closed. Sparks and wisps of smoke and

incense blurred their faces. To her, they became one uncharacteristic maelstrom of faces despite the recognisable features of people she knew.

Liran gazed upwards as smoke drifted into her eyes. She moved her head to the left and then to the right. Like an ominous cosmic joke, the smoke seemed to follow her. Where the sun had been was now a black expanse of nothingness in a sea of stars. Like clockwork, every cycle, the eclipse of Arbonar smothered them.

Beside Liran, Claudya's voice boomed. 'In the darkness, we are the flame.' The flock uttered the words back to their Prime. Liran's senses were foggy. She had inhaled too much incense, and the stars above blurred, disappearing in a murky haze like stones lost below muddy and disrupted river water.

Liran wiped her eyes and peered back into the night. She blinked erratically, tears welling in her ducts. It didn't take long for her to spot a dancing star as it crossed the sky. Spotting one made it easier to see the second, and soon, she counted five streaking through the night as Claudya led the town into a second hymn about the promise of protection.

The melody began as a promise the Prime One gave the people: a commitment to guide the Rahsu and defend them all their lives. The song then shifted to a tale about the old demons and how the first Primes defeated them, bringing about peace on Arbonar.

Liran's gaze was glued to one of the dancing stars as it drifted towards the dark void where the three spheres obstructed the sun. The emptiness now almost sunk below the tree line and rooftops of Xylona. The star dashed towards the void, and Liran kept watching it follow the sun's lead to vanish behind the eclipse.

Her eyes widened. The star passed over the void and remained bright until it fell below the tree line. Liran coughed. Though she had been holding her breath, smoke had snuck into her lungs.

❖

How was the dancing star closer to her than the moons and the great sphere? Liran willed her mind to think clearly as her gaze fell upon the faces around her. Others would be able to recognise the significance of what she had seen, wouldn't they?

Instead, the seas of faces were transfixed on the ornate chest that two guards carried towards the Prime One, the drums and horns building to the chants again. In unison, the men eased the chest before Claudya, unlatched the lid, and lifted it free. The drums and trumpets hit a crescendo before cutting off abruptly, permitting a heavy hush to fall over them. Claudya nodded to the gatekeepers, who, in a heavily choreographed manner, stepped away from the box and stood by two columns on either side of the Prime One.

Liran stepped forward: her part to play in the Rites had come. Liran raised her voice, addressing the Prime One as a representative of the congregation. 'Prime One—the third of the Lyfera line, our protector and mother—we ask you to bestow the Spirits with our bounty,' Liran said as the crowd listened on. 'Prime One, we seek the Spirit's protection from the demons of the world. In the shadows of the eclipse, banish the demons in our name.' Liran stepped back as Xylona chanted 'Protect us; Spirits deem us worthy.'

Claudya drew back the sleeves of her robe and reached both hands into the chest. From it, she lifted a garjee fruit. The soft yellow fruit was difficult to see in the dim light as Claudya raised it above her head as if presenting it to the heavens.

'Spirits of the Rahsu, we offer you the fruits of the forest so you may sow the soils that sustain us,' Claudya proclaimed. 'Hallowed Spirits hear us.' The ring of people chanted as one. 'With this gift, we ask that you protect us from the shadows and demons,' Claudya bellowed.

'Hallowed Spirits hear us,' Liran chanted in unison with a thousand other voices reverberating around her.

'Give us guidance and know our devotion, past, present and future,' Claudya finished as the congregation chanted and bellowed their final blessing.

Claudya's determined eyes bore deep into the fruit hoisted above her head. Silence hung in the amphitheatre. The drummers and trumpeters were focused on the dome. Liran turned to Claudya and followed her gaze to the dim fruit. The masses lulled as every eye focused on Claudya's hands. The fruit began to pulse as golden light radiated from it, illuminating the entire arena.

In her hands, Claudya held the sun's brightness, a golden orb of light that blinded those looking directly at it. Liran shielded her eyes as Claudya stepped down from the dais and walked to the altar behind her, turning her back, her face now visible to the congregation on the other side of the altar. Liran stared at Claudya and could see the face of the Prime One, lit up behind the fantastic light of the fruit. Claudya's eyes burned in the light, her arm a torch to light the path of the Rahsu.

Liran was awestruck; how the Prime's eyes stayed open was a gift. Were those that carried the blood immune to the light?

Claudya approached a basin at the altar and removed one hand from the fruit, placing it on a carving of rings that overlay one another. They were a symbol of something, though Liran did not know the meaning. No one knew the purpose of the marks. Liran believed it was the written script of the Rahsu from over a millennia ago.

Claudya barely brushed the carvings when a flash of light spewed from the altar and devoured the spire above the dome like a lightning bolt. Pure light pierced the heavens in a beam that lit up the darkness. The stone slab where the Prime One stood split in two, sliding apart, pulled by unseen forces. A grinding crunch and whirring rasped from the slab's depths. It was unique to everything else that hit the ears in the village. From the pedestal's opening rose a glossy bowl of a material shinier than copper or silver.

The fruit kept its luminosity as Claudya gradually lowered it onto the dish. Liran, now motionless, saw a sudden gushing force-like wind pass through a tunnel that then swirled around Claudya. It emerged from where the fruit had been set, but within a blink, the fruit vanished, taken and inhaled by the Spirits.

The townspeople cheered and wailed, rejoicing, their faces exuding relief. The Spirits had accepted the offering.

Claudya inhaled deeply, smiling weakly as she repeated the process. Each time, the bright radiating fruit disappeared in a gushing whirl as the Prime One placed it upon the dish. Liran glanced at Ayon who watched his mother; his face was sunken and solemn as Claudya carried the weight of the rituals on her shoulders—the fate of the Rahsu.

Ayon was the only other Rahsu alive who could summon the Spirits. What would transpire if the boy didn't heed his birthright? The sea of faces would never again rejoice at the Manna Rites. How many more would take place if the Scion was the last of the blood? She imagined fear replacing smiles and shuddered; a cool breeze ran through the air, blowing at the flames around them.

Claudya withdrew from the basin as the last fruit beamed and disappeared within the altar.

As the spire above the altar relinquished its glow, cheers erupted from around the ring.

Liran watched Claudya's weakened body stride back to the dais to greet the crowds. Their eyes turned skywards to see the sun emerging from behind the celestial bodies that resumed their traversal of the cosmos. The light was fighting a losing battle, though. The sun hovered on the horizon—washed hues of red and pink stretched across the sky.

Liran closed her eyes, allowing the cool breeze to blow away the incense and clear her head. She inhaled the fresh evening air and exhaled, feeling healthier than she had all day. She sank into her mind as voices stirred within the masses. Distressed murmurs rose as it spread. Liran opened her eyes and witnessed people gaping into the sky, many gasping and pointing above the ceremony. What had captured their attention?

Stars blanketed the sky, sparkling freely as wafts of incense smoke dissipated. At first, Liran noticed nothing unusual until she strode from the dome of the Altar. Ayon, Claudya and Reeva followed as more Xylonans stared into the heavens. Liran converged on the first coil of benches, where villagers craned their necks skywards.

Liran gasped. Above them, a star shone three times the size of all others, a star that did not exist before the Manna Rites.

6

OLBI

The new star pulsed in the sky above the altar. As the braziers dimmed, burning the last of their fuel, the star burned brighter. Olbi had never seen a star shine as this one did. He was mesmerised.

'What do you suppose it means?' Alvar said to a traveller sitting next to Olbi.

The grey-haired man, dressed in the equally grey robes of the Granite Hills, looked up from their row. 'It means it's time to down a few ales, is what I think,' the gruff traveller said, smacking his knees and groaning as he lifted himself off the stone bench. 'Spirits, you Xylonans need to do something about these seats: thirty minutes on this stone and my arse has gone numb.' The man rubbed his backside as he wobbled into the aisle and towards the town square where the largest of the feasts would be held tonight.

Alvar turned his gaze from the star and smirked at Olbi.

Olbi shrugged. 'Maybe it's a dancing star that collided with another. Now it's twice as bright,' Olbi suggested, lifting himself from the bench. He regretted not packing a cushion. Next time, he vowed not to be in such a rush.

'Ah, perhaps you are right,' Alvar said, scratching his beard. 'It sure is bright. Looks like a garjee fruit sitting among the stars,' Alvar commented as he went to stand.

Olbi offered his arm to the aging master of the Stonehall. 'Let me help.'

Grunting, Alvar took his arm and stood, his knee joints cracking. 'Soon, you are going to have to bring me here on the back of a muk cart,' Alvar said, chuckling.

Olbi returned a smile.

'Alvar, you run the Stonehall around the clock without stopping. I've seen you climb the cellar steps carrying an urn of apris wine in one hand and a barrel of field ale in the other. I think walking to the altar every cycle is the least of your worries.'

Alvar gave a hearty laugh before keeling over and coughing into his sleeve. 'Damn, incense smoke will be my death,' Alvar said begrudgingly.

'Running around the Stonehall is different. It's my life, but this …' Alvar gestured towards the altar and the stone rings. 'This is a lot of people without a drink in their bellies and a song about magic spirits in their throats. The real spirits are in my distilling room.' Alvar laughed before the craggy lines on his face furrowed. 'Sorry, my boy, I forgot I had news for you,' Alvar said, slapping Olbi on the shoulder. 'Your father visited the Stonehall this afternoon. He is back from … oh, where did he say? Ah yes! Aldrowen. He has returned and came looking for you earlier. I told him you were out hunting. He will meet you at the feast. Let's go so I can sit and drink myself silly.'

Olbi let Alvar finish, knowing the old man became confused when interrupted. He was surprised to hear his father was in town. Even though he was late returning to Xylona, he thought it odd that he would return the day of the Manna Rites.

Travellers were exempted from attending if they were on the road during the days of the eclipse. And besides, his father was never interested in rituals and sacred days, nor of spirits and demons. Instead, his father was more concerned with ensuring mouths were fed and goods were traded between towns and villages.

The braziers dwindled to flickering embers as Olbi and Alvar made their way to the town square. They followed the last stragglers; some were still prostrate, muttering their prayers at the altar.

❖

'Olbi, my boy, don't lose a spot at the table waiting for my old legs to warm up. I'll be fine. Go on, off you trot. Save me a barrel or two,' Alvar said, breaking into a guttural chuckle.

Alvar was not kidding. Olbi knew no one could sink more ales than the master of the Stonehall. He smiled at Alvar as he began to jog for the town square.

He darted out of clusters of people, many sticking in familial groups. A few grinned and acknowledged Olbi as he trotted by, even sending well wishes his way. 'Glow bright!' a small girl, maybe six years old, yelled at him, her face focused on him as her tiny arms gestured from her heart toward him. He spotted the girl and automatically returned the gesture and replied, 'Spirits protect you.' The girl clapped at Olbi, and an infectious grin shot across her reddening face as she ducked behind her mother's flowing robes.

Aromas of freshly baked bread wafted from up ahead. His stomach rolled in anticipation. Olbi wondered if the fish he left with the kitchen hands at the Prime House had found their way to the square.

As he rounded a wind guard of hedges at the north of the square, crowds of people preparing to feast materialised.

On the rows of tables, he saw the river jacks he had caught mere hours ago. Some folks had already begun searing meat on the long fire trough that divided the square. The pit was rimmed by a narrow, raised brick wall that stretched twenty metres, allowing the many kitchen hands and chefs to cook and converse on either side of the iron lattice that lay above the smouldering coals.

Olbi observed townspeople clasping goblets of ale or sweet waters who chatted with each other over the charred, sizzling bounty. The trench served as a typical fire on cold days, but today, it was the communal heart of the feasts. He approached, salivating as the fragrance of spices engulfed him.

Olbi scanned the expanding crowd for a glimpse of his father. He wasn't at any of the six long tables. Nor was he at the high table that ran parallel to the common house.

❖

Though it was called the common house, it was anything but. The considerable hall served as Xylona's civic space. At the hall's east end, a large archway led to a room filled with chairs: the town's school. On the west side, a chamber operated as a shelter for injured or sick Rahsu. It was a buzzing structure, and the town square, along with its adjoining buildings, was the beating heart of Xylona. The square was uniformly cobblestoned, interrupted only by the fire pit and a monumental statue in each corner.

Xylonans were oblivious to the statues' meanings—a common trait among the Rahsu whose history had faded with time. The sculptures in the gardens and cloisters had lost their faces to erosion, and the memory of who they were faded into obscurity. Olbi speculated they once honoured significant Rahsu figures, though hymns and legends remained silent. Oddly, some ancient Rahsu sculptures in the town's cloisters had detailed histories, a phenomenon Liran, the town's Maven, attributed to people crafting fictitious stories for the unknown past.

A group of townspeople gathered under one of the statues, speaking animatedly. This particular statue, though weathered, retained a faint contour in a recessed area that depicted a hunched figure reaching towards the sky with one hand, and clutching a small orb to its chest with the other. As the group conversed with frantic eyes, one member gestured vigorously skyward. Olbi, following the pointing arm, witnessed the throbbing luminance of the unique star, a vivid reminder of its distinctive place amid the celestial tapestry.

Glancing back to the gathering under the statue, a man he knew well garnered the attention of the others. Dressed in a deep green travel cloak, he leaned against the statue and gesticulated wildly with his arms to calm the people around him. His face was weatherworn, and beneath his wide-open onyx eyes, dark circles and bags from sleep deprivation sat above a wiry, matted beard. From where he stood, Olbi noticed the beard was full of wispy white patches—a recent occurrence for his father.

Olbi approached the group, weaving through the crowded town square. His father had not seen him yet, and as he neared, Olbi began to hear the huddle's exchange.

'But surely it isn't connected. It could simply be a coincidence,' someone said. The owner of the voice had their back to Olbi.

A person dressed in similar clothes to his father spoke over the huddle as some in the gathering laughed. 'Faiyor, see reason! The stars are falling; the celestial dome does not deal in coincidences!' he said before another voice piped in over the top.

'Why now? Have we upset the Spirits?' At this, Olbi's father rolled his eyes.

'The Spirits have nothing to do with this. There have been stories of stars falling for years. The people of Hydoran have many tales of stars plummeting into the Great Lake with waves lapping at the town. Even barges docked at the mouth of the Flow have been capsized. This latest star has provoked panic in Hydoran—never has one fallen so near to a town before. It was as if the thunder and lightning were within grasping distance!' his father said, pointing again to the pulsating star in the sky. 'This could be about to happen to Xylona!' This last admission resulted in agitated outbursts— voices clambered over one another.

'If you think this true, we must inform the Prime One at once,' Faiyor said.

'I did, Faiyor. I told her what we witnessed,' Olbi's father said, standing up straight. 'People in Hydoran are spooked. She understands the gravity of the situation, but I doubt there is anything she can do. The Prime One will seek guidance about the star, but she appeared distracted when I met h—' he halted when his eyes met Olbi's. He grimaced as the rest of the gathering spun and saw Olbi listening in on their exchange.

The group dispersed except his father, who just frowned at him.

'Father, good to see you safe and well.'

His father shook his head. Olbi felt like he was a little boy again, being chastised for his behaviour.

'Olbi,' his father said, walking over to him. Tarak's dark eyes punctured his—a profound, hawkish stare. The man grasped Olbi's shoulders pulling him into a fierce embrace.

'You shouldn't listen to people's private conversations like that; I didn't raise a snoop.'

Olbi's stomach turned. He didn't feel like a lecture. He wanted answers. Besides, his father had hardly raised him. 'If you were concerned about being overheard, I propose meeting in a locked chamber instead of the town square,' Olbi replied.

Tarak went to speak, his mouth opening and closing a few times before he mumbled about hunger.

Olbi followed his father alongside a feast table to a spot beside Faiyor and another person Olbi recognised from his father's gathering. The two took up their seats at the table just as a burly woman with straw-toned hair and a round, cheerful face placed a serving tray in front of Olbi alongside a jug of wine, numerous dishes of steaming bread, roasted tubers, and nuts from the orchards. The serving tray was heaped with steaming, fleshy white meat fillets with brown and gold dotted skin to one side. It was one of his river jacks.

The burly woman then slammed a goblet before Olbi and poured him an apris wine, grinning at him. 'Glow bright, Olbi!' she toasted, raising her goblet before she drained its contents.

'Why is she toasting you?' Tarak said, turning to his son with a wrinkle in his brow.

The woman released a throaty belch that drew cheers from feast-goers before she raised her empty goblet to the mob, dabbing her mouth with a stained sleeve. 'Olbi deserves to be toasted, Tarak! He caught eight of the meatiest river jacks I have ever seen,' she bumbled, digging her wine-soaked fingers into the white flesh of the fish and bringing it to her mouth. 'Outstanding!' she roared, voraciously slurping at her greased fingers.

Another round of applause erupted around her as people lifted goblets to Olbi. He felt a flush of warmth within his cheeks as he sipped his wine.

Faiyor served the fish, filling plates that lay before Tarak and Olbi. 'Tarak told me you were a skilled fisherman as we arrived in Xylona this morning; I can see his boasts were not false.' Faiyor patted Olbi on the shoulder as they continued to load plates and passed them down along the table. There was something in Faiyor's eyes that elicited a feeling of comfort. *Do I know you?* Olbi thought.

A sheepish *thanks* was all Olbi could muster as he crammed bread into his mouth. He hadn't realised how hungry he was.

Tarak smiled, taking his turn to pat Olbi's back. It seemed odd that Tarak would boast about his skills when he was sure his father wouldn't know he was an adept fisherman. Tarak had never taught or accompanied him to the river. It took much trial and error, along with Alvar's old pike that he practised with, before he could consistently snag fish. Nonetheless, his father displayed interest tonight as he introduced his fellow traders.

'Faiyor is from Aldrowen, and Cotsh here is from the northern forests beyond Japheles,' his father said. Faiyor smiled and shook Olbi's hand before the traders wrestled with what to devour first.

Faiyor had a familiar face, but Olbi knew they had never met. Cotsh was a reserved man and was comparable in age to Olbi; his complexion was pale, and beneath his travelling garbs, Olbi could tell he was sturdy and broad. He barely glanced at Olbi before swigging from his goblet and giving a half nod in his direction.

'Listen, Olbi, I have something to discuss after the feast.' Tarak said, not looking at him; instead, his father eyed a platter of muk meat and roasted onions down the table.

'Is it about what you were discussing at the statue? About the star?' Olbi raised his head, checking that the star had not vanished. It shone with fury, unquestionably the brightest object in the night sky now the moons had set.

Olbi scanned the square's festivities. Occasionally, townspeople looked up from their food and drink to cast an eye on the star. Some wore quizzical expressions, while others glared at it with suspicion.

Tarak leant towards him, bringing Olbi's focus back to the table. 'It has to do with your mother.'

Olbi turned to his father. He opened his mouth to speak, but Tarak continued. 'It's not something discussed with ears about,' his father said. 'But I can tell you this, Olbi: what you overheard has many people troubled, and Hydoran is shaken. They fear something is not right. Hydorans didn't want to speak to Faiyor, Cotsh, and me when we docked there.' Olbi perceived his father's travelling companions were listening in to the conversation despite focusing their gazes upon their plates. Tarak's forehead furrowed as he glanced at Faiyor and Cotsh. Olbi sensed his father shared the same concerns and fears as the people he met in Hydoran had. He was intrigued— what had his father seen, and why had falling stars compelled a grown man to worry so?

'What did you see?' Olbi asked.

Tarak looked along the table at the raucous feast. People were engaged in their own stories. The burly woman opposite Olbi had turned her back to them and was engaged with an older woman leaning on a cane; her voice trumpeted loudly as if magnified. Faiyor and Cotsh were the only two people paying them any mind. Tarak glanced around and nodded at his peers before reaching into his travelling cloak.

Olbi watched him remove a small green pouch from his breast pocket. Tarak beckoned to Olbi for his hand.

'Take a look, but under the table,' Tarak said discreetly.

Olbi stared at his father curiously and turned to his companions; both wore grim expressions as Olbi accepted and untied the pouch's drawstrings under the table. The weight of the pouch suggested whatever it contained was small and light. Olbi hesitated. Should he stick his hand into the bag or not? Instead, he peered between his stomach and the side of the table. He tipped the bag's contents onto his palm and out rolled a small object no bigger than a large shirt button. The object was unremarkable as he ran his fingers over its smooth surface. The material was the only thing that seemed odd about it. It was a hard metal, much like copper, but it was the colour of the mica crystals within granite, almost sparkling. He looked back at his father, narrowing his eyes and shrugging.

'What is so unique about a piece of metal?' Olbi muttered.

Tarak raised an eyebrow and nodded at the object. Olbi flipped it over. The other side was different: the shiny metal was now grainy. On this side was a tiny copper box with black strands protruding from it made of a pliable material he had never seen. He held onto one of the black strands and noticed little strings of copper sticking out of the soft material. It was like nothing Olbi had ever seen before. He studied it, intrigued about what it was or where it had come from. As if Tarak read his mind, the man leaned in and spoke softly into his ear.

'What you hold in your hand is a falling star.'

Olbi regarded his father, perplexed. What did he mean? Was his father thinking straight? Tarak grabbed the object from Olbi's grasp, set it back in its pouch, and swiftly returned it to his robes, looking around like a paranoid thief. It was Cotsh who spoke first.

'Do you think it wise to show him the fragment, Tarak?' Olbi looked at the younger man, who stared back into his bronze eyes. Olbi said nothing, but Faiyor clasped Cotsh's shoulder.

'Come now, what we have found cannot be secreted away. We must seek the Prime One's advice. If not the Prime One,

then at least the Maven or another Maven somewhere else. Surely someone would have something to say about it and the other pieces,' Faiyor declared in hushed whispers. Before Olbi could ask about the other pieces, he noticed the table around them had quietened. He scanned the square just as trumpets began to peel over the crowd.

The townspeople within the square all rose to their feet; only elders or those who couldn't stand remained seated. Olbi craned his neck to look towards the north entrance that stood between the hedges.

The Prime One and Scion stood there, heralded by trumpeters on either side. Claudya stood tall, her chin raised, but she glanced towards the glowing star as the trumpets sang.

Reeva strolled out of the shadows behind the Scion and loomed over him. She stiffly scanned the square, appearing even more uptight since the kitchens that afternoon. Olbi felt a chill as Reeva's eyes met his, her grey eyes narrowing, piercing him with a hostile glare. What had he done to warrant that reaction? In front of Reeva, Ayon looked at his folded hands as though praying quietly to himself. Then, he looked up, his face composed.

As the trumpets broke, the Prime One and her entourage strode towards the high table at the far side of the square. She passed between the pit that divided the square and the banquet table where Olbi sat. Claudya's dress glided against the sandy cobblestone, picking up dirt and leaving a brushed trail. Several townspeople cheered while others yelled *burn bright* as she drew near. Olbi caught Ayon's eye, and a subtle smile crept onto Ayon's lips. Olbi grinned back but withdrew as Reeva followed the Scion's gaze, forever casting a shadow over him.

Claudya drew level with the burly woman seated opposite Olbi. The woman hurled herself to the ground before the Prime One, grabbing at the cuffs of Claudya's dress.

'Hallowed Prime One, burn bright! What does it mean? Is there anything in the hymns or holy scripts? The star comes from the demon's constellation, does it not?' The woman sobbed as she clasped the Prime One's gown. Olbi noticed her goblet sat empty opposite him.

Reeva edged herself in front of Ayon, her hand on the hilt of her sword.

Claudya looked down at the woman weeping at her feet and then flung her gaze upon the square, scanning the faces that were captivated by the commotion. The sizzle of meat on the grills became clearly apparent as the musicians stopped playing their tune. Everyone wanted to know the answer, they needed some reassurance that all was well. Claudya's eyes strained. Olbi sensed she was afraid as anguish glistened on her brow.

The Prime One knelt and clasped the sobbing woman's hand. 'Come, Yallon; all will be well,' Claudya soothed as Yallon continued weeping and sat back down at the table. Claudya examined the bursting sea of worried faces gathered in the town square.

'Xylona, travellers from far away, guests, family, friends, hear my words. I know your hearts are troubled but know this: the Spirits will protect us from wickedness,' Claudya's voice boomed and echoed across the square. Her words struck powerfully, and resilience resonated through the people in her vicinity.

'We know not what message the Spirits send with this sign, but I vow this,' Claudya hesitated and looked at her son beside her, briefly putting her hand on his shoulder before turning to the crowd again, 'You will be safe, the Spirits will protect you, and the Manna Rites have proven the Rahsu are favoured. We are worthy in the eyes and hearts of the Spirits, and no ill will befall us as long as we stay true.' Claudya finished by holding her hand to her heart—a genuine smile on her face—and then swept her arm out as if passing her heart on to everyone in the crowd. The townspeople returned the action to the Prime One while she eyed Olbi and kept her smile on him.

❖

'Let us enjoy the bounties we share tonight, from the fields and pastures to the orchards and the streams. Go on, eat; let us celebrate the Manna Rites!' Claudya's eyes twinkled at Olbi, her last words falling upon the fish before him. He felt warmth permeate his cheeks again as Yallon cheered Claudya's speech, provoking further cheers to erupt across the square. Olbi glanced at Ayon who was smiling broadly and clapping at the embarrassed fisherman.

'Come, move forward, Scion, let the people eat,' Reeva barked, pushing Ayon forward. Ayon shuddered as the Guardian's guiding hand nudged him through the crowd. She shot Olbi another indignant glower as she continued to the high table where the Maven was already pouring the Prime One a goblet of wine.

'That was a filthy stare. What have you done now?' Tarak said. His father's hawkish stare had returned.
'Nothing at all,' he said earnestly. He picked a fish fillet from his plate, which had been stacked with more food while he was distracted. Opposite him, Yallon started shovelling food into her mouth, oblivious to Olbi's mood. He searched his memories. What had warranted Reeva's disdain? Perhaps it was annoyance that Ayon had taken so long to collect yar milk that afternoon, and she blamed him for the Scion's tardiness. Or was it because he was in the Prime House kitchens with Ayon when he should have been preparing for the Manna Rites? Regardless, Olbi presumed it had something to do with Ayon.

Olbi ate happily but felt discouraged despite the conversations around him taking on more spirited topics. Claudya's reassurance had dissuaded Xylona's apprehension. However, Tarak and his companions remained wary. They only spoke to pass a dish or refill their goblets. Olbi overheard some girls a few seats down from him gossiping about Ayon. Their voices bounced in rhythm with the clang of cutlery.

'Well, I think it's because he is frightened, look at him; it's not as if he has seen manual labour. I bet he couldn't lift an

❖

empty barrel,' one of the girls remarked—the other two giggled in response.

Olbi recognised them from town, of course, but didn't know their names. They were two or three years younger than him, and even though Olbi didn't keep social circles, they wouldn't have been party to them if he did.

'The Prime One must be coddling him. He must pick a companion sooner or later.' The dark-haired girl continued sipping from her goblet. 'Or perhaps he doesn't like girls?'

'I hear that it won't be anyone from Xylona; the Scion stormed out of the house today and ran for it when his Guardian told him he would be forced to live with Remnants.'

Olbi's eyes met the dark-haired girl when he heard this. He quickly averted his eyes back to his dinner plate. Was this true? Had Ayon run away, and that's why he was on the farm today?

'Dayla, how could you possibly know these things? You were in the markets today looking for zirge root, I'd wager,' one of the girls said, all of them laughing at this.

'Indeed. One of the Monitors told me when she came looking for soaps at the stall,' the girl named Dayla continued. 'I only inquired because the Guardian ordered the Monitors to look out for the Scion, and they asked me to be vigilant. The woman that's always with him: Reeva. She was furious. I can see why. He is risking all our futures if he doesn't pick one of us soon, think! What if it's you, Faran? We wouldn't want future Prime's unable to handle their ale!'

Faran roared as she realised that she had knocked her goblet over, her ale dripping down the side of the table. Olbi shifted his attention to Ayon, who was absentmindedly stabbing a piece of tuber with his knife. Was it true? Would the Scion be sent away to find a companion so he could father future Prime Ones? Olbi's heart sank.

Despite the glow of the star above them and the strange object his father had shown him, Olbi finally relaxed into the comfort of the feast. Food kept appearing on the table, and people came to shake his hand or slap his back to congratulate and thank him for the fish. People that normally wouldn't give him the time of day between cycles.

Musicians played tunes again and people began to dance, including the Scion's grandfather. He circled like a hawk, cornering young women with a lecherous grin asking for a dance. Most agreed, but soon enough, Thessus was standing on the dance floor alone, searching for his next catch.

Faiyor was describing the fish one could find in the Minor Flow and within the canals of Aldrowen when a shriek pierced the air.

'It's moving!' a woman's shrill voice screamed nearby.

Olbi searched for the voice and located the woman pointing to the star. Olbi saw it then, too. The blazing orb now radiated a vivid light as it burned brighter.

The clunk of dropped goblets followed, and people sprung from their seats. Countless eyes snapped upwards. The musicians stopped playing, and the dancers looked around, confused at first before they, too, realised that everyone else was staring up at the sky.

At the high table, Claudya and Reeva shot upright, the growing light illuminating their faces in the night. The crowds gasped and cried out. Bursts of red, blue and green streaked violently across the atmosphere. Olbi noticed Claudya glance at Reeva and the Maven with a sallow stare of worry. He could tell she did not understand what was transpiring. Reeva was hard and fierce, her lips thin and white.

People screamed, and parents called out, grasping their children. Fear swept over the town like an angry surge.

'This is bigger than Hydoran's!' Tarak's voice struggled over the noise of the crowd. Olbi gawked up, unsure what emotions were appropriate for the phenomena. An incredible thunderous rumble resonated throughout Xylona as the star doubled in size. The night sky burned fiery red. The accompanying sound grew louder and shriller. The star was coming for them and fast.

'Remain calm!' Reeva boomed as she beckoned to the guards and Monitors within the square. 'Stay where you are, children. Under the tables, please.' Reeva's commands were ignored as panic-stricken citizens hurried to leave.

'Quick, inside. Olbi, follow me,' Cotsh said. Olbi realised that Cotsh and Faiyor were tugging at his robes, beckoning him to follow.

'Please, we can take cover in the storeroom beneath the Stonehall,' Tarak said.

Olbi searched for Alvar in the crowd, but to no avail. The thunder drowned out everything else. Olbi spun, watching people screaming and trying to speak under the building crescendo that swamped the square.

Reeva ushered the Prime One and Ayon away to the hall behind the statue where their banquet table sat just as a ferocious gust of wind blew through the square. Tables thrashed violently, dishes were flung, and barrels hurled through the air. Cries filled the night as people fled into the buildings that bordered the square. Olbi pursued his father, narrowly avoiding a platter that flew by his head, which smashed against a wall and shattered into jagged shards.

The star was picking up speed; its fiery tail enveloped most of the sky. Tarak raced towards the closest building, his cloak violently flapping in the wind.

Out of the corner of his eye, Olbi watched a banquet table split in two. A cracking and ripping sound followed as shards of wood became airborne, whipping in front of Olbi where Tarak was running.

Tarak took the full force of the collision. Debris hurtled into him and pinned him against the base of the statue he was leaning against earlier.

Olbi's screams were cancelled out by a thunderclap. He rushed over to his father and tried desperately to lift the table off Tarak as his rear was pelted with gnarling debris. He wrestled with the torrent of wind that lashed him as the deafening roar grew louder.

Tarak was knocked out. Blood gushed from an unseen wound. Olbi's fingers throbbed as he hauled the table. A second set of hands appeared to help him pull at the wood. Yallon was beside him, and with one great heave, they shifted the table piece away.

Yallon grabbed Tarak and threw him over her shoulder and headed for the closest building where Cotsh and Faiyor stood at an open door, beckoning them in and helping others to safety.

Olbi turned back towards the star. It appeared to be coming directly for Xylona, flashing a dazzling silver like the object his father had shown him earlier. Another dancing star had fallen to Arbonar. Only this time, it was Xylona that was in its path. Olbi darted across the square to where Faiyor held the door ajar. He was now the last person in the square. The cyclonic wind and thunder were vicious, and the fireball following the dancing star erupted just as he raced inside the building.

'Shut it now!' a voice yelled.

Olbi felt heat rising and he could make out the deathly glow of the fireball behind the barricaded door. The building shook, specks of dust and paint fell onto him and the others that hid and cowered. Children cried. Many Xylonans were bleeding. People aided others, some with injuries far worse than those they helped. Everyone was shaking and afraid.

Someone grasped Olbi by the hand—he looked over to see Tarak with eyes wide open as he grimaced. Yallon propped him up against a beam and Olbi knelt by his father. He looked out at the door, hoping it would hold.

The locked door jerked violently in the whistling howls, its outlines glowing from the light behind it. Something was burning. The door's hinges gnawed at the wood but kept holding it in place. Olbi prayed the Spirits would protect them.

But soon, the clamour of the falling star retreated before a colossal tremor rocked the town. Explosive roars enveloped them. Olbi stumbled as more paint fell from the ceiling and dusted his hair. As the falling star hit the ground, Tarak's grip went limp in his hand.

7

LIRAN

The rolling thunder died as quickly as it had come, leaving behind a chilling silence.

Liran searched the room for a light. In the darkness, she could make out Claudya and Ayon pressed up beside Reeva on the floor. Another twenty or thirty townspeople were scattered around the room, huddled up against pillars and under tables. Amid the inky blackness, Liran's deft fingers found a sconce on the wall and a flint tucked away in a small recess behind it. With a quick scrape and flick, Liran lit the candle, bathing the room in warm light. Faces covered in fear were unveiled from the shadows.

In the rush for cover, some had sustained cuts and abrasions while others had escaped unscathed. Liran could not determine if they were caused by flying shrapnel or the scramble for cover. Hopefully mild scratches were the worst of it. A downward glance revealed slashes in the garb the Prime One had given her, the robe now resembling a dirty rag. Reeva spoke in hushed tones to Claudya and Ayon, who both seemed unharmed. Liran hated to admit it, but Reeva was adept at protecting the Prime family in a crisis. The other people in the hall were silent as if uttering any words would be dangerous. Liran moved towards the door and unlatched the brace that barred it. The door gave little resistance aside from a slight creak in the hinges as she opened it slightly. Peering through, she sensed the danger had passed. She opened the door fully and stepped out onto the cobblestones.

The fire in the long pit still burned, its flickering the only movement she glimpsed in the square. Nothing of the feast was where it had been minutes ago. The square looked as though a tornado had swept through—tables were piled up against stone buildings, and the greenery of the hedges that marked the northern border of the square had been completely shredded. Food, cups and plates were strewn about and smashed across the stones. As Liran stepped further into the square, she noticed two bodies curled up behind the fire pit. Her eyes widened. Some had not made it to cover.

Liran pushed by the smouldering remains of a chair and approached a weeping woman. It was the teacher who taught the youngest of the Rahsu. In her arms, a small girl lay motionless. Blood seeped into her tiny dress from a wound on her head and stained her mother's robes. Liran fell to her knees. The child was barely breathing and losing blood too quickly. A rush of footsteps reached her. It was Reeva, the fires casting her long shadow over Liran.

'I will need your help, Maven,' Reeva said as she moved to the woman. 'I fear this won't be the only one.' Reeva's words were soft, and a rare flicker of sadness haunted the usually stoic guardian as she hovered over the woman. Through wafting smoke, Liran saw nothing but anguish haunting the mother's face as their eyes locked. Soon Claudya appeared, shadowed by Monitors who she commanded to check the square for others who failed to flee.

The mother stroked her child's back and rocked back and forth as Reeva cleared debris around them. Caught in the throes of shock, Liran hadn't noticed the tears streaming down her face. A hand fell onto her shoulder and squeezed. Claudya bent down and beckoned Liran to stand. 'Come with me,' Claudya said. 'Reeva has this one. Let us check other buildings.'

Liran could not speak, only sobs passed her lips as she let the Prime One lead her away. Other townspeople emerged from the buildings, and someone ran over to them from the darkness holding a torch.

Claudya spoke to the face behind the flame. 'Darling, I need you to search the buildings. Find Syrona as soon as you can. Tell her we have wounded people. She is undoubtedly already at work with her disciples, but if she is injured, I need you to let me know.'

Liran looked up. Ayon stood in front of them, his face stern as he nodded to his mother's commands. The injured would likely already be receiving treatment from the town's healer.

'Ayon,' Claudya called after her son. 'Find your grandfather too.'

Liran wiped gathering soot from her eyes as she watched Ayon turn back, nod silently to his mother and dash off on his mission. He called across the square to some Monitors who were attempting to douse the fires with buckets of sand, though it did little to suffocate the flames. Reeva was right about Ayon: he wasn't a boy anymore. The Scion disappeared into a building with two Monitors in tow. Would it still be Liran's responsibility to take him to Hydoran in the morning? Surely, there were more urgent tasks at hand.

Claudya steered Liran to what remained of a bench and sat her down. She crouched down, searching Liran's eyes.

'I will be fine, Claudya,' Liran said. 'I will help Ayon and clear space in the common hall for beds.'

'I won't ask anything of you that you cannot do, Liran. I have seen that pain in you before. Do not think I have forgotten it's been one year today since Hayda passed.'

Liran's chest heaved at hearing her son's name. It felt like fibres in her lungs had snapped.

'I know your loss, Liran. We share that. But now is the time we find what strength lingers in us.' Claudya placed her hand on Liran's cheek. 'We need to ensure people are safe,' she said, biting her lip.

How could Claudya be so calm? Liran surmised that she, too, must be holding back tears. The image of the mother holding her child was burned into Liran's mind, and then she remembered Hayda's cold, soulless stare. She still had no idea how he died. His body had returned to Xylona in the back of a northerner's trading cart. Liran tried to focus, but her mind

❖

kept picturing the grief and anguish on the mother's face as if she were reliving her own.

'Prime One! A fire is ravaging the fields!' The voice tore Claudya's eyes away from Liran as a group of villagers approached them. A man not much older than Ayon sweated, his sallow face glistening. He had been running, and anguish twisted his features. 'There is damage to the market square and anything built of wood … I'm sorry, Prime One; houses have shattered,' the man managed through a wheeze as he clasped his sides and sucked in deep breaths. Another voice in the distance yelled out, 'The fields are on fire!'

'Gather as many people as you can find and head for the river,' Claudya ordered, jerking her head to the man. 'The fields will burn but protect what you can.' The man and his party nodded in unison and rushed off.

'Do you think this is what Hydoran experienced?' Claudya asked as she surveyed the glowing flames and smoke billowing above Xylona.

Liran knew this was worse. There was nothing like this in the pages of history, and she suspected there wouldn't be anything in the scriptures to explain it. No, this was different. If Hydoran had been devastated like this, there would have been an influx of travellers seeking aid and sharing stories.

'I think explanations must wait, like you said. But I fear it will happen again,' Liran said, lifting herself. Her legs wobbled beneath her. 'I will see what help I can offer in the Common Hall.

'I will also find Euyan and ask him to speak with Alvar of the Stonehall about shelter for people tonight,' Liran said. *Judging by the amount of carnage in just this square, I wouldn't be shocked to find half of Xylona is already homeless,* Liran thought gloomily.

Liran left Claudya to the mercy of a swarm of villagers that approached her for guidance. Reeva had returned to Claudya's side, and both were taking questions and delegating jobs to uninjured citizens.

As she tramped through the square towards the Common Hall, Liran looked skyward. Though heavy clouds had rolled in, she could make out through small breaks that the star was gone. That the stars might hurt them down here seemed so unlikely yesterday, yet in just one day, a falling star had threatened Hydoran and now this: Xylona was in ruins.

Liran strode up to the hall. Its doors were propped open and locked to the walls, allowing people to come and go unimpeded. Stepping inside, she saw that Syrona had pre-empted the Prime One's request. The woman had her grey hair tied back against her nape, and crimson stains spattered her robe. She was tending to an older man who had a long piece of wood sticking out of his leg.

Syrona's disciples moved around the room, clearing spaces for beds as people stumbled in carrying relatives or screaming from injuries. Hysterical cries echoed through the large hall—Liran could make out someone speaking of people trapped under rubble, while others seemed to seek out lost loved ones. It all suffocated the air, adding to the commotion.

Liran joined the closest disciple, a young girl who couldn't have been older than fourteen, and helped her move a table from an adjacent classroom into the hall. Others had done the same to provide makeshift beds for injured folk to occupy. The girl looked up at Liran as they pulled the table along the floor, a loud screech sounding as it dragged against the stone. The girl's blue eyes were swollen and bloodshot from tears. Liran put her hand on the girl's shoulder as they stared at each other, sharing their pain. Liran let out a breath and continued tugging on the table.

8

OLBI

Tarak's eyes, once full of life, now stared through Olbi, empty of the vigour they had held minutes ago as they fled the square. There was no light in the room, but voices and sobs indicated a cluster of people was shrouded in the veil of darkness. The sound of striking flint came from behind him; Faiyor had found a sconce.

'Father ...' Olbi's voice was soft as he knelt on the floor. A whoosh sounded as a second sconce was lit and light flooded the room. Olbi saw his father's robes were soaked in blood, something he had missed in the adrenaline-fuelled flight from the square. The table had slammed into Tarak's body just above the navel, where splinters of wood now pierced his skin and were embedded deep in his torso.

Olbi sensed movement behind him. Faiyor brushed by him as they and Cotsh appeared. With effort, they lifted Tarak's lifeless body from the floor. Faiyor moved to place Tarak on a nearby desk.

'Make space,' Faiyor said.

Yallon's previously jovial face was now focused as she cleared people out of the way ahead of Tarak's trading companions. With one arm, Yallon wiped books and paraphernalia off the desk. Faiyor lay Tarak down on the cleared surface, his feet dangling off the edge. Cotsh placed his fingers on Tarak's neck.

Olbi only then realised they were in the weaver's store as he noticed the bolts of deep burgundy, green and strawy yellow fabrics propped up against the walls. He continued to kneel as his legs wouldn't allow him to stand.

The wails of people outside filled his head while he watched Faiyor hover over his father's body and remove his travel robes.

Yallon headed to a rack and violently tore away a scarf of yar wool, handing it to Faiyor, who pushed it into Tarak's wounds. Olbi didn't understand what Faiyor was doing—why was Faiyor barking instructions for Cotsh to find water?

'He is dead, Faiyor,' Olbi stated, deadpan. He knew it was true. He was numb—it was as if his brain had halted. This was a dream and he'd wake soon.

'No. He is not dead yet, but if we don't stop this bleeding …' Faiyor trailed off. They slid a weighty book under Tarak's head. It was the store's ledger that Yallon had swiped off the desk.

Olbi stared at his father, his senses muted by a bewildered fog. Faiyor was not making sense.

Cotsh returned from upstairs carrying a bowl and a jug of water.

'I couldn't find much. Will this do? It looks like it's been there a while; it has a film of dust.' Cotsh placed the jug and bowl on the desk near Tarak's face.

'It will do for now, thanks.' Faiyor poured water into the bowl and, with a clean end of the scarf, began dabbing it into the water. The scarf soon sullied as Faiyor wiped away blood from Tarak's torso.

Olbi stumbled towards the desk. His muscles ached, pulsating thrums of pain throughout his body. He clambered to his father's side. What had Tarak wanted to discuss about his mother? Ideas swirled in his mind. Olbi didn't know his mother; she was from another town and left him in Xylona as a baby. Tarak hadn't mentioned her in at least a decade. He had said she was a traveller from the far north and would never return to Xylona. Had Tarak seen his mother? Was that what he was going to say? Olbi had no way of knowing until his father spoke. His mind spiralled into speculative scenarios, each grimmer than the last.

Cotsh placed a damp cloth over Tarak's forehead. Pink hues started returning to his cheeks.

Olbi locked eyes with Faiyor. 'I saw his eyes. His spirit was gone! What is happening?' Olbi demanded.

'He fainted; shock can do that. Stand back and let Faiyor work,' Cotsh said pointedly.

Olbi's stomach flipped. Tarak's chest barely rose and fell as his lungs struggled for air.

'Olbi, look at me.' Severity streaked across Cotsh's face, adding age to the man's appearance. 'Trust Faiyor—they know what they are doing. In Aldrowen, Faiyor was a healer's disciple, and I've seen them bring people and animals back from the clutches of death. If Faiyor says Tarak has a chance, then he will live. I have no doubt.'

Olbi blinked, trying to decipher the words as his brain was having trouble processing their meaning.

Faiyor commanded the room with an air of authority, and their resolve was evident in how they moved around Tarak.

Olbi shifted his hands and withdrew from the table. He watched his father's breathing as Faiyor leaned over Tarak; the water bowl revealed cherry wisps swirling through it where blood dripped from the now-drenched scarf.

The room felt confined. Two people had moved to the doorway and pushed on the wooden doors, which creaked on their hinges. A cool breeze gushed in and dispersed the stagnant air and dye fumes trapped in the weaver's shop front. The fresh air seemed to lower the tension, much like the breeze that swept between trees in the forest.

'Yallon, could you show me where the well is?' Cotsh asked.

Yallon stood up from a stone step and gathered her messy hair into a loose blonde bun. 'Don't bother; I will grab as much as we need,' Yallon said, striding out the door.

'Cotsh, find the healer. Take Olbi with you,' Faiyor ordered, not looking up from Tarak.

Olbi's jaw dropped. 'I'm staying—'

'Olbi, there is nothing you can do,' Faiyor cut in. 'He will be fine. The bleeding has stopped, but I need fresh water and herbs to stop the wounds from putrefying.'

When Olbi didn't move, Faiyor smiled at him—a smile he could have sworn he had seen before.

'Trust me, Olbi.' Faiyor's smile faded as quickly as it came as Tarak gasped for air.

'Father!' Olbi yelled.

'The water and herbs are not just for Tarak. I see people here with abrasions. Who knows what others in town might need, but medicine and water are a good start. Please, don't dally,' Faiyor urged.

Cotsh put his hand on Olbi's shoulder and guided him to the door. They brushed by a young boy, who was checking others in the room for injuries.

As Olbi and Cotsh passed through the threshold of the splintered door and into the square, he took in the carnage that the star had brought. Nothing like this had ever happened in Xylona, and as far as Olbi knew, it had never happened anywhere. How could a star tumbling from the sky cause a wave of gale-force winds and a trail of destruction?

The breeze was gentle on his face, the earlier thunder now replaced by the clammers of people searching for survivors amidst the wreckage. The sobs of children and those injured by debris were thick in the air.

The devastation and terror of events replayed over and over in Olbi's mind. Why did the star appear to slow down as it streaked above Xylona? It seemed to slow down as people fled for cover. Whatever it was, the apparition he had seen in the forest had almost been driven from his mind. Were the two events somehow connected? Were the spirits instead demons, seeking to inflict pain and suffering on the Rahsu?

'Which way is your healer?' Cotsh asked.

Olbi pointed to the hall behind where the high table had been. Monitors were there, clearing debris away from the entrance to the Common Hall. They marched forward, kicking up dust and ash that blanketed the square.

Snippets of conversations pierced Olbi's ears as he moved past clusters of people who lamented the devastation. He overheard tales of destroyed homes on Xylona's fringe. He thought of his father's small residence, which was a wooden building on the town's outskirts. He shivered at the thought of his father lying on the desk, potentially homeless. At least the Stonehall was large enough to provide shelter to the affected.

Olbi led Cotsh to the healing hall. Faiyor was right, his father was not the only one to have suffered injuries. Syrona's disciples moved frantically between rows of makeshift beds fashioned from mismatched furniture—old tables, benches, whatever they could find. Even a bookcase turned on its back was used to support a dignitary. His robe marked him as a representative of Kanowna.

Olbi spotted the Maven moving between beds and offering water to those who needed it. Olbi nudged Cotsh and pointed at her. 'Maven Liran,' Olbi addressed the woman as he approached the bed of an older man she was tending to.

'Olbi, it's good to see you are alive.' A small smile barely curved Liran's lips. Her eyes were bloodshot; telltale tears formed channels in the dirt upon her face.

'You too, Maven. Is everything okay?' Olbi shuddered. He didn't know why he said that; obviously, *nothing* was okay.

Liran's eyes flickered with indignation.

'Are you busy, or will you ask another inane question?' the Maven said, her words void of emotion as she guided a small water bowl to her patient's mouth. Olbi recognised the man from the marketplace. His brightly coloured stall had stood out, where he made wooden toys for children in the shapes of animals. He tried to smile kindly at Olbi before grimacing and coughing up the water. A disciple had bandaged one of his hands. Would he ever make toys again?

'Sorry, Maven, my father is—' Olbi choked.

Liran's face softened as Cotsh stepped forward and said, 'Maven, I am Cotsh of The Northern Forests. His father is badly hurt, and we could use some assistance. He is being seen by a former disciple of Aldrowen, and I daresay he should not be moved.'

Liran nodded. 'What do you need? Syrona is running low on supplies, but if you tell her the situation, she will instruct on what to do.' Liran bit her lip. 'Better yet, ask one of her disciples. She is overburdened, and I doubt the night will end soon. People are saying fires on the edge of town threaten homes.'

Liran turned her gaze to the young fisherman. 'Olbi, I'm sure this traveller and the disciple he speaks of can help your father. The Prime One is looking for people to assist with the fire.'

Olbi was torn; he wanted to be with his father, and he wanted to see Tarak live. But if the Prime One had prioritised controlling the fire, that was his duty.

'I can help with the fire; where should I start?' Olbi asked.

Cotsh squeezed his shoulder before rushing off to speak with a disciple.

'The grain fields south of the town are burning, near the mill. But help anyone you can,' Liran directed as she moved to the next makeshift bed where a woman was curled up.

Olbi did not recognise her. The middle-aged woman appeared to have no physical injuries, but she rocked back and forth, sobbing softly and muttering whispers. Olbi's heart sank. So much carnage and heartache had befallen Xylona in the blink of an eye. He had to get to the fires soon—they would easily consume the grain fields and devour the edges of the town like a ravenous beast. He pictured the area where he was playing with Boji that morning and how peaceful it had been. What might become of it?

He turned to run, but the woman in the bed gripped Olbi's arm, her face twisting into a tortured scowl.

'They see you; they are watching, the spirits have warned us. The end of the Rahsu draws near. *She* lies, she lies. The demons are here.' The woman's eyes locked onto him, bringing him discomfort. What was happening? Her eyes glazed over, unseeing yet piercing his soul. The woman sucked in a shallow rattled breath, her facial muscles contorting unnaturally as if breathing was painful for her.

'You have seen them, boy of the forest, I know you have. Be wary: they will consume you; they will devour you, and they will inhabit your essence.' She gasped, choking for breath as she let go of Olbi's arm, leaving red imprints on his skin.

'Seen whom?' Olbi said, stunned. 'Do you mean the blue faces?'

The woman's gaze shifted across the chamber; her eyes boring into the wall. She ignored him now, her expression blank.

'Go Olbi, she's in shock,' Liran said.

'But she—'

'She is in shock,' Liran cut in. 'Don't take any stock of her words. Go now. We need everyone that can help.'

Olbi watched the woman rock back and forth. Her smoky eyes, unblinking, remained fixed on the wall.

'Olbi … the fire,' Liran repeated desperately.

Olbi nodded and regarded the strange woman one last time. Her filmy eyes were now drawn closed as she gripped her arms, her fingernails clawing at her skin like a bird grasping a branch in the wind.

****

Olbi was familiar with twisted wood in forests after a storm: branches tangled in a natural bedlam, each tree severed and snapped as if mere twigs. What he saw now resembled that. Wooden structures around Xylona lay decimated in the wake of the star. Doors were ripped from buildings, entire houses were shattered or blown away, and the snapped remains of fence posts looked like fangs jutting from the ground. He passed a row of houses that had been completely flattened, with some still at the mercy of the engulfing flames. They, too, would soon be mere embers. Olbi tried to help douse a fire, but a resigned man stopped him.

'Let it burn. It won't spread, there isn't anything to be done,' the man said as he watched the flames devour the house.

Olbi wondered if the man was watching his own house burn, the fruits of his life fuelling the flames and cascading sparks into the sky above. For the man's sake, Olbi hoped not.

Ash swirled through the narrow streets, and Olbi felt the heat of embers as they flickered like fireflies in the night. His breathing became laboured as he approached the town's wall. Dense plumes of smoke wafted beyond it.

Olbi spotted his footprints leading up to the old wall from earlier in the day when he was with Ayon. Who knew he'd be climbing the mounds for a second time in one day? A glowing scarlet horizon met his gaze as he wiped sweat from his brow. His head throbbed from the smoke as its tendrils spread into his lungs. He was thirsty and wished he had passed one of the fountains in town to relieve his parched tongue.

Looking to the outskirts of the town, Olbi noted that, thankfully, the fields remained untouched, though the areas closer to the mill had not fared as well.

Silhouettes in the distance moved and fought the red glow of an oncoming fire. The breadth of the damage was far greater than he'd anticipated.

Olbi ran for the subsequent rise towards the flames and hoped that the Grand Mill would still be standing as it had been that morning. His father and the many faces of anguish he'd encountered consumed his thoughts. He recalled the words of the woman in the healing ward as she spoke of the end of the Rahsu. Who did she mean by 'they' when she said someone was watching him? Had she seen the faces, too? He shook away his confusion. Answers would come later, all Rahsu would be confused and blanketed in fear. Wallowing in grief would drag Xylonans into a whirlpool of misery. No, he needed to help; that's what a Monitor would do. Olbi coughed up smoke that had seeped into his lungs as he struggled to tear through a grain field to the rise beyond.

Flames danced on the walls of the mill. Its charred white stone glowed in the night's incendiary brilliance. The fabric cloth of the sails had been set alight making the mill look like a tree stripped of its leaves.

Olbi watched people darting around the base with buckets, several of them flinging water at the growing red wall of fire. Olbi ran towards the furnace. He knew the layout of the farm from trading with the workers, and he often used their well to fill his water bladder before heading into the forests.

Ash choked the air as he ran, and thick smoke enveloped him, swallowing him whole. He couldn't breathe. His vision became blurry, and the sound of the inferno roared and crackled as it hungered for wood and grain to feed on.

He reached the well, his lungs suffocated. His cough was getting worse.

Someone approached from the base of the mill, carrying an empty wooden bucket. The figure limped closer, their hand shielding their eyes from the smoke. They had cloth—wet and dirty with soot—wrapped around their face. The figure dropped the bucket beside the well and unwrapped the cloth, revealing a man in his forties who had a gruffness about him.

'Start pulling the bucket up,' the man's deep and croaky voice resonated over the sound of roaring fire as he pointed at the well crank. Olbi grabbed it and lifted the chain from the depths as the man crouched, resting and waiting for the water to reach the surface.

Olbi recognised him—he was a mill worker who often also worked the fields, but they had never spoken. The man breathed heavily, sucking in equal parts smoke and oxygen.

'How many more are coming?' the man asked.

'Not sure,' Olbi replied. 'I didn't run into anyone on the way except for those dousing fires in town.'

The man spat on the ground and swore, exhaustion radiating from his body.

'How many people are here?' Olbi asked. He heard a bucket sloshing in the darkness of the well as he continued to wind the crank.

The man coughed, hacking up phlegm. 'Seven, including the Scion and two Monitors, if you can believe that.' The man stood up again.

'Ayon is here?' Olbi stuttered.

The man nodded, looking down at the well. Twice in one day, the Scion and he would be meeting in this field. The bucket slowly appeared from the darkness of the well. Olbi unlatched the full bucket, placed it next to the man, and attached an empty bucket to the chain. Olbi let go of the lever, allowing the bucket to plummet into the abyss.

'Where is the Scion now?' Olbi asked as the man drank a handful of water from the bucket.

The man rewrapped the cloth around his face as another firefighter appeared from the swirling smoke. It was a woman this time, though comparable in age to the man. She paid them no attention as she approached the well and started winding the bucket up.

'I think the Scion was making sure the herd was safe,' the man said. 'The yar were panicking and fleeing the flames. He should be over at the pens. I hope he gets back soon. We need more buckets, or the fire will take this place down, including the pens.' He picked up his bucket and began running towards the mill.

Olbi felt his gut twist. How could he have forgotten about the yar? Though without a bucket for himself, Olbi would be useless.

The woman still ignored him. She unclipped the bucket of sloshing water and attached the empty one back onto the hook.

❖

Olbi struggled to scan the area, the smoke and ash obscuring much of his surroundings. He would have to head for the pens to see if the Scion was there and whether he had buckets.

Olbi's mind swam with images of Boji happily playing with him that morning. Hopefully Ayon was keeping the yar safe.

The pens were tucked away down a small hill, along dirt tracks nestled between granite boulders. Olbi noted that the boulders shielded him from the flames, and that if things got worse at the mill, this was where they should wait out the fire. He sped further down the road, his aching legs protesting, until he could see the lumbering movement of yar in the pen. They yowled in terror. He could not see Ayon when he clambered to the fence. There weren't as many yar as there should have been.

Olbi looked around until he spotted two people up in a field guiding two beasts towards the pens—one of them was Ayon. Olbi ran up the hill, his shins burning and sending jolts of pain up his legs. Rest would come later. He pushed through the pain.

Ayon was covered in ash, which fell from his frame like dirty snow. When he saw Olbi, recognition flashed across the Scion's exhausted face. Everyone was exhausted.

'Olbi, take these two,' Ayon said. 'There are a few more out there that have run off. We must get them to the pens; it's the safest spot for them.' Ayon handed Olbi the rope tied around the yar's neck.

The Monitor accompanying Ayon continued to stroll towards the pen; the yar in Olbi's charge kicked up the soil as it trotted—the beast was distressed, and fear swam in its eyes. Ayon's eyes belied the same fear, his lips trembling in the darkness, though he tried to avoid Olbi's perception.

'Prime Scion, I can get the others.' Olbi said. Ayon didn't flinch or react like he had that morning to his title.

Olbi started for the rise, but as he did, Ayon pressed a hand to Olbi's chest. He was barring the way. Olbi looked down at Ayon's hand and the palm softly placed over his heart.

'Olbi, please don't,' Ayon said in almost a whisper. Olbi carefully studied Ayon, thin streaks of tears formed rivers in the ash on his face. Olbi's heart froze. What didn't Ayon want him to see? Olbi easily pushed away Ayon's slender frame as he handed over the yar's reins, and with his heart beating like thunder, he crested the hill before him, ignoring Ayon's call.

Grass smouldered near the green wall of the forests at the bottom of the hill. Three yar were swinging their heavy heads by the tree line nudging dark mounds within the grass. Tears welled behind Olbi's eyes—they were the bodies of yar that failed to escape the oncoming inferno.

Olbi's heart constricted as if a hand was clasped upon it. Ayon's voice called for him in the wind, but Olbi continued running towards the yar gathered at the forest's fringe, his chest heaving with effort as he passed more of the charred bodies.

'Olbi, please! Come back, please!' Ayon's strained voice travelled across the field.

It seemed to be increasing in pitch as if the Scion was chasing him, but Olbi couldn't afford to turn back. The forest drew nearer. This was the field where Boji sometimes met Olbi when he returned from the forest. The three yars watched Olbi approach; the poor beasts stressed and huddled around a mound—another yar that had fallen.

Olbi's eyes locked on the mass of fur in the burnt grass. The smell of ash and pungent burnt hair assaulted his nostrils. The dead yar was smaller than the others. His heart sank as dread welled in his throat. Olbi collapsed onto his knees alongside Boji's small, blackened remains.

The breeze carried Olbi's screams. Tears blinded him while he brushed his hand over the small yar where patches of fur remained brown. Boji must have tried to run towards the forest and suffocated in the smoke before falling. The yar around Olbi continued to swing their heads mournfully.

Rushed footsteps approached. Ayon slowed and stepped up to Olbi's side as he continued to sob, his tears falling onto Boji's matted tufts. The Scion crouched down and wrapped an arm around Olbi's shoulders.

'He was waiting for me,' Olbi stammered through sobs, choking on his words. He began to suck in shallow breaths, anxiety gripping and restricting his breathing. Ayon remained silent, his arm still on Olbi's back.

'He was waiting for me to help him, and I wasn't here. I wasn't here when he needed me!' Olbi shouted, screaming into the garjee trees ahead of him. He laboured for smoke-addled air in between coughs, and tears and snot dripped down his chin.

Olbi felt Ayon's hand stroking his back, but suddenly, the hand tensed. Olbi lifted his eyes from Boji and towards Ayon. The Scion was frozen, his gaze set like stone, locked onto the forest. Olbi spun and choked on his tears. His eyes widened— he saw them and knew Ayon could too.

Two glowing blue presences watched them as they hunched over Boji's body. Olbi recognised one of them, there was no mistaking those intense eyes. He had seen them that morning. Now, he knew without a shadow of a doubt that they were real. Ayon's gasps confirmed he wasn't hallucinating.

One of the blue figures was shorter and seemed calmer; its eyes didn't pierce his soul like its taller companion.

Are they human? Olbi thought, unable to see clearly through the wafting smoke and the tears in his eyes. Like earlier in the day, the figures appeared blurry, the fierce blue light obscuring their features.

'Who are you? Show yourself!' Ayon commanded. His voice bellowed with a robust strength Olbi had never heard from him. The phantoms watched them but did not speak or move. Instead, they regarded each other, their eyes intensely

focused. The spirits then veered around, walking away into the tangle of garjee. Ayon tensed beside Olbi; his fists tight.

'Show yourselves! Be you demons or spirits? I am the Prime Scion, and you *will* answer me.' Ayon took a step forward as Olbi clutched Boji's coat. Ayon's severe tone seemed to give the two figures pause.

For a moment, the taller one began to open its mouth but closed it just as quickly, as though it wanted to speak but changed its mind. With a glance at Olbi, it turned its back and, without further movement, disappeared.

Olbi couldn't move, his jaw dropped. No doubt about it: they were Spirits.

Ayon stumbled back at the sudden disappearance. The second figure was still there. It regarded the two men before focusing its stare directly on Olbi with a hint of a sad smile. Then, it vanished too, casting the forest into darkened obscurity.

'Spirits of the Rahsu, why have you done this?' Ayon yelled into the forest. 'Why do we suffer, and why do you bring the stars down upon us? Did the manna offerings not please you? Answer me now!' Ayon's voice reverberated through the forest, and the startled yar near them jolted and began galloping up the hill towards the pens. Olbi stepped to join Ayon and, together, they stared into the shadows of the garjee. No answers came.

9

ZILLAH

Whooping klaxons rang out around the chamber as Captain Zillah Morgana regained consciousness. She felt the cool sting of a gash across her brow, the pain worsening as she recollected the jolt that threw her across the ship's bridge as it slammed into the planet's atmosphere.

Months of training simulations and re-entry drills could not have prepared the crew for such an unexpected electrical disturbance while they waited in geosynchronous orbit. Likewise, years of studying the atmosphere's composition had no explanation for what they experienced. Something electrical on the surface of the planet had surged violently towards them, crippling the craft and skewing its trajectory.

Zillah shifted in her safety harness, her forty-year-old muscles aching in ways they hadn't in a long time. She felt forces pulling at her, a heaviness she hadn't experienced in weeks—artificial gravity was no substitute for the real thing.

The straps holding her into the emergency capsule twisted and dug into her shoulders. She hadn't had the time to secure them properly when she had made a hasty dash to the emergency chamber. The compartment was bright outside her capsule. From its small window, she could see the sleek white walls of the compartment and her crew locked into six identical pods lit up by harsh artificial light. No one stirred.

Zillah fossicked for the release latch with her right hand. She yanked the lever, and her ears popped, adjusting to the pressure change as the capsule door unsealed. Unclipping the buckle, she felt immediate relief from the tension of the straps.

The klaxons rang louder as Zillah stumbled out into the room. Her legs were like jelly as she staggered across the room to the panel on the opposite wall. With a heavy fist, she

slammed on the button that released the locks on the other capsules. Through each of their tiny windows, the quiet and soft faces of her team resembled still-frame photographs.

Other than shutting off the aggravating alarm systems, her priority was to contact mission command back in Quartab.

Quartab—the city they had departed from on the moon of their home planet, Anatara—would be anxious for contact. As the captain, Zillah was bound by Quartab Command's watchful eye and intense scrutiny. She was apprehensive about how QC would react to confirmation of the crash landing. Some of her adversaries wanted nothing more than to see her leadership fail.

Zillah hovered towards the corridor that led to the ship's bridge. Electrical wires protruded from the walls where cladding had dislodged on impact and hissed angrily. She wondered what condition the ship was in—the dread that they may be stuck on another planet lingered in the back of her mind. The list of questions grew with every painful stride as she pushed open the metal door that sealed the corridor from the bridge.

As the door unlocked, she heard voices behind her. The crew were waking and getting their bearings. *Damn*, she thought. *Perhaps I should have waited before waking the team.* A few moments alone to connect to Quartab Command would have been preferable.

The bridge was dark as Zillah entered. The blast shield across the navigational window blocked any light from outside, so the only glow was the flashing amber of the alarms, which illuminated the room in vivid bursts. Zillah navigated the darkness with her hands outstretched while she began piecing together the events that preceded the uncontrolled descent.

Quartab Command would want to know the facts, no matter how insignificant. The crew had discussed this scenario and how they would descend in an emergency. The consensus was to touch down close enough to where their satellites had detected settlements on the surface. Particularly towards one that sat at the mouth of a river and a large body of water.

Zillah remembered Dr Joja Amira suggesting they sit in orbit until daylight to get better bearings on foot. Only moments later, a pulse of electricity nullified those plans. The alarms sounded, the ship shuddered, and the crew were in their capsules within minutes as Zillah attempted to initiate the auto-land procedures and advise command of their situation.

Zillah moved to the communications console. Nothing appeared to be damaged beyond the superficial. If she could get a signal to one of the satellites in orbit, it would take radio waves two and a half minutes to traverse the space between planets and get word to Quartab Command. That was if the pulse of electricity hadn't affected the satellites.

Zillah tapped the touchscreen of the console, which illuminated immediately and hummed to life. The screen flashed, and warning signals popped up to indicate the thrusters were depleted—a problem for later. She read on.

Zillah absorbed as much information from the screen as she could, though her head still throbbed annoyingly. She overrode the warning systems, and the klaxons abandoned their cries of alarm. She sighed, enjoying blissful silence before finding the communications. She licked her parched lips, ready to update Quartab Command that they had, in a fashion, landed.

'QC, this is Zillah Morgana, captain of the explorer-class ship, codenamed Unity. Since the last communication, the mission has hit a setback. An electrical disturbance has disabled our orbital thrusters, resulting in the Unity's involuntary entry towards the Arbornian surface.' Zillah continued to record her message as she moved to the captain's screen and studied the status of the capsules in the next room.

'QC, we have crash landed. I am currently unaware of the extent of damage; however, the shock absorbers have dampened the impact, which no doubt saved the mission from a catastrophic end. I can advise that all six crew members are alive and on the surface of Arbornia. I am pulling up the log from the descent now; please await the incoming data compilation.'

Zillah heard echoes of footsteps down the metal tread of the passageway—one of the crew was approaching the bridge. The console beeped and Zillah scanned the readings, feeding the data through to Command.

'QC, I can advise that despite the ship's uncontrolled entry, there is remarkably little damage to the hull. The automatic safety mechanisms were activated, and the descent thruster fuel cells were depleted, indicating that the ship slowed enough to save itself from irreparable damage. QC, we await your response. Morgana, offline.'

Zillah pushed the prompt on the screen to confirm and send the message to the network of orbiting satellites. A shadow moved across the console. A figure loomed in the doorway and stepped into the room as Zillah found the buttons for the bridge's lighting. It was the man she least wanted to be on this mission.

'Any chance you will illuminate me with what you just sent, or will I need to check the logs?' Commodore Gideon Sloane said. His gruff voice reached her before his profile stepped into the light.

'It is all there,' Zillah said, gesturing to the console. 'If trust is going to be an issue, Sloane, you should step down and let one of your lieutenants take charge.'

She wasn't in any mood to hear another rant about her communication channels being accessible for the military personnel on board. Sloane lumbered closer; his grey eyes boring into hers. Hard eyes. Eyes that held no warmth. Was this part of his training? *Don't let the enemy know what you are thinking*, she thought.

After all, it hadn't been long since their countries had been at war. The fact that the nation of Jaree had managed to muscle its way to claim the top military rank on the multinational Unity mission repulsed Zillah. It had only been four years

❖

since Jaree had launched an attack against the Tarean capital of Aster. Thousands had died, and Zillah was now looking at a man who wore the uniform of those who issued the strikes on her countrymen. Although she was a civilian captain, Zillah had considered taking up arms and joining the defence force during the war. Luckily for her, Tarea's superior technology thwarted Jaree's efforts.

Sloane kicked off his boots as he took a chair. Zillah turned her back on him, returning to face her console. She wrinkled her nose at the smell wafting from his feet, though in truth, they all stank. Sloane cleared his throat, baiting her to turn and address him.

'If you need a lozenge, I daresay there are some in the storage unit to your left,' she said dryly.

'Your humour is lacking, Captain. Please, advise me of our current status,' Sloane said, leaning forward in his seat and looking at a console before him. It sprung to life by the touch of his fingertips.

'We crash-landed,' Zillah said coolly.

'I gathered that, Morgana. Maybe something I don't know.'

Without looking at Sloane, Zillah could tell he had a smug grin plastered across his face. She hated that face. The way his short black hair sat meticulously on top of a high forehead, his broad chin protruding from a sharp jawline dotted with pockmarks, his large, hooked nose, and worst of all: the sly grin that never left the corner of his mouth.

Zillah had resisted the urge to introduce her fist to his face the first time they'd met. She pleaded with the Tarean delegation for the mission, demanding a new chief of security be installed for the expedition. However, the Jaree delegates were insistent. If she were captain, Sloane would lead the military contingent.

Sloane remained preoccupied with his console as she filled him in. 'I have sent a status report to QC advising that we successfully achieved landing after experiencing an electronic disturbance that pushed us off course. Despite the disturbance of unknown origin, the emergency thrusters kicked in, and we are still on track to continue the mission.'

Zillah turned, hearing movement down the corridor. Sloane glanced at her and raised his eyebrows. She sensed he was determining the truth of her words. Before she had time to ask him to check the logs, Sloane shrugged and turned back to his console.

'That explains the fire I saw before getting into the capsule,' Sloane said as he half-heartedly returned to the logs on the monitor.

The two sat silently until a third crew member appeared in the doorway. The small figure of Joja Amira was not an authoritarian one, but what she masked in her petite twenty-five-year-old body, she made up for in her intellect. Her long brown dreadlocks bounced as she stepped onto the bridge. The doctor's dazzling blue eyes beamed, and her smile was wide and childlike. *What could she possibly be grinning about?* Zillah thought.

Joja sprung to her console. 'Good morning, all. Well, isn't this exciting? We did it!' Joja's smiles turned to eye rolls as her gaze fell on the stoic faces of the captain and commodore.

'I see that a successful landing on an alien planet is lost on some,' Joja finished. She giggled to herself and turned on her console. The young scientist and doctor was partly right—this was the first time in sixteen hundred years that people from Anatara had visited another world.

'We crashed, you fool! And there are people already on this planet,' Sloane said, not taking his eyes off his console.

Joja scoffed. 'Yes, but we are alive … and how exciting it is to be the ones to make first contact with another society of humans. I bet they are just as excited to meet us; think of everything we will learn about each other.'

Zillah had long since stopped listening to the chief scientist's out-loud thinking. Joja's chirpy voice blurred into the background as she continued to search for issues with the ship.

Zillah found the internal communication system and chose to update the remaining crew in the capsule room about their situation. After addressing everyone, she searched for the mechanism to retract the blast shield from the bridge's window. Joja was not the only one excited to see what lay outside.

Although Zillah didn't show it, after fifty-six days in space, she was eager to see the planet's surface. She found the command for the blast shield and listened as the locks hissed and metal casings retracted, letting a faint glow of light leak into the ship's interior.

'Sunrise is in about twenty minutes, Captain,' Joja said, lifting herself from her chair and walking to the window. The doctor's face lit up. Zillah rose to join her, feeling butterflies in her chest. She stared out, looking out at another world.

They had landed in an open area, devoid of forest, though narrow waterways weaved through shrubs and grasses.

'It's a marsh,' Joja said. Zillah nodded.

The boggy expanse wasn't what caught Zillah's eyes. At the edge of the marsh stood an impressive forest ablaze with flames. Joja turned to the captain.

'Do you think that was us? Did we set the forest on fire?' Joja pushed her face up against the window. Her childlike awe had spiralled into sombre concern.

'I would say so … likely the descent thrusters. They are hot enough to set the trees alight.'

The flames danced in the trees—only the tallest had not yet caught fire. Zillah clicked her tongue; this was a concern. Her first concern was whether the fire would spread and to what extent. Second, if they were stuck on the planet, would setting a forest ablaze spark diplomatic rifts with the natives? Satellite imagery suggested that these forests were dense and encompassed huge swathes of the planet's surface.

Multiple fields had been selected as landing zones that would minimise the impact on the surrounding environment but were close enough to settlements to allow easy retreat if there were hostilities with the locals. Attempts to communicate via radio had been made over the decades with the inhabitants; however, research teams advised that it might be hundreds of years before the native population reached the level of technological advancement to enable them to respond to the signals.

Sloane's voice yanked her attention from the fire, reminding her that they had been confined on the ship for months.

'Captain, when do you expect we will be able to disembark? The team will be eager to get out of this wreckage,' Sloane said.

Zillah wasn't feeling the effects of long-term containment. None of them should be: extended isolation was part of their training. 'Commodore, we have been on this ship for fifty-six days. Another few hours while we gauge our predicament won't be difficult.'

'Has anyone ever told you how much of a bore you can be?'

Zillah cocked her eyebrow and glared at Sloane before he chuckled. 'With all due respect, Captain,' Sloane finished. Fuck, he irritated her.

'We await the go-ahead from QC, Sloane. If you must, we can suit up and prepare for an initial search around the landing site. You heard what Amira said? We still have half an hour until sunrise.'

Zillah's head throbbed as she wiped her brow, her hand collecting caked blood from the cut across her head, she suspected it would leave a scar.

'Bridge, this is engineering, come in,' a man's voice sounded across the room.

❖

'Come in, Idonea. This is Morgana,' Zillah responded to the distinct baritone of the ship's engineer, soldier and fellow countryman.

If things turned sour with the commodore, Lyra Idonea was Zillah's insurance policy. The other soldier on the ship, Viggo Doxxa, was another concern of Zillah's—a wild card. Despite hailing from the neutral nation of Du-Kan, Doxxa had been less than receptive to taking orders from a civilian. How the crew had survived the last fifty-six days locked on this ship surprised her. However, according to psychological assessments and doctors ensuring a balance of personalities and personnel, all participating nations had given the all-clear. There had been a tense month of diplomacy and Zillah expected there must have been under-the-table negotiations for positions on the mission.

'Bridge, I can advise that the engine's damage appears superficial. I don't expect any issues in repairing them.' *Finally, some good news*, Zillah thought. Idonea's report was interrupted by another beeping on the console before her.

'QC has received our transmission,' Joja said, beating the captain to the message. Sloane raised his brow; curiosity shadowed his face.

'Play the message, please, Doctor,' Zillah replied flatly.

'Explorer Unity, this is Quartab Command,' a woman's voice came through, broken and distorted. The electrical disturbance was likely still affecting communications. Zillah knew the voice; she would recognise it anywhere. It belonged to her older sister, Zaila Tynoch—another of her insurance policies against mutiny.

Her sister's bureaucratically flat tone continued to crackle from the speakers. 'We have received your message and are relieved to hear the Unity's mission can proceed as scheduled. We have reason to believe the electronic disturbance registered in one of our satellites was a pulse of energy emanating from the planet's surface.

'Satellite imagery has recorded the later stages of your descent. The disturbance knocked out several satellites in proximity. We have been analysing the footage fed back to QC. The emergency thrusters have sparked nineteen localised fires, including one within a two-kilometre range of one of the native settlements. You are approximately one hundred and twenty-seven kilometres southwest of your intended landing site.

'Command advises that the coastal settlement will not be accessible within the designated time frame. Therefore, QC suggests that the settlement fifteen kilometres south of your current position is your destination. As you are aware, we have less knowledge of this settlement due to heavy forest cover, but infrared imagery suggests it is likely the largest settlement on Arbornia.

'Your new mission is authorised once you have taken the necessary precautions and determined the ship and crash site are safe to vacate. QC will be on standby and monitoring your progress via satellite surveillance. QC offline.'

The message ended unceremoniously with static. Zillah hadn't expected her sister to offer any sympathy or reaction to the fact she and her crew had crash-landed, but her tone seemed off—soulless and void of emotion. Where were the cheers of success in the background to celebrate the achievement that, for the first time, Anatara as one united planet had come together and put people on another world? There were no congratulations or acknowledgements, only strained silence.

'Well, that's that then,' Sloane said, lifting himself off the chair with a grunt. He lumbered off the bridge, leaving Joja and Zillah alone. Zillah watched the scientist at her panel. Joja quietly shook.

'Everything ok, Amira?' Zillah asked, more as a captain concerned with the mission than a friend worried for the woman. Joja turned, her eyes wet, proof trickling down her face. She sniffed and gave half a smile.

❧

'We have just landed on another world. We are following in the footsteps of our ancestors, Captain. But this,' Joja pointed to the panel in front of her. Zillah shifted and walked to Joja's panel to get a clearer image.

'This is not the way it should have been,' Joja finished, wiping her eyes on the sleeve of her jacket. Zillah understood why Joja was distraught—her monitor was linked to a satellite sending live video to them and QC. The images came from above the settlement to the south.

QC had understated the spot fires. Was this why her sister sounded flat? The fires were expansive, burning around the settlement in a furious ring.

Joja zoomed in on the images. Fires engulfed dozens of structures within the confines of the settlement, and entire fields were ablaze, creating thick plumes of smoke that blanketed the sky. It looked like images of wars back home.

Zillah glanced at Joja and in her glistening eyes, she saw flames reflected in them. They had brought their destructive ways to another world. She hoped QC would censor this from the public eye.

Unity's thrusters were responsible for widespread devastation. How could they prevent a major diplomatic disaster on an alien world? Zillah doubted her crew's ability to adhere to protocol, especially if the natives turned hostile. Vastly outnumbered, they couldn't afford any division or infighting—it would only make an already dangerous situation worse.

Zillah continued to watch smoke billowing on the screen as potential solutions whirred in her mind. She was interrupted by sounds emanating from her monitor screen—a system had detected an issue and triggered an alarm.

'What is it, Idonea?' Zillah called on the intercom.

'Captain, the unity is sinking into the mud,' Idonea's stressed voice radioed back. Zillah walked away from Joja's screen to return to hers—the final image she saw was a bird's eye view of fires spreading to new structures in the settlement.

❖

She could only imagine the debates at QC regarding her
captaincy.

10

LIRAN

Liran, exhausted and sore, lumbered from the crowded healing ward. The morning breeze brushed her skin as she emerged from the Common Hall. The sun had yet to breach the horizon yet the expectant warmth when it did was enough to soothe her weary emotions.

Syrona wished that she take a break to allow her mind to rest and process the shock of the night. So much pain and misery was painted on all their faces and Syrona had seen that anguish on Liran's face before. The healer's side eyed glances all night were not lost on Liran, Syrona was obviously expecting the Maven to mentally crack again. Liran's robes hung heavy, weighed down by the sweat and blood that soaked the delicate fabrics. She had aided countless citizens in the night. At first, she recognised the faces filing in, but after an hour, they became obscured and all she saw were broken bodies. First came a wave of people that had attended the feast, followed by a wave of people who were celebrating in the privacy of their own homes. Once this segment had arrived, in came the burn victims.

A few animals—howling and adding to the cacophony— were also brought in by their owners. The stench of burnt hair and skin lingered throughout the night, consuming the thick air of the ward. Liran wasn't adept in medicines, but Syrona had been grateful and desperate for her assistance.

Liran gazed out at the dimly lit square; the light of the oncoming sunrise was a haunting scarlet that filtered through the trees in the distance. A hazy hue sat on the horizon, brought on by smoke from the fires that still burned across Xylona.

'Burn bright,' Liran muttered to herself as fresh air caressed her face, drying the sweat that clung to her form.

❖

Only stragglers milled around the square at this hour, the fires in the long pits had long since burned into a soft white powder. Liran breathed deeply, feeling raindrops hit her cheeks before they slapped the white ash piles in the fire pits. Each droplet plunged deeply, throwing up dull wafts of ash and leaving small craters in the powder.

Through the raindrops, she recalled the night. The falling star had almost obliterated Xylona from existence. Gentle raindrops trickled into her eyes; closing them, she let the sound of each raindrop hitting the stones at her feet enchant her. She imagined the craters.

Opening her eyes, she gazed into the fire pit and the spots where the raindrops had landed, contemplating the star's own impact site. Perhaps it held answers.

Birdsong danced on the wind as the sun crested the rooftops. Liran smiled. Amid turmoil and loss, the enduring birdsong filled her with hope.

Weary, Liran fought the urge to head home; instead, she'd go to her studio.

The cries and smells of the ward faded as Liran wandered away. The conversations she'd held with Claudya and Reeva before the Manna Rites resurfaced in her mind as she traversed the silent streets of Xylona. She sifted through the exchange; most of it now seemed veiled behind the greater revelation of the star. Did Claudya still expect her to take Ayon to Hydoran?

Liran rounded a stone building: its thatched roof had been torn off, splintered wood littered the street, and objects had been blown down adjacent narrow lanes. Belongings were scattered across her path. The roads would have been death traps in the night, where narrow wind tunnels would have hurtled debris at dangerous speeds. How many people would have been hurt running for cover? Syrona had confirmed four deaths, and before the day was through, she expected another four or five wouldn't make it.

Liran leaned on the healer's strength last night, but Syrona—her own body barely holding together—proved that

Xylona was battered and bruised. She had left knowing that several lives would have flickered out when she returned. Liran wanted to hear their stories and record some facts or features about them, so they could live on in the archives and memories of the Rahsu.

As Liran turned into the final square, her studio's outward appearance exhibited no evidence of damage as she hobbled closer, damp and cold. The debris and flames had thankfully left the western side of Xylona relatively untouched. What debris there was had blown in from somewhere else, thatching from roofs was scattered at her feet like fallen leaves of a forest bed.

Liran placed her hand on the front door. No heat. She rested her forehead against the door with a soft thud and closed her eyes. The reprieve, though restorative, was brief, as it was soon interrupted by a scurry of feet.

Four figures covered in ash approached through the dull light of the morning, dragging their boots through the scattered thatch and dirt as they lumbered onward. Liran didn't know how much more sympathy she could muster as she quickly sank into a quagmire of exhaustion. She averted her gaze back towards the door in an attempt to slink unnoticed into the studio. A hefty hand on her shoulder stopped her cold.

A voice croaked, 'Maven?'

Liran jumped and spun sharply to face a man whose husky pronouncement indicated he must have inhaled overabundant smoke.

It was Ayon.

His gaunt, soot- and ash-smeared face stared back at Liran, the whites of his eyes standing out from the grime. He looked twice his years, tiredness making his boyish features haggard.

'Ay … Scion, what are you doing here?' Liran looked behind Ayon and acknowledged the others—Olbi and two city Monitors in the Scion's party, all covered in the same film of ash and wearing the same spent expressions. Olbi's eyes were red and puffy as though he had been crying.

Liran opened the door. 'Come, step inside,' she said. 'I have water to wipe your faces down and seats to rest your feet.'

Liran wedged the door open with a granite stone weight she kept by the entrance. The boys and the Monitors remained silent as they crossed the threshold. With what energy she could muster, she cleared space for her guests to sit and then handed one of the Monitor's the jug of water and cloth Euyan had given her the previous night. Her eyes strained in the darkness until she opened the louvres of the window, the morning sun scattered upon the stone floors. She turned and gave her guests a look over; none of them had any physical injuries that she could see. Something was upsetting Olbi, though—he had never looked so distraught.

'Thank you, Maven. You are kind to offer us refuge,' Ayon said. His formality was strange coming from someone so dishevelled—no doubt formalities for the sake of the Monitors.

'Please, Ayon, there is no need to be so formal,' Liran said as she gestured for them to sit. She paused before clearing a seat on her day bed. She watched one of the Monitor's eyes widen as they stared at the Scion, though he said nothing of being spoken to with familiarity.

'Have you seen my mother?' Ayon asked.

'No, I have not seen your mother since last night,' Liran replied. 'I spent the evening in the healing ward with Syrona. Your mother was helping someone else when—' The woman clutching the child flashed in her mind.

Ayon glanced at Olbi before locking his eyes with Liran. 'Have there been people taken by the Spirits?' Ayon asked, his voice a whisper. Liran saw the pain in Olbi's eyes; had he lost someone tonight, was that it?

'There have been passings this night,' Liran uttered regrettably.

The Monitors stood abruptly. Liran raised an arm, halting them.

'There is nothing that could be done,' Liran said. 'Some were hit by debris, while others succumbed to smoke inhalation.'

The Monitors paused and slowly sat back down, stricken by the news.

Liran continued to speak. 'We mustn't dwell.' She turned to Ayon. 'The Rahsu need you strong, Ayon. Until we know what has happened, we need strength. Many people are saying the Spirits are punishing us, ridiculous as it is.'

One of the Monitors harrumphed.

'You do not believe that though, do you?' Ayon asked.

'No, I do not. The Spirits would not let innocent people perish …' Liran threw herself into her armchair and rubbed her arms, the stones beneath her feet not yet holding the heat of the sun.

Ayon looked up at the ceiling as if in quiet meditation. Liran knew too well that Ayon's aspirations would clash with his status as a Prime, but Claudya and Reeva had a point. Xylona would only get through this with solid and continuing leadership. Whether that was Ayon remained to be seen.

'I forgot how wonderful your paintings are, Liran,' Ayon said, his eyes raised. Everyone looked up at the fresco of the girl in the meadow standing before gushing waterfalls. Liran gave a weak smile as Ayon looked around the studio. 'I am glad the star spared this building,' Ayon continued. 'Where did you get inspiration for the fresco?'

'I found a sketch among some old crates in a warehouse at the docks in Hydoran. This was in there, locked away for generations. I was able to smuggle it out before Monitors in Hydoran torched the archives,' she lamented, staring at the Monitors in the room. She was also glad that the fanaticism of the last Hydoran Prime line had left Xylonan history untouched.

Until today, but not because of revisionist Primes looking to purge pre-Prime history.

Liran thought of all the damaged houses and what people had lost in the fire amidst the carnage, art and history included.

Olbi remained quiet. The boy looked sullen; his usually strong chin was drooped, his eyes hollow like an empty well.

'Any word on your father, Olbi?' Liran pried.

The boy lifted his chin, his eyes finding hers. He parted his mouth to speak and coughed, it was heavy and thick. He needed Syrona or a disciple.

'We have been in the farms putting out fires and prote—' Olbi paused. He shut his eyes, and his face fell. Ayon picked up where Olbi trailed off.

'Many of the fires have been contained, and the mill has been spared the worst. However, most of the crop has been destroyed.' Ayon looked at Olbi, hesitating before continuing.

'Several yar have been lost, and we saw considerable damage in town. The Prime One will need to know the extent,' he finished.

One of the Monitors passed the Scion the water jug and cloth to wipe down his face. The fabric was black with ash, but Ayon did not seem to care.

'You are right about your mother wanting to know about the farmland,' Liran said. 'We have a lot of work to do— feeding and housing people will be the priority. Traders and dignitaries returning home will send word of our plight.'

'Liran, do you know what it was?' Ayon asked, probing with eyes inquisitive for the truth. She wished she had answers rather than doubts. If it was a message from the Spirits, what purpose did they have for bringing the star down upon them? The Manna Rites had been successful. Liran opened her mouth to respond but was cut off by Olbi's husky voice.

'It wasn't a star, and it wasn't a message from the Spirits,' he said dryly. He didn't raise his eyes from his lap. The Monitors looked at Olbi with unease and Ayon regarded Olbi with a quizzical furrow.

'What makes you say that?' Liran asked.

❖

Olbi didn't speak straight away. The squawk of a bird in the cloister outside broke the silence, followed by the patter of intensifying rain falling on the tiled roof. Ayon finished cleaning his face and handed Olbi the cloth. Olbi accepted it but did not indicate he would speak again.

'Ayon, get yourself some rest, and you two,' Liran gestured towards the Monitors, 'advise the Prime One of what is happening around town. I know she will want to call council to discuss what happens next.'

Liran directed a glance at Olbi, who was cleaning soot from his face. 'Olbi, I want you to stay back for a moment; I should have something for your cough,' she said.

'Will you be alright here, Olbi?' Ayon asked, kneeling before the fisherman. The Scion took the cloth from his hand and dropped it in the water bowl.

Liran was surprised—Ayon had never shown this sort of care for someone outside the confines of his family. Whatever bothered Olbi must be genuinely shattering, not that Ayon was callous, he just always kept to himself. Olbi mumbled something to Ayon.

The Scion stood, gesturing to the Monitors to stand. 'Thank you, Liran. When I find my mother, I will give word that you are well. It will please her to know. No doubt when she calls for council, you will be summoned,' Ayon said. He turned to leave with the Monitors in tow.

The door shut loudly as Liran moved to the window to peer outside. 'I hope they don't get too wet, but I suspect the rain will help smother the fires. Perhaps that is the will of the Spirits.'

She turned to Olbi and returned to her seat. He raised his head but did not speak. She hated to see him like this. Although they hadn't spent much time together, she liked Olbi. Besides a tendency to say exactly what he was thinking, he was an amiable man, albeit that he preferred keeping to himself. She had never seen him hanging around the archives or Common Hall; he was constantly alone on the farms or by the river.

'Olbi, what has you so troubled?'

He cast his gaze down again and spoke.

'Besides the fires, deaths, and my father lying motionless on a desk in the weaver's store?' She was taken aback slightly by his tone, cold like a still winter's night.

He sighed heavily and looked up at her directly through bloodshot eyes. 'I'm sorry, Maven, I don't mean to bother you. Many need help right now,' he said, pain lingering in his eyes.

'That may be true, Olbi, but you are here now, and I am asking you if you are coping. All of you looked exhausted, but I sensed more in your case, or am I wrong to say so?'

Olbi swallowed and bit his lip, his eyes welling. 'I lost a dear friend: one of the yar younglings I had known. He didn't flee the flames and...'

Liran's heart sank. 'It's okay, Olbi, you don't need to relive it,' Liran said. She recalled when people would enquire about her loss, and every retelling would send jolts of pain to her heart as though the death of her son replayed in front of her very eyes.

Olbi coughed and wheezed as he tried to suck in air.

'Oh right, honey. Sorry, Olbi. I almost forgot,' Liran said. 'I think I may also have bread and apris jam.' She shot up and strode to the storeroom where she gathered food on a plate to bring to Olbi.

'Thanks,' he mumbled, accepting the plate offered to him. He ignored the jam, grabbed the honey jar, and poured some on the bread. Liran watched him intently as he chewed on the crust.

'So why do you believe it was not a star that fell from the sky?' she asked.

Olbi stared blankly at her past his sooty brown curls, swallowing the bread.

'For the record, Olbi, I agree. I don't think it was a star. I also don't think the dancing stars are what we believe them to be,' Liran muttered more to herself than for Olbi's benefit. She recalled the star moving before the eclipse during the Manna Rites. No, this transited closer than the moons—the stars were much farther away.

'Because of something my father told me last night,' Olbi said, interrupting Liran's thoughts. 'He wanted to talk to you about it, or if not you, then the Prime One.'

'Tarak was going to talk to me about the star?'

'Well, one in particular: the one that fell near Hydoran.'

'Did he tell you about the Hydoran star?' Liran probed. Tarak was back in town, and she too had planned to speak with him about the matter.

'Not much,' Olbi mumbled, playing with his fingernails. 'But enough to understand why people in Hydoran are worried and that what fell from the sky was not a star.'

Liran felt her intrigue surge. She didn't know where this newfound energy was coming from, but it made her alert and focused, eager to learn about recent events.

Olbi continued. 'I overheard my father speaking with some of his companions. Then, he showed me an object at the feast. When I saw the star fall last night, it wasn't like a shooting star—it slowed down like a bird gliding into a tree. Something didn't seem right—'

Liran held up a hand, and Olbi stopped. This was a lot for her to take in. She stood abruptly and approached her desk, grabbing a pencil and parchment. Olbi finished off the bread.

'He showed you something at the feast?' Liran said, sitting back down.

'I know he didn't want me to tell anyone, but mentioned you, so I assume he meant to show you.'

Liran nodded. 'Listen, Olbi. I wanted to speak with your father because he had already spoken with Cla ... The Prime One about the star.'

'He did?' Olbi narrowed his eyes.

'Yes, I met with the Prime One and Reeva before the Manna Rites. The Prime One said she had spoken to your

father. People in Hydoran are scared. At that meeting, I was tasked to travel to Hydoran to speak with their Maven and hear their stories. But now … well, things have changed,' Liran said, gesturing towards the town square.

'My father showed me something he believes is a piece of the star,' Olbi calmly stated, setting his plate off to the side. Liran's eyes widened at this admission.

'He saw the impact site?'

'He didn't say. I know other pieces rained down from the sky in a flash of light and thunder. It didn't sound as bad as what had happened last night.' Olbi paused for a second, shifting on the bench. Colour had returned to his face, and his sadness had diminished. Liran couldn't remember the last time he had spoken so much.

'What did it look like? The star fragment,' she eagerly interjected, frantically scribbling down the details of his account.

'It felt like metal, but it was unnatural. I have never seen anything like it before.'

Liran realised her mouth was hanging open as she documented Olbi's admissions. When he concluded, she said nothing. Heavy rain battered the studio, and the fading light filtering through the window louvres grew dimmer. The stone floor remained as cold as ice. Liran shivered, mulling over Olbi's story.

'I think you should come with me to see the Prime One,' she suggested, breaking the silence. Olbi cocked his head, his eyes narrowing. Liran crossed the room and grabbed her shawl, wrapping it around her shoulders. 'Whatever your father showed you and what happened last night and in Hydoran, it is all somehow connected. I want to get some rest first, and then I want to see if we can locate the impact site of the star or whatever it was.' Liran walked back to her desk. Her eyes landed on the book she'd written on the dancing stars. She picked it up and flicked through the pages.

❧

All wrong, she thought and began laughing. It felt wrong to do so at a time like this, and the shocked expression on Olbi's face reinforced this.

'I cannot believe how misguided I had been,' Liran muttered to herself, still amused.

'Maven, there is one more thing,' Olbi revealed. His eyes darted to the door and then to Liran.

'Just one?' she said.

Olbi shifted uncomfortably. 'Do you think the Spirits walk among us?'

Whatever she expected Olbi to say, it wasn't that. Liran examined Olbi closer. She had seen no proof to confirm the Spirits existed. But then, who were the Manna Rites for and where did the fruit go when placed on the altar? 'Some people believe so. What makes you ask?'

Olbi fidgeted his fingers again. 'I think I saw something in the garjee forests last night with Ayon,' he admitted. 'And I believe Ayon saw it too.'

'You *think* you saw?'

'I *know* I saw,' Olbi said adamantly. 'I just don't know what I—what we—saw. There were two … people in the forest, and it was not the only time I have seen them. They don't speak; they watch. Olbi looked away, continuing to fidget with his fingers.

It was not the first time Liran had heard anecdotes like this. Her belief in the Spirits had never been strong, but she could not deny the accounts or admit to them publicly, given her position.

'Others have told me similar things, Olbi. Monitors speak of faces in the trees, of queer light shifting among branches.'

Olbi looked up, his eyes wide.

'The common factor is the forest, Olbi. Some think it is the Spirits—others, demons. I haven't been into the forests since I was a girl hiding from chores. The garjee give me splitting headaches,' Liran admitted.

Olbi nodded silently. 'I don't think they are Spirits; the Spirits would not watch yar burn.' Olbi's sullen mood changed to full-blown, radiating anger. The boy had been through so much. They all had. But within minutes, Olbi had relaxed as if a weight had lifted from his shoulders. He sniffed and looked up at the fresco.

'I have never seen Ayon care about someone like he did for you just now. I was unaware you were friends?' Liran said, smiling. Olbi jerked.

'We aren't friends,' he rebutted quickly. 'I barely know him.'

'Few people know him, Olbi, that's why it makes me happy to see him open up. I heard you were teaching him how to fillet a fish?'

'Reeva didn't like that,' Olbi said, and Liran chuckled.

'No, she didn't,' Liran said slyly. 'She thinks it's undignified for a Prime to learn how to feed themselves.' Olbi gave up the first half-smile since he had arrived.

'Do you like him?' Liran asked.

Olbi shrugged, but his cheeks flushed. 'Why did he run away?' he inquired.

Liran sighed, Claudya's request at the front and centre of her mind. 'Because he is being asked to do something he doesn't want. His position comes with a responsibility that contrasts with who he is.'

'That he needs to find a companion and strengthen the bloodline,' Olbi offered.

'The pressure is getting to him,' she conceded. 'I can't blame him. Soon, every young woman in town will eye him like he is a well-marbled slab of muk meat, and to be honest, I imagine some will link the destruction of Xylona to the Scion's apprehension to continue the line.' Liran shook her head. Unfortunately, the fates of life had woven a destiny of torment for Ayon.

'It's already happening,' Olbi said. I overheard some girls at the feast mocking the Scion.' The rain pelted the roof with fury.

'Yes, as tragic as that is. He is at the age when the Prime family is to do their duty. Do you know the rumours, Olbi?'

Olbi shook his head.

'In the last two hundred years, we have witnessed the bloodline diminish.' Liran leaned forward in her chair. 'Once, there were several families with the blood vying for power. They turned against one another, and the Rahsu fought brutally amongst themselves. We now stand at the precipice of annihilation, all because the Rahsu hungered for power and dominance.'

'It's what we are all taught,' said Olbi. 'What then happens if a Scion doesn't want to have children? What if the offspring does not have the blood?'

'That's something the Rahsu will need to deal with when the time comes. We may need to get used to the notion of life where the reign of the Primes ends.'

Olbi looked incredulous. 'That's unusual for a Maven to say,' he replied.

Liran laughed and leaned back in her seat, running her hands over the smooth wooden armrests.

'I am the only Maven with half a brain,' she puffed. They shared a laugh until a knock at the door interrupted them.

'Maven, are you there? It's Euyan. Are you safe?' The muffled voice behind the door echoed into the room. Liran rolled her eyes.

'Speaking of half a brain,' she said, smiling at Olbi. She started gliding towards the door but then hesitated. 'Best not mention anything about the Scion or the star to Euyan; he can be quite the zealot.' Olbi nodded and Liran continued to open the door.

Euyan panted as he stepped inside, dripping rain onto the entryway stones.

'Maven,' he started to speak, his arms gesticulating wildly as he propped his umbrella against the wall. 'The Prime One has called for council, and reports reach my ears concerning destroyed farmlands. There are also accounts the star behaved strangely as it approached Xylona. I can vouch for that. Before I ran for cover, I saw the star flaming from underneath its silver form, shooting jets of fire to the ground, setting buildings ablaze a—'

His beady eyes fell on Olbi and he stopped in his tracks, visibly gulping. 'Maven, I had no idea you had guests,' Euyan said contemptuously.

'You didn't give me time to speak, Euyan,' Liran replied casually.

Her assistant glared at Olbi as if he had done something wrong merely by being there. Euyan was the last person she had time for right then, but she ushered her assistant in. He was dressed as though ready for a day in the archives. He even wore a sweet perfume. His dark blue robe that clung to his form, and his wet but clean hair looked out of place next to Olbi's dusty and sooty Manna Rites garb. Somehow, Euyan had found time to change and, judging by his energy, somewhere to rest overnight.

Liran gestured for Euyan to sit. He took her armchair, soaking the upholstery in rainwater. Liran held her tongue. 'You spoke of a council. Do you know what time?' There was an edge to her tone that Euyan didn't pick up.

'Council will begin in an hour at the Prime House,' Euyan said, tripping on his words as if trying to get the information out as fast as he could. He took a couple of breaths before continuing.

'A few Monitors and I have been asked to gather those who have been requested to attend. The bell tower has been … destroyed, so we are sprinting across Xylona.' Euyan keeled over panting as if he'd run a marathon, yet not a drop of sweat shone on his forehead. Liran fought her eye muscles that threatened to roll in distaste.

'Thank you, Euyan. I will see you at the council meeting. Olbi and I best make our way to the Prime House,' Liran started. Euyan's eyes bulged.

'But he wasn't called for council,' Euyan said, ignoring Olbi.

'Well,' Liran rebuffed, opening the door for Euyan, 'I am inviting him. You best be off. Let the other guests know of the council meeting as you've been charged and be careful not to scuff your fresh robe.'

Euyan glared at Liran and then at Olbi. Miraculously cured of his exhaustion, he trotted out the door, huffing.

Liran closed her eyes and the feeling of being depleted returned. 'Come, Olbi. Unfortunately, rest must wait. The Prime One beckons.'

'Should I join you? I'm not on the council?' Olbi stood up as Liran guided him out the door and into the damp streets.

'No, you are not, but your father's story must be heard,' Liran said as the room was briefly revealed by a dazzling flash followed by a thunderbolt cracking above Xylona.

11

ZILLAH

Zillah sat in the Unity's sterile medical bay, staring at Joja Amira's chest as the doctor attended to her cut. Zillah hadn't thought the injury a priority; getting the ship stable and out of the marsh was her first job. However, the doctor conveyed she did not want to take any chances with an open wound in an alien environment, particularly while it rained. There were, after all, hours of walking through unknown forests ahead. Zillah hoped the rain would stop soon and spare them a soggy day.

'How are we going to dodge a political incident, Captain?' Joja asked as she cut a bandage to size and applied a thick glob of antiseptic cream to her fingers. The pungent smell of the cream made Zillah's eyes water.

'With tactful honesty,' Zillah said. 'I am hopeful the natives will understand it was an accident, if they understand us at all.'

Joja raised an eyebrow.

'I think you'd agree, Doctor. For these people, the very idea of us will be jarring. It may take considerable convincing for them to understand just who we are. Remember, they are a primitive society. Who knows how they will react. That's why those military fucks are here,' Zillah said.

Joja gave a chuckle that didn't quite reach her eyes before nodding in agreement.

Zillah liked the doctor—it was hard not to. She was young, yet her talents shone through. Joja was a part of the Tobanian delegation to QC, which had other highly skilled and more experienced candidates—nevertheless, the advanced ages and unwillingness to cope with the journey to Arbornia had stood as a hurdle for the other candidates. Joja had a determination and resilience that Zillah admired, and the doctor had proven her skills in the comprehensive training simulations and scenarios they had all undergone. Zillah's hesitation was eventually dissuaded by the doctor's double degree—ultimately, a scientist who also acted as a medical officer cemented her in the highly coveted role aboard the Unity.

'All done,' Joja said, removing her gloves. 'I will be closely observing everyone. Even though the planet is deemed hospitable, we should monitor for any unexpected problems. We don't want Arbornians infected by a deadly pathogen we may inadvertently introduce.' She began packing away the medical kit into her travel bag.

'That's what your academy is notable for, isn't it: pathogens?' Zillah asked.

'Hophnam? Yes, it's where our scientists eradicated the Jaree virus before it spread throughout Tobania,' the doctor said. Her casual approach to the matter struck Zillah. Tobania had avoided mass infection of a deadly virus that was the precursor of a Jareean invasion on Zillah's home country, Tarea. Although the Tareans may not have wanted to admit it, they owed a lot to Tobania's effective cure for the virus that Jaree had weaponised. Zillah fell silent, remembering the countless friends and family lost to the ugly virus.

Joja must have noticed her mood shift as she piped in with her trademark, perky voice. 'Hey, let's go make first contact with some aliens; what do you say?' Joja said, smacking the captain's arm.

Zillah raised an eyebrow and cast a wary gaze at Joja. Just because she admired Joja didn't mean she was ready to start playing favourites.

The rain outside the Unity grew in intensity; like an angry barrage of stones, it pounded against the ship's hull. The mood was sombre as the crew gathered in the cargo hold. From here, the belly of the Unity would be lowered to the surface. However, from Idonea's reports, they were not sitting flat on the surface. Instead, they were wedged in a marshy bog, and the heavy ass of the ship—where the engines were—was sinking into the mud, exposing the landing pads to the elements on an ever-increasing angle. Zillah knew that her first steps, the first of any Anatrian's onto another planet would instead be a first swim.

Zillah stood at the centre of the platform and faced the expedition crew. She eyed each team member assembled before her—everyone had survived the crash landing without significant injury. Viggo Doxxa had a laceration across his left cheekbone and grazes along his left arm. The cut had Joja's trademark antiseptic cream, but judging by his stubborn and steely stare, the man had declined the bandage.

Each person was dressed in attire befitting their position. The military personnel wore deep green uniforms marked with their rank insignia of their respective nations. A committee at QC had chosen the green colouring as a tactical decision: forests could be used as cover in a hostile environment.

Lyra Idonea wore the Tarean navy uniform with a few modifications to the pants that were cut off at the knees. Dark red tattoos depicting faces enveloped in smoke, a cultural symbol of one of Tarea's religions, ran down his legs. She knew he would have similar tattoos beneath the strands of fair hair sticking out from beneath his cap.

Dr Amira wore a simple jumpsuit, and a sky-blue backpack adorned with easy-to-access compartments. She also carried a knife, tucked into a band around her leg, for cutting samples of plants for analysis, or so she had said. Zillah hoped she was skilled enough to use it if things turned sour on the mission.

Everyone looked at Zillah fiercely, all well-rested and ready to get off the ship holding them captive.

'Temperature readings suggest it's twenty degrees above zero outside,' Zillah began, thinking of no better way to initiate the final briefing.

'Well, I'm inspired,' Sloane said under his breath.

Zillah knew she was expected to deliver a speech with grandeur. Despite all that time in the void between worlds, she hadn't written out anything fitting for this moment.

Zillah stared at Alrin Sandol, the scrawny, young, red-haired man from Manakria. He carried a camera to log the expedition. Of the six crew members, Alrin offered negligible value; however, he was crucial in one aspect: accountability. His camera was linked to a satellite network orbiting Arbornia and would feed everything the mission would see and do back to command, including Zillah's decisions. She felt like she was being watched—the lead character in an interplanetary television show. Alrin fumbled the camera as Zillah tried to conjure up what inspiring words to say before the platform was lowered and they found themselves on the surface.

'Well,' Zillah uttered, suddenly aware that hundreds of millions of people would soon be watching her back home. Her hands oddly felt alien, and she had no idea what to do with them. Likewise, she became all too conscious of the gash on her forehead. The crew, too, suddenly aware of public perception back home, appeared to stand taller. She wasn't sure if she imagined it, but was Idonea wearing eyeshadow?

Alrin gave a thumbs up to indicate he was ready to go, his sallow face half hidden behind the viewing lens of his camera. Zillah cleared her throat ready for the most important speech of her career. 'Today, we stand at the brink of a new frontier for all Anatrians. On this mission, our core objective is unity. The unification of all Anatrians, where we set aside our long-ingrained differences and instead work together for a common goal.' Zillah watched Alrin turn the camera to scan the crew, spotlighting the different nationalities of the team.

He does know his craft, Zillah mulled before continuing. 'Finally, as history demands, we are reclaiming our birthright. Within the very fibre of who we are, beats the blood of the masters of the stars. The children of the Injai now follow in the footsteps of those who came before us.' Zillah paused for dramatic effect. 'Moments ago, we landed on the surface of

Arbornia. The children of the Injai have returned to their verdant paradise. This distant world in our skies reminded us of the great civilisation our ancestors lost. Together now as one people, we reclaim it. Anatara and Arbornia have finally been reunited!' Zillah finished with much bravado in her tone.

Straightening her back, she stared directly into the lens. She imagined the crowds of people cheering and clapping back on Anatara. Homes and buildings in her hometown of Aster, the capital of Tarea, would be in awe of her—their hometown icon would adorn banners and screens in cafes and along the beachside promenade, places she missed dearly. Captain Zillah Morgana and her crew would be the most famous people on Anatara, once the relays fed the visuals back to Quartab and the images were edited for global consumption.

'Communication severed,' Alrin called. 'It will take a moment for another satellite to be within range to transmit.'

Shoulders around the cargo hold slumped. No cheers went out and no smiles adorned their faces—only quiet and stoic visages of determination. Zillah could barely hear her racing heartbeat beneath the rain slamming violently against the ship's hull.

12

LIRAN

The sun had well and truly begun its journey to its zenith as Liran and Olbi stepped into the Prime House Plaza. Rain droplets glistened on the manicured plants and flowers, and birds serenaded the square. Before too long, an ominous opaque cloud blocked any warmth the sun offered as the pair hurried, their feet kicking up mud and ash.

Liran shivered and looked down at her garments, she couldn't believe it: she had forgotten her shawl again. She swore at herself before turning to Olbi.

'Don't say anything unless I signal that it's appropriate. I'm unsure what direction the conversation will take, but I think it wise to listen first. I don't know whom Claudya called to council nor its whole purpose, it may just be about moving forward,' Liran said.

Olbi nodded his agreement as they climbed the steps up to the main hall of the Prime House. The house appeared untouched by the onslaught of the previous night—its robust stone structure and exterior walls aided in its protection.

The great hearth was already lit and a dozen people milled around its crackling flames, whispering in hushed voices. Liran strode across the hall and guided Olbi with her hand on his shoulder. Faces that brimmed with curiosity turned and scanned them, clearly wondering who else had been called upon for council. Some nodded at her as she approached, while others glanced at Olbi, including Alvar, the owner of the Stonehall.

'Good to see you alive and well, boy. Couldn't very well run the hall alone,' Alvar said, beaming a smile at Olbi. Olbi picked at his fingernails, this was all evidently new to him.

Liran scanned the gathering and found it was full of the faces she expected. Thessus, the Prime's father, was there, his face sullen and leg bandaged around the knee.

Because of the star fall or another dalliance with booze? Liran thought.

Phran, the aging head Monitor, stood with his back to the fire, his black hair peppered with ash alongside his regular grey streaks. His dark red attire was smudged with dirt and grime, his usually pristine hands stained in charcoal. Phran offered Liran a solemn nod.

Syrona was nowhere to be found, but two fledgling disciples that Liran recognised were gathered. Liran hoped Syrona would be given a reprieve from the meeting—it was a prudent measure to ensure she could rest before another day of tending to the wounded.

Reeva was speaking with a guardsman who had deep blue eyes under a stern brow. Reeva—engrossed in her conversation—ignored Liran and Olbi as they gathered with the other guests, her face set and severe as the guard nodded.

Liran approached Syrona's disciples with Olbi in tow, though she had to step around a merchant to avoid tripping over his long cloak.

'How fares, Tarak? Any word? Did they move him to the hall?' Liran asked one of the disciples. She didn't know the young girl's name but had seen her grinding herbs and changing bandages the night before. Dark circles hung under the teenager's eyes, and her voluminous red hair was matted and messy.

'Sorry Maven, I know not that name. By the night's end, I could only see bloodstains,' the girl said, fighting back a sob. She was shaken.

Liran reached out and took her hand. 'No need for apologies—last night was horrible, and you did an honourable deed in helping those that needed it.'

The girl dropped her head and sobbed. Liran glanced at Olbi and searched for any belied emotion; she hoped to ease the boy's anxiety by getting some good news about his father.

The creaking of heavy wood drew the huddle's attention. The great doors to the council chamber were being opened, sending a booming thud that reverberated through the hall. Two Monitors stood at either side of the entrance as the Prime One emerged. Gone were her ceremonial robes; instead, she wore an austere red top with loose pants. Her hair was tied back, and like most of them, her face was laced with tiredness. Liran had never seen the Prime One in public without makeup, not since she had been a young Scion with a rebellious streak.

'Friends, if you follow me, we have much to discuss,' Claudya said, guiding the party into the council chamber. It was not lost on Liran that this was her second meeting with the Prime One in two days.

Claudya remained by the door, offering small smiles and words of comfort as people filed past her. When Liran and Olbi approached, she gave Liran a grim smile and glanced at Olbi. Liran merely gave Claudya a nod and ushered them into the room.

The council chamber was an impressive room with high ceilings and tapestries sprawled across the walls. The tapestries, made with the finest threads, narrated stories of the history of Xylona and were vibrant and colourful against the bland stone walls.

Long ago, when the Prime Ones were viewed as Spirits among men, the room had been used as the throne room. That was in the days when the Rahsu had been fractured into five city-states. Xylona had held the seat of power over the southern forests and as far north as the walls of Hydoran.

Where the throne once sat now stood a modest statue of Cayden Adira, the first Prime One of Xylona. The statue was illuminated from behind, where the only window to the room brought in natural light. What light pierced the clouds outside basked the chamber in yellow rays filtered by multi-paned stained glass. The light danced across the statue and highlighted the wooden Cayden's features as if the carved effigy were alive.

The sculpture was said to be the only piece of garjee ever carved. The tree was nearly indestructible and blunted any axe or saw that dared touch it. The statue, which would have rotted away centuries ago instead—after a thousand years—looked as if it had been carved yesterday. The figure of the young Prime One appeared to dance with a garjee fruit in his hand, gazing at it with awe and reverence. Liran's eyes fell on the carved face of Cayden, the Prime who had built Xylona— perhaps his statue would see its demise.

The crowning feature of the chamber was its long table carved from marbled onyx stone, which glistened under the sconces and the light from the window. The glassy surface was unlike any other stone in the Rahsu lands.

'Please take your seats,' Claudya called from the doorway as two more latecomers arrived. Liran knew the faces of everyone in the room, but the two people who appeared at the door were unknown to her. They bowed to Claudya as they joined the gathering. Surprisingly, Olbi betrayed recognition as he pulled out a chair to sit on. Liran nudged him and gestured with her eyebrows towards the strangers.

Olbi leaned in as she sat beside him. 'That is Faiyor, and the younger man is Cotsh. They are part of my father's trading party and the ones that showed me the—' Olbi dropped his voice to a whisper. 'You know … The Prime One must have invited them instead of my father.'

Liran nodded, not breaking eye contact with Faiyor. She had heard the name before, just over a year ago. Faiyor had known Hayda; of this, she was sure.

The Monitors closed the doors and Claudya's last guests took their seats just as lightning illuminated the room. The crack of thunder reverberated throughout the chamber, and the tapestries rippled and moved slowly in the wind created by the

❖

closing doors. Liran felt chills as the warmth of the fire from the hearth was denied entry into the chamber.

'Thank you for coming. I know many of you are tired, and I thank you for your hard work. However, this meeting could not wait,' Claudya said as she glided from the doors to the head of the table. The Prime One's seat—positioned beneath the wooden statue of Cayden Adira—was ornate, its wooden backing depicting a garjee tree with a gold-painted carving of its fruit at the apex. Though Claudya was expected to take the Prime seat, she rather stopped short, pulled out another chair, and sat down adjacent to the ornate seat. Whenever possible, Claudya shirked the pomp and ceremony of her title. Liran scanned the table, each face was trained on the Prime, waiting for her to address them.

'Look,' Claudya said, interlacing her fingers. 'We face a new, harsh reality and one that cannot be overlooked. Our crops are destroyed, a dozen people have died since last night, and Xylona lies in ruins.' She locked eyes on the young disciple Liran had spoken to before. The girl lowered her head, her face twisted in distress.

'All of you here have done wonderful work helping the town get through the night—more than anyone could ask. Xylona owes you all a great debt. The town has suffered, and many have seen and experienced horrors they should never have to witness.' The young disciple continued to sob as Claudya paused.

'Lives have been lost, livelihoods and property destroyed. Despite the past day's events, we have only seen the beginning.'
All eyes were locked on Claudya; her expression was grave, and the silence across the chamber was palpable. Claudya sucked in a breath. 'Our world is about to change, and I fear that we will never return to the lives we have lived.'

Liran looked across the table. Something was off; Ayon's seat was empty. Why had Claudya not included the Scion in a meeting about the future? Guests were beginning to whisper.

❖

133

What did the Prime One mean? The world about to change? What had Claudya learned in the last few hours that Liran did not already know? Claudya's face was fraught with agony. The Prime One's hands were clenched as tight as her jaw was set, her posture stiff and unnatural.

'These are dark words, Prime One,' Alvar spoke. 'I am here because I am ready to help as many Rahsu as I can. We will get through this and rebuild.

'Why, before your time when great storms ravished the town for nine days and the river flooded, homes and livelihoods were destroyed, but we rebuilt.' He banged his hand on the table gauging the reactions of the sullen faces. A few nodded at Alvar in agreement. 'How is this any different?' he added at the finish.

Claudya's face remained unchanged, turning to Liran briefly, her lips trembling. Alvar's words rallied the townspeople like a beacon of hope. Their spirits uplifted and they burst into discussion around what they could do to assist in rebuilding. Claudya, having had her lead rein taken away, struggled to get a word in edgewise.

Suddenly, a ponderous slam shocked Liran, and several people jumped in their seats as Reeva stood, her fist firmly planted on the stone.

'Do not speak over the Prime One,' Reeva demanded, eyeing every person at the table—her stare filled with a fire that dared them to contest. Nobody did.

Claudya closed her fatigue-ridden eyes and with a heavy sigh, said 'Thank you, Reeva.'

Clenching her knuckles, Reeva lowered herself back down.

'Events of the last week have rocked our world and not just here in Xylona.' Claudya rubbed the bridge of her nose and returned to the topic at hand. 'Our guests here, Faiyor and Cotsh, are from the northern reaches of the Rahsu lands and along with our own, Tarak,' she paused and glanced briefly at

Olbi, 'they witnessed a phenomenon, which as an isolated incident would have been cause for concern in itself.'

No one spoke, but several sets of eyes darted to the travellers, who, in turn, scanned the gathering. Olbi shifted in his seat as Claudya raised her hand. A Monitor rushed over from the wall, holding a small box. It was ornate like the one Liran had seen in the inner sanctum, but unlike the garjee chest, this one fit neatly within the Monitor's hand. The Monitor placed the box on the table and withdrew quickly to his spot beneath the tapestry, where he drooped his head.

Liran glanced at the chest, confused, though her curiosity surged. She straightened in her seat and leaned forward, placing her elbows on the table. Claudya stood and delicately touched the box, her fingers massaging and toying with small copper latches.

'For years, we have been watched,' Claudya said, her hands unmoving. Her eyes lifted to the gathering with a deliberate, slow blink that curbed the guests' murmurs.

'Watched? Who is we?' Alvar said, his eyes narrowing.

'We as a whole, Alvar: the Rahsu. Every one of us has been watched from the stars,' Claudya elaborated, her voice no longer meek.

Liran stared blankly at the Prime One—it was clear Claudya was serious. Why hadn't she discussed this with Liran before the Manna Rites yesterday? A knot tightened in Liran's throat. She cleared it loudly. 'Years, Prime One?' Liran said, her tone cut thin as heat rose beneath her skin.

'You forget yourself, Maven,' Reeva warned.

Claudya raised her palm to Reeva, ushering her to pause. Reeva obliged yet daggered Liran with a cold and menacing glare.

'Watched by whom?' The sound of a mousy voice came from farther down the table. Eyes fell on the disciple who had been sobbing. She melted back into her seat as people stared.

'The spirits are watching us, you fool. Who else would be watching?' Alvar's voice boomed across the table, and the girl

shrank farther into her seat, her face obscured by a veil of wavy hair.

'Alvar, please,' Claudya implored, unlatching the box. The room fell silent again, watching the Prime One. 'Please, let me speak. I will tell you all what is about to happen and what may happen. We must be prepared! Rest assured, whatever transpires, we face it together.'

Liran listened intently as a nervous energy filled the room. Stares of curiosity and confusion morphed into expressions of concern and worry. Who was watching them? From the stars? This made no sense.

Olbi looked up at Liran. He must have sensed it, too. Whatever it was, Tarak's tale was somehow involved.

Claudya waited for silence, and when all eyes returned to her, she parted her lips. 'The Spirits are not the ones watching us, people from the stars are. These people are not Rahsu, and they have been observing us, learning about us for over eighty years.'

No one spoke. The patter of rain on the windowpanes and the flickering of the sconces lining the walls was all Liran could focus on.

Claudya opened the box lid, pushing it back on its hinges. Liran's mind raced. Something didn't make sense. How was it that she, as the town's Maven, did not know of this? She again scanned the bewildered faces that sat around the table. An ugliness squeezed her chest, welling up inside her … the Prime One had lied to her.

'Prime One, how long have you known of this?' Liran found herself on her feet. Claudya continued to stare into the box; her hand delicately delving into it.

'Liran, you must understand that this information is sensitive—' Claudya began.

'How long, Claudya?' Liran demanded.

Reeva burst to her feet and brandished the hilt of her sword, her eyes trained on Liran. Others around the table stood now, some shocked at the use of the Prime One's first name in public. Even Alvar's jaw was dropped, his face glistening with alarm.

'Answer the question, Prime One,' Liran demanded again. 'You told everyone at the feast that no harm will befall us, so what truth do you hide?' Her blood pumped. Olbi rose beside her, his eyes trained on the box.

'Do not make demands of the Prime One, Maven, or I will have you thrown into the holds,' Reeva spat, beckoning the guards at the door. 'Guards, if the Maven makes another demand—'

'There will be none of that, Reeva,' Claudya said sternly. 'I will answer the question; please, everyone, sit down.' Claudya's eyes pleaded with Reeva before she turned to Liran. Liran had never seen the Prime One look so fearful.

She had thousands of questions for her leader.

'What is in the box?' Olbi questioned, trying to peek at what lay before him. Claudya's eyes flickered towards Olbi, avoiding Reeva's heavy breathing and Liran's piercing stare.

'I believe you have seen one before, Olbi. Your father showed you a piece last night, I have been told,' Claudya said. Olbi nodded as he flicked a glance towards Faiyor.

Now Liran knew what the box contained.

'Fragments of the fallen star,' Liran whispered as she fell back into her seat.

'Yes,' Claudya said, pulling an object from the box and sliding it across the table to Liran. She placed three more fragments on the table before her, each piece remarkable and unique.

'As you can see, these fragments are not of this world. They belong to a people that travel the stars. They are not the Spirits of the Rahsu, and they have been watching us all of our lives, as well as the lives of our parents and grandparents. We do not know why, but we can no longer ignore this truth.'

Claudya turned to the Maven. 'Liran, my friend, I have only known about this for a day. However, there have been rumours and reports of Rahsu finding pieces of these stars for decades. They were often observed and lost—nonsense traveller stories for taverns and halls. There is no denying it now, we cannot ignore the truth anymore,' Claudya alleged ominously.

'I've heard these stories in the Stonehall,' Alvar cut in, shifting in his seat. 'Those travellers spoke of artefacts, not of the Rahsu, and then, strangely, I never saw them swilling ale in my hall again. But how do you know all this? You say that you only just found out? Who told you?' Alvar's face was sceptical as nods of agreement went around the table. 'You tell us that people have been watching me? Why? Where are they and how do they see us? These bits of twisted metal don't prove squat!'

'I told the Prime One, and it's true,' Reeva interjected.

Alvar looked incredulously at Reeva, though the Guardian's face was calm and composed.

'You?' Liran cut in. She was done with games. What exactly was going on? How many people had known of these revelations? The Monitors lining the walls exchanged nervous glances as tensions in the room grew. 'How would you know? What knowledge do you possess, or are these lies that you feed into the Prime One's ears? What hold do you have on her? On Ayon?' Liran felt anger and resentment heaving within her, resentment that had built up over the years.

'How I know is not important, Maven. Accept facts—we are not alone, and believe me, these people are a threat to the Rahsu,' Reeva said calmly.

'Not *important*?' Liran scoffed. 'Reeva, I suggest you go see Syrona, you have lost your mind if you think none of this is of concern.'

'How I know does not change anything,' Reeva said with a clenched jaw.

'It bloody well does,' retorted Alvar. 'You think we accept your word without any proof?'

'Here, here,' one of the merchants exclaimed, nodding at Alvar's words.

'But we have the pieces of their stars,' Faiyor said, pointing at the chunks on the table. 'Surely that is proof in itself, Alvar?'

'Rubbish! How do we know that these came from the star? You say you saw a star fall—did you find anything?' Alvar asked.

'These are the pieces we found,' Cotsh said, pointing at the fragments. 'Among many more, too many to carry. Believe us when we say this object was not of this world. No Rahsu could make such a thing.'

'They *are* the dancing stars,' Liran cut in, intrigued by Cotsh's words.

Alvar scoffed with derision.

'No, listen,' Liran said. Alvar let her speak.

Liran nodded her thanks. 'After writing about the history and purpose of the dancing stars, it was said they appeared recently in our history.' Liran recalled her research for her book, though she'd not considered this possibility. Confusion etched the faces around the table—she had their attention.

Liran stood. 'The dancing stars appeared in our skies suddenly and unexpectedly during the last days of the Hydoran Prime Era. My research found no records of this phenomenon before that time. In other words, the dancing stars may be the eyes of these other people. According to Claudya's words, the dates match up, but what has changed?' Liran was verbalising her thoughts, more for herself than for the benefit of anyone in the room. 'Why have they begun to fall from the sky?' She trailed off, her mind racing with a hundred different possibilities.

'We are missing something,' Cotsh said. 'Suppose they have been watching us for eighty years; why now have the Prime One and Reeva shared this information? Why the alarm?' Cotsh drew the glances of Reeva and Claudya as Liran felt Olbi shrink into his chair beside her.

'We have lived in peace with the dancing stars for generations, they had never posed a threat,' Liran said. 'Olbi,

tell them what Tarak told you about the star.' No one appeared to be listening to her.

The guests were talking over each other. Some spoke fearfully, while others remained unconvinced, suggesting that what mattered most was repairing Xylona and reaching out for aid from other towns and villages.

Liran turned to Olbi. He sat quietly, listening to the conversations around the table. He looked at Faiyor, who was regaling Alvar about finding the pieces, the flash in the sky and the star falling from above as they sat on the riverbed. Faiyor described the fire, noise and brightness, the roars as it battered the forest.

'So, the fire destroyed the land around it, like it did here last night?' Alvar asked Faiyor.

It was Cotsh who replied, 'No, that's just the thing; the fire didn't burn anything. It just left a huge hole in the ground. It was over in mere seconds. There was no wind and no flame.'

Liran listened, intently taking in Cotsh's tale, deciphering as much as she could. Faiyor and Cotsh spoke further about approaching the spot where the star had crashed. Liran was most surprised by Cotsh's admission that the most prominent fragment was the size of a barrel. Liran studied the pieces on the table again and then the grim-looking Claudya, who was speaking in hushed tones to Reeva beside the statue of Cayden Adira.

Liran assembled the pieces of information she had gathered about the stars until a cohesive pattern emerged. Somehow, everything was connected. Despite this, something didn't add up, there was more to the story, and Liran wasn't going to stop until she had the answer. Liran approached the Prime One, someone she had trusted unequivocally … until now.

'Claudya, the object that fell from the sky near Hydoran, that gave us these fragments, didn't cause a fire. It was small, relatively speaking,' Liran said.

❖

The council guests quietened as they listened in on the Maven, Claudya nodding as Liran pressed on. 'Whatever fell to Arbonar last night was much larger. So much so that it caused great devastation, setting fields alight unlike what our friends from the north here confessed happened in Hydoran. Several Xylonans have revealed that the star last night slowed down as it approached; yet that doesn't make sense unless it too was man-made,' Liran surmised, pacing back and forth.

Claudya gazed upon Liran through eyes that revealed a soul in turmoil. Something had spooked the Prime One. Reeva's face, on the other hand, was twisted in anguish. Liran turned back to the gathering.

'If we believe that there are people amongst the stars, watching from their magical eyes,' she addressed the sprawl of attendees, 'then what do you know about the star that consumed Xylona in fire? Claudya, what was it that fell from the sky last night and what is it that threatens to change our lives forever?'

Liran stopped pacing, her eyes searching Claudya's, looking for a hint of truth. The Prime One drew in a long breath, staring back at Liran before parting her trembling lips.

'What fell from the sky last night, Liran … It was them— the ones who have been watching us. The people of the stars have arrived and now walk among us.'

'Spirits protect us,' Alvar whispered as a rolling thunderclap reverberated through the halls of the Prime House.

❖

13

ZILLAH

Bone-chilling rain hindered the landing party as they squelched through the brackish marshes. The Unity lay behind them, an otherworldly silver monolith. Its nose stuck fifty metres above the surrounding thickets and small trees, whose bark was stringy like a snake shedding its skin. Alrin had filmed the historic descent of the cargo elevator and the first steps Zillah took on the planet, but since that landmark moment, his camera had been stored in a waterproof pouch hanging from his jacket. Zillah was glad that the live broadcasts would not be a regular distraction. Instead, they would be carefully choreographed and edited for the audience's viewing pleasure back on Anatara.

'Make for that tree line,' Sloane yelled over the rain. The soldier trudged a few paces ahead of her, grimacing under the barrage of rain. The downpour was unrelenting, resulting in a painstakingly slow process through the bog that oozed and squelched under every step.

Zillah nodded in Sloane's direction and turned around to see the crew carefully treading the muddy ground. Putrid smells of disturbed mire consumed her nostrils, the moisture thick and hot against her clothes. Joja's teeth were grit with fierce determination, but she managed a smile. Clearly, she was the only one enjoying herself, although even Joja must have resented the mud as her legs sank deeper. Behind them, the Unity faced the same battle. Zillah could swear one of the ship's windows was now semi-submerged in the marsh.

Sloane appeared to be right about the best way forward. The lumbering wall of trees was anchored on a subtle rise of firm ground. Zillah squinted as water trickled into her eyes, the forest was close. Zillah saw boulders the size of houses within the trees.

❖

'How far to the settlement, Captain?' Idonea called, scraping mud off his gun. Zillah looked at her communication tablet for readings.

'Approximately fifteen clicks to the southeast,' she yelled. Zillah could feel fresh mud seeping into her boots. The sensation between her sock and boot made her question whether her footwear was still on her feet or if mud had replaced them.

At this rate, reaching the settlement would take them until nightfall. Arbornia cycled through daylight similar to Anatara, so midday was still hours away. Thick clouds masked the sun's warmth and even the planet Oaga, the enormous gas giant in orbit between Anatara and *this god-forsaken swamp*, could not be seen.

The party travelled silently with all communication limited to only physical gestures to avoid specific hazards in the mud. Soon, Zillah realised that the depth of the slush no longer submerged her boots, though they were caked in black sludge, the original green fabric no longer visible. Up ahead, Sloane rose from the swamps and darted towards the cover of the trees, the gun never parting from his muscled grip.

'There is strong footing here,' Doxxa called from behind Zillah. She'd begun to climb up to the tree line, taking care not to get her foot tangled in the expansive network of roots that broke sporadically through the red-tinged soils. The roots resembled thick spiderwebs, glistening as the low light hit the soggy wood.

Up close, the trees were giants with a grandeur greater than they originally appeared from afar. They towered forty metres above her head with girthy and smooth trunks the colour of dark aged pewter. Their limbs weaved into chaotic twists that spanned outwards at their heights like an umbrella. Zillah spotted small yellow orbs sporadically clinging to the highest branches that appeared like dull streetlights in the darkness beneath the canopy of mammoth leaves. Zillah hadn't seen a fruit or tree like this anywhere in Tarea.

❖

As Zillah turned back to check on the crew, a meandering river, broad and calmly snaking through the marshes, caught her eye. Occasional islands rose above the waterline.

From this vantage point, she could also see Unity's body stuck awkwardly on a slight rise. The scars of the crash had torn a grotesque path through the swamp, along which fires battled with rain and smoke wafting across the mud. Wiping rain from her eyes, Zillah grit her teeth and grimaced at the angry scorch marks dotting the marshes along a straight canal where the Unity had slid before reaching its final resting spot. The Unity had dug its own grave, she surmised.

'Lucky we landed where we did,' Doxxa called out. He looked out at the Unity, his back perched against a large, exposed root of one of the colossal trees.

'It's a double-edged sword, Doxxa,' Zillah replied.

Doxxa straightened his back and cocked an eyebrow. 'The ship avoided the forest, Captain. We wouldn't be standing here if we hit these beasts,' Doxxa responded by slapping the root under his rump. Had he not thought of what was beneath the Unity?

Zillah pointed to the river. 'The ship sits on mudflats of a river delta. With Unity's weight, she will sink. Even if these granite boulders suggest bedrock is close to the surface, we don't have the resources to lift the ship out of the muck.'

Doxxa shrugged with nonchalance. How could he be so cavalier? Unity was the only way for them to get off the planet. The ramifications of having limited resources played in her mind as she turned back to their ticket home, a towering structure that was sitting on proverbial thin ice.

All but one of the crew gathered under the protection of the trees, their thick and expansive leaves functioning as an effective shield that barred the heavy rain. Grateful for the reprieve, Zillah scanned the bogs and glimpsed Joja standing in the marsh with a glass beaker in her hand.

The doctor was wading through knee-deep water, scooping up the brackish soup—so much for wanting to keep any potential pathogens or parasites at bay. Joja weaved towards the tree line to join the rest of the party. Suddenly, she tripped over a hidden root, falling face-first into the mud. Half the contents of the beaker splashed over the lip of the rim, but she steadied herself. The soldiers burst into laughter, only exacerbated by the sticks, slime and mud that now decorated Joja's dreadlocks. Zillah was irritated by the effort it had physically taken them to get this far.

'Dr Amira, please get a move on. You will have plenty of opportunities to take samples and conduct tests, preferably when it is dry and pleasant,' Zillah stated.

Joja gave a resigned look and joined the party, several of them using the thick roots as seats.

'Remarkable. Simply gorgeous,' Joja exclaimed as she ran her hand over the smooth roots of the tree. 'This is an entirely foreign species that must be indigenous to the planet,' she continued, grabbing her knife and scraping it against the roots to gather a sample, despite Zillah's stated reluctance to waste more time on her scientific pursuits.

Zillah gazed up at the colossal trees crowned with a lush canopy of oversized leaves, each one casting a verdant umbrella over the forest floor. Their trunks were even more impressive. If all six of the crew linked hands, they wouldn't be able to encompass a quarter of the tree base.

'Tough bark!' Joja said. 'I can barely cut out a splinter.'

'Can't you just use a stick or a leaf on the forest floor?' Alrin queried as he turned on his camera to gather footage of the expansive root systems tangling through the dirt and into the forest's depths. Zillah thought it looked dark and foreboding in there. She scanned the forest floor—besides tufts of grass and the occasional moss-covered rock, the forest floor was void of debris. It was as if someone had swept the forest floor before their arrival.

'It's okay. I should have enough shavings here,' Joja said, depositing a few fibres off her knife blade into a small plastic sleeve.

'That's enough of a break. Let's move,' Zillah announced with one last nervous glance at the Unity.

The forest darkened as they delved into its depths, the trees strangling out what light was available. Thunder rolled above the tree line, and an occasional stray rain droplet hit Zillah's face as they trekked. One by one, they switched on their torches for guidance in the dark. Sloane, Idonea and Doxxa had the advantage of lights attached to their guns. Despite having a sidearm in her pocket, Zillah walked with her torch attached to her breast strap. Before long, only the narrow beams of their torches gave them visibility of their surroundings, that and the occasional flashes of lightning that pulsed and illuminated the green blanket above.

They trudged farther south through the trees, each tree growing in uniquely twisted forms. The silence unnerved Zillah—forests in Tarea were full of predators that lurked above on branches or below in burrows and caves. It was common for something to crawl into your bag or clothing when stopping to rest. Here though, the forest was dead by comparison.

All that accompanied them through the dark was their own stench, of rot and sulphur from the mud caking their boots, which stung at Zillah's nose. Sloane had tied a bandana around his face to cover his own nose. A flash of lightning illuminated his figure; the thunder rolled faintly, muffled on the other side of the canopy. Sloane had stopped ahead of Zillah, waiting for her and wearing an irritated expression.

'Morgana, what's our status? How far to the settlement?' he said, pulling out his comms tablet.

Why's he asking me? she thought. They all had access to the same information on their tablets, including direct access to the GPS. 'Something wrong with your tablet?' Zillah asked.

He shot her a resentful glare before muttering under his breath and tapping aggressively at his device. 'Must have been the mud or rain, fucking thing is playing up,' he said, putting it back into the pouch hanging from the strap of his bag. Zillah pulled out her tablet and the small screen flickered to life in the darkness. She tapped her finger on the touchpad, but the usual feeling of haptic feedback was gone.

Alrin called out before she could announce that her tablet wasn't functioning either. 'My camera isn't uploading to the Unity computers, and I can't connect to the satellites.' He, too, checked his tablet, and the same flashing glow illuminated his red hair and confused face in the darkness. Soon it became evident that none of their tablets were working.

'Some sort of interference?' Alrin offered as he held his tablet above his head and walked around, watching the screen intently.

'I think that would be the most logical assumption. I've seen nothing but trees and the odd rock for the last hour,' Sloane said, using the unscheduled break to take a swig of water.

'Could this be linked to what happened with the Unity?' Joja asked. 'Some electromagnetic anomaly we didn't account for?'

Another roll of thunder rumbled above. The long rolls were softer but sonorous, lingering well after the flash. The storm was moving on. Zillah glanced at her tablet again, but it continued to glitch; though, she could still see the clock on the screen.

'We have been walking for a few hours. I'd estimate we should be out of the forest within an hour at our current rate,' she said, pointing her torch in the direction they were heading. Nothing ahead suggested the forest was any less dense.

'How do we know we aren't going in circles without GPS?' Idonea said.

'We haven't been, I've made sure of that,' Sloane said. 'Military training prepares us for situations like this—I'm surprised Tarean combatants don't have that skill, Idonea. We can find our way without any navigational aids.'

Idonea didn't take the bait.

'Does this forest seem a bit off to anyone else?' Alrin asked as he pulled out a small bottle. He unscrewed the lid and tipped a purple pill onto his open palm before popping the pill between his teeth and taking a chug from his water bottle.

'Something wrong, Alrin?' Joja asked, watching him with narrowed eyes.

'Just a throbbing headache. That and my back is killing me! Oh, and a change of socks would be great too,' Alrin replied, refastening his drink bottle. He smiled faintly at Joja and shrugged.

'Just isn't an amicable place. A bit grim if you ask me. Being an explorer on a new planet isn't living up to my expectations,' he continued, brushing hair from his forehead and massaging his temples.

'Let's move on,' Zillah said. 'Perhaps our equipment will return online as we walk. As for the back pain, Mr Sandol, we all have it. Your spine is recompressing and getting used to a planet's gravity again.'

Zillah, too, felt a headache coming on and compression in her spine. The forest's stagnant air was suffocating and cold. Arbornia was further from the sun, so it was expected that the temperature would not soar as high as it did at home. She longed for the warm beaches that lined the promenade of Aster and, for a split second, questioned why she had left home.

Dark lumbering trees continued to twist their limbs in every direction. The forest was a quiet and desolate place. The long and ghostly tones of a melancholic bird that called above their heads gave Zillah a shiver. She shifted her focus to the sound of her footsteps on the forest floor. Occasionally, she thought she saw pulses of light coming from between the trees, hoping it was slithers of sunlight finding gaps in the canopy. She was unnaturally drained, her energy levels depleting fast. One glance at the strained faces of the others reflected her emotions. They barely spoke. Occasionally, someone would sporadically pull out their tablets and whack the screen in an attempt to fix the issues.

'Got any more of those painkillers, Amira?' Sloane shouted from up ahead. The request broke Zillah from the trance of counting her footsteps.

'A few,' Joja replied, 'but we should use them sparingly if you've used up the few in your packs.' The doctor sounded flat.

Sloane swore under his breath as the party weaved through tree roots and endless granite boulders.

The monotony drained Zillah. She trained her torch on the ground; the grass looked inviting, soft and light against the forest floor. More grass came into view; the green tinge lined the surface everywhere a tree and its roots didn't take hold. She lifted her head, and a smile reached her lips momentarily. Sloane saw it, too; as they looked up, a slow, placid beast was grazing in the grass.

Joja gasped in delight. The lumbering four-legged animal—covered in thick brown fur—had its face nuzzled deep into a tuft of grass, a leather harness hanging loosely around its neck. *It's domesticated*, Zillah thought before turning to Alrin and gesturing for him to turn his camera on.

A loud bang suddenly ricocheted off the trees around her. Zillah turned, her ears ringing as she watched the animal collapse and cry out in pain. Sloane stepped forward, gun raised and fired again between the animal's eyes. It fell silently as it slumped into the grass.

'What the fuck is wrong with you?' Idonea yelled at Sloane. Idonea wasn't the only one who raised his voice, Alrin also dropped his camera from the shock of the deafening sound of Sloane's gun.

'It could have attacked us,' Sloane said, kicking the beast with his boot.

'It was *domesticated*!' Joja shouted, anger flickering in her eyes.

'Can't be too careful,' Sloane mouthed, offering a blank expression and shrugging.

❖

The party was dumbfounded by Sloane's actions until Doxxa called out for them to look up ahead and pointed into the trees.

Zillah lifted her gaze. Slivers of light stretched into the forest, fingers bringing energy to the base of the trees. The light danced beneath the columns, illuminating the dust particles suspended in the still air. Jubilant shouts came from Doxxa and Alrin.

The edge of the forest beckoned, and not a moment too soon. Zillah felt as if her health recovered with each step closer to the light. She picked up her pace, leaving the beast's carcass behind them. Light shone through gaps in the leaves and she glimpsed blue sky and clouds breaking through. The storm had passed. Zillah stepped into a beam of sunlight, feeling warmth caress her skin as six simultaneous beeps chimed from each of their chests.

'My tablet is back online,' Idonea called, shielding his eyes from the sunlight and tapping the screen.

Zillah grabbed her tablet and tapped it too: everything was functional. Joja, still in the shadow of the trees, immediately crouched down and began feeding tree samples into her analyser, the screen shining vivid light on her face. Zillah switched off her torch and tried to reconnect with the satellite network. They had moved through the forest slowly. The tracking dot pulsed on the screen half a kilometre within the dark green patch of the forest. She zoomed out and analysed the location. 'We are just two kilometres from the edge of the settlement,' she announced. 'We should clean up and prepare for contact. Remember the protocols people.'

Zillah knew Alrin had his camera trained on her as she briefed the team, and she hesitated when she locked eyes with the lens. 'We will stick together and approach with caution. If the first native we see runs, we do not follow. If they become aggressive, we will not fire. Is that clear?' Zillah stared at Sloane as she spoke, the urge to punch him lingering.

The man smirked, though Zillah ignored him and continued, 'We will defend ourselves as necessary but inflict no deadly force. Remember, the natives do not know who we are or where we come from. They have been isolated from us for sixteen hundred years and likely have evolved new languages and cultures. Please be calm and respectful. They *are* us, separated by millennia.' Zillah wrapped up and watched the recording light fade away on Alrin's camera.

She relaxed her shoulders, slinging off her backpack slightly annoyed that she cared what the camera captured.

Others were already scrubbing the mud off their clothing, while two sat with their heads between their knees. Idonea raised his head, and Zillah's heart tightened. His eyes were bloodshot, the colour of his tattoos, and what colour he did have in his skin had fled from his cheeks. Before Zillah could call out, Idonea stood and dashed into the trees.

'Idonea, are you alright?' Joja called out, watching the soldier stumble on shaky legs.

Idonea responded with a visceral gurgle before a stream of vomit erupted from his mouth, splattering onto the ground. Joja threw a worried glance at Zillah as she ran to Idonea.

'Something feels very wrong about this forest,' Alrin repeated. 'I don't think we should be in here.' He looked up into the leaves with apprehension as if he expected some evil to present itself.

'I agree. My head has been throbbing for hours,' Doxxa called, coming out from behind a tree and zipping up his pants.

Zillah glanced at Idonea and returned to watch Joja as she spread out her medicine bag, unclipping a needle. The doctor plunged it into a small bottle of clear liquid.

'What are you administering?' Zillah called, walking over to the doctor.

'It's a serum that reduces fever and will, hopefully, settle his stomach. We need to get out of this forest, Captain,' Joja muttered sternly.

'What is it, Doctor?' Zillah asked, looking over Joja's shoulder at Idonea. His face was as pale as the clouds above them.

Joja flung a glance back to Idonea as he vomited again. The doctor dropped her voice to barely a whisper. 'My money is on acute radiation poisoning. It explains the issues with our equipment and the headaches we are all experiencing,' Joja said. The doctor stared into her eyes, no doubt Joja knew Zillah had been experiencing a throbbing skull.

'Captain, we are all sick. Some won't admit it, but you can see it in their faces.'

'Are we in danger? Are the levels dangerous?' she asked quietly, though Joja merely shrugged.

'Our sensors are designed to monitor anything hazardous. It's possible that the levels are relatively low, and we haven't been exposed to anything deadly yet,' Joja said as she packed away her equipment.

The last thing Zillah wanted was six corpses. Why didn't they have more warning? She had seen nothing since entering the forest that signalled danger. Zillah turned and studied her team, some appeared worse for wear than others.
'We move out, people. We haven't got far until we are out of this forsaken forest,' Zillah mustered. The crew were quick to their feet and moved towards the light.

Zillah kept a close eye on Idonea. Whatever pain she was feeling was nothing compared to how Idonea looked, sweat now beading down his forehead. His pupils swam in a burning sea of crimson. The soldier stumbled as he tripped on a scrag of roots. Joja lifted Idonea but struggled under the weight of the heavier man. Zillah rushed over and assisted by grabbing Idonea by the arm and hoisting him up. The three of them scurried through the last trees where a wall of light beckoned them.

Zillah felt the first rush of cool, fresh air touch her face. She sucked it in while Joja grunted under Idonea's weight. They passed the last colossal trunk of the forest and soon, they were out, greeted by the first direct sunlight Zillah had felt in over forty-seven days. She collapsed onto her knees, savouring the sunlight.

An expanse of dirt mounds ran in uniform rows before Zillah, each perfectly straight. The uniformity of a farm. The crew sat up ahead, catching their breaths and soaking in the sunlight. It was the same sun that warmed Zillah back home in Aster, only slightly smaller in the sky and weaker.

Joja was seated nearby on a mound, her tablet beeping as she swiped it from her pocket and looked at the screen. Idonea lay motionless at Zillah's feet, shallow breaths escaped past his dry and cracked lips. What else could she do? She glanced at the doctor who was fixated on the screen before her. The doctor's lips were parted as her eyes darted erratically across the screen.

'What is it, Doctor?' Zillah asked.

Joja jumped, looked up at Zillah, and then down at Idonea as the soldier groaned.

'Well, are we going to live?' Zillah asked for a prognosis as Sloane sidled over to the group.

'I haven't had the chance to look yet. The analysis of the trees came in,' Joja said flatly.

Zillah didn't give a fuck about the trees; she was more concerned with their mortality and the success of the mission. 'The trees can wait, Doctor. What about the radiation?' Zillah said firmly.

Joja's eyes darted from Zillah to Sloane. Zillah had forgotten that Sloane didn't know about the radiation; his eyes glared at her angrily. She knew she'd pay for keeping that news to herself even for a moment. Joja turned her tablet around to Sloane and Zillah.

'That's the thing, Captain. It's the trees that are giving off the radiation,' Joja said as Idonea coughed up a fresh stream of bile.

14

OLBI

After the council meeting, Olbi rushed to his father's side, while still processing what he'd heard. Outsiders had been watching them all his life, all his father's life. How could that be? He had hundreds of questions, but the Prime One took none after Liran's deductions.

Instead, discussion moved towards what each person was to do to aid in Xylona's recovery. How could the Prime One give them life-altering information and then expect them all to undergo mundane procedures like nothing had changed?

Olbi left the meeting in a struggle to keep up with the Maven's strides. All through the meeting, he could almost feel the heat of rage radiating from Liran. He was surprised that a Maven didn't know this secret. Furthermore, Liran wasn't the one who told the Prime One of the Outsiders. They had rushed out of the Prime House as the storm broke overhead, Liran muttering angry words under her breath as they marched through the square and into the garden cloister.

'What do you think they want, the Outsiders?' Olbi asked.

Liran let out a huffed laugh. 'Well, if they have been watching us for that long, then they have likely been studying us. Working out our patterns, how we live, what we do. Maybe assessing our weaknesses,' she said.

It was just what Olbi would do on the banks of the river. He would watch the fish, learning where they liked to gather and their favourite pools for food. Was that what the Outsiders were doing? Learning about them so they could attack?

A surge of fear coursed through Olbi's chest, and he was suddenly short of breath. Liran glanced at Olbi and paused. They'd stopped next to a statue of a small girl holding a basket of flowers. A statue that had adorned Xylona since time immemorial.

Biting her lip, Liran began to pace. 'If they are here, then there is not much we can do. They must want to meet us,' Liran said, halting her pacing as a thought seemed to capture her. 'Surely they are just as curious about you and me as we are of them. I wouldn't be worried.' She placed her hand on Olbi's shoulder. Judging by the way she bit her lip, he was less than reassured.

'Run off to Tarak; I think you should see how he is doing,' she added. 'I am sure he is going to be okay.'

'What will you do?' Olbi asked.

Liran stared off towards the Prime House. Did she have unfinished business there?

'I am going to do what I was asked, Olbi.'

'What did the Prime One ask you to do? It seemed like you already knew what she wanted,' he pried carefully, recalling Liran's look of bewilderment when the Prime One had called a close to the meeting and left the council room.

'I was tasked with'—Liran paused— 'I am to protect the Scion, take him far away from here.' She set off again towards the southern arch of the cloister.

'Isn't that Reeva's job?' he called after her, quickening his pace to catch up to her.

'See your father, Olbi. I think he will be okay.'

Liran left Olbi standing at the archway as she rushed towards her studio.

****

Sunlight filtered through the windows of the healing hall and pierced Olbi's eyelids, rousing him from sleep. He had drifted into an uncomfortable slumber, hunched over in a chair beside his father's improvised bed that had been cobbled together from two desks. Yallon had visited in the night, bearing fabric from the weaver's shop to craft makeshift blankets.

Syrona, tired and under the directive of the Prime One, had departed the healing hall hours ago. Now, two of her dedicated disciples crept through the aisles of beds, diligently traversing the hall to ensure the well-being of the patients. Tarak lay silent, his chest's sluggish rise and fall the only indicator he was alive. His condition had not changed.

While watching the rhythmic breathing of his father, Olbi had drifted off into a dreamless sleep. Tarak's mortality stared him down. Olbi had never been close to his father, but he needed to know he would live right now.

He wanted to know what his father had to say about his mother.

One of the disciples approached him, noticing he was awake. 'He has not stirred while you slept,' the young man said.

Olbi nodded quietly, his eyes returning to the rhythmic movement of Tarak's chest.

'Can I get you some water or anything to eat?' the disciple asked.

Olbi looked up at the man, he was younger than Olbi, maybe seventeen or eighteen. He had soft blue eyes hidden beneath bushy blonde hair. Olbi recalled seeing him around, though they had never talked. Olbi was sure his name was Augun.

'I am okay, thanks,' Olbi mumbled through a yawn. Augun nodded and stared at Olbi as if he wanted to ask something but lacked the courage. Instead, as all other surfaces were used as beds, he placed a cup of water on the ground by Olbi's feet.

'Do you know when my father might wake?' Olbi asked.

'I do not, sorry …' Augun said.

Olbi politely nodded again.

'Is what they are saying true, about the star? You were there, weren't you? At the council meeting?' the disciple asked. Olbi scrutinised Augun's blue and searching eyes.

'Yes, the star was a vessel,' Olbi responded. Augun's features lit up, and a smile spread across his face.

'Visitors! I wonder what they are like?' he said, walking off and leaving Olbi alone with his father.

❖

Olbi thought about the meeting—the meeting he was not invited to. He wouldn't have known about the vessel without telling Liran his stories. Sitting at that table wasn't reassuring. Emotions were flaring, and many at the meeting had left fearful of the news. There was much talk about what would happen in the next few days and what everyone's role was, but for him, nothing. The Prime One hadn't spoken to him, and why would she? He wasn't a Monitor; he was just a fisherman who held no authority in Xylona.

Olbi's mind drifted to Boji, and a fresh twinge of grief hit him. He decided he would return and find a place to bury the young yar, near where they used to play. He didn't want to go back and face the calf's lifeless body, yet the harrowing image was etched in his mind. With everything going on in town, it was up to him to ensure Boji's body wouldn't be left to decay or be taken by predators. After that, he would help Alvar as much as possible at the Stonehall and visit his father until he was well enough to speak.

Olbi sat with his head back, looking up at the ceiling, his eyes following the cracks in the paint. Tarak groaned and moved atop the table before him. Olbi's heart raced as he noticed his father stirring and moved to his father's side. Tarak struggled to lift his eyelids.

'I am here, father. Be careful, your injuries are severe,' Olbi said, placing his hand in Tarak's.

'Where am I?' Tarak said. His voice was dry and raspy behind weathered and cracked lips.

'In the healing hall. You are going to be okay.'

Tarak tried to sit up, but Olbi held him down. The school desks underneath rocked on the uneven surface. Olbi grabbed the cup of water by the leg of his chair and brought it to his father's lips.

'Drink. You must be thirsty.'

Tarak drank the water, draining the cup—his face grimacing. 'What happened? The star … It was like Hydoran, wasn't it?' Tarak said, opening his eyes. He peered down at

his bandaged body on the table. He grimaced again and poked a bandage with his finger—he convulsed in agony.

Olbi's lips trembled. He brought his father up to speed about the events following him being hit by debris in the square. Olbi explained how the fire had swept through the fields, how strong winds had levelled houses, and then his chance meeting with Liran. Olbi skipped over Boji, not ready to relive that story; meanwhile, Tarak sat quietly without interrupting. Olbi paused after mentioning the council meeting. Olbi took a sip of water, catching his breath. So much had happened.

'Why did the Prime One call for a council?' Tarak asked, urging Olbi to continue. The vision of his father handing him the piece of the star at the feast played in his mind.

'She wanted to discuss the recovery and …' Olbi paused again. 'To tell the Rahsu about what the star was.'

Tarak's eyes widened. 'And?' he urged.

'And how our lives are about to change.'

Tarak's stare back at his son was hollow. 'What did she say?'

Olbi cast a look around the room. He had the feeling that others were listening, so he dropped his voice. 'The star is a vessel bringing visitors from another world. The fragments you found are the eyes of people of the stars. They have been watching us for eighty years.'

Tarak's grim face turned into a grin.

Olbi was shocked by his father's sudden burst into laughter. 'How could you be laughing right now?'

Augun glanced in their direction.

'Why are you smiling, father? People have died.' His father's laugh faded, his smile receding.

'She finally came clean then. We knew it—however they try to hide it, there is no denying it.'

A grimace returned to Tarak's face as he clutched at his side.

'You aren't making sense,' Olbi whispered.

Tarak lifted his head, looking around. Several patients had stirred, they were listening in, so Tarak lowered his voice. 'Not here, Olbi. Have you seen Faiyor or Cotsh since the meeting?'

'No, I came straight here. I don't know where they went,' Olbi said.

Faiyor and Cotsh had left the meeting before him. As visitors to Xylona, they likely would be staying at the Stonehall. Tarak struggled to sit up; his groaning filled the hall. With effort, he propped himself up. The young healer, hearing the commotion, sped over to them.

'Please, don't aggravate the wounds,' the healer said, his eyes wide with alarm at the outbursts of pain. Tarak raised his arm towards the man.

'I will be fine, don't worry about it,' Tarak said, pushing his legs off the desks. Augun stepped forward.

'You have lost a lot of blood. Syrona advised you need to stay here for observation,' said Augun, keeping an arm's length away from Tarak.

'I need fresh air, boy, and a chance to relieve myself. Get us a chair, will you?' Tarak ordered.

The young man froze for a moment, torn between Syrona's instructions and Tarak's demands before he ran off. He returned quickly, pushing a chair fitted with smooth and well-worn wooden wheels.

'This is the only one we have,' Augun said. 'Please get it back to me before Syrona returns.'

Tarak winked. 'Our little secret, boy,' Tarak said as Olbi aided his father off the desks and into the chair.

'We will just be outside in the square,' Olbi said, smiling at the young healer. Augun sighed and nodded before turning back to his duties.

Olbi wheeled Tarak into the town square, his father slumped in the wheelchair; it did not look comfortable. Olbi sat on a splintered barrel left from last night's feast. The sun was high in the sky—rain clouds drifted towards the forests and horizon beyond—drying the puddles left by the storm.

They were alone, save for the occasional figure hurrying through the healing hall or slipping into one of the buildings that bordered the square. Olbi could tell Tarak was still in pain. His father was a strong man, but the blow from the falling debris had been brutal.

He flinched, remembering the moment his father collapsed after the feast.

Tarak sighed.

'Olbi, she is right—the Prime One. Things will change,' Tarak said, looking up at the sun. His dark eyes glistened in the sunlight; he was smiling.

'The Prime One is worried,' Olbi said.

'And she should be. Her whole system is about to collapse. When the people learn the truth behind the lies she has told Xylona and the Rahsu, there won't be anywhere to hide,' Tarak said, a devilish smile lingering on his lips.

'What do you mean? How do the Outsiders have anything to do with the Prime One and Ayon? This isn't another one of your stories about despising the Primes, is it?'

'It has everything to do with the Prime, Olbi. Don't you see?'

Olbi furrowed his brow. 'I don't understand, father. The Prime One would never lie to us.' Olbi rocked on the barrel as cries from within the healing hall spilled out onto the square.

Liran had been angry at the meeting. Had the Prime One lied—was Tarak's distrust of the Primes valid?

'Son, why do you think the Prime One forbids people from entering the Forbidden Lands?'

'Because it's where demons' dwell. The Spirits keep us safe so long as we stay in their realm,' Olbi answered.

'Let's come back to that,' Tarak said, leaning forward in the chair, which creaked with his movement.

'Why is knowledge hoarded? Why do those who speak against the Prime One's vanish or are suddenly locked away or exiled?'

It was like Olbi was back at school.

'No one speaks ill of the Prime Ones—I have never known someone to. As for knowledge, I don't understand what you mean; we learn it all at school,' Olbi said.

Tarak shook his head and laughed.

'The Prime Ones have been keeping secrets from us and the true nature of things—truths we never learn at school and that are banned from the texts. I have known this for some time, but those who question it are silenced, Olbi. Some of us know the Primes are dying, and their power over the Rahsu is about to end. I know it, Cotsh and Faiyor know it … your mother knows it.'

'My mother?' Olbi interrupted, his voice sharp. The suddenness of it startled a bird in the square.

Tarak's gaze followed the bird as it fluttered to the ground, pecking at a loaf of bread beneath one of the statues. 'Yes, your mother,' he continued. 'She was the one who revealed the truth to me, and not just to me—there are others she's entrusted with this knowledge.'

'Is this what you had to say about my mother?' Olbi asked. He watched his father intently. They had never spoken so openly before.

Tarak shifted in his chair again; the bandages around his stomach were damp and tinged red. His wounds would not seal up properly if he kept squirming.

'It is strange to think this is how I would tell you about your mother, Olbi—sitting in this chair. It doesn't seem fair to tell you now,' Tarak said, averting eyes towards his lap.

'Tell me what, father?' Olbi said.

'Your mother is sick, Olbi,' Tarak said, his features falling into sorrow. 'She learned I was in Hydoran and came to see me; alas, she is but a wisp of her former self.'

'Okay' was all that he could muster.

'I know you have never known her, but she wasn't in your life for a reason, and she wanted you to know that. It wasn't that she never cared. It was *because* she cared and wanted you to have a normal life.'

'*Normal* life?' Olbi snorted. 'Father, a normal life is a family home not used as a storage room for traders. Normal is two parents that live and sleep in the same bed, brothers and sisters …' Olbi stopped as Tarak raised his palm and nodded.

'I know, believe me. When you were younger, and I left you with the teachers and Alvar, I too questioned your mother's choices,' Tarak said.

'Then why?' Olbi asked, his ears flushed as a streak of resentment welled beneath his skin. 'What was more important than raising me?' Olbi asked.

'Because of who your mother is, Olbi. Specifically, *what* she is,' Tarak elaborated, dropping his voice to a fraction above a whisper.

Butterflies fluttered in Olbi's chest. 'Enough secrets, father.'

Tarak sighed and rubbed his knees. 'Olbi, your mother is a Remnant from the previous line of Primes.'

Olbi opened his mouth to speak, though no response emerged, his jaw remaining dropped.

Tarak breathed heavily, and through gritted teeth, he applied pressure to his bandages.

Olbi's mind wrestled with shock, his head spinning as he splayed his fingers, reaching and grasping for threads of reality. His body had forgotten how to function.

'We kept it quiet for obvious reasons. Your mother hid her pregnancy, joining me on the road. We fell deeply in love, and she opened my eyes to a wealth of forbidden knowledge. Knowledge reserved only for the Primes.

'Eventually, you were born here, and she returned home to her family. They were unaware of your existence; she did not want to risk you being caged into that life. If you showed the traits of a Prime, you would have no freedom or choice on what you wanted from your life, you would belong to them.' Tarak gestured around him.

Olbi sat back down on the barrel. Remnant children were prized or considered threats in the past.

❖

'Olbi, you would have been a threat to the Prime One. Especially if you showed stronger connections to the Manna Rites than her recently born offspring.'

'You mean Ayon?' Olbi asked.

Tarak nodded.

'Ayon was born in Xylona one year before you. You were born of the Hydoran line—a fiery divide would have fractured the Rahsu if your mother's pregnancy was common knowledge and it turned out you had the blood,' Tarak said.

Olbi observed his hands as if expecting them to suddenly reveal a difference.

Rivalry between regions of the Rahsu had been responsible for men taking up arms against one another. It was decided by Rahsu long ago that one Prime family would take dominion over all cities and hamlets at a given time. But Remnants would still occasionally battle for power.

Olbi's mind raced. His father was being ridiculous. 'I don't believe you—I don't feel like a Remnant.'

'Olbi, trust me. Your mother would be the Prime One if she had the power to perform the Manna Rites.'

'Why didn't she want me to know? Wouldn't she want Hydoran to take back the Rites? Hydorans still hold a grudge that the seat of power has moved,' Olbi said, still thinking about what it all meant.

'Weren't you listening, boy? The Prime line is about to end. The Outsiders will see to that—' Tarak began, but Olbi had more questions.

'I know what you said, but what does anything we do have to do with these Outsiders? Why would my mother want you to tell me now?'

Olbi stood up from the barrel and paced, he was confused and growing annoyed. The urge to run into the forests crossed his mind. Too much had happened. Dryness crept into his mouth as his heart pumped louder. Pumping *Remnant* blood. His father watched him, shaking his head.

'Your mother says the choice is yours to make. By law, you can test your blood if you wish to. The Remnant blood may yet reside in you and if it does, then it's your choice to reveal yourself. If you do, then you can challenge Claudya. But whether the Prime seat exists when the Outsiders arrive is another thing. Don't you see? Don't you get it? Our world will change, whatever happens.'

Olbi paced. His chest heaved; it was heavy. Too much was happening all at once. How had he come from sitting with the Maven in the Prime House for a council meeting he wasn't invited to, to learning about others arriving from the stars to realising that maybe, just maybe, he could have Remnant blood coursing through his veins? Blood that may activate the garjee fruit and give him the right to claim the Manna Altar. For Hydoran? He had no connection with that place, nor had he been there. Olbi's father had never trusted the Primes and his trade missions bordered on the clandestine. Tarak appeared thrilled about recent events—why, and what of Ayon? The Prime Scion's face swam in his mind. Ayon did not want children; Ayon was ready to let the Prime line die. Would that matter?

'What sickness befalls my mother?' Olbi asked.

Tarak scratched at his beard. 'It is a sickness that has stripped away her strength, all too common for those of the Prime lines, I am afraid,' Tarak said.

'Wait, if that is true, will I succumb to this sickness one day?' Olbi sat on the barrel again. It rocked on the sandy ground, which only worsened his light-headedness. Tarak reached out his arm and placed it on Olbi's leg, squeezing slightly.

'I know it is a lot to take in, but I made a promise to your mother. All she asks is that if you have the blood and wish to take the Prime title, you will be honest with the Rahsu. Do not hide the truth of the past.'

Olbi gazed at his father with newfound curiosity, sensing an air of secrecy surrounding him. Something wasn't right.

❖

164

Tarak was guarding a significant revelation, holding his tongue.

'You know something, don't you? What past? What truth are the Prime Ones hiding?' Olbi's voice betrayed intrigue as he confronted his father, looking into the older man's weathered eyes. Olbi saw Tarak's eyes flash, a glimmer—not of fear but of anticipation.

'Olbi, my dear boy,' his father began, leaning forward. 'The Prime Ones have concealed everything about who we truly are.'

15

ZILLAH

'They aren't real trees.'

Dr Amira's declaration hung in the air like a joke with no punchline. Zillah looked back towards the verdant wall they had come from, the trees swaying in the breeze. They appeared real enough.

After fifteen minutes of waiting for Joja to run tests through her analysis machine, they all breathed a sigh of relief when she advised that their radiation exposure had been minimal and their symptoms would remain superficial—little comfort for Idonea, the soldier's complexion signalling uncertainty about his ability to continue the mission. Joja had assured them all that Idonea would survive. Zillah had grown to appreciate the Tobanian scientist, she was proving to be the most helpful crew member.

Joja kept injecting Idonea with serum in between checking the beeps on her tablet. The last beep indicated further analysis regarding the forest they had emerged from was completed.

'Look pretty fucking real to me,' Sloane said, sitting atop a dirt mound, his gun propped across his legs.

Alrin began filming the tree line—his camera panned the trees. Alrin's eye seemed glued to the viewfinder, the camera shifting around and seemingly focusing on the immense leaves of the trees above. Though it would make for interesting footage later, Zillah wasn't sure how one could film only leaves for minutes on end. Wouldn't a quick snapshot suffice? Though Zillah had to admit that she was appreciative of the protection the leaves had provided from the rain before. The leaves—now soaked in the sun's rays—were the largest she had ever seen, longer than she was tall and at least two metres wide. The central stem of each leaf was a bright emerald, which gradually faded to darkened green at the extremities.

'No wonder the rain didn't get through. Look at the size of the leaves; it's like a tiled roof,' Alrin said. He packed his camera back into its snug pouch. Beneath his ginger hair, his forehead glistened. 'You sure they aren't real trees, Doctor?'

Joja looked up at the young photographer. 'Their organic signature is weak. They are hybrids. Structurally, they comprise wood, but they are also interwoven with a metallic composition,' Joja said.

'Metal trees?' Zillah asked.

'No, they are wood. But now I know why I couldn't cut it with my knife,' Joja said, closely studying a bug that was crawling across her tablet.

'Will it burn?' Sloane inquired.

'I doubt it. If it does, it would take a while to penetrate the trunks. The flame would need to burn hot,' the doctor answered while swatting the bug away, 'unlike the tree species that burned under the immense heat of the thrusters, these trees are practically shielded in heat resistant bark.'

'What of the fruits they produce?' Zillah asked, remembering the yellow growths dotted in the highest branches upon entering the forest.

'You saw fruit?' Joja asked.

'Big yellow balls?' Sloane cut in. Zillah nodded.

'I must have missed that. Perhaps Mr Sandol captured them in his footage,' Joja said, shrugging.

'Any other dangerous plants or animals we should be worried about?' Doxxa cut in. He was looking out at the field with his back to them, grasping his gun. The area was bleak, almost barren, as if freshly sowed—the odd puddle of rainwater pooled between the ridges of rich soil.

'The plant and animal life are remarkably similar to what we have on Anatara,' Joja explained. 'So much so that I could name most of the species I have seen; however, there could be some, such as these trees, that are endemic to the planet.'

Zillah rose to her feet, brushing away the earth and dried mud clinging to her pants. The freshly tilled field extended

gently up a rise, concealing what lay beyond. The settlement must be just over that hill, where the first signs of structures and perhaps even native inhabitants awaited her. A nervous energy moved through her. The others took her lead and began preparing for the next part of the journey.

'Doxxa, stick close to Idonea, he may need help,' Zillah ordered. Doxxa hesitated, flicking the briefest of glances towards Sloane.

'You heard the captain, Doxxa. Stick with Idonea,' Sloane cut in, offering Doxxa a modest nod.

'Yes, sir,' Doxxa replied, saluting Sloane. He moved to pull Idonea up from the dirt.

Though Zillah said nothing, she knew she should have—her authority was already tenuous. Idonea struggled to his feet, his legs wobbling as he tried to walk. Zillah needed her countryman to recover, and with haste.

The dry dirt beneath their boots crunched and kicked up in the full sun as they marched up the field. Warmth licked at Zillah, tiny beads of sweat forming on her brow. Although marginally farther from the sun than Anatara, Arbornia was not all that different. Concerning climate, the warmth, the land and the air all appeared to mimic Anatara's. The only difference was that, unlike Anatara's vast oceans, Arbornia had lakes instead.

Zillah guided the party, with Sloane trailing behind. She reached the top of the rise and halted. The farmland rolled down a graceful hillside dotted with green stems and sprouts of grass. The crops rippled in the breeze, and the smell of rain lingered in the air as the storm loomed menacingly on the horizon. In the distance, another grove of trees clustered together like an island adrift in a sea of turned soil.

Zillah quickly rummaged through her backpack, pulling out a pair of binoculars. She used them to examine the grove ahead, noticing immediately the difference in the trees—they were a different species, with fewer limbs and far less dense foliage. While some trees were green and untouched, some were spindly and jagged like the deathly claw of charred bones. Glimpses of white stone buildings peeked through the grove, and above, a swirling cloud of smoke wafted into the air. Adjacent hillsides—also tilled into lines—were scorched and desolate. Zillah's chest constricted with knowing apprehension.

The fires sparked from Unity's entry were still burning. Others joined Zillah at the crest; each fixed their eyes on the grove, trying to spot the settlement beyond. From the grove, dirt roads snaked through the fields, intersecting each other and sprawling in different directions. Based on their satellite feed, the largest road wound from the settlement's edge and cut through the fields to their left. It then disappeared within the cover of forests and re-emerged into view by a large lake. It would be a few days walk to the north from here.

'Get down, I see movement,' Doxxa called as he crouched down and pulled Idonea down with him. Zillah and the others followed suit. On the road below them, small figures moved along with carts pulled by lumbering beasts. The same species of animal that lay dead by Sloane's hand behind them.

'They appear to be quite primitive,' Alrin commented. Zillah hadn't noticed he was filming the natives slowly ambling towards the settlement. Alrin turned the camera towards Zillah. She scowled, quickly turning from the lens.

'Care to narrate what we are looking at, Captain?' Alrin said. He was all business, his eyes wide behind the lens, clearly enjoying himself.

'Let's get this over with,' Zillah snapped. She wasn't in the mood to be the face of first contact, not after the misfortunes since landing. 'Remember, don't bring the camera out, it might unnerve them,' she said to Alrin.

The young man nodded and packed away the camera.

They trod down the field between rows of fledgling crops that emerged from the soil. Zillah almost forgot they were walking on another planet instead of the rural hills of her country. Before the war, Tarea had farms just like this.

'Captain, what's the plan? What's our angle regarding the fires?' Joja whispered, asking for directions.

Zillah watched a bird cross above her as she mulled things over. 'We don't raise it unless they do. For all we know, they don't know how the fires started,' Zillah replied.

'I think we should tell them,' Joja proposed. 'We shouldn't initiate contact on the wrong foot.'

'I agree with the captain,' Doxxa offered. 'By examining their technology levels, I'd say they would assume the fires started naturally.' Doxxa still had Idonea at his side, but it appeared he was walking alone, albeit unbalanced. Whatever Joja had given him was working. The smoke billowed ahead of them; Zillah resented the electrical disturbance that had created this mess.

Joja pursed her lips. 'I do not deny that they appear primitive, Doxxa,' she said, 'but let us not forget that the electrical disturbance came from this region. It would be naive to think that the locals aren't aware of what starts fires.' Zillah kicked a clump of clay with her foot and watched it tumble into a puddle.

'Remember, first, we establish communication. Then we find artefacts or confirm the connection between our world and theirs. We need to establish trust and friendship. Otherwise, we might not be able to find what we are looking for,' Zillah said as the terrain levelled out. Not far ahead lay the well-worn road.

Sloane snorted, his own humourless form of a chuckle. 'And if they are hostile, Morgana?' Sloane was gripping his gun in a way that made Zillah uncomfortable. The last thing they needed was hostility or the native's sustaining injury—or being killed—due to diplomatic breakdown.

They stood a hundred metres from the side of the road, which vanished between hills to the north. The farmer they saw earlier had disappeared into the settlement, which appeared extensive and larger than Zillah expected. Impressive white stone facades stood between towering trees, some long and dotted with windows and doors. Some of the buildings displayed evidence of being licked by flame. The path into the town was well worn, and under the sand, smooth stones a metre wide spanned the street. Zillah threw a glance back to her party as she stepped onto the road.

Where was everyone? For a town this large and in the middle of the day, surely they would have been spotted by now. It wasn't right to walk in unannounced. She imagined meeting the natives of the planet with pomp and ceremony; instead, she stared down a dusty street shrouded in silence. Zillah paused and bit her lip.

'Doxxa, I want you to stay back here with Idonea; you too, Alrin,' Zillah said, noticing Doxxa was whispering something to Sloane. 'We don't want to spook them. Joja, Sloane and I will make contact, and when we establish that things are progressing peacefully, we will radio for you to join us.'

'And if the tablets malfunction again?' Alrin asked.

'Let's rendezvous at the top of the hill in two hours. Doxxa, establish a lookout,' Sloane said, pointing to the rise they had walked down.

Idonea slowly lifted his face to Zillah. 'I am well enough to continue, Morgana,' he insisted, though clearly struggling to stand. His eyes were less bloodshot, but he still needed medical attention. *Maybe Joja should stay?* Zilla thought.

'Idonea, it is best to wait here and recover. Your illness might spook the locals,' Zillah explained, casting a gaze towards Sloane. His face was blank, showing no indication of what he thought of splitting the party in two.

Alrin stepped forward and cleared his throat. 'I insist I join you, Captain. I must log the mission and report back to QC. They are being kept in the dark by asking me to stay back. They will ask questions and billions of people will be eager to know what these people are like,' Alrin said. The defiance in his voice was like a slap to Zillah's face. Of all the crew, she expected Alrin would be the least likely to push back against her orders.

'QC will understand the diplomatic sensitivities of such a request, Mr Sandol. It is for our safety as much as theirs. You must advise QC that the mission is jeopardised if something were to go wrong. If you accompany us and we are all put in danger or incapacitated, who will transmit that message?' Zillah clicked her tongue. She did not like having to explain herself.

Alrin was silent, his gaze darted to Idonea and Doxxa for backup, but they were turning around to head back up the hill. Alrin stepped back, defeated. He followed the others and announced, 'I will take footage of the forests and the farms then.'

Zillah breathed a sigh of relief. *You do that then*, she thought. She didn't want to test just how far her authority as captain would go.

Sloane and Joja joined her on the road, peering towards the native town.

'Let's conduct a sensible approach. I will open a dialogue—please refrain from sudden movements or raising your weapons,' Zillah said, scrutinising the entry to town.

Joja nodded, while Sloane gave her a severe stare before walking down the road. Zillah followed, with Joja in tow. Her heart raced. This was the most crucial moment in her life, the weight of an entire planet rested on her shoulders.

The road ahead was lined by gently swaying trees that permeated a tangy aroma akin to lemon. The small leaves, still heavy from the morning's rain, glistened. The wind shifted through branches and grasses like waves on a beach.

The crew walked beneath a stone arch that spanned over the road like a picture frame for the town beyond. Stone facades with dark wooden doors stood on either side, each building lined with verandas that wrapped around the long structures. To her right, a pen full of animals like the one Sloane had killed grazed on dried straw and grasses. Their heads lifted briefly, big brown eyes flickering with idle curiosity as they regarded the group, then drifted back to their chewing, uninterested in anything beyond their next mouthful.

'Where is everyone?' Joja whispered. Her footsteps were barely audible as she crept forward.

Unease took over Zillah. Were they being watched? 'It's possible they know we are here. The farmer with the cart may have tipped them off,' she said. From what they knew, thanks to satellite imagery, the town stretched outwards a few kilometres. It was almost a perfect square—filled with dozens of smaller squares—with one large square in the centre and a perfectly circular clearing to the north. Ahead of Zillah, small streets and narrow lanes jutted off in all directions.

'No defensive buildings or battlements that I can see,' Sloane remarked. 'A good sign.'

Zillah had noticed that too. The population may not be hardwired for conflict. The same couldn't be said for the war-torn Anatara.

Zillah cautiously strolled a few hundred metres farther down the street, closed doors and windows meeting her at every turn. To her right, she heard rattling and a loud squawk as a white bird took flight. Joja jumped and gasped as the bird flew across the street into a thick clutch of trees.

The road ahead skewed to the right, restricting their view into the belly of the town. Rubble and debris lay scattered on the street while plumes of white smoke slowly billowed overhead. Zillah debated whether to knock on a door or peer through a window. She slowed her pace, eyeing a large building that stood alone, detached from the others.

'Look down,' Zillah said, gesturing to the others. She knelt in the sandy street and pointed out the visible footsteps. Many footsteps. This was a high-traffic area and was recently used. She peered back towards the long building of grey stone.

Zillah narrowed her gaze. The windows on the ground floor were boarded up. She took a few steps towards the structure and exhaled quickly. From behind the boards, she saw shadows of movement and heard muffled footsteps. She raised her hands as if in surrender and edged towards the large building as if the ground beneath her would give way.

'Captain, what are you doing?' Joja whispered, her eyes darting anxiously between Zillah and the building.

'Morgana?' Sloane said, his hands flicking closer to his gun.

'Don't make any sudden movements,' Zillah ordered, barely loud enough for them to hear. 'We are being watched.' She took another step closer to the building, close enough to see the shiny new nails that were used to board up the windows.

An awkward silence hung over them as Zillah weighed her options. She was only a few steps from the window. She glanced again at Joja and Sloane who both still stood in the middle of the road. A rustle behind the boarded-up window redirected her attention back to the building.

'Hello, my name is Zillah Morgana,' Zillah said, projecting her voice towards the building. Several seconds passed with no response. Her heart thumped in her chest. Joja and Sloane remained silent, but Joja's feet crunched in the sand as she rocked on her heels.

'We are here to talk with you. We mean you no harm,' she continued, speaking now to the vast emptiness of the town. Nothing. She backed up into the street towards Joja and Sloane.

'We have come far to meet you and learn from you.' She closed her eyes and listened for movement. A response. Anything.

'Captain!' Joja urgently called out in a strained voice. Zillah followed the doctor's gaze to the door: it had opened.

Zillah's heart skipped as the door swung ajar, creaking on its hinges, the sound filling the quiet street. She held her breath as a man stepped out of the shadows. She glanced at Joja and Sloane, adrenaline jolting through her body.

❖

'Stay back,' she mouthed to her companions. Neither of them moved; instead, they regarded the man as he moved gingerly into the street. He was elderly with a strong face topped with wispy hair that had long been grey. He limped forward, putting his weight on a cane. His squinted eyes darted to Sloane as they adjusted to the light, then to Joja, who briefly returned a half smile. His expression furrowed as if confused as he stepped closer to Zillah. His blue eyes penetrated hers, eyes that sat behind dark bags and wrinkled skin, though she sensed he was sharp and alert, studying her. His hands sat perched on his cane as he halted three steps from the door, which closed behind him. He was human, with familiar enough features that he could have been from Tarea.

'Hello, my name is Zillah Morgana,' Zillah repeated. She tried to drop her voice, speaking only to him. Zillah pointed to herself as she said her name. Did he understand her? The man squinted at her finger pointed to her chest.

'Alvar,' the man said, pointing to his own chest. His voice was deep. Strong but shaky. Her heart leapt and pounded against her ribcage.

'Hello, Alvar. This is Gideon Sloane and Dr Joja Amira,' she said, pointing to her two companions. Sloane remained silent, but Joja raised her hand as if to wave though dropped it quickly. Instead, she smiled again and nodded politely. Alvar nodded to the three of them.

'You understand our words?' Zillah asked.

Alvar nodded. He hadn't yet smiled or given anything of himself.

'As I was saying, Alvar, we have come from far away to meet you,' Zillah said. Alvar continued to stare at them, a searching stare, a look reminding Zillah of wary prey, wondering if he were in danger.

'I know who you are, Outsider.' Alvar's voice was firm. The shakiness had left him. Joja gasped.

'You came from the stars, did you not?' Alvar said, straightening his back. His accent differed from theirs, but their language was the same after all these years. Zillah cleared her throat and cocked her head to Joja. They knew about them. Zillah swallowed saliva that built up on her tongue. She steadied her disbelief.

'That is correct, Alvar,' Zillah acknowledged. 'We come from a world called Anatara, a planet close to Arbornia.'

Alvar listened, narrowing his eyes and pausing. He let out a gruff laugh, revealing his yellowed teeth.

'You've been watching us for eighty years and yet can't get our name right.'

Zillah took half a step back. 'What do you call this world?' Zillah asked, taking her turn to study Alvar. She was stunned that he knew so much, even about the satellites that orbited the planet.

'Our home is Arbonar. You stand in Xylona, the seat of the Prime, the protector of the Rahsu,' Alvar said. He eyed Sloane now; his eyes fell on the gun hung at the soldier's side.

'Why have you come? You speak of peace, yet many Rahsu lay dead by your hand. Farms and homes have been destroyed as you fell from above and from our good graces,' Alvar said, his eyes misty.

Zillah felt Sloane and Joja's eyes on her. She was lost for words. She knew the landing thrusters had set fields and forests ablaze, but she hadn't considered that lives had been lost. Alvar didn't look away. She saw pain there—no anger, just pain and loss. Zillah fumbled for words, finding no response. This is why she was chosen to be the face of first contact, but it wasn't supposed to be like this. Alvar raised a hand as she opened her mouth.

'You will answer to the Prime One; may the Spirits guide us all,' Alvar said as a tear rolled down his cheek.

16

LIRAN

Liran spent mere seconds in the studio gathering supplies for her journey to Hydoran. She was in dire need of rest; every fibre of her being was thoroughly drained. Despite its protest, her body moved mechanically as she packed her old rucksack, which still carried the fetid scent of decaying leaves and paint from its last use—a day spent painting beneath the trees in the gardens. Now it held spare clothes, a water bladder, her sketchbook and charcoals, and whatever food remained in her storeroom. With everything packed, she scampered out into the street.

It was apparent why Claudya wanted Ayon removed from town—she desired to withdraw him from Xylona before the strangers arrived. Liran doubted Ayon would be safe regardless of his location.

I shouldn't be leaving, she thought. *Why am I to be the one to safeguard Ayon?* She wanted to remain in Xylona for when the Outsiders arrived—after all, the Maven was usually at the forefront of delegations to receive any travellers.
Since learning the star's identity, she yearned to find this vessel that fell from the stars. Instead, she would be slipping away on a fool's errand. Ayon wasn't at the council meeting, nor did Claudya hint at his whereabouts. Liran half expected Reeva to have locked him away until Liran came for him.

Liran recognised every stone on the road between her studio and the Prime House, each step as familiar to her as the next. She sharply turned a corner and collided with a tiny figure. She recognised a blur of Monitor's robes as the man fell to the stone.

'Maven, they are here! The Outsiders arrived from the north,' the man squealed as he picked himself up from the stoney street, his eyes wide with alarm. 'The Prime One has asked everyone to remain in their homes until we know their intentions.'

'How far away are they?' Liran asked as the Monitor dusted off his robes.

'A farmer bringing wheat stock saw six strangely dressed people emerge from the northern garjee forest. They approach the arches of Xylona. Hurry to wherever you are going. Don't let yourself be spotted and tell anyone you see to hide themselves away.' With that, the man sprinted down the lane, jumping over a smashed flowerpot that spewed dark soil and stained the white stone.

****

Panting and short of breath, Liran climbed the steps to the Prime House. At the top, she pressed her palms against the intricately carved doors of the building, but she heard the jarring rattle of a chain locking her out. Liran pounded her fists against the wood.

'Hello,' she yelled. Liran spun. The empty plaza was quiet behind her. *What is Claudya thinking?* she thought.

If there was a risk of violence, where were the defences and the call to arms? Liran heard the rattle of chains again before the door creaked open, and a pair of eyes appeared from within the shadows. The hollow stare belonged to the Head Monitor, Phran. He scrutinised Liran, though for a moment she saw fear flicker in his eyes.

'Maven, what are you doing? Come inside, quickly; the Outsiders are coming,' Phran said, ushering her in.

The hall was dark, the light from the cracked front door cast shadows across alcoves and cornices. The great hearth lay dormant, the familiar hub of the room now abandoned, and all that remained was a chilled ambience. Liran shivered. Boarded windows let in slivers of light, enough for her to see Phran's aging and anxious expression.

'What is going on, and why the hiding? This is ridiculous,' Liran said.

Phran was taken aback at the question and looked over Liran's shoulder. She pivoted, and her eyes met Reeva's tall physique. The guardian was dressed in polished armour, her sword glistening at her side. In the darkness, Liran noticed Claudya seated at the base of the stairs like a small child. The Prime One, adorning a lavender dress, had her hair up—loaded with ornamental jewels—and her hands were clasped tightly together, apprehension riddling her weary complexion. Reeva strode towards Liran and blocked Claudya from view, her metal armour squeaking with every twitch and gesture.

'Maven, you are late. The Scion waits in the kitchen,' Reeva said. 'Make your journey east and follow the river north until you hit the road to Hydoran. The Outsiders have stopped in front of the Stonehall and—,'

Whatever Reeva had said was lost as Liran sidestepped her imposing frame. Liran knelt by Claudya, who offered a sheepish smile. Red pillows swelled under her eyes: she had been crying. Liran had never known the Prime One to weep.

'Claudya, am I to go ahead with this flight to Hydoran? You know, if these people mean us harm, then there is nowhere Ayon can hide. They have the power to swim with the stars, they will know where we are going.'

What anger she had harboured at the meeting had vanished. It was evident that the Prime One and Reeva held secrets about the history of the Rahsu. Liran swallowed the bitter taste of resentment building within her.

Claudya sniffed and dabbed the corner of her eye with a sleeve. 'I should have told you the truth from the beginning,' Claudya murmured.

Liran reached out her arm to the weary woman who took it and squeezed. Reeva paced in the middle of the hall; her eyes fixed on the entrance. 'The truth about what?' Liran asked.

❈

179

'The secrets that the Primes are sworn to keep. It does not seem right to hide the—'

'Prime One!' Reeva's hushed yet severe voice carried across the hall. The two women on the steps raised their heads—there was a noise from outside, the crunch of footsteps on the plaza's gravel and stone. Somebody was approaching the Prime House.

Reeva hovered by a window with its wooden panels latched tight. She peeked through cracks between the wood, her hand on the hilt of her sword. Liran had never witnessed Reeva use the blade and wondered how effective it would be if required. Reeva pressed her body against the window. No one uttered a sound.

Claudya squeezed Liran's hand tightly as the sound of shuffling outside grew louder. The slow crunch of footsteps unnerved Liran—it sounded like footsteps were coming from all around. Were they being surrounded?

The footsteps seemed to hurry and now sounded as if they were within the house, muffled by the rugs that lined the halls. Liran twisted to peer down one of the corridors. A shadow moved in the darkness and a lone figure appeared in the passageway. Reeva's armour rattled as she shifted her stance to face whoever was looming. The figure moved into the small bit of light. Ayon, wrapped in a travelling cloak, stood before them. Claudya's eyes widened as he surged towards his mother.

Tears rolled down Claudya's cheeks as she cradled her son. Liran stepped away to give them space. Who was outside?

She shifted to the window and peered out, though she spied no one at first. Soon, Alvar materialised.

The older man—limping ever closer with his cane—wasn't alone, others escorted him. The columns on the veranda obstructed Liran's view of the plaza; however, she speculated the Outsiders were with Alvar from the tensing of Reeva's jaw at the adjacent window.

❖

'Prime One,' Alvar bellowed from the plaza. His voice filled the unlit hall as if amplified by the emptiness. 'The Outsiders desire to talk.'

'The fool,' Reeva spat in a hushed tone, her face twisted as if she had eaten something sour.

Claudya sniffed. 'It's alright, Reeva, we cannot hide forever as you would have it. We must confront them,' she said. Ayon helped his mother off the stone steps and proceeded towards the window. The next voice sent shivers down Liran's arm—a voice she didn't recognise.

'Prime One, my name is Captain Zillah Morgana. We mean you no harm and wish only to introduce ourselves.' The voice belonged to a woman with a peculiar accent. Liran's skin prickled with excitement—someone not of this world had spoken their tongue. Questions formed in her mind.

'If it pleases you, we will forfeit our weapons. Alvar will retain them if that provides you peace of mind,' Captain Morgana said. 'You must be just as eager as us to meet people of another world.'

Liran crossed to the next window, and her eyes found a gap in the boards. She now saw four people standing in the sunlit plaza. Alvar had both hands on his cane, looking towards the sealed door that divided them. He appeared ancient and frail beside the two women and the man he was with.

One woman stood tall, her obsidian hair swept back from a strong, weathered face. She appeared to be around Liran's age.

The other woman was considerably younger and had eccentric hair—tufts of thick, matted cords fell down her back and jutted out beneath a hat. The man stood the broadest, comparable in stature to Reeva, who retained a watch on the Outsiders from the window. Only three travellers. There was no sign of the other three the Monitor she had bumped into in the streets had alluded to.

Liran studied the black-haired woman as she placed an object before Alvar. The thing was slight and had no blade. Was that the woman's weapon? Liran failed to see how it would stack up against the sword that hung at Reeva's side. The other woman relinquished an identical item; however, the man hesitated. His hands firmly gripped an oversized metal item. The two women spoke to him, not audible enough for Liran to hear. The man sneered at Alvar before placing his weapon at the old man's feet.

'Prime One, I urge you not to welcome them,' Reeva said. Phran stood by the door, eyeing Claudya, the keys to the locks hanging laboriously around his neck.

'I must meet them, Reeva, ploy or not. They are being reasonable and have conveyed no reason to mistrust them.'

'Only that they scorched half of Xylona! Do not forget the deaths they have delivered,' Reeva snapped, shaking her head as Claudya started for the door.

'Reeva, I want you to escort me. Liran, you as well. We may require your—'

'Sense of humour?' Liran cut in.

Claudya chuckled. 'Your diplomatic prowess. But perhaps that, too, to help diffuse any awkwardness. I understand the gravity of this moment. The people will be afraid, and we must do what we can to engage peacefully,' Claudya said before turning to the Scion. 'Ayon, my darling, please follow Phran and stay in the inner sanctum with the guards. I think your journey to Hydoran will wait for now. If you leave now people will think you are fleeing out of fear. The future Prime One must face challenges head on,' she added, straightening a crease in her dress. Ayon looked timid yet he appeared to accept his mother's request.

Phran glanced at Claudya, who nodded back. The head Monitor lifted the key from around his neck and unlocked the chain before approaching Ayon and guiding him from the room.

'Let us meet our guests,' Claudya declared as the doors opened, flooding the hall with light and illuminating the lavender hues in her dress.

The mood was tense as Reeva led Claudya out of the Prime House and onto the landing before the plaza. Liran followed in tow, her legs trembling with apprehension. Reeva drew an imposing figure as she marched, her cutting gaze sharp enough to sever the strongest garjee.

Liran peered down at Alvar and the outsiders in the blazing sun, observing them like a painting. Their shadows tarnished the white stones that fanned out from the steps. There was no denying that the Outsiders looked much like them—they could be Rahsu, for all she knew. The only difference was their garbs—the three dressed in a similar style made from a weave that Liran could not determine. No yar wool would make fabric like that. The woman she assumed was Zillah Morgana offered a thin smile as Claudya descended the steps. Liran eyed Reeva's fingers playing with the hilt of her sword.

Alvar leant heavily on his cane and wobbled. From cravenness or frailty, Liran was unsure, but the master of the Stonehall looked uncomfortable as if he wanted to be far gone from the plaza.

The Outsider man puffed his chest, and though he was without his weapon, he was nevertheless imposing.

Claudya radiated regality in her purple gown, the gemstones woven into the lace catching the afternoon sun as she stopped four paces from the black-haired woman. The woman's lips curled into a faint, amused smile. 'I am Claudya Lyfera, Third of the Lyfera and Prime One of the Rahsu. Welcome to Xylona, the seat of the Manna Altar. May you burn bright, and the Spirits protect you,' she announced in all her formality.

Captain Morgana's eyes lit up and a wide smile erupted across her face. She nodded with deliberation and began to speak, 'Claudya Lyfera, my name is—'

❧

183

'You will address her as *Prime One*,' Reeva cut in, her steely tongue as pointed as her blade.

A small gasp escaped the slighter Outsider woman, but Captain Morgana appeared unfazed by the interruption. She retained her smile and nodded gently. 'Prime One, my name is Zillah Morgana, Captain of the Unity mission. To my left is Commodore Gideon Sloane and,' her arm gestured towards the younger woman, 'this is Doctor Joja Amira. Thank you for your kind welcome. We are honoured to have the opportunity to meet with you at last.' Again, Zillah smiled politely and nodded.

Claudya returned the nod.

'This is Liran, Xylona's Maven, and this is Reeva, First Guardian of the Primes—why have you come to Arbonar?' Claudya asked.

Liran noticed a shift in the captain's voice, which became less eloquent as her shoulders relaxed.

'Arbonar, yes, Alvar enlightened us. We have always known this world as Arbornia. Time changes many things, but it delights me that we still share the same tongue and substance behind those words,' Captain Morgana said.

Liran took in a shallow breath, what did she mean by still sharing the same tongue? Zillah looked at her companions, raising her arms to them.

'We represent the many nations of Anatara, a planet that neighbours Arbonar. We are explorers and are here to learn more about you and, in turn, more about ourselves,' Zillah said as the smaller outsider woman with strange hair slightly bowed to Claudya. Liran noted that the captain was being careful with her words, though something about her tone made Liran wonder how rehearsed those lines were.

Reeva's armour squeaked as she took a step forward. 'We have reports that six of you came out of the northern garjee grove. Where are the others of your kind?' Reeva inquired bluntly.

❖

184

Zillah glanced deliberately at Reeva, seeming unfazed by her bluntness. 'Yes, I do not deny it. The others remain outside town. We thought it unwise to overwhelm you,' she sturdily answered.

'The garjee grove? The smaller outsider said in a younger voice. 'That's the name of the trees in the forest we travelled through?'

Liran gazed at Joja Amira—her eyes were wide, cheerful and enthusiastic.

'I would very much like to know more about them,' Joja said, 'we have nothing like them on Anatara.'

Claudya smiled.

'The garjee are most hallowed, and to the Spirits of the Rahsu, they are precious,' Claudya said.

'Are they genuinely trees?' Joja said.

Liran was baffled by Joja's question.

'Prime One,' Reeva cut in, 'I suggest we discuss matters in a more appropriate setting.' The Guardian shot Joja a glare.

'Of course, Reeva,' Claudya said. 'Let us show the guests to the council room. Alvar, can you please instruct any Monitor you see on your return to the Stonehall that people can resume their daily tasks by order of the Prime One?'

Tasks *is one word for it*, Liran thought. In essence, Claudya referred to the clean up after the fires. Alvar stared at his feet.

'What of their weapons, Prime One?' he asked.

'I will have a Monitor fetch them and put them someplace safe,' Claudya said, turning to Zillah.

The captain nodded approval. The Outsiders followed the Prime One into the hall while Captain Morgana peppered Claudya with courteous chatter.

'Such a marvellous building, Prime One. I must say that the architecture and stone works are truly inspiring,' Zillah said.

Claudya smiled. Liran still felt nervous in her gut, shaken by the casual nature of the Outsiders. It was as if they were

traders from beyond the Great Lake—such was the nature of their arrival.

Claudya looked upon the stone walls as they approached the doors to the Prime House. 'They are wonderful. A gift from the early Rahsu. They were masters of stone and built much of what you see before you.'

Liran marvelled at the Prime House in this new light. She hadn't thought about how the early Rahsu built the stone buildings often, despite intentions to author a book about it as stone had long since fallen from favour as a building material. The trade had been lost to time, and the last quarry sat idle within the Granite Hills close to the Eastern Forbidden Zone. Still, she understood some people continued crafting small sculptures from stolen quarry stones. Those statues now stood within the gardens and cloisters in towns and village centres, such as those in Xylona.

'What is a Maven, if I may be so blunt?' Joja asked Liran, distracting the Maven from her reflections. The doctor smiled at Liran, and she reciprocated. She was looking into the eyes of someone who travelled the stars. Her throat was dry.

'A Maven is the town scholar, a counsellor to the Prime One, or when the seat is not within that town, a Maven is the town administrator,' Liran explained.

'Ah, like a mayor or a bureaucrat?' Joja said.

Liran did not know those terms, though she was awestruck.

'I assist the Prime One with delegations and the governance of Xylona along with the Head Monitor. I am also a historian and keeper of the archives,' she replied.

'Liran is being far too humble,' Claudya said, overhearing their conversation. 'She is the right hand of the Prime One, and I praise her for her skills. She is responsible for Xylona's stability.' Claudya smiled at Joja before winking at Liran.

Joja raised her eyebrows, and Liran sensed the young doctor's inquisitiveness. The only one who didn't seem interested was Gideon Sloane, his silence and blank demeanour differed from that of Zillah and Joja. He went extended intervals without blinking, and his eyes did not seem to wander far from Zillah … or Reeva's sword. He appeared bored as they strolled through the great hall towards the council chamber.

Ayon was nowhere to be found, and Liran expected he would be in the inner sanctum with Phran. Reeva followed behind the Prime One, the metal armour at her hips squeaking as she strode.

'Will the others of your party be joining us at any point?' Claudya asked Zillah, standing before the doors and ushering them into the council chamber. 'I can call upon a Monitor to go and collect them if you wish?'

'We can call them when they are needed,' Zillah said, looking at her companions. Liran saw something in Joja's eyes. Was she troubled? Outnumbered and in a foreign land, they had a right to be cautious, but was there something else?

Phran was whispering instructions to his Monitor's, some immediately disappeared towards the kitchens while other Monitors filed in and stood at attention beneath the billowing tapestries, throwing cautious glances towards the Outsiders as the visitors begun sitting at the table. Zillah's eyes wandered around the room, scanning the various illustrations that adorned the tapestries with wide eyes. Joja was fixated on the water goblet in front of her and ran her hand across the marbled onyx stone with a smile. Meanwhile, Sloane glowered across the table from Reeva staring at her. She reciprocated the watchful stare.

Two Monitors materialised at the door carrying a large copper platter stacked with a decadent spread of foods. Fruits, bread, cheeses, nuts, honey and jam from the farms and orchard—enough for twenty people.

Liran abruptly felt sick with what had just happened, the thought of people in town rationing food and making ends meet would be a hardship Xylonans would soon face. Here, the finest bounty was being served to the people who had caused that suffering. The platter was positioned at the end of the table. Joja's smile lit up as she scoured the tray with greedy eyes.

'Fresh fruit, we haven't had any in weeks,' Joja said.

Claudya, the last one standing, smiled softly and gracefully assumed her seat at the head of the table. Liran noted that unlike the council meeting earlier, this time, Claudya opted to sit in the ornate Prime chair.

The doors shut, and for the second time that day, Liran found herself in the same chair at the council table with the Prime One. Only now, the company she shared was unimaginable only hours ago and would be set in the histories. She barely had time to process that people from another planet had landed on Arbonar, and now she sat across from three people—who looked like Rahsu—that had journeyed among stars.

'How did you get here?' Liran asked abruptly. She hadn't realised she had spoken out loud when all eyes fell upon her. Liran's chest tightened, and a warmness swelled in her cheeks.

Zillah turned to her companions and then to Liran before speaking, her hands resting gently on the stone table. 'We have a ship. One capable of travelling through the space between our worlds. We set out once we knew it was safe for us to visit,' Zillah revealed.

'Safe how?' Claudya chimed in.

'That we could breathe the air and find the resources necessary to return home.' Zillah took a sip of the water in front of her.

'What resources do you need to return home?' Claudya asked.

The doctor leapt in now, her eyes breaking from the food platter. 'We can extract fuel from water, but if there were some heavier elements, we might be able to excavate them with your permission. Our scans and analyses of Arbornia show signatures of deposits within the area north of a large lake. We had intended to land near the settlement there.

'Failing that, considerable deposits were detected southeast of here in what appears to be a large area of ridges and quarries. That is our preference as it is also an area of keen interest.'

The Eastern Forbidden Zones. Liran knew that was what they meant.

Reeva's eyes flickered. 'Those lands are forbidden,' she exclaimed.

'Why is that?' Joja said, her eyebrows raised.

'Demons roam those lands—none may enter,' Claudya extrapolated.

Zillah leaned forward.

'Demons?' Sloane uttered, speaking for the first time.

Liran could see Zillah's mind ticking behind her eyes, she was holding something back. Liran cleared her throat and turned to Claudya. The Prime One nodded permission to speak.

'You mentioned that you are pleased we still speak the same tongue, Captain? How is it that you understand us?' Liran asked. A fog of mystery descended upon them.

'Yes, many were sceptical about how much change could have transpired between us. After all, there are nations on Anatara that differ greatly. But this is truly fortuitous,' Zillah said.

'I don't quite catch your meaning,' Liran responded, turning to Claudya. The Prime One lowered her head, her posture heavy with weariness. Zillah took a deep breath, straightened her spine, and slowly raised her hands from the cold stone table.

'What do you know of Anatara, Maven?' Zillah asked.

Liran furrowed her brow in bemusement. How could she know anything?

'I am a Maven, not an all-knowing oracle, Captain. I know nothing of Anatara.'

A wrinkle appeared on Joja's face. The doctor bit her lip.

'What aren't you telling us?' Liran inquired.

Reeva and Claudya were strangely quiet. Zillah leaned back in her chair.

'Maven, we have a shared history,' Zillah stated as a matter of fact.

'I beg your pardon?' Liran blurted, the words tumbling from her lips. Reeva shifted, her metal armour creaking. Zillah took a sip of water and weaved her hands together.

'Long ago, our worlds were connected, Maven. Anatara and Arbonar shared a destiny, one that was severed some sixteen hundred years ago. We are on a mission to understand why. We believe the answer may be here, in your *Forbidden Zone.*'

Liran's heart thumped, what madness was this? She became lightheaded.

'None will enter the Forbidden Zones,' Reeva muttered, loud enough for Joja to hear.

'You would deny us our history and opportunity to learn who we are because of superstitions?' Joja responded heatedly.

'You have no proof you are who you say you are,' Reeva said, abruptly standing up.

'Then how do you explain this?' Joja said, slapping her hand onto the stone table. She stroked at the wispy white streaks flowing through the onyx. Liran thought the doctor was batty—what did a stone table prove?

'This stone is only found in Tobania,' Joja continued, 'mined for its conductive properties from a unique geological structure outside Edwar,' Joja said.

Liran goggled at the table with newfound interest. It was true, she had never seen a stone quite like this, but that was hardly proof.

Reeva scoffed.

Zillah stood up as Joja returned to her seat.

'We can trade for safe passage to your Forbidden Zones and will share what we find. We understand your culture

differs from ours, but we have come a long way to learn about our shared past.

'Our intentions are simple and respectful. We will not disturb your traditions; we merely wish to observe and establish a dialogue between Anatara's respected governments and the Rahsu. Do you speak for all the Rahsu, Prime One? Is the land forbidden for all?' Zillah asked.

Claudya sat up straight and nodded. 'I speak for those under the protection of the Spirits, but all Rahsu speak for themselves. Xylona is the seat of the Manna Rites. It is where the offerings are given. There are a great many Rahsu spread throughout the forests of Arbonar, each with their own customs and ways of life, but yes, the Forbidden Zones of this world are places that Rahsu may not enter,' Claudya said.

'There you have it. We are *not* Rahsu,' Joja said.

'No, you are not, so how does studying Arbonar help you?' Liran invited.

'Is there a way we can speak with other Rahsu?' Zillah said.

'If you wish to speak with all Rahsu, then a Grand Meeting would need to be summoned,' Claudya said.

Liran turned to Claudya. 'A Grand Meeting? One has not been called in living memory,' she said. Their purpose was often reserved for challenges to the Manna Rites.

'I believe a request to meet with people of another world would merit a summons,' said Claudya.

The last time a Grand Meeting took place was over fifty years ago when the Forbidden Zones accord was declared, before Liran's time.

'We would welcome this,' Zillah said. 'In a few years, we could dispatch another ship and reestablish a genuine trade link and dialogue between our worlds.'

'How many ships do you possess?' Reeva asked, her eyes set on Gideon Sloane.

'Many,' Zillah answered. 'We have already established a colony on our moon, and the Quartab Command Centre is a

multinational installation used as a launch point for exploring the solar system.'

The captain's words threw Liran off. What did she mean by the *solar system*?

'It sounds like you have a truly great society that can explore the stars,' Liran said. 'What can we possibly give you in return? We are simple by comparison, and a voyage among stars is something we could not imagine.'

'Why, Liran, you can offer us so much,' Zillah said, wearing a bemused smile. 'We, too, are students of history. Surely you want to know of our shared histories. The ruins of the Injai have left us in awe of the past, you must be just as intrigued as we are?'

Claudya shifted in her seat while Reeva appeared to be seething in her armour.

Zillah didn't seem to notice. 'Our studies of Arbonar suggest ruins of the Injai and their relics lie all over this planet. I must say, it is peculiar to us that you have confined yourselves to a diminutive domain of such a vibrant and exquisite world. We hope you will allow us to study these relics and ruins in greater detail, so we may better understand who we are.'

Joja nodded in agreement as Zillah took another sip of water. 'That is why we are here; we are all scholars, nay?' The captain gave Liran a meaningful stare.

'Ruins of the *Injai* … what do you mean?' Liran questioned. 'And what relics?'

Reeva's nostrils visibly flared as she huffed out a breath. Liran watched as Joja became alert and tense.

'The place you name the Forbidden Zone is a treasure trove of Inj—' Joja started.

'We must discuss the other matter at hand,' Reeva interrupted, her steely glare stabbing Joja.

'What matter is that?' Zillah asked calmly, turning to Reeva.

'The destruction of Xylona and our fields by your hand,' Reeva stated firmly as a suppressed awkwardness boiled to the surface, followed by a chill that gripped the room like a bout of winter. Sloane showed the first ounce of emotion as a flicker of a scowl registered on his brow. Joja abruptly appeared troubled and shrank into her chair as Zillah uncrossed her hands on the table and laid both palms flat against the stone.

'Something powerful on Arbonar forced our ship to spiral out of control. I did what I could to mitigate the thruster effect.

'We understand the anger and resentment you rightly feel. We feel for your loss. I strive for peace between us and know that what has regrettably transpired has tarnished what should be a momentous occasion,' Zillah said with sincerity.

Liran detected sorrow in Zillah's cadence.

'What on Arbonar could affect your ship?' Liran asked.

'A great surge of electricity and radiation erupted from the planet's surface yesterday,' Joja divulged.

Liran blinked and realised what she may be referring to.

'The Manna Rites,' Liran mumbled to herself.

Were they condemning the Manna Rites for the crash? Claudya breathed in, her face betraying nothing. Liran speculated if Claudya and Reeva had surmised the offering of garjee had that power. The light beam and the crackle of lightning swallowing the spire above the altar during offerings crossed her mind. *Surely not?* she thought.

A sudden crash outside the hall pulled Liran's attention.

Voices began to bicker behind the door, and abruptly, a strange noise that Liran had never heard came from the three Outsiders. Each of them dug into their pockets and drew out a small black rectangle that emitted shrill beeps like the chirp of a bird in anguish. None of the Outsiders looked at it; instead, they pushed a small button and placed it back in their pockets. Confusion replaced the silence as Claudya stood up, beckoning to the Monitor closest to her.

The yelling outside grew until the chamber doors were thrust open. The Outsiders jumped to their feet, Thessus stood at the door. He panted heavily, his clothes unkempt—likely he hadn't bathed or changed since the feast. Stains dotting his garb confirmed this.

Every face was trained on the intruder as he stumbled in, tripping on the yar rug. He steadied himself before the food on the table, his breathing laboured. He coughed onto the platter. Had he been running? Reeva wore an expression of disdain.

'You *murderers*,' Thessus muttered through gritted teeth, his arm outstretched toward the three guests. Zillah and Sloane abruptly stood up, and Sloane looked like he was enjoying the sudden change in atmosphere.

'Father, please, we are discussing—' Claudya began, but Thessus ploughed right over her.

'They should be made to pay the Time Oath seven times over!' His sonorous declaration blasted across the hall, shaking the very foundation under Liran. 'The Rahsu will not allow the scum of Anatara to walk on Arbonar after what they have done.'

He dug his hands into a loaf of bread and then dipped his fingers into a pot of honey. Sticky strings of golden syrup dripped down his arm and onto his already stained garments.

'The Time Oath is reserved for Rahsu, Thessus. Outsiders do not have the luxury of service to another under our justice system. No, they deserve much worse,' Reeva said, her eyes glinting with malice.

Zillah's focus was on Claudya. The Prime One stood and ushered Monitors to remove her father as the shrill chimes from the rectangles resumed. The noise from the contraptions resounded, and this time Zillah looked at hers. Her jaw plunged. She turned to Sloane and Joja as they reached for their devices. The colour from her face drained as she declared in a meagre voice to her comrades, 'Idonea is dead.'

The Outsiders exchanged glances.

❖

Liran wasn't sure who this *Idonea* was, but she assumed this was why the others hadn't entered Xylona.

Dr Amira raised a hand to her lips. 'I left Idonea and Doxxa with enough serum to ward off the radiation. It makes no sense, he was recovering,' Joja said, her fingers tapping frantically on the glass front of her noise-maker. Zillah's sombre expression shifted to the Prime One. Claudya sat patiently like a parent waiting for an explanation.

'Prime One, I do apologise. We know there is much to discuss, including the ship's entry and our relationship as two peoples, in the future; however—' Zillah started, but Thessus cut in.

'However, one of your crew has succumbed to the Spirits of the Rahsu. Do you not see, you *fool*? The planet knows you no longer belong here,' Thessus said as two Monitors grabbed each of Thessus's arms on Claudya's cue, tearing him away from the table. Thessus swatted their hands away.

'Get your hands off me! Do you not know *who* I am?'

Claudya shook her head wearily and brought her hand to her brow. Reeva grabbed Thessus as he continued to thwart the Monitors' attempts to restrain him. He thrashed in her iron grip as she hustled him out of the room.

Finally, thought Liran, releasing a pent-up breath. The nuisance was rectified, and she could get on asking the swarm of questions whirring in her mind.

Joja looked nervously at the Maven; the fact that the Outsiders had inflicted pain and death and destroyed their town was not lost on Liran. The Rahsu would be cold and distance themselves from the visitors unless she could help reopen a dialogue. Liran was also frustrated that those around the table knew more than they were letting on, including Claudya and Reeva.

'What are the ruins of the Injai? What is the Injai?' Liran asked Zillah.

The captain closed her eyes and breathed out. The room settled, awaiting her response. They lit as she flicked them open, colour returning to her cheeks. Zillah looked deeply into Liran's eyes, as if searching for a grain of commonality, and airily said, 'You, me, everyone on Anatara, everyone on Arbonar. Everyone we know Liran. We are all children of the Injai.'

Liran tried to swallow while her heart skipped a beat.

17

OLBI

An hour had passed since Alvar's return to the Stonehall and Olbi was still nervously excited about his tale.

Alvar had rushed into the cellar, letting those who were sheltered within know that the Outsiders were with the Prime One. Olbi had followed the other townspeople to the Stonehall when the Monitors had delivered the Prime One's decree to remain indoors. He felt like a rat hiding and cowering from a predator in the cellar … he hated it.

His curiosity about the Outsiders had compelled him to sneak upstairs when he heard the footsteps and the calls of a woman with a strange accent. He hadn't been able to see the Outsiders through the boarded-up windows, though, and after Alvar had left, Olbi had run upstairs to his room to retrieve his spear. He had collapsed from exhaustion, dreaming of flashes in the sky and Ayon glowing in blue light and smiling at him from under a garjee. The details had faded in the moments after he woke yet a part of his body remembered.

Alvar had been hounded the second he returned. People clustered around him, demanding answers.

Many of the guests of the Stonehall were frightened, some were even angry that the Prime One or the Spirits had not protected them. However, the visitors had been amiable enough, according to Alvar's exchanges with them, which seemed to calm people's nerves.

Alvar had spoken of the strange way the Outsiders dressed and their mannerisms. People were uneasy when he spoke of weapons, though nothing in Alvar's descriptions suggested the Outsiders were different to them except for their clothing and accents. Before long, Alvar was tired of the peppering of questions and soon shooed people away.

Olbi ran out the door carrying his spear and water bladder and flew through Xylona as quickly as possible to the farm he'd been at the previous night, fighting the urge to run to the Prime House to catch a glimpse of the Outsiders. His stomach did somersaults—it would be difficult approaching Boji's corpse, but he knew that if not for him, the yar would not have a burial.

Olbi skirted past the central cloister, aware that the Outsiders were gathered in the Prime House on its far side. He caught a glimpse of Reeva through the trees. She was speaking with two Monitors. Thessus stood nearby, swaying and seemingly speaking belligerently to himself.

Olbi soon found himself at the edge of the still smouldering fields. Many fires had been extinguished but small scrub blazes still dotted the fields like candles floating on a charred landscape. The smell of soot and ash mixed with the morning rains smothered the air.

Muddy soil stuck to Olbi's shoes, but what dirt had dried was flicked into clouds behind him. The mill lay ahead. Last night's efforts by the workers had spared most of it.

Two people—straddled on ladders that leaned against the singed stone of the mill's walls—tore at the damaged sails. Olbi approached them—noting the fresh cloth on the ground below them—he had a new purpose for the old cloth.

'Hey,' Olbi yelled to the two farmworkers as they yanked at the windmill. They looked down at him. 'Can I take this?' he asked, pointing to the pile of mostly burnt cloth.

The man up the ladder regarded him below, sweat beading down his face and into his beard. Olbi didn't recognise the man; he looked like a traveller. The bearded man said nothing as he threw down a part of a sail; it glided in the air and landed in a ruffle at Olbi's feet.

'Thanks,' he said, picking it up in a bundle. The man nodded and turned back to his work.

Olbi approached the mill's barn knowing it would have tools he needed. The barn doors had been scorched black, licked by flames and splintered by the intense heat, and, as Olbi pulled the doors open, blackened soot dragged in an arch across the floor.

On the back wall, an array of tools hung from metal hooks. There Olbi saw a small shovel—its head was stained with rust, but it still appeared sturdy. He grabbed it and, with the cloth, headed to Boji's final resting place.

Each step weighed Olbi down. He fought the pain, determined to give his friend the burial he deserved. He would remember Boji as he was when they would sit by the forest's edge and the yar would nudge him affectionately. He was small back then, small enough for Olbi to pick him up to carry him over small brooks. He'd tried before to coax Boji to cross by himself, but the young yar would always sniff cautiously at the brooks before jumping away frightened by the smallest splashes.

Olbi approached the familiar rise, dreading what awaited him on the other side, but stopped short when he heard the telltale scrapes of a shovel digging into the dirt. Someone was nearby.

Olbi crested and ran down the hill towards the forest line, passing several dead yar. He would bury them, too—they all deserved a proper burial.

The back of a familiar slim man came into Olbi's view, digging at the dirt near the forest line, under the roots of a large garjee tree. The man turned at the sound of Olbi's approaching footsteps. Instant recognition flashed in the man's eyes.

'Ayon? Why are you here?' Olbi said. He looked down at where Boji lay, and his heart broke again. Boji's body rested under a fine rouge shroud covered in delicately sewn flowers and green and black leaves. It was beautifully made and of high quality. It rested gently over Boji, whipping lightly in the soft winds.

'I knew you would be here, and I wanted to help. I did not want you to do this alone,' Ayon said, wiping his brow. He then rubbed his thumbs over his palms, massaging a red callous.

'The shovel is making my hands red and sore,' Ayon said, looking into Olbi's eyes.

Olbi was silent, regarding the Scion before him. The last of the bloodline was here, holding a shovel and helping him bury a yar, while the Outsiders sat with his mother. Olbi strode up to the hole Ayon had been digging, the soil rich and soggy.

'Thank you, Ayon, truly. And for the shroud,' he said sheepishly. Olbi examined the windmill sail in his hand, and he felt like he might start crying all over again. What would Ayon think?

'Did you see the Outsiders?' Ayon asked, plunging the shovel into the soil.

'No, but I heard them. A woman spoke. Did you?'

Ayon nodded. 'I saw them for a moment. Three of them came to see my mother. Phran told me there were more of them.'

'How many more?'

'Not many, but Phran's Monitors spotted two strangely dressed people to the north. He believes the garjee sickness has befallen them, that is why the others did not enter Xylona.'

Olbi pictured the harvesters he'd seen in the past, vomiting and withering away after being in the forest.

'How long were they in the forest, I wonder. Most people can't stand to be among them for more than ten minutes before getting headaches,' Olbi said.

'Phran did not say. The northern forests are some of the oldest and deepest. It could have been hours.'

Ayon stopped digging for a second and surveyed Olbi.

'Why do you not succumb to the sickness?' he asked.

Olbi shrugged. 'I don't know, maybe I have built up a tolerance?'

'You should become a Monitor and harvest the fruits,' Ayon said, scooping up some dirt. 'It would be an asset; it is a rare gift from the Spirits.'

Despite his overwhelming sadness, Olbi's eyes opened widely. 'I want to become a Monitor, truly,' Olbi said emphatically.

He fell silent. Was what his father told him true? Did he have the blood, and that was why he was immune to the garjee sickness? Perhaps it *was* the blood that protected him from the headaches and nausea the trees caused.

'Have you ever been into the forests?' Olbi asked. 'They say Primes don't get sick.'

'A few times, but seldom for long. My mother would never allow it. I have never felt sick but do not want to risk it.'

Ayon stopped digging to catch his breath, so Olbi hopped in and started to deepen the hole. Water gradually seeped in from the walls, and tree roots sprung out sporadically, making the job even more gruelling.

'I wonder what their world is like. What sort of towns and people they have and how they travel the stars,' Ayon said.

Olbi dropped his shovel and began to clear out some of the larger rocks by hand. Ayon looked up at the sky, his face soft, though Olbi sensed a heaviness.

'Do you ever want to leave Xylona and see what is out there?' Ayon asked.

Olbi paused, thinking about the stories travellers shared at the Stonehall. 'I would like to see the Great Lake someday,' Olbi said. 'And the Great Flow—it must be so wide and deep and full of delicious fish.'

'But beyond that, Olbi—surely there is so much more. What lies beyond the Forbidden Zones? What is across the lakes and the Northern Forests? What lands span south of Xylona, over the mountains and the Cayden Plateau?'

Olbi heard stories from his father that the shores of the Great Lake had many scattered villages by its beaches and hidden inlets. Small enclaves of Rahsu lived in simple wooden huts, hunting and gathering food from surrounding forests and the lake. People who had never seen a Manna Rites, something

that the Prime Ones scorned. There was so much he did not know, so many possibilities.

Ayon looked mournful.

'Is that why you don't want to be the Scion?' Olbi immediately regretted the question as Ayon glared at him. 'I'm sorry, I forget myself. Please forgive me—I have no right to ask that of you,' he said, lowering his head and returning to his shovel.

'Part of the reason,' Ayon replied. 'That right there, that apology, is another reason.' The Scion pointed to his necklace, where a garjee pendant glistened. 'The reverence people have for the Prime Ones. We are not special, yet people treat me differently for something I was born into. Can you imagine people treating you differently because of something you can't control?'

Olbi said nothing but flicked his eyes towards the forest. He could see an unripe garjee fruit hanging from a high branch. Would people treat him differently if he touched one and it burned bright? Olbi understood all too well. He climbed out of the grave—it was deep enough now to be called that.

'People love the Prime's for what they give the Rahsu and the Spirits. Your mother is loved, and so are you. I do not know your pressures, but I understand. I would hate people expecting more of me than I can give,' Olbi said.

Ayon smiled. It was soft at first, but the corners of his mouth then creased into a grin. 'Are you saying you love me, Olbi?' Ayon said, his smirk reminiscent of the teasing Olbi remembered him for.

Heat rose in his cheeks. 'Don't tease me, or I'll start calling you by your full title again, my *Prime Scion*.'

Ayon's smile slowly faded, and he looked at Olbi longer than what Olbi was comfortable with. Olbi turned to the red shroud on the ground, remembering why they were there.

'Will you help me lift him?' Olbi asked.

Ayon nodded and, together, they lifted Boji and placed him into the pit. Ayon laid him down gently, delicately placing

Boji on the damp soil. Olbi was touched by Ayon's respect and care. He would make a great Prime One, even if the world changed as Tarak envisioned.

'Are you ok?' Ayon asked, noticing Olbi's sallowness. A tear rolled down Olbi's cheek.

'I will be, but my heart will hurt,' he said, looking down into the hole and picking up the shovel. 'I'm glad that he will rest peacefully, though I will miss him dearly. He didn't deserve this.' Olbi began to feel more tears welling in his ducts but fought them back. His gaze fell on the other yar in the field, their bodies like boulders strewn across the hillside.

'We will get help for them, Olbi. For now, let's finish this,' Ayon said before adding, 'I promise.'

The shovelled dirt stained the shroud covering Boji as each heap of soil took the yar away from Olbi and back to the Spirits.

'He lived a life of love, peace and happiness,' Ayon said. 'He will burn bright; let him frolic with the Spirits now.'

Another tear rolled down Olbi's cheek. Ayon shifted and lay his hand on his shoulder again.

Olbi's muscles tensed.

'I'm sorry, did I hurt you?' Ayon said softly, pulling his hand away.

Olbi didn't know why Ayon was apologising, he had done nothing wrong. It was Olbi who felt awkward when someone touched him. He had never known genuine affection in his life.

'It's not you, Ayon. It's just not something I am used to. It's a bit of a shock,' he confessed quietly.

Ayon nodded slightly and kept his hand by his side.

'Let's go and see if we can spot one of the Outsiders,' Ayon said, changing the subject. The winds picked up and rushed through the trees like a raging river, the blue sky was fleeting as clouds on the horizon loomed darkly and menacingly.

'It will rain again soon,' Olbi said.

Ayon merely shrugged his shoulders. 'Come now, are you not curious, Olbi? People from another world are more exciting than returning to Xylona. Let us see if they are still on the outskirts.' A cheeky grin returned to Ayon's face.

Olbi *was* curious about the Outsiders and what they looked like. 'Let's take a shortcut through the forests,' Olbi proposed.

Ayon raised his eyebrow at the suggestion.

'It will only take ten minutes and, remember, you won't get sick,' Olbi said as Ayon peered into the trees hesitantly. Ayon smiled and nodded like a child scheming to do something he shouldn't.

'See this is why I like you Olbi, you shirk the rules.'

Olbi smiled. *He likes me?*

They left the shovels propped against the tree that Boji now lay at rest beneath. But before they departed, Olbi decided that a small stone cairn should sit above where the yar's head lay beneath the soil.

He scoured the grasses for rocks that had flat surfaces and brought them back to the grave. He piled four upon each other and stepped back.

Ayon offered Olbi a sad smile. 'Okay, let's go,' Ayon said, tearing Olbi away and towards the forest.

18

OLBI

The sweet scent of wildflowers in bloom welcomed them into the forest, patches growing lusher wherever the canopy faltered and allowed sunlight through. Today, however, no sun fell beneath the gathering clouds. Blue and yellow petals floated on a sea of grasses that swayed carefree in the breeze. Ayon looked around and marvelled at the trees as they walked.

'The garjee are so much larger than I remember,' Ayon said, touching one of the enormous roots that bore into the earth. He looked shorter among the trees as if dwarfed by their majesty.

'Do you think we will see them again?' he said, running his hand over a root.

'The blue spirits?' Olbi asked.

Ayon nodded.

'Maybe,' Olbi uttered quietly, looking around.

He had seen them twice in mere days, so it must be for a reason. Olbi didn't think they meant to harm him; otherwise, they would have. He was frightened and eager to see them again. Did they know his secret?

'Do you think they wish us harm?' he asked Ayon. *Maybe he has a better idea of what they were*, he thought.

'I do not think so. If anything, I think they were trying to tell us something, only I believe they cannot speak,' Ayon said, jumping up onto a granite outcrop that sat like an island in the grasses.

'What makes you think they can't speak?'

Ayon bit his lip, clearly thinking. 'They made no sound when they walked and moved. They were silent, and it was as if they were not there at all,' Ayon said before pausing. 'Have you seen them before?' Ayon shot Olbi a glance.

Olbi's chest constricted. How much should he tell Ayon? The last time he saw them was just before the Outsiders' arrival. He grimaced, conflicted.

'It's okay. I think I know the answer,' Ayon said, sparing him from answering. 'Someone that spends as much time as you in these forests is bound to see things others have not. Again, this leads me to believe that they do not mean you harm. People who speak of visions say that they are of the forest. Have you ever seen them in the fields or Xylona?' Ayon spoke as if he was building a case.

Olbi furrowed his brow, straining to pull forth his memories. Ayon was right.

'No, only ever in the forests. Like the others, however, they have never approached me or been as close as last night,' he said.

Ayon clucked his tongue. 'See! They have something to do with the forests. It may be that they are forest spirits, protectors of garjee fruit.'

The fleeting warmth of the sun faded as they cut through the forest's undergrowth. They were west of Xylona, and this was the closest forest to the town. In parts, the garjee almost touched the town, hanging above the buildings and brushing their giant leaves against chimneys. Because of the sickness, people's homes were nowhere near here. It was instead where the town's many storehouses stood, including the timber mill and town foundry.

Through the twisting jumble of tree limbs, Olbi saw glimpses of the Xylona timber yard and heard the rhythmic sawing of wood. Two figures pushed a saw through a large log: it was Karjon and his daughter, Tauva. Olbi knew Tauva well: they had sat next to each other in school when they were younger. She was always lovely to him, one of the only people in town his age that was. She had never teased him for his blemished skin nor shunned him for his quiet nature.

Tauva lifted her head and looked straight at him, watching him move through the forest. They were now only a few paces from the edge of the woodyard. Tauva appeared ready to speak, opening her mouth, but stopped when she saw Ayon. Her face turned crimson, and she quickly returned to sawing with her father. Karjon scowled at her for losing their rhythm.

'Do you know her?' Ayon asked, picking up his pace to match Olbi's strong legs.

'From school and around town. Sometimes, her father comes to the Stonehall after a day's work. I expect he will soon venture there.'

Whenever Karjon was present at the Stonehall, Olbi could find him purely by the smell of the wood shavings on Karjon's clothes. Karjon didn't talk much and mainly kept to himself, merely grunting when Olbi would bring him his pot of ale.

'I don't suppose you have a companion?' Ayon asked. His question came across as uncomfortable, yet there was a mischievous glint in his eye. Olbi blushed—he never had a companion, nor even considered it. Olbi shook his head and ducked under a root, thankful to lose line of sight of Ayon.

'Do your parents pressure you as to why you don't, or is it not expected of you?' the Scion asked.

Olbi forgot how little of his life Ayon knew, and why would he?

'My father has not been around for much of my life. He is a trader. My mother is from another town, far up north. I have never met her,' he said.

Ayon stopped in the grass under a garjee root that arched up and dove into the ground, his expression solemn in the dying light. 'And you have no brothers or sisters?' Ayon added.

Olbi shook his head.

Ayon strode towards him, his hand raised as if to put it on Olbi's shoulder, but he quickly lowered it.

'I had no idea. Forgive me for my prying; it is not my place to ask,' Ayon said, returning to formality.

Olbi had an urge to continue.

'And you? You do not want a companion? Are the rumours true or a falsehood of idle gossip?' Olbi asked.

Ayon's eyes opened wide. 'People are talking about that?' Ayon probed, turning from him.

Did Ayon not know the rumours? Olbi dropped his head, feeling ashamed to spread gossip.

'You would not understand,' Ayon muttered in a sullen voice. He sighed deeply. Fading sunlight cast shadows across his face. What light there was twinkled in his eyes.

Olbi thought he shouldn't have asked and wanted to apologise.

Ayon sniffed. 'To be the only Scion. The weight of expectation on me is too much to bear. You would not know the pressures thrust on me every day. Reeva would have me parade in the streets and offer myself to every girl I saw, all to delay what we all know. That the blood is dying. We are finished Olbi.'

The ambience of the forest filled the void where silence should have been. Olbi took a step forward, listening to Ayon's heavy words as emotion poured out of him like a floodgate that released an ocean.

'Every day. Reeva, my mother, Phran—even the Monitors and Euyan, the Maven's apprentice, tell me that I must sire the next in line. They say that the fate of the Rahsu hangs in the balance. I see it in the eyes of Xylonans as I descend to the altar, from Hydoran and Kanownan dignitaries, watching me, sensing weakness. Fear and anger engulf me everywhere I go.'

Olbi listened intently as Ayon vented his frustrations. Somewhere in the distance, the town bells rang, they must have been repaired. It marked the end of the workday. Olbi knew people would be working well after the bells to help rebuild the town. Ayon lifted his head and stared in the direction of the bells.

'Maybe I should give in to the pressure. What would you do, Olbi? Would you betray who you are and succumb to what people want you to be?'

Olbi stared blankly at Ayon, seeing him not as the Scion but as a frightened young man trapped in a web of constraints.

Olbi would never let others dictate his life. All he wanted was a peaceful existence within the forests. Maybe he would be lucky enough to be chosen as a Monitor, or perhaps he would take over his father's trading cart and travel the roads, seeing the world and its vast forests and array of animals. Ayon watched him intently, reading him.

Olbi was in turmoil. The very thought that a Prime was asking his opinion flew against anything he had experienced.

'I would stay true to myself, but I have never known the pressure. Some must relate to not wanting to parent children. But is there no one in town you would want as a companion? If you do not wish to be Scion, maybe your child will be of age when your mother …'

Olbi trailed off when he saw a torturous twitch in Ayon's eye.

'My heart does not work like that, Olbi.' Ayon spoke in a pitch barely above a whisper with a sad stare through his darkened eyelashes. He strode through the archway of the roots and ran his hand gently against the wood.

'There are few in town who understand or have given me support. Liran appears to be the only one on the council who understands me. But then, she has been there all my life, she knows me better than my own family, and she can understand the pain of such a betrayal to my heart.' He turned, eyes falling on Olbi again.

'You are *the Scion*, there must be someone you can confide in?'

Ayon huffed a sarcastic laugh. 'I have no one Olbi. Reeva won't let me mingle with others my age or let me wander the streets alone. The people of Xylona bow to me and offer polite and rehearsed dialogue before retreating into formality and returning to life beyond the Prime House walls, all the while I remain in the shadows of the Sanctum …'

❖

'I support you, Ayon. If you don't wish to be the Prime One, then a Grand Meeting or a Consanguine will sit in Xylona. The Remnants will meet, and the trials will commence.'

Would my mother travel to Xylona for that? Olbi thought suddenly. Would he recognise her among the many visitors? He didn't even know her name.

He looked up, searching for the fruits, and Ayon followed his gaze. Tucked behind the closest branch, a sizeable yellow orb hung mockingly—dull yet full of questions and possible answers—gently swaying in the breeze.

'As for whether my child would have the blood and be of age ...' Ayon started.

'I didn't mean to suggest—' Ayon raised his hand to Olbi as he spoke.

'My mother will not live to see my child. She will not live to see many more cycles of the Manna Rites.'

Olbi stared at Ayon, perplexed. What did he mean? Ayon appeared sullen, a grimness consumed his eyes and his lips trembled as he spoke. He must have seen the confusion on Olbi's face because Ayon moved towards him and whispered.

'Few know this, but she is not long of this world,' Ayon said.

Olbi blinked and let the words sink in. *Claudya was dying?* Was that why there was a sudden push to see Ayon step up and take her place? He understood now the pressure Ayon must be under. Ayon dropped his head and sobbed quietly. He spoke the truth. Olbi was numb. Claudya was dying, and the Rahsu didn't know.

Ayon shifted his weight on his feet, and in that slight movement, Olbi saw through the archway of roots—with its undeniable and familiar glow—loomed a blue figure, the same one that Olbi assumed was a woman. He froze, fear spiking in his chest.

The Spirit glowed in the archway, the light creating a ring around her, illuminating the darkness. Olbi's mouth hung open, his eyes transfixed. Ayon faced the figure, his jaw dropping while he instinctively reached out and gripped Olbi's wrist, squeezing it.

The woman observed them, her curious eyes flitting between them. Olbi could make out her features clearer than through the previous night's tears. She had a gentle face, like a youthful woman, but her eyes were fiery, filled with years of wisdom. Her slender neck was long and rose from a snug line of her garments—she was human.

'I don't think she is there; it's a Spirit,' Ayon's whisper was scarcely audible over the breeze. Unlike their clothes that moved in the wind, the woman remained motionless, unaffected by the wind—it passed through her unimpeded.

'What do you want?' Ayon said, his voice quivering. He still gripped Olbi's wrist, but now more gently.

The woman turned to Ayon, taking her gaze off Olbi. She moved gracefully; her step towards them was deliberate and calm. Olbi felt his heart pound in his throat, while her steely eyes pierced Ayon. What was she considering? She raised her long, slender arm. Her spindly hand pointed into the trees from the end of a wide sleeve. Through the dying light, they saw nothing but endless forest.

'You want us to go north?' Ayon asked.

The woman offered no acknowledgement that she heard him, remaining still, arm still extended.

Ayon let go of Olbi's wrist and stepped in the direction the woman was pointing. She dropped her hand and nodded. Olbi took his eyes off the apparition and calmly pursued Ayon. The woman was pointing towards a granite outcrop deep within the trees. They took a few steps towards a garjee trunk.

Olbi scrutinised the woman as a smile crept onto her face. It was a soft smile, comforting and warm. She reminded him of how older women at the Stonehall would beam at him when he helped them. At that moment, Olbi sensed that he was being guided and his fear melted and dissipated. He returned the smile, but the figure disappeared instantly, darkness returning to the archway of roots.

'Let's see what she was pointing at,' Olbi said, looking through the twists of garjee. Despite the sense of vulnerability, he clung to his spear. He knew the forests well, though he was unfamiliar with this region. It was dense and cold, the garjee trees dominated and were closer together here like bars of a gaol keep. It was suffocating, yet the final wisps of golden light filtered through the trees and hit the granite outcrop before them. It was the size of a building and resembled a jagged spearhead covered in lichen, rain channels staining its facade black.

'Do you hear that?' Ayon asked.

Olbi paused mid-stride. He could hear a peculiar chiming, like a bird call, yet unlike any bird he had heard. Ayon's eyes flickered, searching for the source of the sound.

'It's coming from the rocks,' Olbi said.

The Scion nodded.

'Let me go ahead of you,' Olbi whispered. He brought them into the forest, and now he regretted dragging Ayon in.

The chirping pulsed ahead of them, beckoning him forward. The sound was only metres ahead, somewhere at the base of the granite crag. At this distance, Olbi could see the rock face shooting straight upwards from a depression. It rose into a sheer cliff face, rivalling the height of the Stonehall's rooftop. How had he never seen this rock before? The chirping—ear-splittingly loud—ricocheted off the rock. Ayon turned to him nervously.

Olbi climbed over one last root that ran like a snake through the grasses, its head hidden from them. He looked down into a ditch at the base of the boulder. The sun was hidden behind the rock, casting this side into shadow. The void was blacker than a moonless night, but something at the bottom of the hole chirped. How deep it was, he did not know, but it was large enough to be called a cave.

'There is a red light flashing down there,' Ayon said, pointing. Olbi followed Ayon's finger and saw it, a red light flashing in unison with the chirps. A surge of fear rushed through Olbi's body. He grasped his spear tightly and shot glances around them, feeling like they were being watched. Doubt about the Spirit's intentions resurfaced; she was nowhere to be seen.

'What do you think it is?' Ayon questioned.

Olbi listened to the forest around them: nothing moved, the stillness he was so used to now seemed cold and haunting. The chirps from the depths were like clockwork compared to the randomness of the woods.

'Only one way to find out,' Olbi said as he stepped forward.

A section of the cavity lit up briefly with every flash of red light, opaque surfaces became illuminated in pulses, only to be snuffed moments later. Olbi edged himself closer to the slope at the edge of the pit, it was much steeper than he expected. He looked up, the intimidating rock wall hanging above him like a waterfall fixed in motion. He felt small.

'Be careful, the ground doesn't look solid,' Ayon advised, kneeling beside him.

Olbi placed his foot on a rock, jutting out a metre down. It held his weight, but Olbi felt tremors in the soil.

'I will be fine,' he said.

Olbi stepped farther into the abyss with one last look around the forest, one last chance to see the Spirit woman again, hoping this was what she intended. For some reason, he trusted her.

Olbi guided his feet gently down the slope, sometimes scooting on his rump and digging his heels into the soil to stop sliding down to the bottom. The hole was deep. Deep enough to break his neck if he slipped in the mud that built up beneath his fingernails as he steadied himself. The high-pitched chirping continued like a bird in distress. Olbi peered down, darkness consumed his feet. This wasn't a good idea, yet something compelled him to continue. Whatever was down here was important enough for the Spirits to approach him. The red pulses guided him towards the bottom of the ditch.

'Everything okay?' Ayon called from above his head. He sounded much closer than he was.

'It smells musty, but I'm okay,' he called back.

Ayon murmured a sound that resembled a nervous laugh. 'Well, if the smell is the worst of it …'

Olbi felt around for a firm grip. Moss and small stones were discernible to his touch as he searched for a footing to anchor himself on for the next drop. The soil was wet from water that had likely leaked out of the ground from the morning's rain and it soaked through his clothes. He found a sturdy rock and carefully lowered himself the remaining metre. He landed at the bottom of the hollow with a splash.

'I'm at the bottom,' he called.

Ayon waved down at him; the Scion's silhouette was sharp against the dull light.

Olbi focused his eyes and approached the flashing light. The pulses were brighter, and the shrillness of beeps pierced his eardrums. He navigated his feet through sludge and puddles, his movements echoed against the stone as he covered the ten paces towards a small mound. The noise was all around him as shrieks bounced off the rock face. He stood directly over the flashing and loud mound. Something was wrong. The flashes illuminated the bottom of the hole, the rock face and the black form at his feet.

Olbi gasped. He took a step back, stumbling. He slipped, and water splashed around him as he hit the floor.

'Olbi, what happened? Are you okay?' Ayon shouted.

Olbi struggled to pull himself up. His legs trembled and his breathing was shallow as he brushed mud off his face.

'Olbi? Are you hurt?' Ayon called down again.

Olbi watched the red light flash in even intervals; it pulsed every second, and with every flash the outline of a corpse burned into his retinas. There was no mistaking it, it was one of the Outsiders.

Dead.

With every flash, ghostly eyes stared at him. Visions of a young man with red hair around his age, his neck crimson with blood where a gash sliced open his throat. Red light illuminated gore that now glistened on Olbi's hands. He looked up in terror.

'Ayon, it's one of the Outsiders.' Olbi tried to tear his eyes away from the face, but it flashed before him. Bile bubbled its way up his throat. Beside the man lay the beeping object, a small black rectangle. He peered closer. The flashing was a word written on the tablet.

\- E-BEACON ON -

Olbi studied the gruesome scene before him and peered up. He couldn't see the Scion's profile anymore. He called out again but could barely hear his own voice above the blood rushing to his ears. His heart thumped when Ayon didn't respond. Stumbling as he stood, he pushed himself towards the slope. He pawed at the dirt, grabbing roots, moss and rocks as he climbed. The smell of blood seeped into his clothes. He wanted to vomit. A voice inside his head told him to keep climbing.

Olbi called out for Ayon again. Nothing. *Ayon, please say something.* The top of the slope was two metres away … one metre.

Olbi stepped onto the first rock he'd used to lower himself into the hole. This time, it was a springboard to push himself up. He grasped blades of grass, clinging to tufts to pull him onto the forest floor. In the last slivers of the day's light, he saw Ayon standing as if a statue, unmoving. His spear lay in the grass—Olbi used it to lift himself off the ground.

'Ayon, it's one of the Outsiders; his throat has been—' Olbi paused.

In his rush, he failed to see the second person in the forest. A tall man dressed in the same clothes as the dead man below.

❖

In his hand, a weapon was pointed directly at Ayon's head. In the other, the same black tablet that Olbi had seen lying beside the body below.

A bitter taste filled his mouth, and before his brain registered what he was doing, he pushed himself in front of Ayon and shielded him from the weapon now pointed at his own face.

Olbi lifted his spear, thrusting it forward at the man. He swallowed the bitterness building in his mouth and clenched his teeth while his heart thumped like a drum.

The Outsider's weapon was metal and had a beam of light affixed to the end, casting Olbi in pure white light. He squinted, trying to see the man's face and to discern where best to impale the man that threatened Ayon.

Olbi looked down; the light stung his eyes. He wished he hadn't—his whole body was red, licked in sickly blood. Some was his own, but most of the crimson fluid was from the corpse below.

'What have you done with Alrin Sandol?' the man said in a strange accent, the weapon still aimed directly at Olbi's head.

Olbi blinked in the light. They were in trouble.

Olbi knew Ayon needed to be protected, even if it jeopardised his own life.

'Ayon, run, get out of here,' Olbi whispered. His heart thumped.

'Do not move, or I will shoot you,' the man said before adding, 'Both of you.'

Sweat trickled down Olbi's forehead and stung his eyes, the light moved away from him and towards the ditch. Olbi kept Ayon behind him, holding onto the Scion's hand. Ayon squeezed back, his whole body trembling.

The Outsider shone the light at Olbi again, blinding him.

'It's strange to find two … what do you call yourselves? Rahsu? To find you at the coordinates of an activated emergency beacon. Whose blood are you covered in?'

Olbi breathed heavily. *Can we run?* he thought. Ayon might get away if Olbi could distract the man for long enough.

'Where is Mr Sandol? I won't ask again!' The voice was harsh and caustic.

Olbi tried to speak, but his voice was lodged deep in his throat. What would the man do if he looked down behind them?

'Why are you in the forest?' the man demanded.

He looked around, darkness shrouded the forest—only a faint slither of light stained the sky above them, it too was soaked red. *Too much blood.* Olbi swallowed the acid pooling in his mouth. His throat was dry, but he choked out what words he could.

'Please, let us go,' he said. He felt stupid and feeble, but nothing else came to mind. The man laughed and stepped to the edge of the ditch, shining his light towards the granite wall before him.

They should run. Surely, he would not kill them. What of Ayon? If he died and Ayon lived, then that would be okay. He would die making sure the Outsiders didn't end the Primes. Olbi could take that chance. He had his spear, and he knew how to use it. Instead, he remained still. Ayon pressed against his back.

The man shone his glowing weapon around the forest, casting shadows and ghostly shapes onto the broad tree trunks of the garjee. Dread filled Olbi as the Outsider hovered over the ditch. He trembled in horror as the man's light pierced the depths.

Time stood still for Olbi. The torchlight shone directly on the corpse. Olbi could see the dead face in the light, the pool of blood leaking into the puddle of water at the bottom of the ditch.

The man said nothing. His light remained fixed on the body of the young red-headed Outsider. The chirping sound of the tablet was the only thing Olbi could hear. The man turned towards them, his fingers sliding across his contraption, punching a long finger onto its surface. Suddenly, the sound of the woman Olbi had heard earlier in front of the Stonehall escaped the object.

'Morgana here, what is it Sloane? Did you find Alrin and his beacon?' the voice from the device said in a monotonous tone.

'Morgana, we have a situation. It appears Alrin Sandol has met his demise at the hands of these savages: his throat was slit by two Rahsu and thrown into a ditch in the forest. I am placing them under arrest,' the man declared.

Olbi's heart sank.

The man stepped closer and scrutinised Olbi and the spear he clasped. The Outsider smiled, striding forward and laughing as he shook his head. He pushed the spear away and gripped Olbi's jaw and examined his eyes. Olbi felt strength in the man's grip and smelt the man's repulsive body odour.

Glee danced in the Outsider's intense militant eyes, which scanned Olbi from mere centimetres away. Sloane licked his lips and sneered.

'You boys have just doomed your entire planet.'

19

LIRAN

'They have the Prime Scion at the Stonehall!' Reeva announced, storming into the Sanctum with a fury that could melt snow.

Liran jumped at the shout. She had been sitting with Phran and Claudya who had both been growing increasingly worried. It had been an hour since Ayon was declared missing and the alarm had been raised.

Phran had been the one to raise the alarm. He had taken the Scion to the inner sanctum as talks with the Outsiders had begun, but Ayon informed Phran he'd left something in his room. When the Scion had not returned, the fear and anguish Phran had expressed was palpable.

Liran had been forced to listen to the older man's sobs and apologies for over an hour before he settled into a shaking mess. She seemed alone in not being concerned with the boy's disappearance. Ayon had likely sneaked off to somewhere secluded, using the distraction of the Outsiders to figure things out. But now, as Reeva entered the room claiming the Outsiders had Ayon, fear coursed through Liran.

Claudya lifted her head. Her skin was flushed and her gaze sullen after the talks and constant updates from Monitors about the status of repairs and problems around town. When was the last time she had eaten? She appeared old, like a frailty had consumed her, no longer filled with the vigour she had exhibited in the talks.

'Thank the Spirits,' Claudya exhaled with relief. 'Where is he? Please bring him to me.'

Reeva grunted, her nostrils flaring. 'It's not going to be that simple. The big one—named Sloane—has made it clear that the Scion was found by the corpse of one of their own.

❖

They have him and Tarak's son in custody. They have accused Ayon of *murder*. Who gave them back their weapons?'

'The Monitors returned them after the talks, at my request,' Claudya muttered feebly. Liran expected the Prime One was doubting the trust she bestowed upon the Outsiders.

'Trusting these people will doom us, Prime One,' Reeva said with a hint of acid lacing her words.

Liran leapt to her feet. Phran yelped from the sudden movement and upon hearing the news.

'Bring me my son, Reeva,' Claudya ordered, struggling to stand.

Liran rushed over to Claudya and lifted her weight, which seemed near negligible like a leaf.

'What proof do they have of this claim?' Liran asked, shooting Reeva an anguished look as she steadied Claudya on her feet.

The Guardian began to pace, uncharacteristically shaken; the creak of her armour reverberated around the room. 'That boy, Olbi,' she started, rubbing her temples, 'was covered in blood. Sloane led him and the Scion out of the western garjee. I saw them myself, being escorted into the Stonehall.'

'What were they doing in the forests?' Liran asked. There was nothing in there besides kilometres of trees. *Were they running?* 'Anyway, I know Olbi. The lad is harmless—he was crying just this morning at the loss of a *yar*!'

Reeva said nothing in return and continued to pace the room.

'And Ayon? What of his condition, Reeva?' Claudya's voice was meek.

'He looked shaken. Alvar advised access to the Scion is denied by the Outsiders until we arrive. After escorting Thessus away, I approached the Stonehall. Sloane ordered that no one was to leave. I suggest we take a full contingent of guards and head to the Stonehall now. Alvar has assured me he won't let anything happen to the Scion.'

220

'What of Zillah, their captain? She only just left, surely she had nothing to do with this?' Liran said.

Zillah had stayed back to talk to Claudya about the political makeup of Anatara and how the Rahsu are governed. The dialogue had not been contentious, so Sloane and the doctor had been granted access to their weapons and were escorted back to their companions on the town's outskirts to examine their dead crewmate.

They stated they would bring the others into town, and Claudya had agreed to allow the Anatrians to stay at the Stonehall after Reeva adamantly rejected the idea they stay in the Prime House.

'Zillah was not at the Stonehall when I was denied access to Ayon,' Reeva said.

Liran studied the woman, clad in her armour, closely. The Guardian's arrogance and zealous attitude towards the Primes had always given people a harsh opinion of her. Still, her abrasiveness appeared to be in the best interest of the Primes and the future of the Rahsu. Was she shaken because she was powerless to protect Ayon?

Claudya remained silent, staring vacantly at the rug where Reeva now paced. Liran watched her leader, whose son was in the custody of foreigners. If it had been Hayda, she wouldn't have stopped fighting until he was home safely.

The Maven shuddered as Claudya stood and started for the door.

'Where are you going?' Reeva said. Claudya threw a casual glance at her.

'To get my son, Reeva. We leave now,' the Prime One said. 'Phran, please inform the Monitors to carry on with the plans.'

'What plans?' Reeva asked.

Claudya stood by the door and did not turn to face the room. 'We are preparing to assist the Outsiders in a journey to the Forbidden Zone to see if we are descended from the same ancestors.

'They will also search for this mineral they seek and, before you protest, Reeva, know this: I want them back on their ship and gone as much as you do. If that means entering the Forbidden Zones and breaking the Grand Meeting edict, then so be it.'

Reeva puffed her chest. 'That won't keep them away, they know too much about us now. We must crush them before—'

'Reeva, enough! We stand no chance.' With that statement, the Prime One left the sanctum with Phran in tow.

Reeva shot a glance over at Liran. Anger pulsed on her face as she marched out of the Sanctum, leaving Liran alone.

****

The still coolness of the night air sent shivers up Liran's arms as she walked the streets towards the Stonehall. In the distance, she could see the Monitor's lanterns guiding the Prime One through the darkness. Reeva was nowhere to be seen.

Everywhere she went, Liran spotted dim lights within windows. It was easy to forget that some people lived their everyday lives while the world changed around them.

The Stonehall loomed large in the distance. Usually, at this hour, it would teem with the energy of people enjoying the end of the workday or travellers seeking a roof, yet tonight, it bathed in ghostly silence. Figures moved silently about the building. Liran looked up at the windows. Many remained boarded shut, but dull light leaked from within.

Liran observed at a distance as Claudya and Phran entered the front door of the Stonehall. She spied Alvar, who led them in, looking shaken and grim.

Liran started to follow, but movement in the corner of her eye drew her attention. A figure moved quickly from a backdoor of the building and out towards one of the garden squares. Although the figure was dark, it moved with purpose. She recalled what Reeva had said: the Stonehall was locked up, and no one was to leave. Whoever it was might be fleeing. She changed direction and began following the figure into the archway, keeping her distance in the shadows.

The garden and surrounding cloister behind the Stonehall was a neglected square of lofty trees. It was one of the oldest groves in town and it was usually devoid of people. No one had any reason to visit at this hour. Liran stood by the deteriorating archway, wishing she had a better robe to keep herself warm.

Suddenly, a bright white light appeared in the figure's hand that illuminated a hard face: Gideon Sloane's face.

Liran kept her distance and debated whether to turn back for the Stonehall, but something compelled her to stay hidden. She moved behind a crumbling wall, loose bricks scattered at her feet. The way Sloane kept looking back made Liran believe he had snuck away.

The white beam of light searched the trees, and as it passed near her, Liran ducked, holding in a gasp. His movement was swift—had she moved quickly enough? Liran held her breath and remained motionless. The light continued to move around the trees, the beam illuminating the branches. What was he searching for? Suddenly, she heard a beep, the same strange noise that their machines had made when they were at the council table.

'Commodore Sloane, this is Officer Einar Roosk. Do you read? Please confirm the passcode on receipt of this message,' a man's voice said.

Liran remained silent. Was there a second man in the cloister? She looked back towards the archway. No one was there.

'This is Sloane, I confirm this is a secure and scrambled line. The passcode is Dormant Bird,' Sloane's gruff voice replied.

Another beep.

Liran listened intently, steadying her breath. She guessed the devices were some form of communication with Anatara.

She found a small hole in the wall—no larger than a keyhole—and peered through the crevice. She could see Gideon Sloane urinating against one of the trees. He was still alone.

For a few moments, Sloane sat silently beneath the trees all the while Liran shivered, rubbing her hands together for warmth. She needed more answers and to learn about the Outsiders, and this could be that opportunity. The beeping returned, and Liran pushed her eye against the peephole.

'Commodore Sloane, your clearance code has been approved,' the voice of Einar Roosk said robotically.

He continued, 'Your last update regarding the natives is as we expected. The primitive nature of their capabilities suggests that the resources we seek will likely be untouched by the population. Further, to your query regarding the scrambled line, we can advise that every measure is being made to ensure transmissions from your device are being hidden within the standard operational systems of the satellites. Any foreign interference will not be able to detect the information you send through.'

Liran's ears strained to hear the man's message as Sloane paced between the trees. She slinked along the wall closer to the voice. Whatever Sloane was here for, he was keeping it from the rest of his team. Sloane remained silent as he listened.

'Please be advised that the removal of the Jareean president has been achieved. Forces stormed government buildings in Owayln some eight hours ago. Currently, Jareean government facilities are under the control of General Jakkus. Your mission is now officially authorised.'

The Jareean president had been removed? Liran recalled that Zillah mentioned Jaree was where Sloane was from, after he and Joja had left the Prime House.

'Please advise the status of the mission. We have reason to believe if Zillah Morgana learns of the coup in Jaree, it might compel her to act against you. The concerns raised by her and the Tareans prior to the Unity's departure would be validated.

❖

224

She is cunning and it won't take her long to deduce that Tarea
will be the first target.

'The same goes for the Tobanian—our files on the doctor
are sketchy but we have intel that places her deep within the
Hophnam Institute. We must keep up appearances to capitalise
on the mission we have been tasked with. Roosk ending
communication.'

The voice coming from Sloane's contraption fell silent,
replaced by the croaky timbre of frogs in the grasses that had
been brought to the surface by recent rains. Liran's heart
thumped. The Anatrians were fractured, and their journey to
Arbonar was fraught with division. News like this might
benefit Claudya if they were to negotiate the release of Ayon
and Olbi. What had the two boys gotten caught up in?

Liran's thoughts were interrupted by the beep of the device
again. This time, Sloane cleared his throat to respond.

'Officer Roosk, the message has been received and
acknowledged. This is excellent news, and I am glad President
Jodol has been removed. His ineptitude and weakness shown
to the Tareans and Tobanians was unspeakable.' Sloane's
voice had strength as he relished in the news.

'I have positive updates for General Jakkus. As you would
be aware from the footage supplied by Alrin Sandol, the Unity
has crash-landed, making this mission's success crucial. I am
pleased to inform command that the current circumstances
weigh in our favour. Not only that, but I also believe that
success is guaranteed. Arbornian assets will be under Jareean
control sooner than anticipated.'

Liran held her breath, her heart thudded.

'Soon, I will be in position to take command from Captain
Morgana. The natives have killed Alrin Sandol, and the
Tarean soldier, Idonea, has officially died from radiation
poisoning. Unofficially, Doxxa helped speed up Idonea's
demise. Doxxa and I are now ready to forego the diplomatic
niceties Morgana is clinging to and will begin the trek to the
Injai facility east of our location. If the intel gathered is

correct, we will secure the assets there, no matter the cost. I will maintain radio silence until the agreed-upon schedule. Commodore Sloane, ending transmission.'

Liran rested against the wall, her heart thumping so loud Sloane might hear it. She listened as the cloister returned to silence. The only sound was the beep of the Outsider's machine and the rustling of the leaves in the trees.

Thousands of thoughts went through her mind. They were in danger: not just Xylonans but all Rahsu. The Outsiders meant to take control of their assets, but what did that mean?

Zillah and the Outsiders were eager to travel east. She knew of no ruins or a facility—whatever that was—but knowledge of the Forbidden Zones was outlawed. The Grand Meeting fifty years ago had restricted access due to the demons of the Rahsu and its dangers. With it, the burning and destruction of texts swept through the Rahsu lands as Mavens were dictated to restrict teaching that didn't support the Primes. Liran had long thought that the Forbidden Zone edict was a fabrication to scare off travellers, but now she wondered if it was more sinister.

Fifty years ago, someone or some group knew what was there. The Forbidden Zones were made forbidden for a reason. Who was here before the Rahsu, and what was it Sloane was after that he didn't want the rest of his team to know?

One thing was certain: his amused and bored expression during the meeting made sense now. He had just laid it bare. He wasn't here to meet the Rahsu, he was here to steal from them. Hot fear radiated through her body as Sloane's heavy footsteps crunched towards the Stonehall.

20

ZILLAH

The embrace of the Stonehall was roasting compared to the chill that had settled in for the night outside.

It was clear the Stonehall was a much-loved communal drinking hole for Xylonans—the ambience was comfortable with cozy wood-beamed ceilings, bookcases in nooks, the aroma of wafting spices from an unseen kitchen, and a roaring fire crackling brightly, which filled the large room with a welcoming glow. A few elderly Xylonans sat at the far end of a bar with their heads down. They were likely farmers or the like judging by their dirtied attire.

Tables and booths filled the large hall, all scratched and wearing signs of heavy use. Well-worn armchairs faced the fire with side tables piled with goblets and used plates. Zillah sat in one of these chairs beside Dr Amira, her tablet held in front of her. Amira had a goblet of local wine that she sipped at hesitantly, sniffing it as one would a pungent cheese. Zillah watched her over the top of her tablet. Joja's mood had changed since the death of Alrin Sandol came to light.

The crew was dropping like flies, and the mission was in danger of falling apart. The power shift at the loss of Idonea was a disruption that favoured Sloane. Zillah was outnumbered.

Zillah tried to convey this to her sister and QC when she left the Prime House, but now she wished she had come to the Stonehall sooner after receiving Sandol's distress beacon. She would have handled the situation of Alrin's death a little more tactfully.

In Sloane's defence, he would have had no idea that the person Doxxa guarded upstairs was the Prime One's son. Even so, they were strangers in an unknown environment, and when the Prime One and her head official had walked in earlier, she spoke as any politician would, with thinly veiled messages. Zillah was no stranger to threats, but Claudya's anguish and anger came from concern for her people and her heir. It was a situation not helped by Sloane's arrogance and knee-jerk reaction. He had left to cool down, or so he had said, leaving Zillah and Joja to bear the stares and scorn of the few locals on the far side of the room who had been left homeless by the Unity's arrival.

Zillah tried to calm matters down by allowing Claudya to see her son and his friend. She had seen them both covered in blood and grime, yet they pleaded their innocence. According to Sloane, Alrin's throat had been slit and he had been thrown into a hole deep within the forest. The Scion's friend carried a spear. In Sloane's eyes, they had been caught red-handed.

'What was Alrin doing, defying my order by wandering off by himself into the forests alone?' Zillah muttered under her breath.

'You believe Doxxa's story then?' Joja quietly responded.

'I have no choice, do I? As captain, I can't very well question the legitimacy of my team's reports.'

But that was exactly what was going through her mind. Idonea and Alrin had met their demise and the only one who should have been with them both was the soldier from Du-Kan. Was Doxxa to blame? Could he have killed Idonea to weaken Tarean control of the Unity mission? No, Du-Kan would never subvert the mission like that … unless Sloane had something to do with it or there was some hidden dialogue between Jaree and Du-Kan.

'I am sorry about Idonea, Captain. He was an Emberchild wasn't he? I saw his tattoos. Are you going to burn him?'

'As much as I would like to, I don't have the proper authority to do so. Only followers of the faith can perform such a rite.' Zillah leaned forward and picked up a cloth from the side table. She rubbed away the moisture building in her eyes and massaged her temples.

❖

Joja hadn't noticed. The doctor sipped her wine, a sad, fatigued smile creeping onto her flushed face. Her eyes were puffy—she'd been crying too, and Zillah could still see the lines on her face where tears had fallen.

'Tastes like a mountain fruit we have back in Tobania,' Joja said. 'It's sweet. Reminds me of my grandfather—he had an orchard in the hills outside Hophnam.'

Joja was interrupted by a pounding at the door. From behind the bar, Alvar dropped a rag, muttering under his breath as he limped towards the barred door. Sloane's order that no one could leave was still in force. Alvar removed the brace and opened the door.

Reeva marched in, sword hanging at her side. Four men marched behind her, each in armour and carrying large halberds. Joja's interest in her wine disappeared as she glanced at the arrivals with a brisk inhale. Reeva scanned the room like a ravenous predator in search of prey. Under the table, Zillah felt for the small handgun tucked away in her waistband.

The townspeople at the bar shrank into hushed silence. A few turned to look at the Guardian as she stepped forward, her men following in unison. The sound of their footsteps rang around the hall. As much as she disliked Sloane, his presence right now would bring her some comfort.

Zillah lifted herself from the chair, keeping her hand close to the gun. Reeva stepped towards the fire as her men fanned across the room to form a wall. Zillah stared her down; flames reflected in Reeva's glowering eyes.

'We have come to take the Scion; you have no right to imprison him. If you hope to leave Xylona, then I advise you to heed my warning,' Reeva declared coldly.

Straight talk and threats. Zillah had been in positions like this before; however, she had nothing to do with the men being detained. As the captain, it was her responsibility to de-escalate the tension. She scanned the room; all eyes were on her. Joja stood by her side, tiny in comparison to the men blocking their exit.

❧

'Reeva, we merely want to learn what has happened. We understand that one of the boys was found covered in the blood of one of my men. Would you not question them if our roles were reversed?' Zillah said. She was calm on the surface, but in her head, she was already running through Reeva's next moves.

'Tell your people to bring him down. We can discuss this in the open,' Reeva demanded.

Zillah knew Reeva held the advantage, and it seemed Reeva did too.

'Your Prime One is with him now. I am not being unreasonable, but I will ask Doxxa to escort the men down as a sign of good faith,' Morgana said. Slowly, she reached for her tablet. Reeva's eyes followed her every movement with suspicion.

'Doxxa, bring them down,' Zillah spoke into the tablet. Doxxa did not respond, but soon, shuffling could be heard from the stairwell in the back of the room.

Claudya was the first to emerge, followed by the two men. They were mere boys, both looking around with vacant expressions, searching the room and those gathered. Doxxa followed behind the pair, gun in his hands, his fingers lightly caressing the trigger. It was aimed in the direction of the boy soaked in blood.

'Where is the Commodore?' Doxxa asked, eyeing Zillah suspiciously. A look that wasn't lost on Reeva. A thin smile curled onto her face.

'Oh, I am here.'

Zillah spun sharply to look in the direction they heard the voice. Sloane appeared behind Reeva and her guards. The back door behind him let in a chilled rush of night air. His gun was planted firmly in his hands. Unease flitted through the eyes of Reeva's men. The advantage they held had diminished.

'For the Spirits' sake, please lower your weapons, all of you,' the Prime One said in a stern voice.

One of the boys had the same black hair as the Prime One. This must have been the Scion—her son.

Zillah watched the other boy: his clothes were torn, and blood stained his shirt and plastered his matted brown hair and face. He wore an apprehensive expression. What purpose would two timid young lads have for murdering Alrin?

Sloane would not have allowed the boy to wash away the blood. Another tactic of his, she did not doubt.

Reeva eyed Sloane, who returned a smirk. Both lowered their weapons, but Sloane kept a firm grip.

'Now, Ayon and Olbi have assured me that they found the body by chance in the forests,' Claudya said in a calm, steady voice.

'What are the chances? Next to none. Lies and deceit,' Sloane replied mockingly.

Zillah saw the boys raise their heads at the accusation.

'Please, I don't know what happened,' Zillah said, raising her palm to stop Sloane's tirade. He was not helping the situation. The last thing they needed was emotions clouding facts. If Zillah could keep tensions from boiling over, she might yet salvage the mission.

Olbi and Ayon recounted their afternoon leading up to the moment they found themselves in Sloane's custody. Only once did they stumble on how they came by the body. Ayon referred to being shown the way to the outcrop, *shown by who?* she wondered... Meanwhile Olbi suggested they happened across the sound of the emergency beacon by chance. Zillah agreed that the loud sound of the tablets would attract them towards it, seeing as it would have been foreign to their ears. When they finished their account, she nodded at the boys and thanked them for detailing the events.

Reeva interrupted them once to ask why they went into the forests, noting that the headaches and sickness hadn't affected them.

'I don't get sick in the forests,' Olbi replied quietly, and Ayon backed him up. Reeva twitched, her eyes widening, then

231

narrowing her gaze at Olbi, as if he hid something from her. Sloane glared at the young men with a smirk and flash of disbelief. The room was silent for a few moments. The fact remained that Alrin Sandol had his throat slit.

'Doxxa,' Zillah called, pulling the soldier's attention, 'why did you not try and stop Mr Sandol from defying a direct order?'

'You asked me to stay with Idonea. I wasn't there to babysit the photographer,' Doxxa responded in a contemptuous manner.

'And yet Idonea was dead already, was he not?' Zillah asked. Doxxa merely stared at Zillah—he wasn't giving anything up.

'Doxxa is not the one on trial, Captain,' Sloane rebuked.

Shut the fuck up Sloane, Zillah uttered under her breath before turning back to the Scion and his friend.

'Did anyone see you go into the forests? Anyone that can support your tale?' Joja piped in.

Ayon shook his head, but Olbi's eyes suddenly lit up.

'Tauva, the timberman's daughter. She spotted us in the forests as the bells rang,' Olbi said.

Zillah nodded, she peered into Olbi's bronzed eyes, she saw no malicious intent in them. 'The boys are free to go,' Zillah said, 'we don't have enough evidence to incriminate. I will speak with this Tauva,' Zillah said.

Immediately, there was an uproar from Sloane.

'Are you fucking joking, Morgana?' Sloane snapped. He looked incensed, eyes flickering with hatred no longer veiled. Zillah knew he would not be happy with her decision, but she was quickly trying to figure out how she could maintain control of the mission with the death of two aligned members. Joja was all that remained of the civilian part of their team, and the Tobanian wouldn't likely be skilled enough to defend Zillah should Sloane attempt to seize leadership of the mission.

'I ask one thing,' Zillah said. She was addressing Claudya, who held her son tightly now. 'That some of your people accompany us to the Forbidden Zone.' Zillah scrutinized Olbi and Ayon as the beginnings of a plan formulated in her head. 'From my understanding, many of these garjee trees are between here and the Injai ruins. I propose that the boys accompany us, especially considering Olbi doesn't get sick.'

Olbi said nothing but cocked his head towards Claudya, shocked by the request.

'I will go,' Ayon said, pushing past Doxxa.

Claudya's eyes bulged with fear. 'No! He is the Scion; I will not allow it,' she said, shaking her head and reaching for her son.

The Rahsu at the bar gasped. Reeva stepped forward, her eyes wide and alarmed.

'Ayon will not go,' the Guardian protested, turning to the Scion. 'You have a duty to your people.'

Heavy energy charged the room, the fire crackled as a log collapsed into the coals, sending sparks up the chimney. Ayon turned to his mother; Claudya's face was ashen as she shook her head, her hands trembling as Ayon reached for them.

Zillah watched tears roll down the Prime One's face as she cupped Ayon's face in her hand.

'My sweet boy,' Claudya mumbled as she caressed Ayon's face. 'I cannot protect you. The Rahsu will never forgive us.'

'Mother, this is what I want. The Spirits will protect me,' Ayon said. His eyes were wide and filled with determination.

'I will accompany the boy. It is my duty as Guardian,' Reeva said, stepping forward.

Of course you will, Zillah thought, expecting no different. Anyone who kept a watch on Sloane was vital to the expedition.

'I see no issue in that at all. Anyone else you suggest, Prime One?' Zillah asked.

'You give these people too much lenience, Captain,' Doxxa interjected. 'Don't forget, Alrin Sandol is dead.'

'By my count, many more Rahsu have perished by your hands,' Reeva snapped.

'Quiet,' Claudya ordered. The Prime One furrowed her brow. Zillah could tell she was formulating a plan inside her head. Why were these people afraid of the Forbidden Zone? What would they find there?

Claudya sighed, her face was the portrait of a mother realising her child was leaving the nest, her tormented soul revealed by creased worry lines across her brow. 'I believe the fewer people that venture forth, the wiser. We need strength to rebuild Xylona.' She paused, looking at Reeva.

'Reeva, take Liran with you—her linguistics will assist. If a connection between Anatara and the Rahsu can be uncovered, it may go a long way to truth-telling and healing between our peoples.'

Claudya then turned to Ayon and Olbi, 'Remember, the forests will be treacherous, and within the Forbidden Zone, the Spirits cannot protect you. The dark lands to the east are dangerous and will test your mettle.'

Finally, Claudya turned to Zillah with defiance in her eyes. 'You have much to prove to us if we are to establish a bond, Captain. I pray that you find the proof you seek and a way for you to return home.' Claudya sounded weary until her gaze brushed over her son and Olbi. Suddenly, Claudya, as if speaking to a large audience bellowed an edict, 'By my order as the Prime One, I declare your safe passage. You leave at first light.'

21

OLBI

Somehow, Olbi had slept that night. He didn't know how long he'd lain there examining the splintered wooden beams that held the roof up in the cramped Stonehall room. Usually, he'd sleep in the larger hall, but the Anatrians took over that space as it had enough room for six. Olbi kept his spear close at hand in case Sloane or his comrades decided to come to his room in the night to finish him off. He assumed it wouldn't compare against their weapons, but at least he would die defending himself. He wouldn't go down a craven.

He lay in bed reflecting on the last few days. His life faced new realities, while the raw emotion of losing Boji was still lodged in his heart. He rolled onto his side and peered at the curtains illuminated by the soft glow of the morning sun. He could almost imagine today would be a typical day, but he knew last night wasn't a dream.

His bloodied clothes lay beside a water bowl where a damp washcloth was soaked red—getting the blood out of his hair had taken him a while. The haunting face of Alrin Sandol staring at him was still prominent in his mind. Though he didn't know the man, he would never forget him. They were forever linked, having been wrongfully accused of his murder. Who else would have killed one of the Outsiders, and how? Why did the Spirits lead him there? The Spirit woman hadn't appeared as if she wanted to frame him. And what of the raving woman uttering nonsensical threats at him in the healing hall? Was she following him into the forests? Could she have slit a man's throat? Olbi's head ached, slammed by the avalanche of questions swimming unanswered.

He pushed himself out of bed and pulled on fresh shorts and a shirt. He donned the same green yar-wool pullover he normally wore when heading into the forests. It helped him blend into the trees when hunting rabbits.

Olbi approached the door and stood silently, pressing his ear against the wood, listening for activity. Murmurs drifted from downstairs, and the smell of freshly baked bread wafted in from the gap under the door. His mouth watered. The events of last night had left him anxious, and his desire to eat had vanished, replaced by a fear of being told he would be heading into the Forbidden Zone to search for the ruins of ancient people.

Slow, laboured stomps approached before stopping outside his door. The light rattle of knuckles against the door sounded louder with his ear pushed against it. A gruff voice spoke through the wood, 'Come boy, breakfast is ready.' Alvar did not wait for a response before he moved down the hallway.

Olbi started downstairs, pausing to peer into the open room where the Outsiders were staying—it was empty, the Anatrians were already up—before he descended the staircase.

He scanned the great room where the standoff had occurred last night. Someone had re-lit the fire in the hearth, the fresh firewood crackled pleasantly, and he could see a few travellers in the booths eating oats and fresh bread.

Only one of the Outsiders was downstairs: the petite girl with strange hair. She spotted him at the base of the stairs and beckoned him forward, rising from the table. Olbi stood frozen on the spot. Alvar was nowhere to be seen, and the Rahsu travellers in town for the Manna Rites seemed more interested in their food than the lone person from another planet.

'Olbi, would you like to have breakfast with me?' Joja asked. An honest, wide smile stretched across her face. She had the energy of a young yar calf bounding through the meadows, giddy and excitable. Olbi hesitated. Boji was dead because of these people. A surge of anger rose within him, a sensation he abhorred. He tried to suppress the emotion as he regarded the woman in front of him. Surely, she wasn't responsible for the death of so many yar.

'I could eat this apris jam for days, it's so good,' Joja said, reaching for a chunk of bread. She closed her eyes as she licked the jam off the end of her fingers.

Olbi shuffled forward as Joja pointed to the seat in the booth opposite her. He said nothing, but he eyed the bread, cheeses, and smears of butter, apris jam and honey that lay in small lumps on her plate. His stomach growled in anticipation.

'Olbi, I can't imagine how you must be feeling. Sloane is an arsehole, and Zillah is just trying to keep the peace. I think they both know you didn't kill Alrin.' Joja spoke like a close friend he had known for years. She grabbed a chunk of bread and placed it on another plate before him. He stared at Joja, while her wide eyes darted, scanning the room.

'Alvar seems nice. Well, he makes the best tea. He said he would bring me a special tea that might help us on our journey. I'm hoping it will relieve the headaches everyone talks about,' she said.

'You didn't get sick in the forests?' Olbi queried, watching her smear butter on a piece of bread. His voice came out meekly and croaky, his throat dry.

'No, I didn't'—Joja smiled, pouring a glass of water and pushing it across the table to him—'but us Tobanians are a tough lot.' She chuckled as she spilled water on the table. 'Oh well, guess I wouldn't make a very good barmaid now, would I?'

Olbi nibbled on his bread. The girl was quite friendly, and he was not sure why. 'What is a Tobanian?' he asked.

'Well, I am. Tobania is my country. Just like you are Rahsu.'

'And the others are not Tobanian's?'

She snorted at him and slipped a wedge of cheese into her mouth.

'We are all from different countries', Joja mumbled, her mouth still full. 'It was supposed to keep us all in line and foster international cooperation, but some of us have never gotten along.' She sighed. 'It was a good idea but flawed the second we took flight from Quartab.' She stared into nothingness, deep in thought.

He stared at her, puzzled. He understood her words but none of their meaning.

'I must not be making much sense.' She laughed again. 'Let's talk about something that does.' She paused and buttered more bread. 'What's so special about this *Forbidden Zone*? It did not look all that special from satellite imagery.'

Her words continued to confuse him, and her accent was difficult to understand, but he discerned she was trying to get information from him.

'There are many Forbidden Zones. It is said to be where the Spirits imprison the world's demons, so they do not harm the Rahsu.'

'What do these demons look like?'

Olbi thought about the glowing woman last night. *Was she a demon?* He held back his answer as the door to the Stonehall creaked open.

Reeva entered, looking annoyed and angry as she always did. She shot Olbi and Joja a piercing stare. 'We are waiting for you both—finish up and let us depart. We have much distance to travel.' With that, she headed back out the door.

'She seems very friendly,' Joja said, leaning forward conspiratorially.

Olbi couldn't help but smile, at least someone else could see it.

After returning to his room to grab his spear and stuff his bag with what he could find for the long journey, Olbi headed out onto the street.

Outside the Stonehall, the party had gathered and were milling around, sorting through their bags and filling water bladders from a nearby pump. Claudya was there with Phran, who checked and rechecked Ayon's bag. She made no effort to hide, biting her lip in between each question of a barrage she was throwing Ayon's way. Reeva was seated nearby, glaring at the Outsiders and their weapons while making a point to sharpen her blade on a whetstone.

The Anatrians were gathered in a small circle, all dressed in dark green uniforms. Joja, now wearing an odd hat, was chatting with Alvar, who looked very comfortable with her. He handed her a small bag, no doubt the tea she had requested. Her smile was infectious and Alvar's nervous laugh made Olbi smile. A gust of wind carried the bag's bouquet on the breeze—there was no doubt about it, zirge root had a pungent smell. Olbi noticed the only one not there was Liran. She soon appeared, walking up the street with a sack that clung to her back like an oversized snail shell.

Anticipation and a strange excitement spread throughout Olbi's body. He felt numb about the journey but also happy that he would return to the forests where he belonged.

Ayon broke away from his mother and Reeva, smiling as he approached. 'A strange couple of days. Are you ready for the journey?' Ayon asked. Under his shirt, a medallion hung around his neck.

Ayon followed Olbi's eyes. 'From my mother. For protection, she says,' the Scion said.

'How are you feeling?' Olbi asked.

'Excited but uneasy. I'm a little worried about Reeva, but exploring the Forbidden Zone is something I have always wanted to do; I can't believe my mother allowed it.'

'What do you expect we will find?' Olbi asked, recollecting his schooling. He expected danger and death inflicted by demons. Ayon smiled at him; it was the same smile he'd given him when they were in the forests the night before.

'I expect we will learn the truth of who we are, Olbi.'

While the party huddled together in the street, townspeople wandered by, gazing at the mismatched group. Some gave the

Outsiders knowing glares, whereas others bowed at the sight of the Prime One, several yelling out their blessings.

An older woman caught Olbi's attention as she approached him. She smiled, it wasn't wide, but it was warm, like the flicker of a candle on a chilled night. He flinched as she reached out and took his hands in hers. 'Burn bright, be safe,' she said before disappearing into the crowd of people. The nature of their journey was quickly becoming common knowledge in Xylona.

He accepted a small bag of supplies from Phran. Upon inspection, it contained a sleeping pouch, a smaller bag of cheese, bread and dried apris fruit, and a small clear stone marbled with black clouds. The last item confused him a little; he wasn't sure what it was for. It felt smooth in his hand, like a river stone carved by the forces of water over eons. He turned it over and saw scratching's engraved on its surface. The lacerations were fine and appeared like a symbol, so he gave Phran a quizzical look and held it up. Phran smiled at him and reached out his hand. Olbi thought he would take the stone, but instead, Phran closed Olbi's hand around it.

'It's for your protection. It will keep you safe,' the old Monitor said.

'How can a piece of rock do that?' Olbi inquired.

Phran looked at the medallion against Ayon's olive skin. Maybe it wasn't to protect him, but rather to ward demons away.

The head Monitor shifted away to help Liran, also giving her supplies. Olbi was so engrossed in watching Liran stuff a book in her bag that he didn't notice that another person was approaching him.

'Olbi, my child,' the voice said.

He turned and was met with the eyes of the Prime One, eyes that were warm and made Olbi feel safe. Could it be true that she was sick? If so, she gave no hints to her health.

'I want you to do something for me,' Claudya said. Her smile was meek and didn't reach her eyes.

❖

Olbi felt uneasy, he gave her the subtlest of nods.

'I name you Guardian of the Primes, if you would accept it. The task I bestow would be solely this: to protect my son, protect the bloodline and ensure no harm comes to him.'

A few moments passed as blood rushed into his ears. Had she asked him to be a Guardian? The position was held in high regard, and it was most hallowed, more hallowed even than the Monitors. His palms became clammy. He wished Claudya would break her eye contact with him—instead, she reached out and grabbed his arm.

'Please, Olbi, I must know Ayon will not be alone and will forever have someone in his life.' A hint of sadness swept over her. In the corner of his eye, he could see Ayon talking with Joja Amira. Something Joja said had Ayon smiling. He turned that smile towards Olbi.

Could he do it? Could he protect the Scion even though he was unsure what the Forbidden Zones would hold? He thought about what Claudya had said, she needed to know that Ayon would not be alone and have someone in his life. Was Reeva not also a Guardian, or was there more to this?

Claudya let go of Olbi's arms as if retreating from the vulnerability of asking the question.

'Prime One, I don't know how to protect someone,' he said.

She smiled. This time, her smile was genuine.

'But you do, Olbi. Ayon tells me more than you might imagine.'

What was she referring to?

'From what I hear, you stood before the Outsider last night, brandishing a weapon for him. That sounds like a Guardian to me.'

'Prime One, that was—'

'Was what? Instinct? Or was it that you cared for him?' Claudya's eyes were warm. She reached into her pocket and took a step towards him, grasping his shirt.

'I think you have been his Guardian for longer than you presume,' she said, placing her palm on his cheek. He held back his instinct to flinch, rather soaking in the warmth of her hand. She stepped back and studied him.

Olbi looked down. A glistening golden garjee fruit was pinned to his chest: the symbol of the Prime family. She had made him a Guardian. Olbi bowed to Claudya and nodded as the Prime One stepped forward and caressed his cheek again.

'Ayon will need you by his side, the future of our people depends on it,' Claudya said before turning and leaving. The weight of the garjee pin felt unnaturally heavy.

****

They converged by the Eastern Arches of Xylona. Here, the river flowed thick with ash from the flames. Still, a few fishermen sat on its banks, rods cast out into the murky waters. Their wide glances greeted Olbi's party as they trooped on by.

The road out of town crossed a stone bridge that arched across the slow-moving Flow. The stonework was so flawless it seemed new, as if it had only been built a year ago, though no one knew its exact age. The bridge had been here for generations.

Over the bridge, orchards grew. Some trees here had their foliage ripped clean by the Outsiders' ship, leaving spindly skeletons. Farmers had gathered dead branches in the fields and placed them into small wooden carts, ready to wheel them into town for firewood. The party was leaving Xylona while so much work was left to do.

Olbi had mixed feelings as he walked with the others—he had wanted to see his father before leaving, but there was no time. Alvar had assured him that he would let Tarak know where Olbi was going and with whom.

Reeva led the party—after all, it was she who had chartered their course—along a path that would avoid as much of the garjee as possible.

Liran was already proving integral to the journey as she handed out three identical maps she had made. She gave one to the Outsiders, one to Ayon and then kept the last one for herself, folding it into a square that she tucked into her pocket. Ayon showed Olbi his map. The map indicated they would be heading southeast towards the base of the Cayden Plateau and, from there, they would follow it eastward to the Forbidden Zone beyond. It was a path few Rahsu had travelled.

Olbi used his spear as a walking stick while staring at the two Outsiders before him: Zillah and Viggo Doxxa. They both looked at their tablets and tapped their fingers on the screens. He wanted to hold one, hoping the Outsiders would let him look at a device. Liran was eyeing the machines too. A wealth of knowledge in the palm of your hand and able to take it anywhere you could go. Olbi overheard Joja talking with Liran, who seemed to be struggling underneath the weight of her bag.

'I am interested to see if anything remains of their technology myself,' Joja said. 'Their understanding of biology must have been far superior to our own. We could learn so much about our genetics, that's to say if they were like us at all. But we have been able to piece together that not much would have changed in the last sixteen hundred years.' Joja continued speaking as she strolled the lane that ran through the apris tree orchard. Liran grunted, languishing with every step. Joja seemed oblivious and continued to talk, more to herself Olbi guessed.

'We determined their decline happened quite suddenly. If we can find ruins that haven't been exposed to the elements, shifts in climate and natural disasters, then we might be able to understand them better. Unfortunately, years of war and many natural disasters on Anatara have left most of our ruins destroyed or lost to time. Tobania has the best archaeological records, and we have a whole museum in Hophnam dedicated to the Injai,' Joja said before Sloane cut in.

'Much of which was stolen from Jareean archives.'

Joja scoffed. 'Your archivists did not know what they had and were useless at identifying items.' Joja turned back to Liran and burst into laughter. 'My friend recovered some of the items and said that a small silver tube was listed as part of a musical instrument; it turned out it was just a *drainpipe*.'

Olbi couldn't help but smirk at Liran's expression. It was a mix of confusion, apathy, and annoyance that she was the only one sweating from the hill they climbed.

Ayon was quiet. He had barely spoken a word since parting with his mother. Olbi wondered if he knew Claudya had asked him to be the Scion's Guardian. His garjee pin rested underneath folds of fabric in the hood of his travelling cloak. He wasn't sure how Reeva would react to that. For now, he thought it best to act discreetly. No one needed to know—even Ayon.

The outer orchards appeared to be untouched by the fires; however, they abruptly ended as rolling green hills dominated the path forward. Small huts dotted the crests of the undulating lands ahead, and yar peacefully fed in the lush grasses. They were larger yar than the ones by the mill as their grains were fed by rain collected in brooks that crisscrossed the meadows. It was peaceful.

When Olbi turned, he could see all Xylona laid out behind him. He nudged Ayon. The Scion turned as well, looking out at the village, his mouth dropping.

'Picturesque,' Zillah said. As she lifted her tablet, Olbi could see the view on the screen. She noticed him looking and showed him the device's screen.

'It's a photograph. It lets you look at something you've seen, like a painting of a memory,' Zillah explained.

She pointed the tablet at Olbi and Ayon. There was a click, and Olbi's heart jumped, alarmed at what Zillah was doing.

'See, I just took a photo of you both.' Zillah turned the tablet over, and Olbi saw himself and Ayon on the screen. He stared, bewildered at his face trapped in the tablet, looking back at him. Olbi appeared startled and in that split second, he had shielded Ayon's face with his arm, protecting the Scion.

****

As the party walked on, Joja was the only one of them who talked. Olbi would see her ducking into a shrub or approaching a bush and remarking on its colours and shapes. She, too, was taking photographs and making notes about her surroundings. They had trekked for half the day, and the green rolling hills transitioned to fields of low, wide-reaching shrubs and trees.

Olbi had been here only once before, with his father, when he was very young. He couldn't remember why they had ventured this far east of Xylona, though he recalled catching frogs and building mud pools in the shallow brooks that cut through the fields. He had enjoyed that day. His father had been happy that day, too, but a memory returned to his mind as if dormant and being awoken by the place's proximity. He recalled someone had approached them from the east. They had been injured, and his father had helped them. Was that why they had been out this way? Ayon looked at Olbi with a curious stare.

'Everything alright, Olbi? Why do you scowl?' Ayon said.

'I'm not scowling, I am thinking. I have been here before and—' Olbi stopped talking. He remembered what the person had looked like. It was Faiyor.

It all came back to him in a rush as if a dam wall had burst. His father had told him that they were going on an adventure to meet one of his friends. Olbi remembered the journey across the bridge and through the orchards. He must have been about eight or nine years old. He remembered the huts, where they had stopped to chase yar calves in the fields and to tumble down the grassy hills. His father had told him that they needed to move quickly.

Ayon continued glancing at Olbi. The Scion's eyes searched his.

Olbi remembered everything.

'Ayon, I have been here before,' Olbi said, just loud enough for Ayon to hear.

'The last time I was here was when my father had met someone who had travelled to the Forbidden Zone, telling him of the Spirits that had hunted them, and of deathly blades in the trees.'

Ayon gulped.

Olbi clenched his spear tightly.

22

LIRAN

Liran gave thanks to the Spirits when the hills levelled out. The bag straps had cut deep, red lines into her shoulders that she knew would bruise quickly. Liran chucked her bag on the grass, the items rolled out and splayed across the ground, as Reeva and Zillah announced they would set up camp for the night.

They had entered a strange land of circular granite boulders larger than houses. It was as if a giant had scattered marbles across the fields. Some looked as though they would roll away with the slightest push. They camped in the shadow of two of these boulders, blocking the cool wind from the north.

The sun loomed in the sky, a glowing orb that diminished in brightness and warmth as it slipped beneath the horizon.

Liran watched as Sloane unfurled a bedroll on the ground. He sat down on the makeshift bed and reached for his tablet. He had been silent most of the journey, not even giving Liran the benefit of an eye flinch to indicate he might have caught a whiff of her in the garden listening in on his transmission. Liran shuddered to think what would happen if she divulged the information she learned to Zillah or Reeva and they acted on it. But could she trust Zillah or any of the Outsiders?

'Reeva, how long until we reach the garjee forest?' Ayon asked. He had his nose in his map, looking at the crude sketches Liran had given him, his usually well-kempt hair was a mess.

'If we maintain our current speed, we will arrive by mid-morning tomorrow. Then it's two days to the Forbidden Zone,' Reeva replied, appearing more agitated than ever. Clearly, the Guardian had not approved of the Prime One's mandate that they travel with the Anatrians.

'Two days in the forests? Doctor, I hope you have enough medicine for everyone,' said Doxxa, picking up dry leaves from a small bush near the granite boulder. Joja appeared unfazed.

'There is enough,' Joja said reassuringly, 'but before we enter tomorrow, everyone should drink a local tea I am told keeps the headaches and nausea at bay.'

'Tea? Stick that up your arse. I'll keep to Anatrian pharmaceuticals, thanks,' Doxxa said.

Joja scoffed at the soldier's gruff retort.

Liran was thankful for the zirge supply Joja had received from Alvar. 'It will prove effective, it's what the Monitors drink before entering the garjee for the harvest,' Liran assuaged Doxxa.

Joja nodded as Zillah walked over with the kindling she had found. Zillah and Doxxa had the same idea about getting a fire going while Joja kicked off her shoes and ran her feet through tufts of grass.

'I agree with the Maven,' Joja said. 'This zirge root does contain enzymes known to act as stimulants that suppress pain receptors. You will still be exposed to low doses of radiation, but your brain won't register it.'

'It is taboo to use, though. Only harvesters are sanctioned to use them, and Syrona sometimes will use it for Xylonan's stricken with incurable maladies,' Ayon added.

Liran shifted uncomfortably, only too aware that the supply of zirge she had received from Syrona after Hayda's death was gone. *Perhaps Alvar will sell me his stock,* Liran pondered.

Zillah raised a brow at the doctor, though Joja dismissed the look and turned to Liran.

'What is it about these trees that are central to your religion? I must say they do fascinate me, the way they give off radiation. How did they come into being?'

Liran pondered the question as the doctor pulled out her sleeping mat. 'It is said that the garjee fruit feeds the Spirits, giving life to the world around us. Every eclipse, we offer the fruit to the Spirits at the Manna Rites,' Liran said.

Joja sat down and tapped on her tablet, taking notes.

'What is *radiation*? Is that what causes the illness?' Liran asked.

Joja nodded. 'Low doses, mind you,' she said. 'It's like an invisible energy and is often magnetic and electric. So, I want to learn as much as possible before it interferes with our technology. How long have they been part of your culture?' Joja pushed dreadlocks out of her face.

Olbi and Ayon appeared beside her. They, too, had collected kindling for a fire, but it looked like sizeable dry wood was hard to find in the vicinity.

'The trees have been part of the Rahsu since the dawn of time. They will be here long after we return to the soil to be with the Spirits.'

Joja nodded, taking in Liran's every word.

'This fruit?' Joja asked, looking up from her tablet and realising she had a small audience. 'What about it makes it special to the Spirits? Does it taste heavenly?'

'You can't eat them,' Ayon cautioned. 'They are like stone and warm to the touch.'

Joja's eyes lit up as she turned to the Scion. 'I look forward to analysing one of these fruits; they sound fascinating. However, I now wonder if they give off the same radiation as the—'

'You will not touch a fruit, Outsider,' Reeva cut in. 'Only Primes and their sworn harvesters may handle them.' She walked into the circle that had formed around the pile of sticks and leaves. Joja fell silent.

Liran rolled her eyes. 'That is not precisely true, Joja. When it is needed, anyone can touch the fruits,' she said.

Reeva gave Liran a steely glower.

'What would that need be?' Zillah asked, taking out a small object and placing it in the pile of sticks. Within seconds the wood crackled, and a bright flame licked from within the

sticks as sparks flew and smoke bellowed into the air above them. The Rahsu watched wide-eyed as she put the object back in her pocket.

'When the blood is threatened,' Liran elaborated.

Reeva almost burst with frustration. She walked towards Liran and towered over her. She looked fierce and more menacing than the Outsiders ever could.

'That is enough, Maven. Must you tell these people everything about us? They are not our friends nor our kin, do you understand me?'

Everyone fell silent. Liran heard her blood pumping alongside the crackling of the fire.

Zillah pushed herself between Reeva and Liran. 'Reeva, we are a curious people,' she began. 'We mean no offence by asking questions. We merely wish to learn. You may ask us anything you desire as well. We harbour no secrets.'

Liran appreciated her trying to bring things back under control.

'There is nothing we need from you except for you to fix your ship, leave Arbonar and never come back,' Reeva spat. The guardian turned and walked off from camp into the dusk.

'It is clear that the garjee is a touchy subject, I do apologise,' Joja offered meekly.

Liran brushed her off. 'Please don't let Reeva's nature cause you discomfort. She has always been like this, ever since I first met her,' Liran said. 'She once lashed out at me because I suggested we open a public space where people could read scriptures, scrolls and books instead of them being sealed in archives behind lock and key. She asked the Prime One to reconsider my position.'

'Is reading not allowed?' Zillah asked.

'It's allowed, but many writings are taboo. Historical accounts for example. It was not always so, once archives were full of scrolls and texts, but over the years things have gone missing or have been destroyed. Intentionally if you ask me,' Liran said as she unpacked some dried apris fruit.

'Sad indeed,' was all Zillah could muster before their thoughts turned to food.

Liran and the others sat in silence for what felt like an hour. The remaining sunlight streaked across the sky, diminishing to the horizon and then, as if being sucked down, vanished. Above them, a blanket of stars grew brighter, no clouds impeding their view. Joja stood up and studied the night sky, searching. She gasped as she focused on a bright star that did not twinkle. Liran watched as tears trickled down Joja's face.

'What is it?' Liran asked.

Joja smiled yet tears still fell. She pointed at the star.

'I've never seen Anatara from the surface of another world. It looks so small, so fragile,' she sobbed.

Everyone around the fire looked up at the star. Liran had seen it many times. Hayda loved the stars, and when Liran would chart them on research nights for her book, Hayda would often come along and name the stars and constellations with her.

'Are you sure that is Anatara?' Olbi asked.

The question snapped Liran out of her trance; she knew why he had asked. Ayon did too. The Scion regarded Joja cautiously, suddenly solemn.

'Of course, it's Anatara. It's so bright because it's closer to us than all the other stars. Why does that trouble you?' Joja asked, apparently noticing the soured mood.

Ayon pointed to the star.

'It is part of a constellation we call the Daemon,' he said, his voice soft, yet everyone in the circle heard him. 'The constellation depicts the demons fighting the Spirits of Arbonar. It brings fire and destruction and that star'—again Ayon pointed at Anatara—'that star is its heart.'

The gathering fell silent, each face glowing with a graveness in the light of the campfire. Liran felt a surge within her. There was something about this story that stirred a realisation.

Joja shifted her gaze to the eyes of the Rahsu before her, looking cautious and pained. 'So, to the Rahsu, Anatara is the heart of all evil,' she said.

No one answered. However, Liran sensed a profound truth as she watched the agony spread across Joja's face. Somehow the ancient Rahsu had known more than they did. Their religion, their stories and history, Anatara, all of it. All of them were connected.

****

Reeva must have returned sometime in the middle of the night because when Liran opened her eyes, she saw the Guardian's lumbering figure leaning against a boulder. Her eyes were shut, but Liran expected she was feigning sleep. Reeva would watch the Outsiders until they were on their ship returning to Anatara, only then would she rest.

The sun breached the horizon as the party stirred from their slumber. Liran wrapped her sleeping roll and brushed off the dead leaves that had stuck to it in the night. The grass here was wet with dew, and her toes were slow from the chilled frost. She glanced over at the ashes of the fire, though they offered no warmth.

Ayon and Olbi were already awake, and she could hear Olbi teaching Ayon how to wrap his roll. The Scion's first attempt would not fit into its buckle.

Like the others, Liran nibbled on some cheese and drank cold zirge tea. She wished they could wait for a fire to brew a hot tea to invigorate her, but Sloane and the ever-alert Reeva demanded haste.

Yesterday's stunted conversations were lively compared to the deafening silence of the mood this day. The Anatrians asked no questions, and Liran wondered if the tension in their midst would ever dissipate. She wondered if Arbonar was visible in the skies of Anatara. What would it be like to see your whole world as a sparkling dot in the sky? For the first time, Liran fantasised about travelling the stars and setting foot on an alien world.

They trudged through low grasses that glistened, first amber in morning glow and then resplendent gold in the noon sun. They hiked with a singular purpose, to make as much ground as they could. The farther east they walked, the more Liran found herself outside the comfort of familiar surroundings. As the sun crept up, drying the grasses beneath their feet, the sound of animals scurrying in the undergrowth and bird calls surrounded them. It wasn't long until a green haze of trees appeared in the distance, and the garjee forests drew near.

The silence was eventually broken when Doxxa yelled for them to stop. He had inadvertently found himself at the head of the party. He turned to the rest of them, his tablet in hand. It was beeping incessantly, a sound that pinged in Liran's ears.

'I'm picking up something on the scanners that's worth a look,' Doxxa said.

Zillah, standing by Liran, pulled out her tablet, the pinging also coming from her tablet. She stabbed a finger at the screen, bringing up an image. Liran looked over the captain's shoulder. The image resembled a map with lines running across it. Was this how they knew where they were going? Zillah tapped the screen and focused on something.

'Looks like a small ruin. Let's check it out,' the captain shouted to Doxxa.

'A ruin?' Liran asked.

She knew of no Rahsu ruins that had been mapped this far east. Besides the trees and farmlands behind them, this part of Arbonar was untouched and had been for over one thousand years.

'Could be Injai. Worth the detour, don't you think?' Joja said, gleefully looking at her tablet.

The Anatrians mentioned their satellites could see things on the surface of the planet. The dancing stars. Liran still couldn't believe the stars belonged to the very people she was walking with.

The party shifted course towards the mystery location on the Outsiders' tablets. The detour would see them veer off course temporarily, but as Liran looked up ahead, she frowned. They were entering a boulder field, a foreboding mass of giant granite crags.

Jagged and imposing, the rocks loomed ominously, their uneven terrain appeared unnavigable. The next hour saw them negotiating a treacherous path with limited routes ahead. Liran knew she would struggle climbing over the granite, even with less in her pack, thanks to Olbi offering to carry some of her things. She had done next to no exertion in years. Her shoulders slumped, her muscles aching just watching Olbi dart across the boulders before her. Even Ayon had a massive grin stretched across his face as he jumped from rock to rock. The Scion's mood had changed. Never in his life had he been out in the public eye like this—his dirty face and messy smile lifted her heart.

It took longer than expected to pass through the rocks. Zillah was the only one who had misjudged a rock and fallen. Her arm was grazed, but she recovered quickly. Liran helped her up as Sloane chuckled to himself when Zillah revealed the scrapes across her arm.

The sun hung directly overhead, and the chill of the morning had been replaced by searing heat unusual for this time of year.

They moved through a twisted copse of trees that leaned parallel to the ground. Unlike the tall and dominating garjee, every tree here was stunted. It was as if they were crawling across the landscape, pushed low by howling winds. Joja spoke of a similar forest in a country neighbouring Tobania, but Liran only half listened. She felt tired, and blisters developed on her feet.

Zillah studied her tablet closely as they wound through the leaning trees, their leaves thick and waxy. The path forward, much like the boulder field, was a labyrinth of thick gnarly shrubs teeming with spiderwebs and darkened burrows.

'We should be out of the trees in one hundred metres. The ruins are just beyond that,' Zillah said.
'No need to tell us that, we can see them already,' Liran said, lifting her gaze and craning her neck upwards. She had never seen anything quite like it. Soon, everyone stopped in their tracks and gazed upward with awe spread across their faces.

The imposing structure soared higher than any tree. Twisted metal covered in vines shot from the ground over one hundred metres tall. Liran marvelled as the structure glinted in the sun. Its metal beams, as thick as tree limbs, were a patchwork of orange and brown branches, marred by rust and on the brink of collapse.

'What is it?' Ayon asked no one in particular.

Liran didn't expect anyone to respond, but Joja spoke up.

'It's an Injai communication tower,' the Doctor said matter-of-factly.

Liran was astonished. She was face to face with proof the Outsiders spoke the truth.

'It was used to transmit messages across the planet,' Zillah said, 'much like our devices here.' The captain lifted her tablet.

'How do you know that?' Liran asked, staring at Zillah. Reeva sighed heavily, eager to get a move on.

'Because they were found and catalogued across Anatara. See here,' Zillah held out her tablet.

Liran looked closer. She saw a dozen images of similar structures on backdrops far different from the landscapes of Arbonar. The Maven was awestruck.

Joja turned to Reeva, who had begun walking towards the structure. 'Does this not prove we are connected, that we are siblings born of another planet?' Joja said.

Reeva turned, and Liran saw the fire of hatred rekindled in her eyes.

'We are not the same,' the Guardian said coldly. 'I know what you are doing. You would have us think you are forging a common future for us. Instead, you would seek to control us. Your world is fraught with war and death. Here we live in an eternal peace crafted over millennia, and we will continue to do so without you.'

Liran bit her tongue. Did Reeva also know what Sloane's plans were? Zillah remained quiet during Reeva's outburst but watched with great interest. Liran sensed that the puzzle pieces were coming together, but Zillah couldn't quite see the whole picture.

Zillah stepped towards Reeva; the Guardian of the Primes was an enigma in herself.

'Reeva, how do you know all this? It appears you are the one being dishonest. What are you hiding from your people? You already knew something about Anatara and so did Thessus. How can that be?' Zillah probed.

Everyone focused on Reeva, Sloane uncharacteristically lowered his gun and listened in, but the Guardian stood her ground. She regarded Zillah with a sly smile, malice building in her eyes.

'Oh yes, I know of the Injai … and Anatara is following in their footsteps,' Reeva said. 'There is only one path for you Zillah Morgana, and that is to your own demise.'

Shivers shot down Liran's spine.

With that, Reeva walked off towards the looming tower, her metallic armour reflecting the sun into Liran's eyes.

23

ZILLAH

The ruins proved to be of little value, despite Joja's insistence they stay longer to study debris that may have crashed and been buried at its base. If anything was left of the Injai beneath the pillars of the tower, it had long succumbed to the elements. Zillah wondered how long it would be before the tower fell, returning to the soil. The tower's plight prompted her to check the Unity's signal, dreading the prognosis would confirm it was still sinking.

She replayed Reeva's words in her mind. Somehow, this Rahsu knew far more than she was letting on. Far more than anyone else on the planet and perhaps more than any of the Anatrians. Curious as it was, their mission was far from over and answers would need to wait—the true challenge lay ahead of them.

The Prime Guardian led the party out of the twisted trees and towards the green haze of garjee that lay foreboding on the horizon. Zillah had already lost men to those trees, delving in again was absurd and dangerous. The terrain sloped downward, and here grasses had returned and wildlife was abundant. Ahead, a flock of massive birds took flight like none Zillah had ever seen. Their feathers shimmered in the light, an iridescent cascade of blues that shifted with every movement of their flight. Their long slender sapphire necks were elegantly sculptured and reminded her of swans, but their wings were the span of an outstretched human arm buoying them with grace amidst the winds and updrafts. Were the birds watching them, curious as to what they were?

Something about the planet seemed off. Zillah wondered how a society could flourish on a planet and yet, by her estimation, be confined to such a small slice of it. They couldn't be more than fifty kilometres from Xylona, though

✦

the landscape here was as foreign to the Rahsu as to the Anatrians. Had they no desire to discover the wonders of their world, or had the taboo teachings Liran told of artificially stifled their development? Perhaps if the Rahsu society hadn't endured stunted growth or strict societal norms and expectations, their technological capabilities would have outshined the Anatrian's.

Soon, the green blur of the garjee materialised into an imposing wall before them—each tree a sentient soldier set to oppose their every step. They stopped on a rise where the doctor brewed tea by crushing some pills and adding zirge to the mix until they dissolved into an increasingly purple concoction.

'It's best to gulp it down, I think,' Joja advised, her nose screwed up as her eyes watered. 'It smells foul.'

Ayon laughed as Joja passed him a cup.

Zillah took a cup from her bag and poured some tea into it. The smell wasn't as bad as the doctor had made it out, but she wouldn't rush to drink it if not necessary. Everyone except Olbi drank the medicinal brew per the doctor's insistent beckoning.

'This should help with headaches and nausea. If possible, we should stop again and brew more tea by nightfall. I imagine we will be in the forests for the night,' Joja said with a hint of trepidation.

Zillah shuddered at the thought. She hadn't experienced headaches to the extent that the others did, but she knew the pills in her pocket would not last for the return journey through the forest. Maybe there would be a better way back to Xylona.

Silence festered as they sipped their tea. Doxxa had initially refused, but glancing towards the trees, he resentfully downed his cup.

The zirge coursed through Zillah. She felt remarkably better as her body lifted, and her head swayed as if riding an ocean tide.

❧

'Does anyone else feel high?' Joja asked, giggling to herself.

Zillah agreed, this was amazing. The forests ahead lost their arrogance and force. She could do this. Still, what bothered her most was how quiet Sloane had been. He seemed almost bored and withdrawn, as if he was waiting for something … or weaving plans in the shadows of the garjee.

Night started to set in early as the twisted limbs and foliage blotted the sunlight, and within an hour, torches were necessary.

This forest was more alive than the one they had walked through from the crash site. They made camp early in a clearing ringed by garjee trees, listening to the animal yowls and bird calls circulating in abundance around them.

'Captain,' Joja called, 'these trees have lower radiation levels, but it's still higher than recommended—' She aggressively smacked at her tablet. 'Damn!'

Doxxa was also tapping his tablet against his leg with a look of irritation and checking if it helped fix the screen. Zillah pulled her own tablet out and noticed the same screen issues.

'It's the trees … they are electromagnetic. Quite fascinating,' Joja said, pursing her lips.

Zillah took a swig of water. Her head had begun to pound as if a new heart sat beneath her left temple. Fascination was not what she would use to describe the trees—she resented them—instead, she imagined setting them alight and watching them burn.

'Let's get a fire started. Ayon, help me with the firewood,' Liran said.

Zillah watched the Scion bounce up on his toes and eagerly follow Liran. While others seemed drained, Ayon and Olbi were alert and awake.

'I need to analyse some samples,' Joja whispered to Zillah. The doctor seemed almost too alert and focused, as if she had

been dipping into the stock of pills. Zillah felt a surge of resentment rising from within, but she fought the feelings.

'Come on, Olbi,' Joja said, turning fervently to the young man who seemed entranced by running his hands through blades of grass. 'I want you to tell me what some of these plants are called and describe what lives in these forests. Some predator won't eat me in the night, will it?' She offered a hand to Olbi, but he declined, smiling and shaking his head as he stood up.

Zillah hadn't thought of what predatory animals may lurk on Arbonar, but now it was front and centre of her mind, tucked nice and close to the pulsating pain encroaching on her skull.

Before long, a warm fire radiated from a small pit Doxxa had dug. The wood had been gathered from small shrubs that dotted the forest floor under the garjee trees. Liran had explained that the garjee wood could not be burnt or cut. Perhaps Joja was right that the trees around them held more secrets than first realised.

Zillah ambled towards a trunk, analysing the trees as if they would suddenly reveal something. Instead, she saw nothing but the slow flutter of a moth landing on the bark and the shimmering of the leaves above her.

'Liran, you said that it was the fruits of these trees that are harvested?' Zillah said.

Liran inched away from the fire, hugging herself and shaking despite the warmth of the flame. 'Yes, the garjee fruits are harvested in the days leading up to the Rites. The Monitors, some designated harvesters, will go into the forest and find fruits ready to harvest,' she explained.

'And no one here is authorised to touch them? Who is allowed?'

'Only Ayon may, as the Prime Scion,' Liran paused and looked over at Reeva, who was out of earshot. 'Designated Monitors and the Remnant lines are also permitted to hold them.'

❖

Zillah raised her brow.

'"Remnant lines"?'

Liran nodded. 'The ancestors of those who have been Primes. A dwindling number of people, I am afraid. Long ago, Primes—and those with the blood—were plentiful. Then, they were targeted, victims of power struggles and geopolitics. The Prime One is the provider and the leader of all. They govern over all Rahsu, but in the past, there were many. And with the many came clashes of personality and battles for control. Rahsu numbered in the tens of thousands. Now, we are diminished and ruled by one leader, one Prime.'

'How many Rahsu live today?' Zillah asked.

'It's hard to say'—Liran shrugged—'perhaps twenty thousand. How many people live on Anatara?'

'Considerably more. Last estimates put the figure at two billion, but that was before the war.'

Liran eyebrows shot up and her eyes widened. 'I would be interested in learning more about your past, as no doubt you are about ours,' she said enthusiastically. 'If we are of the same roots, I would be curious to know if any of the Outsiders share bloodlines. It would go a long way to convincing us that you are indeed the "lost" Rahsu.'

Zillah nodded and thought of the political consequences of that for the Rahsu, the possibilities seemed endless.

Abruptly, Liran's enthusiasm faltered. She appeared torn and weary, the radiation exposure was sapping life from them all, yet her eyes betrayed concern, as if she wanted to say something else but was hesitating. 'Is there anything else, Maven?' Zillah posed carefully.

When the Rahsu woman remained silent, Zillah turned to the warm fire. But then Liran grabbed her arm, panic-stricken eyes boring into Zillah's.

'I fear we are all in grave danger,' the Maven whispered through her teeth. Reeva looked over at the two of them, and a hollow stare bore into them both. Liran removed her hand

from Zillah's arm and smiled, regaining composure and unleashing a fake laugh.

'*Of course* I will explain the Manna Rites to you,' Liran said loudly, emphasising her words as if to ensure they were heard by all.

Zillah stared at Liran and then at Reeva. The Guardian was watching her intently. *What is going on?*

24

OLBI

That night, Olbi and Ayon laid their bedrolls beneath a blanket of stars. The others were as close to the fire as possible, which dwindled in the centre of the clearing as the moons crossed the sky.

Even with the combination of the Outsiders' medicine and the zirge root tea, the others struggled with nausea. Liran was the worst affected in Olbi's opinion, her shaking had worsened despite Joja's claims it wasn't because of the trees. Perhaps Liran was just ill.

Olbi rolled over and felt a rock digging into his hip. He grabbed it and realised it was the stone that Phran had given him. He ran his thumbs across its smooth surface, feeling the slight rifts where the runes were etched. In the moonlight, the stone seemed akin to that of the council table in the Prime House.

Olbi watched Ayon's face in the shards of moonlight. He slept peacefully; no sign of any sickness touched him. Perhaps they both hadn't been sick like the others because of the blood. Were the Prime's immune to the illness the trees cast upon them? He thought of the countless times he had delved into the forest and wondered what his future would have been like if the Outsiders hadn't arrived. Not getting sick would put him in high regard as a Monitor. He pictured his life protecting Ayon as a secret Guardian and retrieving fruits from the garjee for Ayon to gift at the Manna Rites. Then he imagined himself holding the fruit for himself and it beginning to glow.

Olbi then thought of his mother. What she might look like and whether she would be proud of the man he became—thoughts that lay dormant in his mind for a lifetime surfaced like an island emerging from an ocean. *One day I will meet you,* Olbi promised.

He wanted to know more about who he was. He wasn't just a quiet fisherman squatting at the Stonehall anymore, he was something more: a Remnant, a son of past leaders, and now a Guardian of the Primes. He stood alongside a lineage of remarkable Rahsu.

Olbi watched Ayon for some time. His hair was messy and unwashed, his face serene, and his thick lips were slightly parted. Olbi studied Ayon's face, every curve, every freckle. He had never slept beside someone before.

'Are you watching me sleep?' Ayon whispered, not opening his eyes.

Olbi gasped, blowing his cover. In the soft hues of the moonlight, Ayon's lips stretched into a deviant grin before his eyes fluttered open.

'I can't sleep,' Olbi whispered as Ayon rolled onto his back. 'How are you faring? Are the garjee affecting you?'

'No, but my body aches.'

'It's called walking, it's something you do when you are outside.'

Ayon stifled a laugh and put his hands behind his head, gazing into the night.

'This journey is the first time I've slept beneath the stars. They are beautiful,' Ayon said.

Olbi couldn't help but stare at Ayon's smile. He turned to Olbi.

'What did my mother approach you about before we left Xylona?'

'When?'

'Outside the Stonehall. I saw her touch your face.'

Olbi paused. He wasn't ready to tell Ayon about his mother's request.

'She told me that you are hard to deal with and to try and not murder her only son.'

'I am a delight and you know it.' Ayon smirked.

Olbi pouted. 'Scion, can I ask you something?'

'Please, don't call me that.'

Even in the moonlight, Olbi could see Ayon's eyes roll.

'What does a garjee fruit feel like? Do you feel different, knowing the blood is in your veins?' Olbi asked.

Ayon furrowed his brow and ran his hand through his messy hair. 'The fruits are warm, like they have been in the sun all day, even when they are in a cool dark place,' Ayon said, rolling onto his side to face Olbi. 'As for if I feel the blood, I don't know. I feel and look like everyone else.'

Ayon removed his hand from under his thin travelling cloak and raised it before Olbi. 'Tell me, do I feel different to you?'

For a moment, Olbi was unsure what Ayon was suggesting, but as the Scion continued to hold his hand up it became clear what he was asking. Olbi brought his hand up and slowly pushed his palm against Ayon's.

Ayon's hand was soft, and a sensation of warmth travelled up Olbi's arm and enveloped him. Ayon smiled and intertwined his fingers into Olbi's. The physical link made Olbi breathe in sharply as they held hands for what seemed like a lifetime.

'So, do I feel different?' Ayon asked softly as he broke his hand gently away. Heat rose in Olbi's cheeks as he processed the question.

'Your hands are clammy,' Olbi said, unsure if the warmth in his body was Ayon's blood or something else.

Ayon smirked and rolled back over. Olbi stared at the dancing stars crisscrossing the heavens until sleep took him.

****

'The faster we get going, the faster we are out of these forsaken trees,' Doxxa thundered, waking Olbi. He opened his eyes, expecting it to still be the dead of night. The trees around

him were shrouded in darkness, but above them, wisps of light streaked across the sky.

Olbi propped himself up on his elbow and scanned the clearing. Most of the party had already packed their things, while Joja was brewing the zirge tea for the day. Sloane stood beside her with a cup, waiting like an impatient child. He downed the tea in one long gulp once it was brewed.

'Morning, snore face!' Ayon said, smiling at Olbi.

'I don't snore,' Olbi protested.

'Yes, you do. And you mumble in your sleep. Let me see, something about me?'

Olbi froze as Ayon grinned.

'I think it's sweet that you were dreaming about me,' Ayon said with a wickedness in his eye.

Olbi felt his face go red. 'Shut up!' was all he could say as Ayon continued to smile while rolling up his bed. Olbi strained to remember his dream, but it had faded quickly, vanishing from his memory.

According to Liran's map, they would be out of the trees within a few hours. The Outsiders' tablets were still not working, and Olbi sensed the tension this created amongst them. Sloane was annoyed, his jaw forever tensed, and Joja kept mumbling about access to their health readings. They began their trek only once everyone had drunk their zirge tea. Olbi had refused, but Liran forced Ayon and him to drink.

'Just because you aren't sick doesn't mean you won't develop symptoms later. Now drink, or I'll force it down,' Liran demanded.

Olbi was glad she was here. Besides maybe Joja, Liran was the closest thing he and Ayon had to support. Not that he needed it, but for Ayon's sake, Liran was a comfort in a sea of uncertainty.

They rushed through the forest on well-rested feet. Even Liran moved quickly despite mentioning sore muscles and aching bones. Olbi was glad that Reeva had said nothing since

last night and that she opted to walk behind the group, watching them like a skulking predator.

Ayon, walking beside him, was in a good mood and uncommonly chatty, talking Olbi's ear off. He asked Olbi about the teachers at the school and the forests around Xylona, all things that Ayon had never experienced. Olbi obliged and told him everything he could. He spoke for so long, his mouth went dry and his voice went hoarse. Liran shot smiles at the two of them several times as they journeyed further east. Ayon—oblivious—continued talking, not realising that Olbi was just mumbling answers back.

The party halted by a shallow forest stream for rest in a welcome clearing. The babbling brook was not on Liran's map, but it was more expansive than the stream in Xylona, perhaps even comparable to the Flow.

'No, the Flow is a kilometre wide in parts,' Liran said. 'There would be many streams that pour from uncharted parts into the great river. Imagine what lies beyond the Cayden plateau. There is a whole world out there we know nothing about.'

'Once we are out of this forest and our tablets are working, we could show you just how large Arbonar is,' Zillah said. 'Your world is vast—there are deserts, mountains, canyons and glaciers that dominate the poles.'

Olbi saw the unbridled glee burning in Liran's eyes.

'I'm still surprised that so much of your world is unknown,' Joja said.

With everything that had happened in the last week, Olbi wondered if that was by design.

Olbi continued to glance into the trees that formed endless columns, half expecting to see the Spirits again. Would they be out this far into the wilds, or did they stay close to Xylona? A longing to see the blue woman resurfaced. He felt less safe and didn't know why.

By the clear and pure stream, the party filled up on water while Joja took samples from nearby bushes and tried to scrape the garjee with no luck. Zillah and Reeva had agreed that they would stop for an hour. On this news, Ayon lay down in the grass and was soon dozing.

Olbi did not feel the need for rest and so resolved to explore the stream. He followed the fast-flowing currents downstream armed with his spear, hoping to catch river jacks for dinner. The dry, preserved food was bland, and the bread was stale and almost gone. He skirted each bend expecting to find a pool where fish might shelter, but the stream never sank deeper than his ankle. The torrents splashed around his feet, creating eddies in their swift descent down the slopes.

Olbi continued, spear at the ready, and eventually reached a small rocky outcrop that obstructed the river's flow. As he approached, the sound of rushing water grew louder—a waterfall. Instinctively, he sensed a nearby water hole. Persistent, he scaled the granite rock, ascending into the canopies of the towering garjee. He reached the summit, and a sight left him breathless and unsteady.

Before him lay a cavernous abyss that plunged into an endless darkness, forming a perfectly round void that devoured the surrounding forest, spanning as wide as the Manna Alter. It was unlike anything he had ever witnessed. The stream cascaded into the chasm, throwing up wafts of mist. The hole was like a well built for giants, its depths remaining concealed in obscurity. What captivated him most was the sheer precipice. He could not shake the feeling that this couldn't be a natural occurrence. Could it be proof that the Outsiders were right, was this the work of the Injai? Lost in fascination, he gazed out over the expanse before reluctantly turning away with no river jacks in hand. His companions were likely preparing to depart.

Olbi tore his gaze from the chasm and found himself facing a hanging garjee branch within his reach, and there a golden fruit hung, nestled behind budding leaves. The fruit was suspended like a glistening golden orb, naked yet mystifying.

❖

Its skin gleamed in the low light as if sapping the sun, stealing its warmth and glow.

Olbi's heart raced.

One touch.

A light brush to test himself is all it would take. His father's words spun in his mind. What would it feel like to glide his fingers over its surface? Ayon's warm hands intertwined with his flashed in his thoughts. He yearned for that warmth again. Would there be consequences if he did touch the fruit before him? There was no one around, only him and the gushing stream below. He paused a moment before reaching out his arm.

Olbi's hand trembled as he outstretched his fingers, hovering just above the orb. Its golden surface appeared to pulse with his heartbeat. He was mesmerised, as if in a trance. This was wrong, he should turn and run. Yet his heart told him to stay. Olbi sucked in a deep breath and lowered his hand, touching its hard surface. Olbi felt the smooth, solid skin connecting with his fingertips. The world vanished; he was numb to everything but the fruit.

Olbi waited.

Nothing happened. He placed his whole palm on the fruit and felt a warmth radiate in his palm, his fingers tingled, and his heart pushed against his chest. A sensation ran down his arms like a jolt. He gasped. The fruit was hot to the touch as it began to glow. The golden light was intensifying, its pure white light shone with the intensity of the stars. It pierced the forest with fiery shards illuminating the stalwart trunk that grew the fruit. Olbi shielded his eyes and panicked, letting go of the fruit.

It still clung to the branch, pulsing. The fruit's skin was replaced with a light, swirling like whirlpools. The light gradually dimmed until the fruit appeared as the others in the trees.

Olbi didn't know how long his gaze remained fixed on the fruit. He drew in heavy breaths and raised his open palms to

❖

his face. They trembled and his heart thudded with anxious realisation. His father had spoken the truth: he had Prime blood in his veins. And he was the son of a Remnant.

Suddenly, he laughed. The nervous laughter echoed through the forests, louder than the babbling of the sinkhole behind him.

He scrambled down the rock face, shaking with excitement. He was a Remnant! That's why the forest embraced him, he belonged to the trees, this was his realm.

Olbi felt the weight of expectation on him as he returned to the forest floor. As he lifted his head, ready to trek back along the stream, he was stupefied to see a profile lurking on a nearby sandbank. The woman was staring directly at him. He froze mid-stream, his feet rocking on river pebbles. There was no glow about her, this woman did not belong to the forest.

Zillah stepped forward, her face glowing with astonishment.

'I can see there is more to this fruit than the Rahsu let on,' Zillah said with an inquisitive glint in her eye.

25

LIRAN

Liran's head was spinning. The trees danced and swayed in her vision. Their branches were arms, reaching out to her, pulling her into their deadly embrace. The air was stagnant, musky and fetid. Decomposing leaves clawed at her olfactory. Her tired legs dragged through the dirt, screaming out for rest. How much farther did they have left of walking through this infernal forest? The break by the stream had been hours ago, and as they walked beneath the trees, the garjee grew larger and more looming. The hard ground devoid of grasses sent jolts of pain into her ankles, while the darkness suffocated her. They could only navigate the lengthening shadows by the grace of the Outsiders' torchlight. Liran longed to be out of this endless labyrinth, to feel the sun caress her skin once more.

Paranoia had her in a firm hold; the forest felt like a vacuum sucking away all their vitality. The young men striding in front of Liran resembled ghosts of the abyss. At one-point Olbi turned to look at Ayon, and a torch beam revealed a face drained of colour, hollow and pallid, influenced by the artificial illumination.

Besides the sound of their footsteps, the atmosphere was eerily quiet; nothing lived here where it was deathly and hostile. Still, Liran saw shadows moving in the trees, following and disappearing into the nothingness beyond the torches. For all she knew, it could've been her fancies deluding her into conjuring preternatural phantoms.

'How do we know where we are going?' Liran said, voicing her concern. 'We could be walking in circles. I half expect to see our footprints soon.'

'Just walk,' Reeva uttered from the shadows.

With the tablets being out of commission, they only had Liran's crude maps to go by. Reeva marched on unconcerned, like the rudder of a fishing barge slowly guiding them in the right direction. Or so she hoped.

'We must stop and rest,' Joja called after an hour of silent drudgery.

'I agree. Let's take a few minutes,' Liran said. 'These trees send shivers down my spine. I keep thinking I see flashes of light and figures looming in the dark.'

She half expected Reeva to protest from behind her. Instead, she was met with deafening silence. The others took a seat where they could on the stony forest floor. Liran fumbled for her bladder, searching for salvation in the last trickle of zirge. It was apparent it wouldn't be enough for the return journey. Given their current situation, she doubted it would get her safely out of the forest.

She wanted out. This was Hayda's calling, not hers. Where were her books, wine and comfort foods? Back in Xylona, where she could mull over old texts and maps. How much longer before the gnawing headache ate away the last of her sanity?

'I could climb up and get a look over the canopy to see how far we have to go,' Olbi suggested as if reading her mind. He approached a tree, intending the impossible.

'What are you doing? You want to break your neck?' Ayon's concerned baritone stopped him dead. 'No way. Besides, these trees are too tall; there are no lower limbs to climb up onto.'

Liran regretfully agreed.

'Reeva seems to think we are heading in the right direction. Perhaps she can tell us how far we must go?' said Liran, turning to look behind her. Reeva was nowhere to be seen. Joja's torchlight searched for the Guardian but fell on empty space.

'Reeva!' Liran yelled. They paused in silence, waiting for an answer. There was none.

Zillah strode over, shining her torch into the trees, concern creasing her brow. Nothing but columns of thick tree trunks were revealed by her torch beam.

'Roll call!' Zillah pitched her voice into a deafening blast, doing no favour for Liran's headache. 'Joja!'

'You know I'm here,' Joja announced from next to Zillah.

'Sloane?' Zillah called out next.

'You can't get rid of me that easily, Captain,' the commodore drawled from the gloom.

Liran could see Olbi's and Ayon's faces in the dull light beside her.

'Doxxa?' Zillah continued.

There was no response as Zillah rattled off the soldier's name.

'Doxxa,' Sloane bellowed into the trees several octaves louder than Zillah but, like the captain, he was met with an eerie silence.

Zillah swore under her breath and grabbed a small item from her pocket. She handed it to Ayon. 'Start a fire, will you? We will need the light to find our way back,' she said, unbuckling her backpack.

Ayon stared at the strange gadget with awe before searching the ground.

'Start a fire with what? There is nothing to burn,' Ayon stated bluntly. The forest was void of any substantial undergrowth and the rotted leaves were soggy under their feet.

'Joja, lend them your stove. The flame should provide enough light if you can't find anything to burn. Liran, Olbi, Joja, Sloane, will you join me, please?' Zillah said with urgency, pointing her torch in the direction they had come from. Liran noticed Zillah's firm grasp around her small weapon.

Joja extracted the small stove from her pack and handed it to Ayon, then quickly turned and started heading into the forest the way they had come.

'You can't leave the Scion here alone,' Liran said, trying to keep the desperation out of her voice as she gauged their reactions.

Zillah was creeping forward into the trees, heedless of Liran's plea.

'I will stay with Ayon. I have my spear if there is something foul at play,' Olbi said. There was a confidence in his voice she had never heard before.

Zillah grit her teeth as if to protest, but Olbi's steadfast resolve overruled Zillah's hesitation. Liran turned and wandered with Sloane and Zillah into the darkness, leaving the Scion and Olbi behind them.

Liran felt the sickness leaching out of the trees and seeping into her extremities. Her limbs faltered with a tiredness she had never known before. As if mocking her, a root in the darkness tripped her feet. She softened her fall with her hand and landed on her knees.

'That's fine, I don't need a light!' Liran grumbled from her diminutive position.

'Stick close to me,' Zillah whispered, helping her up.

Sloane continued edging forward, his gun pointed into the void. They tread with caution, minimising all noise as they waited for any sound or sign of Reeva and Doxxa.

It had only been ten minutes since Liran had heard Reeva's coarse mumbling as the Guardian followed on her heels.

'Surely they haven't gone far, that's to say if they were together,' Liran said.

'And you are sure no predator is lurking in these forests?' Joja asked nervously.

Liran mumbled a 'no', though she too was beginning to wonder if something could indeed be hunting them.

Their spotlights moved through the trees erratically. Liran felt dizzy. How much longer would they search for the others before they succumbed to sickness? Zillah's grey face was focused, her eyes trained to the streak of light. Liran looked

❖

down towards the forest floor checking for roots. As Zillah's torch brushed by, Liran spotted something.

'Look,' she said, tapping Zillah on the arm.

The captain spun around, and Liran found herself blinded by the light. She stepped back, her eyes overwhelmed.

'Sorry, what is it?' Zillah said, looking into the trees to the left of them.

'Nothing now except a blinding sensation,' Liran replied. Her eyes began to refocus, but the flash had stung, and her tear ducts were welling. 'Look at the ground.'

Zillah turned her attention to the forest floor and nodded, confirming what Liran had seen.

'Something has been dragged through here,' Liran said, eyeing the disturbed dirt. They could see their footprints from earlier close by.

Sloane noticed they had stopped and were staring at the ground. He ambled closer, hands firm on the trigger of his gun.

'We are being watched,' he announced in a low whisper, staring at the scrapes. Liran registered little in his face as he followed the drag marks, training his gun before him. The drag trail led behind the tangled roots of a nearby tree. Liran and Zillah followed Sloane as he disappeared behind the root.

Liran watched Sloane's cone of light as it scanned the forests. Through blurry eyes, she thought she could see the figure of a person in the trees just beyond the next garjee trunk. She rubbed her eyes and refocused. There was nothing there but a dull blue light that quickly melted into nothing. Her eyes were playing tricks now. *Damn, these trees,* she thought.

'Well, I found Doxxa,' Sloane called out to them, his voice casual, though Liran detected hints of anger.

At this angle, she couldn't see what Sloane's torch was focused on. Joja stayed back as Liran rounded the roots of the garjee, its ribbon-like curves and hollows formed dark cavities in the tree trunk.

Doxxa was there, resting against the trunk in the darkness of one of the hollows. Blood seeped from his neck, and several

slashes on his torso told the story of a bloody and violent end. His face was cold and stared blankly into her eyes, those icy windows haunting her. She shrieked and covered her mouth.

Zillah approached Doxxa's body and with a trembling hand leaned down and closed the soldier's eyes.

'Reeva did this,' Sloane asserted with disgust. His steely eyes met Liran's with a visceral anger, as if she was somehow the enemy.

'We do not know that commodore,' Zillah said, turning to them.

'You are right. It's exactly how I found Sandol,' Sloane spat. 'I think your Prime Scion and his friend have answers.'

'Ayon wouldn't have done this, and Olbi would never—' Liran started.

'Would never what, kill? The boy is carrying a spear, a blade that could slice through a neck and slash us easily in this darkness,' Sloane said, continuing his allegations.

'Olbi and Ayon have been by my side the whole time since we stopped at the stream,' Zillah said.

Liran's muscles relaxed, comforted that the captain was calm and collected. Jumping to conclusions would stir yet more distrust.

Sloane's cold stare shot to Zillah, something in his eyes had snapped. He suddenly pointed his gun at his captain.

'Or perhaps it was you, getting Doxxa out of the picture. Do not think I don't know your game, Morgana,' Sloane seethed as anger akin to Reeva's boiled beneath his skin.

Liran's muscles began tensing with nervous energy, her eyes darted uneasily between Sloane and Zillah.

'What is going on back there?' Joja called from the far side of the tree's expansive base.

'Sloane don't do anything rash,' Zillah said, ignoring Joja's calls. 'You aren't thinking straight. You need to stand down. Now!' On the surface, Zillah's voice seemed firm, but Liran detected a quiver.

'You do not have the authority to command me, Morgana,' Sloane spat.

He was becoming unhinged. Liran wrestled with whether to turn and run back to Olbi and Ayon before events unravelled further.

'I am the captain of this expedition, and Quartab will reprimand you,' Zillah warned him.

Sloane laughed a devilish guffaw, his eyes flickering with a fiery indignation. 'Our equipment isn't working. All I need to do is leave your tablets in this forest and advise QC you went missing, no one would be the wiser.' Sloane's eyes flickered with malice in the unnatural torch light.

'You will be locked out of Unity's systems, Sloane. There will be no way to return to Anatara. Stand down and think straight, Commodore. Why would I kill Doxxa and Idonea?' Zillah asked.

'Doxxa killed Idonea,' Liran whispered loud enough for the captain to hear. Zillah's gaze, now shifted to Liran, was one of incredulity.

'*What?*' Zillah snapped.

With unease, Liran divulged what she had overheard in the garden of Xylona, 'I overheard Sloane talking to someone through your devices. He said Doxxa killed Idonea. I wanted to tell you before but …'

In the torchlight, Zillah's anger contorted her face like a gnarled tree trunk. 'I fucking knew it!' Zillah seethed through gritted teeth. Before Liran blinked, Zillah had a smaller weapon pointed at Sloane. 'Jaree lied its way onto this operation! How many bribes did it take to get you here? What does Jaree want with the Unity mission?' Zillah asked.

'The Unity is lost, Captain. It sinks as we speak. I have the same reading. You are stuck here, admit that to yourself,' Sloane cackled. 'Jaree wants what it is owed. You would build a coalition against us. Well guess what, Morgana: you fucked up.'

Zillah shook her head. 'You idiot, you are trapped here too! Unity is under my command. It is programmed to me.'

Sloane wiped spittle from his chin. 'The Unity's systems can be reconfigured. Quartab will understand that change of command was necessary. Your leadership is over, Morgana!' Sloane said, his fingers flexing on his gun.

Liran took a step backwards. Sloane flinched as if forgetting she was there. His eyes were bloodshot, sweat glistening on his flushed skin.

The trees!

It was the trees—the sickness was affecting them all.

'Please, we must get out of this forest,' Liran begged. 'If we don't, we will all perish.' Liran's shout was filled with dread and urgency.

Zillah began to lower her gun, but Sloane showed no sign of lowering his. The commodore's eyes flared, burning like the radiation seeping into their pores. Sloane's clammy hands fumbled, his grasp on his weapon faltered.

'We can settle this outside of the forest, Sloane. If that is what you want, then so be it,' Zillah said.

Joja approached from behind and joined them from the shadows, her gaze straight away fixed onto Doxxa's corpse. She turned her head from the grizzly sight and closed her eyes with a grimace.

'Damn it, how did he die? Where is Reeva?' Joja exclaimed.

Liran's eyes darted to the forest behind Sloane. Again, she saw shadows moving towards them, her mind was playing tricks on her. Sloane cackled and swayed on his feet like a drunk, leering at them.

'How long have you been planning to pick us off individually?' Sloane asked. 'Doxxa dead … and the snivelling archivist. Afraid Sandol would record your treachery, were you?' Sloane goaded the captain, his voice booming through the forests. Sloane fumbled in his hip pocket of his bag with one hand, the other still on the trigger of his gun, and pulled something out. Liran couldn't see much of the item in the darkness, but what she could make out looked like another of their machines, only this one had a glassy black eye on the front.

'I have Sandol's camera,' Sloane announced, holding it up, 'and once the tech heads at Quartab give me the codes, your gig is up, Morgana. Tarea will have to answer for what you have done.'

Sloane waved the camera around. Zillah stood calmly in the face of accusations.

'I was the one who picked Sandol for the mission, Sloane,' Zillah said. 'He was here to provide transparency should the military contingent of this party try to overthrow a civilian-led mission.'

Liran was confused. Neither Sloane nor Zillah appeared to know who killed this Sandol. She feared that perhaps it was a Rahsu that murdered this Sandol person after all.

Liran was about to step away when she saw shadows approaching. They loomed larger, and then Liran heard movement. Sloane heard it too but turned too slowly. The shadowy form hit Sloane at lightning speed, knocking him down with a crunch. Liran took a step back and tripped on a root. Sloane's weapon was flung into the darkness but not before a barrage of projectiles sprayed from the end of his weapon. The projectiles bounced off the trunks around them. Liran smelt sulphur as she watched Sloane rearm himself and fight with the dark silhouette that had hit him.

Zillah grabbed her firearm and pointed a light at Sloane as he rolled on the ground in a tangled, thrashing fiasco of limbs and bodies with another human-sized form.

It was Reeva.

She had rammed Sloane to the ground, and blood stained her armour as she found her feet and tackled the Outsider again, her blade in one hand. Moving with surprising agility, she thrust the metal towards the man. Sloane growled like a beast and aimed his gun at Reeva, but with a smash of her armour to his arm, Reeva forced Sloane to relinquish his weapon.

Zillah moved silently towards Sloane's gun and seized it.

Recovering his balance, Sloane knocked Reeva to the forest floor with a powerful sweep of his leg.

Liran froze up, she knew she had to run. Yet, like Joja, she couldn't look away from the two warriors tangled in rage before them.

Zillah holstered her firearm and gripped Sloane's larger gun with both her hands.

'I will shoot you both if you do not stop,' she shouted ballistically, her hands trembling.

Liran helplessly watched Sloane wrap his hands around Reeva's neck. She began to wheeze, but she had an arm free and thrust a blade deep into Sloane's knee. Liran heard a crunch. Sloane released his choke grip on the Guardian, growling in agony. Gasping for air, Reeva lashed out again at Sloane.

Just then, the sound of a gunshot tore through Liran's ears; Zillah had fired Sloane's gun, hitting Reeva's leg. The Guardian collapsed mid-run as the blasting sound of the gun reverberated through the trees.

'I will take you both down if I have to,' Zillah said.

Liran regarded Reeva, noting the blood running from the wound where Zillah's bullet had entered, shredding straight through her armour. As for Sloane, blood dribbled down his chin from his lip. The Jareean soldier laughed maniacally, spitting out blood that clung to his teeth.

'You don't have it in you to kill anyone, Morgana,' Sloane garbled coughing up phlegm.

'Try me,' Zillah coaxed, pointing the gun directly at the commodore. 'Move. We will settle this out of the forest.'

Sloane sneered and stood up. Blood soaked his knee. The knife that had done the damage now lay in the dirt by his feet. He glanced at the blade.

'Kick it over,' Zillah said.

Sloane nudged the knife with his foot, and it slid through the dirt.

'Liran, pick it up please,' Zillah ordered.

Liran bent down and picked up the blade covered in Sloane's blood. The soldier was unarmed, and yet he continued to smirk. Zillah didn't react. Instead, she turned to Joja, 'Doctor, restrain Commodore Sloane's wrists.'

Joja looked terrified but removed something from her bag and approached Sloane. He didn't stop smiling as Joja secured a black cord around the commodore's wrists.

Reeva still had her sword but stood fixed to the spot where she had been shot. Sloane flashed her an almost lecherous sneer.

'For a woman, you give it good. Poor Alrin wouldn't have stood a chance going up against you, hey?' Sloane said to the guardian, maintaining the nauseating smirk.

Liran wondered if Sloane smiled because even though Zillah now had the upper hand, the captain was unaware of the coup that was taking place on Anatara.

'Well, after you, Captain. But watch your back, the Rahsu are more dangerous than they look,' Sloane mocked.

Slowly, Reeva and Sloane followed the light beam from the gun Zillah now had in her hands. Liran followed at Zillah's side. Ahead, a glow radiated between the colossal garjee trunks. Olbi and Ayon had managed to light a fire; they scurried towards the beacon.

26

LIRAN

Reaching the fire, Liran beheld the troubled expressions on the boys' faces as the flames cast their wary shadows. They had found a few tufts of grass and had doused one of Olbi's shirts in disinfectant Joja had left with them, which burned long enough to act as a beacon.

'What happened? We heard a woman's scream and loud blasts,' Olbi said as the light of the fire flickered through the garjee.

'Doxxa is dead,' Zillah said, no grief in her delivery.

Joja collapsed by the flames, distressed.

'And them?' Ayon said, his eyes darting to Sloane and Reeva.

'Unhinged and suffering from the sickness of the forest,' Liran jumped in. Reeva gave the Maven a look of disgust. 'I suggest we leave the forest as soon as we can.'

The adrenaline that coursed through Liran's body dissipated, and the throbbing headache returned with a vengeance. She despised these trees and longed for her studio—apris wine was abundant there.

'I agree. But first, I need to treat those wounds,' Joja said, going through her backpack.

Zillah nodded but kept her gun pointed squarely at Sloane.

'I can do that myself, Amira,' Sloane said, grabbing the ointment and bandages from the doctor's hand despite his hands being restrained. He dabbed his knee with the brown liquid and lifted his shirt, smacking the plaster on the stab wound. He then tied a bandage around his knee.

Joja held out a bandage for Reeva, who took it without a word. She wrapped her bullet wound and, with gritted teeth, stood up.

Liran and the dwindling party progressed slowly after leaving Doxxa's body behind. Ayon and Olbi, who still showed no signs of sickness, walked beside her.

'How are you feeling, Maven?' Ayon asked. She could feel warmth in her skin, but her insides were frozen.

'I feel like my energy is being sapped. Like an unseen force is drinking from my spirit,' she replied.

Ayon's face dropped in the torchlight that Zillah had given him. He asked no more questions, instead focusing the torchlight in front of Liran so the ground was visible to them all.

Sloane rasped and stumbled; his body was battered but he pushed on. Even Joja, who had warded off the sickness up to this point, appeared weary. Gone was her chatter and the vigour from her step.

With every stride, Liran's vision blurred. She followed swirls of colour through the trees—blue hazes in the dark. *What was it?*

Fatigue crept up on Liran as more colours flashed in her peripheral vision—blue, green and red swirling with white embers at the fringes of her consciousness—fading into a comforting obliviousness as her eyes slid shut only to moments later flutter wide open from a burning white light that jolted her awake and alert. She peered through a squint to a pleasant revelation about the intense sizzle that almost permanently stunted her vision.

It wasn't torchlight.

Through the trees, Liran felt the warmth of sunlight fighting its way in, beckoning through breaks in the canopy. They were finally leaving the forest. She regained a sense of her surroundings as if breaking from a trance.

Sloane and Reeva were leading up ahead, dragging their feet. Joja and Zillah were behind them, weary and on guard. Olbi and Ayon brought up the rear, still full of vim.

In the sunlight, Liran observed how different Ayon looked. He cocked his eyebrows at her, but she just smiled back. The Scion looked dishevelled.

'What is it?' Ayon said, smiling back awkwardly.

'*You*. Look at you—a real explorer. I told you that one day you would be,' she said.

Ayon beamed, glancing down at his travelling cloak.

Liran laughed. It seemed wrong to laugh right now, but she did anyway. 'The only difference, Ayon, is that I thought you would tell me stories of your journeys as I sat in one of the cloisters,' Liran confessed, 'with cheese and wine in my hand. Never did I think I'd be joining you.'

'I'm glad that you are here, Maven. You were always the better storyteller,' Ayon said.

They weaved their way through the last of the trees. The grasses returned, softening the forest floor, radiating life that dared not delve into the darkness. Without the canopy above, the sun was able to warm their bodies. Liran shielded her eyes, days of darkness had changed their eyes, and the brightness stung her retinas. As Liran passed the last tree, a kaleidoscope of vivid red butterflies fluttered on the precipice of the forest, dazzling her.

'Wow, so beautiful,' Joja said as she was swarmed by them. The doctor began to laugh as Liran stepped into a sea of grasses. Beyond that, her vision remained blurred. She collapsed into the soft grassy bed and wept.

A vast meadow stretched out into the distance. The grasses danced in the wind like ripples in an emerald ocean, the fields alive and vibrant in contrast to the deathly nothingness among the garjee trees. Liran could lie there all day, she wanted nothing more, thankful that the garjee was behind them. She deeply inhaled fresh air into her starved lungs, each breath bringing a cleansing relief to her foggy thoughts. She exhaled, as if the sickness of the forests was being banished.

Olbi and Ayon scouted for water when Liran heard the familiar beeping of the Outsiders' devices. She pricked her ears, straining to listen as Zillah spoke. She was updating their commanders back on Anatara.

'Quartab Command, this is Captain Zillah Morgana of the Unity mission. We are back online after several days of interference caused by—' Zillah paused and spoke a few words to Joja.

Liran sat up and listened. The grasses were long and dense enough that Zillah couldn't see Liran listening in. Zillah cleared her throat and began speaking again.

'A mix of factors, including electrical signatures within the trees and the heavy foliage, cause our technology severe interference. Our tablets cannot connect to the satellites due to the unique nature of the trees' leaves; Dr Amira is therefore seeking answers to the phenomenon by analysing leaf samples collected while in the forest.

'Further, we are now within a few kilometres of the ruins. We expect to be there within an hour. Zillah Morgana ending transmission.'

'Why did you not update QC about Doxxa's death and Sloane's infringements?' Joja asked.

Liran knew why Zillah wouldn't have said anything, she could tell Zillah was a leader who would only play her cards when necessary.

Sloane was the one to respond. 'Because she knows that telling them half her crew are dead will put her leadership into question. Who do you think they will get to replace her?' Sloane cackled to himself. He was sitting on a patch of grass out of Liran's view.

Silence hung awkwardly over them like a shroud until Liran heard Olbi and Ayon yelling in the distance as they ran through the grasses towards the group. Liran lifted herself from her grass nest, leaving an indent of her body in the squashed blades. Ayon and Olbi's excited chatter seized on the spot as they halted before Sloane and Reeva. Liran ambled over towards the panting boys.

'What is it? What did you see? Are we in danger?' Joja asked as Ayon and Olbi caught their breath.

'Waterfalls,' Olbi said.

Ayon cut in, 'Bigger than anything we have ever seen. They plummet off huge cliffs, hundreds of metres tall and as wide as Xylona.'

Liran tried to picture such a scene, but her mind's eye was still unable to picture anything but suffocating forest.

'Then we must be close,' Zillah said, far less excited than Olbi and Ayon. 'From the infrared satellite pictures, that's where the strongest signal came from.'

Liran stared at her, confused.

'You'd know that half of what you say makes zero sense, right?' she said.

Zillah gave a sly smile in a rare glimpse of levity; the flicker in her demeanour lasted but a split second.

'You two, up; we move now,' Zillah commanded Sloane and Reeva. Liran had no idea how things would play out. Did Zillah honestly believe she could constrain them both?

'I am no threat to you,' Reeva stated as she picked herself up from the grass.

'Is that so, Reeva? You did attack one of my crew and are the key suspect as the executioner of the other. Or do you deny it?'

Reeva said nothing, her face blank and cold.

The meadow comforted Liran, embracing her like a long-lost friend, every shade of green sprawled out beneath their feet as the party followed a gentle rise. The fields met the blue sky in the distance, and the buzz of insects flying through the breeze surrounded them.

Liran pulled out the map she had drawn before leaving. It was tattered and smudged with dirt, but she could still see the outlines of features other travellers had mapped out. The maps she had found in the archives had been old and faded with time and neglect. She placed her finger on the etches and ran it across the page, retracing their steps. Xylona, the fields, the garjee and then to the grey haze where a notched line marked the beginning of the Forbidden Zone. The line was immediately next to the forest on her map. She was astonished, this wasn't at all what she imagined.

'Reeva, is this the Forbidden Zone?' Liran said.

Olbi and Ayon glanced over, both wearing curious expressions on their faces. Reeva continued to limp forward, yet the guardian glanced momentarily towards Liran, giving her a skewed half-nod before turning back to the horizon.

'It does not seem dangerous at all. It is quite pretty,' Olbi said, running his hands through the blades of grass. 'Where are the demons?'

'I think someone did not want you to know about your past. I would say this place is as safe as the Rahsu lands,' Joja responded with a glance at Liran.

'Sometimes the past can haunt you,' Liran said. 'Maybe our ancestors thought it would be better for us not to know.'

Reeva paused, readjusting her bandage. 'For once, Maven, you speak more truths than you could know,' she said.

The grass sea continued endlessly towards the horizon, which didn't seem to be getting closer, yet Liran heard roars of churning water. Thunderous movements and rumbles that never subsided.

Liran's legs ached, and her feet were swollen and pushing against her shoes. Despite the soft soil of the meadow, there was no reprieve for her aging body. Beneath her tattered shoes, Hundreds of small white flowers grew in the lush soil, beneath her tattered shoes, and blanketed the meadow in white patches like large snowdrops defying the sun. She leant down and picked one, holding it to her face. The soft, velvety petals glistened in the daylight. In the middle of the flower was a blue disk of seeds.

'I've never seen so many beautiful flowers,' Joja said. She, too, leant down to pick one up to observe before removing a petal and slipping it into her pouch. More tests, Liran assumed.

❧

287

'I have never seen these kinds of flowers. They do not grow in Xylona,' Ayon said.

Liran was silent, staring at the delicate flower between her fingertips. Recognition crept into Liran's memories. Her chest tingled. *It can't be,* she thought. She jerked her focus from the flower bed as tears ran down her face. She brushed quickly through the long rustling grasses and up a hill. As she reached the top, Liran looked out at the grandeur of the Forbidden Zone. What lay ahead of her was not the home of demons and the prison of the dark spirits. Instead, she saw unbridled wilderness and beauty before a vast wall of water stretching for kilometres.

The thundering sound of water boomed across the fields as torrents fell from cliffs, shooting upwards from the ground. They must have been a kilometre high in places. Great clouds of mist rolled out towards them and, somewhere beneath the fog, a river flowed that Liran could see glinting in the sun. Rainbows sprawled across the blue skies, suspended in vivid arcs against the misty shrouds of moisture in the air.

Liran dropped to her knees, the damp soil seeping into her clothes. Tears rolling down her face met the mist that had blown forth from the base of the cliffs.

The others joined her, and Zillah almost dropped her gun away from Sloane and Reeva as they looked at the tremendous arching wall of water. Joja took photographs on her tablet, while Ayon and Olbi sat in the grass admiring the majesty of the falls.

Liran flung the bag off her back and rifled through it for her sketch pad. Zillah glanced over curiously as she flipped the pages.

'There is no time to draw, Liran, as beautiful as the landscape is,' Zillah said.

'No, it's not that, look at this,' Liran replied, flipping through the large pages. She settled on a page and pointed at it. Zillah's gaze broadened.

'I thought you had never been here. Isn't this your Forbidden Zone?' Zillah said.

Tears streamed down Liran's face, tears of happiness. Liran looked down at the drawing. It was a copy of a painting, almost remembering every scratch of pencil and smudge of charcoal on the paper. She stared at the young girl in the meadow, with her sad smile and the waterfalls in the distance. Liran lowered the paper and watched those same waterfalls gushing before her. The girl, *she* had been here.

Reeva picked herself up from the grass, glancing wearily at Zillah's gun. Her eyes wandered to the page in Liran's hands. Before Liran could react, Reeva tore the sketch from her hands. Zillah lifted her weapon, but Reeva paid her no mind, scanning the sketch with intense focus.

'*Where* did you get this?' Reeva demanded.

'I drew it. Copied it from an old painting I found in a warehouse on the docks of Hydoran,' Liran said.

Reeva appeared flummoxed. Liran felt the woman searching her eyes, somehow the picture inflicted Reeva with sorrow and anguish, warping her hard features. The sketch slowly slipped from Reeva's grasp and glided in the wind, landing in the grass by Olbi.

He picked up the sketch and walked to Liran, who couldn't take her eyes off Reeva. Why was the stony woman suddenly so emotional? Olbi read out the tiny scribble of script at the bottom of the sketch that Liran had also copied.

'A new future born of love,' he said, handing it back to Liran. 'What does that mean?'

Liran had never known the meaning behind those words but as Reeva shed a tear, Liran expected that somehow Reeva knew.

27

ZILLAH

Within minutes, mist had penetrated Zillah's clothes, and cool droplets of water clung to the grime and dirt on her face as the crew descended the rolling meadows to the foot of the cliffs.

This planet is too fucking wet, Zillah thought.

'How do you suppose we get over them, Captain?' Joja said, studying her tablet. 'The cliffs span fifteen kilometres in either direction, it's one giant plateau. Then there is the river at the base of the cliffs. By my account it will be too wide and dangerous to cross.' Joja's voice was almost lost, drowned out by the angry water ahead that crashed into the rocks.

Zillah scanned her tablet. Joja was correct. There appeared to be no breaks in the cliffs, and their destination, according to the map, was a few hundred metres past the ridge. She glanced up at the torrents above them. Ledges covered by green grasses and small shrubs dotted its face, wherever the water did not fall. Thick vines hung from some of the ledges, draped across hard grey rock like idle lengths of rope.

'Do we climb?' Olbi asked, craning his neck to scan the impermeable wall.

Zillah felt twinges of frustration, there had to be a way around the cliffs. She glanced at Liran, who was looking at the cliffs knowingly and smiling.

'Do you know the way up, Liran?'

Liran slowly turned, still smiling. 'Not up, but I have a feeling we won't need to,' Liran said, raising her arm and pointing to a spot along the cliffs. The river churned ahead of them, violently bubbling. Though it was largely shrouded by fog, Zillah could make out a bridge of white stone, the same stone as that used for the buildings in Xylona. It commanded the river, unmoved by the tumultuous water that flowed beneath it. What lay beyond that was hidden, shrouded by thick whirling mist clouds that moved and stirred with restless energy.

'We should cross the bridge. I think there is a chance we won't need to climb,' Liran said.

Zillah hoped she was right. There was no way that Reeva and Sloane, tied up and with their injuries, could climb, and as for Liran and herself, they weren't exactly in their prime.

They began their scramble down the hill towards the river. The grass was damp and thick, licking their wet legs and boggy shoes. Joja slid in the mud ahead of Zillah, scraping several metres down the bank towards the furious river.

A narrow slate path appeared that snaked along the river's banks in both directions. The party fought muddy footings on their way forward, descending the final slope onto the path, and found themselves within metres of the river. It resembled a cauldron of boiling water—no section was still, and the churning forces would carry even the best swimmer to their demise beneath the falls, where they would be torn apart.

Zillah's eyes stung despite her attempts to keep water out of them. Ahead, Joja's mouth moved. She was clearly speaking, but no sounds besides the rushing torrent reached Zillah. The waterfalls deafened them to all other sounds.

They walked to the foot of the bridge; its glossy stone became more apparent and brighter as they approached. Zillah's eyes were only half open, but she could see the bridge had been crafted from a single rock. If she hadn't seen the ornate curves of the stone and the parapets lining the span, she would have assumed it had been carved by the force of the water beneath it.

The bridge was more expansive than she had expected— wide enough for vehicles, it spanned the width of twenty men. The stone was rippled beneath their feet. Zillah bent down and ran her hand along the ribbing. *Traction for the wet environment*, she thought.

Sloane and Reeva crossed first, guided by the point of Zillah's gun. The three Rahsu followed Zillah and Joja, all drenched by the whirling rain. They were walking into an unknown, blind faith pushing them forward into the swathes of endless mist and gushing water.

Zillah propelled herself through the spray, the others appearing as shadows in the mist behind and ahead of her. She strained to keep an eye on Sloane. When she drew level with the walls of water on either side of the bridge, her ears ached from the booming onslaught, the sheer immensity of the water falling beside her was intimidating. Thankfully the gushing water did not fall onto the bridge, the narrow path through the falls appeared to be the only way forward. This had to be the right way.

The bridge opened to an oval clearing where moss grew between grey stones lining the ground. The stone glistened, continuously wet from the spray of the waterfall. A hundred metres in front of them, the cliff face dominated, looming and imposing.

The towering rock face loomed above them, and Zillah felt a creeping sense of dread. They were insignificant beneath its weight, staring up at what seemed an impassable wall. The path to their destination lay just beyond, yet all she saw was stone, cold and unyielding. It made no sense—this place was man-made, yet nothing suggested a way through. Had they been wrong all along? Time may have eroded whatever had once been here, leaving them stranded. What if they found nothing? After all their effort, no tangible proof of the Injai besides a fallen communication tower decaying into the soil. The thought gnawed at her, and for a moment, it felt like a dead end. But then, through the thinning mist, an archway emerged at the far edge of the clearing. Relief swept over Zillah as the tunnel came into view, its once-small opening expanding as they drew closer, until it towered above them, offering hope once more.

'You could fly the Unity through here,' Joja said from beside Zillah. She was drenched head to toe, her dripping dreadlocks pooling water at her feet.

❖

Zillah turned back towards the bridge. It had disappeared, consumed by mist. They were now on the other side of the waterfall, hidden from the world, whoever had built this place wanted it to remain hidden.

The cave delved deep into the ancient rocks, with a mouth that sought to swallow them whole. Zillah would, without a doubt, pick this rocky maze over the forest every time. In fact, it gave her a brief sense of familiarity. Quartab Command was a series of tunnels beneath Anatara's moon's surface, and they had spent three months before their departure wandering the labyrinth.

'What exactly do you expect we will find in here?' Ayon asked as they studied the mouth of the tunnel. Warm air from within blasted Zillah's face like the breath of a snarling beast.

'Answers. More questions. Proof of our connection,' Zillah said, looking down the tunnel, the darkness swallowing their torchlight.

'There are a lot of dark places in your world,' Joja said.

'You will find dark places on Anatara too, Doctor,' Sloane rebuffed.

Zillah spied Sloane grimacing under his breath. His wounds may have stopped bleeding, but the pain clearly lingered.

Good.

Reeva, on the other hand, appeared sullen. The bullet must still be in her leg. Yet the woman showed no signs that it caused her grief besides a slight limp as she led them down into the depths.

Zillah welcomed the warm, dry air with each step taking her further from the roars of the waterfall behind them. There was a sudden flash and deep hums behind them, and they all froze as lights appeared along the top of the arched passage. The lights sprung to life, illuminating the cave at even intervals, the pattern continuing deep into the murk. They had awoken the cave; Zillah knew the sleeping truth of Arbonar was within her grasp.

❖

The walls were clad in metal panels, rusted and peeling at the edges, that warped outwards. Long spindly mushrooms, with putrid yellow powder on their heads, grew in the gaps between panels, as did thick vivid green moss that clung to the wall. The deeper they walked, however, the conditions improved until the passage appeared newly built.

'The tunnel is curved,' Ayon said, looking behind them. Olbi seemed entranced as he ran his hands along the walls. Zillah glanced over her shoulder. The tunnel entrance was no longer visible, and the bombarding waterfall now echoed as a distant rumble.

'Is it Injai?' Liran asked, looking up at the lights.

'Yes, I think so,' Zillah responded. 'Unless the Rahsu built it.'

'It is remarkably well preserved,' Joja said. 'No Injai ruins on Anatara still have functioning electrical systems, although that may be a blessing as well as a curse.'

Ahead of them, the tunnel opened like a funnel. They were moving into a space that defied the notion they were underground. The passage ended and opened into a large cavern, large enough for the entire network of Quartab Command to fit into twice over.

'Whoa,' Ayon exclaimed.

The ceiling loomed above, where lighting strips illuminated the cavern. Despite its grand size, it was barren. An oversized metal door was built into the stone at the far side of the immense cavern.

'This is it; this is the door to the facility. Doctor, get as much footage as you can,' Zillah said.

She had access to Alrin Sandol's camera if needed, but there may be evidence about Alrin's death she didn't want to risk erasing. Despite her prowess with most technology, she also didn't want to admit she had no idea how this type of camera worked. Joja complied and started taking photos with her tablet, while Liran had her sketch pad out, scribbling in charcoal as she took in the surroundings.

❁

After years of research and travelling, they were finally on the doorstep of their ancestors. Zillah felt insignificant as she crossed the cavern, heading for the door.

Zillah soon stood in front of the doors; an entrance so large it would take a monstrous amount of energy to open. There was a small panel on the right-hand side, but apart from that, nothing adorned the rock face.

'These are some serious doors, Captain. If the power isn't on, I do not see another way in,' Joja said.

Zillah bit her lip. Would this trip come undone because there was no way into the facility? She walked to the panel—the flat surface glistened like onyx, and its texture looked like a cross between glass and marble. Zillah still had Sloane's gun in her hand and didn't want to turn her back on him.

'See if it's working, Doctor,' Zillah said, gesturing to the panel.

Joja approached, studying the smooth surface of the panel before reaching out and lightly touching the glass. Ripples radiated from where her hand had made contact. She jerked her hand away and gasped, the waves ran to the edges of the glass, consuming the entire panel until the silky onyx lit up.

Zillah's chest leapt. The Injai facility was still very much alive. Beside her, Liran gasped.

The panel displayed a handprint, surrounded by a myriad of holographic lines and symbols that she could not understand.

Joja spun, astonishment glinting in her eyes while a smile etched wider onto her childlike face.

Somewhere within the panel, a voice spoke, sending shivers down Zillah's spine.

'Authorisation required,' a female synthetic voice said.

'The Spirits speak,' Ayon whispered. The Rahsu searched for the voice's keeper, yet no one appeared.

'No one is there, it's a machine,' Zillah said. 'Go ahead, Doctor. Place your hand on the handprint.'

'What if it's rigged with a defence mechanism?' Joja said as a glaze of trepidation appeared on her brow.

Reeva gave a barely discernible smirk.

Joja raised her hand slowly towards the panel, her fingers outstretched to match the image on the screen. As her palm connected with it, she closed her eyes, a wrinkle forming between her brows as she concentrated on the task before her.

The holograms and graphics changed and whirled around the screen. 'Access denied,' the panel said bluntly. The handprint glowed, striking tones of yellow at the edges before returning to a static blue tinge.

'Should we all give it a go?' Joja said, stepping away from the panel.

Zillah studied the faces of those around her. The Rahsu wore dumbfounded expressions. Liran was sketching the panel, her face alive as her charcoal flitted across the parchment. Reeva glared at Zillah. A flicker of hesitation appeared on the Guardian's face before a cold defiance returned.

'You, Reeva. Put your hand on the panel. You know about this place, do you not? Somehow you knew of Anatara. What else are you hiding from us?' Zillah said. She was careful not to raise her gun in Reeva's direction. Reeva did not move.

'I said put—'

'You do not command me,' Reeva snapped, her smirk disintegrating and turning vile. Hatred burned in her eyes.

Zillah's chest tightened—she raised her gun at the guardian as Sloane moved out of the way.

'You know I will shoot you, Reeva. I have every right. Do not make me ask again.'

'You cannot harm me Anatrian,' Reeva spat.

Zillah stood her ground, her feet planted on the hard stone. She had come too far to fail now. Her mission was to prove that Arbonar and Anatara had a shared history, and the success of the mission, she knew, lay behind those doors.

❖

Liran stopped sketching as the standoff boiled. Reeva glowered before irritation took over her, marching to the panel and placing her palm on the handprint. Again, the holograms danced around, only this time glowing purple.

'Access granted. Welcome, Third Officer Adela,' the synthetic voice said in monotonous apathy.

As the panel spoke, a crack appeared down the middle of the door, serrated like a knife. The two halves moved away from each other and beyond, lights flickered on, revealing more grey and dark halls.

'Adela?' Liran said.

'Who is Adela? Why did it call you that?' Ayon demanded.

Reeva turned from the panel, all eyes on her.

Who is she? Zillah thought, holding her gun up. Not for protection, but because she was unsure what to do. Reeva was staring directly into her eyes.

'You have been granted access. I suggest you act on it,' Reeva said, turning towards the doorway. She walked gracefully, the bullet in her leg appearing to no longer be a hindrance.

'Who are you?' Olbi said, his voice croaked yet it echoed around the cavern.

Reeva stared at him through narrowed eyes. 'I could ask you the same thing, son of Tarak,' Reeva responded.

Zillah hadn't forgotten what she witnessed in the forests with the fruit.

Olbi's face glistened with dread, but Joja interrupted, her voice only marginally louder than a whisper.

'It is obvious, is it not? She is Injai.'

28

OLBI

More darkness. More dim light struggling to brighten the next room.

Olbi cautiously followed Reeva—or the woman the voice within the door called *Adela*. Ayon had the same look of confusion on his face, was Joja right? Was Reeva *Injai*? How could that be?

Reeva was Rahsu, a part of the fabric of Xylona for as long as he could remember. He never gave her much thought, but now every fibre of his mind reached for memories of her. As Guardian of the Primes, she was afforded a comfortable residence in the Prime House, but before that, where had she come from? Did she have a family? Reeva had ignored him for most of his life, their exchanges had been brief until recently. In the last week her demeanour had been nothing short of hostile. Did Reeva know his secret, who he was and the blood that flowed through his veins? He shuddered, nervous that those around him could sense his Prime blood.

Beyond the door was another extended corridor that sloped downward into depths unseen. Olbi wondered how much rock was compressed above them. He felt as though the walls were constricting. Liran quickened her steps to meet him and Ayon as they walked down into the stone-lined tunnel. Again, lights appeared along the curved ceiling.

Olbi glanced at the Maven, while she gaped at Reeva's back, a searching stare.

'Do you think Reeva is Injai?' Olbi whispered.

A shadow of concern flickered on Liran's face beneath the harsh artificial light.

'It makes a lot of sense,' Liran said. 'I can safely surmise Reeva knew about the Outsiders before they arrived, and she has been feeding a narrative to the Prime One. For what

purpose, though, I do not know. I fear the Rahsu are being played, and I sense turmoil ahead.'

Olbi gripped his spear more tightly.

'Does she have any family?' Olbi asked. 'What of her parents?'

'No,' Ayon whispered, 'she once told me she came to Xylona from the Granite Hills. This was before I was born, when my mother first became the Prime.'

'I am ashamed to admit that before I became Maven, I thought nothing of her. As time went by, I realised the unnatural hold she had on your family, Ayon,' Liran said, talking softer so Reeva and the Outsiders couldn't overhear.

'For as long as I can remember, Reeva has been a part of the family,' Ayon said. 'There were times my mother and Reeva were at odds … it was worse after my brother died in childbirth. Since then, Reeva has overseen every aspect of my life—she was my teacher, my shadow …'

The Scion stopped talking. Ahead, the path forked off in three directions—each passage lit by different coloured lights along the ceiling.

'Which way, Injai?' Sloane mouthed through harsh rasps, his chest heaving as dark blood welled beneath his bandages and soaked his clothes.

Reeva turned to face them, and Olbi watched the Guardian transform into a metal-sheathed creature as green, red and purple lights from three intersecting corridors danced across her face, hitting her mocking grin at odd and jagged angels.

'Now is not the time for silence, Reeva. Speak!' Zillah's demands echoed down the passages.

The Guardian resentfully clenched her knuckles into fists. 'For your power source, to the right. The left will take you to the living quarters—there is nothing of value to you there.'

'And straight ahead?' Zillah added when it was clear that Reeva had stalled.

'Operations,' Reeva finally mumbled with reluctance. 'There is nothing for you there either.' She took a step forward, prompting Olbi to move closer to Ayon. Whoever—or whatever—this creature had been to the Primes; it was as clear as daybreak to Olbi that he was Ayon's only genuine Guardian now.

'What is this place? How can you be an Injai? They died out sixteen hundred years ago,' Joja remarked.

Reeva smiled. Though her voice had lost its malice, she was still clearly mocking them. 'This place is beyond your comprehension, and I will not allow anyone to jeopardise its operations,' she bluntly stated.

'So it's functioning and not a ruin at all.' The doctor's eyes filled with wonder as she worked out pieces of the puzzle in her mind.

'Grab your power source and leave this world while you still have a chance,' Reeva said.

'What good will that do? We will be back. Our worlds belong together—we mean you no harm,' Zillah said, lowering Sloane's gun and inching towards Reeva. 'If you truly are Injai, then we are family. Think of what we could learn from this place, what potential both Anatara and Arbonar could benefit from and share.'

Reeva's smile turned into a snarl. 'Admirable, but not all of you share in that promise of a brighter future,' she said. 'You speak of friendship yet friends you are not. The Rahsu have lived for millennia in peace, thriving, hidden away from the rest of the empire that collapsed. I will not let that carnage return to Arbonar.'

'That is not true Reeva,' Liran interjected. 'The Rahsu have not lived in peace. History is riddled with tales of deceit and power struggles.'

'Petty squabbles, Maven,' Reeva said dismissively. 'Anatara would bring annihilation to everything you hold dear.'

Reeva's eyes fell on Olbi briefly before settling on Ayon. Her lips parted but Olbi cut in. 'How is it that you are still alive?'

Reeva's eyes appeared purple in the pulsating lights. Eyes he had seen for years, but now they felt different. Olbi detected sadness leaching from her eyes as if cracks were appearing in her defensive charade.

'It's the garjee fruit, isn't it?' Joja asked. 'That's what's keeping you alive. It's not for the Spirits—it's all to keep this facility functioning.'

'What are you saying?' Olbi blurted. Ayon stepped around Olbi and confronted Reeva.

'What is going on, Reeva? Tell me, now! What lies have you been telling me?' Ayon asked softly.

Joja flipped her tablet allowing Olbi to see an image of a garjee fruit.

'These fruits,' Joja said, pointing to the image, 'there is a reason they aren't consumed: it's because they aren't real fruit. They are batteries. Highly concentrated energy sources, powerful enough to sustain the Unity for a month.'

Olbi witnessed a glint in Zillah's eyes as she looked upon the fruit—she knew his secret. But even Olbi didn't understand what Joja meant.

'Amira, we would have detected a power source so abundant, long before arriving,' Zillah glared at Reeva. 'Is this true? Is it the fruit keeping this facility alive?'

Reeva flared her nostrils as she leaned tiredly against the wall, steadying herself as blood trickled down her leg.

'I have done what is best for the Rahsu, guided you through the darkness. Arbonar became the shining beacon of what life should be,' Reeva said through teeth caked in blood. She stumbled forward towards Ayon. Olbi pulled the Scion back. Reeva laughed to herself, spitting blood onto the stone. 'To think that the Rahsu have been safe for hundreds of years and within days, the future is threatened. Did I not warn you Liran?' Liran inhaled, but before she could reply, Reeva was speaking again. 'I have protected this world from the evils out there—the Anatrians will destroy what has been created. A haven for life, away from the chaos of the Injai, away from the wars and toxic seed that runs deep in your species. You destroy, whereas I have created.'

Gone was Reeva's malice, she appeared defeated—a gallant soldier falling on her sword, resigned to the fact she had fought her final battle.

'Reeva, we are not evil. That notion is based on false assumptions,' Zillah started.

'You do not know your own past, Captain,' Reeva said. 'The scourge of treachery runs deep in your veins. Your ancestors have bred you in their likeness. When your machines appeared in the skies to watch us, I knew it was only a matter of time before you would spread your disease to Arbonar.'

'Our satellites?' Joja asked.

Reeva nodded. 'Yes. Your desire to pollute the universe means you will never understand us. We nurture our surroundings; we care for it. That is why I strived to destroy as many of your satellites as I could, to stop you from learning about the verdant paradise here.'

Joja's eyes lit up. She scanned the hallways, her mouth agape.

'Reeva'—Joja stepped forward and looked around at the Injai halls—'this place is your home, isn't it?'

Reeva's spirit wavered into sadness as she gazed at them all.

'A very long time ago—when I was but a young child—these halls were the home of people fleeing the empire, the home of a people that realised the truths of what was happening to them.'

Olbi could not believe how human and vulnerable Reeva had become. 'Reeva, do the Anatrians speak true? Are we all connected?' he asked.

'The Anatrians are not to be trusted. Your days are numbered.' Reeva slicked back her grey hair.

'Why should we trust you, Reeva?' Ayon growled. 'You are the one we cannot trust!' Ayon looked ready to lunge at Reeva in a fit of anger, but Olbi held him back.

✦

Reeva smiled as Ayon struggled in Olbi's firm grip.

'Good, Ayon. Do you hate me?' Reeva said, smiling as Ayon struggled in Olbi's firm grip. 'Use that anger to defeat the Anatrians.'

Before Ayon could react, Olbi's attention snapped to a sudden movement beside him.

Sloane, fuelled by adrenaline and perhaps desperation, charged at Zillah with a ferocity that even his injuries could not suppress. He had worked his hands free from his restraints. Joja registered the danger, but her reaction lagged. Zillah's body collided with the unforgiving concrete floor of the tunnels, a cry of pain escaping her lips.

In a heartbeat, Olbi reacted, thrusting his spear towards Sloane, but the man was too quick. With a swift motion, Sloane wrestled the gun from Zillah's grasp, his fiery gaze fixated on her with an intensity that sent shivers down Olbi's spine. Sloane's fingers found their place on the trigger. Zillah's eyes widened in fear, her attempts to rise hampered by her injuries.

Sloane's disposition was of a man unhinged; a maniacal grin appeared as he pointed his gun at Zillah's head.

'Please, stop this!' Ayon yelled.

Sloane snapped around and pointed the gun at the Scion.

'This doesn't concern you. But I will kill you, do not think I won't,' Sloane spat.

Olbi thrust himself in between Ayon and Sloane, his spear jutting towards the soldier's neck.

'Lower your weapon!' Olbi roared.

Sloane lunged at Olbi, swatting away the spear, but Olbi was quicker. Repositioning himself, Olbi found Sloane's weak spot, thrusting the spear into the Outsider's already wounded knee. The man collapsed as Reeva, sensing an opportunity grabbed at Sloane's weapon. But she wasn't strong enough and Sloane fought off her attempts and spun around to face the Injai.

Just as chaos threatened to consume them, Olbi felt a strong tug on his arm. Liran tried to pull him towards the shadows of the tunnel bathed with an eerie green glow. Ayon was already sprinting ahead.

'Olbi, hurry! We must escape,' Liran pleaded.
Olbi heeded the Maven and pulled backwards. His heart pounded as Sloane's gun swung with deadly intent, and its barrel returned to Zillah's temple. Would Sloane dare pull the trigger? Ayon's and Liran's frantic footsteps echoed down the tunnel, their figures blurred as time slowed to a torturous crawl.

Olbi's gaze flickered between the impending horror behind him and the fleeing shadows ahead.

Joja's desperate cries pierced the air, a futile attempt to reason with Sloane. 'Gideon, stop!' she screamed, her voice thick with terror.

Sloane was not listening. Then, without warning, he whirled around, unleashing a barrage of gunfire. Reeva's lifeless form crumpled to the ground, etching itself into Olbi's mind as he fled, following Ayon and Liran deeper into the tunnels.

❖

29

OLBI

'Keep running, Olbi! Don't stop,' Liran shouted as she ran, appearing to Olbi as a distant silhouette—a shadow moving through ghostly hazes of an ancient world that was grinding back to life. Ahead, more tunnels beckoned him onwards. At times, they were met with dead ends, but as Olbi and Ayon approached, the walls moved, and they opened into rooms filled with treasures and contraptions Olbi had no understanding of nor could even begin to fathom their purpose.

One room contained crates and stacked coloured boxes with strange words and symbols, the next had giant black cubes hanging from its ceiling and giant clear tubes on its far wall. Further along the corridor was a white walled chamber with three odd white pods protruding from the floor, while another space housed thousands of books which turned Liran's neck so quickly Olbi thought he heard a snap. They turned several times, pivoting left, right, straight ahead. In the confusion and adrenaline, Olbi struggled to track their movements—finding their way back would be near impossible—he was lost in a subterranean maze. Meanwhile, the echoes of gunshots rang and pounded his eardrums.

The tunnels all looked the same to Olbi. There was no way to differentiate them unlike the trees he was used to. They had personalities, this place was soulless. They turned into a narrow passage lined with coloured tubes and wires. They darted right and followed a hallway to a single door. Like the other doors, when Ayon approached, it opened. Liran—clutching at her side—followed the Scion into the room as the door began to close on its own. Olbi ran through just in time before the metal barrier shut behind him.

'It's a dead end,' Ayon said as Olbi smacked into Liran's back. She stumbled but was quickly able to steady herself.

Ayon was right—the room was a small, dimly lit circular chamber. As Olbi caught his breath, they listened for footsteps chasing after them. None could be heard in the lonely tunnels.

'I hope Joja and Zillah are okay,' Ayon said. Ayon's concern was lit upon his face in the dim purple glow.

'Never mind that now, we need to find a way to get Ayon out of here and back to Xylona,' Liran said.

'What about you?' Olbi asked, but the look of resolve on Liran's face said it all.

'I will stay here,' she said, scanning their surroundings.

Olbi's vision steadily adjusted to the low light. The same tubes and wires they had seen in the halls circled the entire room near the ceiling. Several pipes shot downwards to the floor and converged at a central pylon—covered in holograms and glyphs—under a metal grating.

'What is this place?' Ayon asked, scanning the room.

'I don't know,' Liran said, her brow furrowed. 'There are lifetimes of wonders we have passed to study and learn from. We have barely scratched the surface of what this place is and what it means for the Rahsu ...' She trailed off, her eyes squarely fixed on the column in the centre. She stepped forward, observing the dancing words that floated near its surface, slowly rotating around it like orbiting moons.

'I recognise some of these symbols,' Ayon said. He pointed to one of the images.

'How? Where have you seen it before?' Olbi asked. The images were foreign to him.

'The holy texts in the sanctum and on the altar.' Ayon raised his hand towards one of the images. 'My mother told me that this symbol initiates the offerings. It's within the handprint on the altar, the symbol of the Spirits.'

Olbi tried to study the images, though they mostly mesmerised him. Liran pulled out some parchment and busily sketched the column into her pages making use of what little

light she had. Ayon walked around the room, his eyes rarely straying from the pedestal, such was its allure.

Olbi was drawn to the pedestal too, transfixed as if pulled towards the otherworldly glow. He had never seen something so foreign and so beautiful.

Olbi stepped closer, holding out his hand. The images shone brighter, slowing their movement around the column. He focused on the images and symbols. How could all this be on Arbonar? Were the Outsiders right all along? They were all connected to forgotten people who spanned worlds. Reeva was one of them, she had been using them for power, for her own survival. But was there something more? So many questions were still unanswered. He distrusted Reeva but felt as though her death had closed a book that they would never finish.

The lights had an allure like that of a drug—he wanted to know what the images felt like. Would they react to his Prime blood? Blood that no one else knew he had. He stepped closer again, more cautiously. The lights shimmered, and new ones formed in the air before his eyes. The symbols reacted to his movement much like the door panel had for Joja. His fingers inched closer to touch the lights. A surge of warmth jolted across his fingertips, where they passed through the light. The column lit up, filling the room with a kaleidoscope of dazzling colours. Liran and Ayon's gasps felt distant as the brightness moved down Olbi's arm, swallowing him, becoming a thin fabric sleeve that warmed his skin. Olbi stared at his arm and held it up to his face. It was lit up in a vivid array of dancing white sparks of pristine light.

'Olbi, step back! What have you done?' Liran's voice was fading. There was alarm in her eyes. Olbi turned to her as the light moved over his chest and towards his neck.

Ayon rushed over, dread filling his face.

The warm, tingling light reached Olbi's lips. His nose. As it reached his eyes, he closed them. The sensation blanketed his entire body. He felt weightless as if he was floating in a river. He opened his eyes again.

Liran and Ayon were gone.

Olbi couldn't move his body—he felt nothing—unsure he even had a body anymore.

Am I dead?

White nothingness consumed him. Olbi screamed, but no sound came, he could hear nothing, feel nothing. It grew too bright, burning his eyes. Olbi closed them tightly, but his eyelids offered little help as the brightness engulfed everything.

****

When Olbi came to, he had no idea how much time had passed. Minutes? Hours? He had no way of knowing. Olbi opened his eyes. The whiteness had vanished and been replaced by a void of darkness.

'He wakes,' a woman's voice said.

'Good. Get in there and ensure everything is recorded. We may only have a few moments,' another voice said. It sounded like a man, but Olbi hadn't heard the accent before.

Olbi tried to steady himself, convincing his mind that something was distorting the voices of Liran and Ayon. The darkness softened, and faint shadows began to take shape— like the ones he'd glimpsed on moonlit nights in the forest— silhouettes slowly materialising before him.

'Ayon?' Olbi called. He couldn't hear his own voice— maybe he hadn't said anything and that's why Ayon and Liran weren't answering him. The shadows shuffled around him.

He tried moving but felt numb, though a tingle started in his feet and hands. He wasn't sure if he was lying down.

Soon, he could move his hands, though he couldn't feel anything around him except the tingling that remained. He shifted his legs and tried to stand. It soon felt as if his entire body had pins and needles. He looked down and discerned colour for the first time.

His body shimmered in the dimness. What was happening? Panic grew inside him.

'Are we ready?' the man said.

A different voice answered—a woman, but her voice was soft and ethereal.

'Remember, he will be anxious and alarmed. His society is still developing. We must not scare him,' she said.

The figures approached through the blur. More colour filtered into his retinas, and suddenly, a face materialised.

'Hello, Olbi.' A woman's face appeared in the blur. She was smiling. Her lips, full and pink, came into focus first, followed by eyes that sparkled with boundless joy. They seemed old on her young face. She looked familiar to Olbi, though they had never met.

Olbi blinked, feeling tingles in his face. Where was Ayon and Liran? Had the light also consumed them? Olbi dreaded what the column had done to him. He couldn't feel the air on his skin, only pins and needles. Olbi broke his gaze from the woman and raised his arms.

His hands were transparent, made of light. Olbi gasped. No sound passed his lips. He moved his fingers; the edges of each finger were blurred a hazy blue. Blue that he recognised. His mouth gaped as he looked back at the woman.

She took a step towards him. She had a slim neck and wore a clean-cut white top that clung to her body.

Olbi took in his surroundings. A circular room came into focus, but this one differed from the chamber he had been in moments ago. There was no pedestal, no tubes, no wires. The room was lined by reflective glass. His reflection stared back at him, his face contorting as he screamed in terror. He was a blue figure, standing on a raised platform, surrounded by his reflections.

'I know how you are feeling, Olbi. You mustn't be frightened,' the woman said softly. 'It is a strange sensation, the first time you holoport, but trust me, you are quite safe. And so is your body back on Arbonar.'

Safe? He didn't feel safe. Who were these people, and how did she know his name? He opened his mouth to speak, but he had no idea what to say, so he closed it again.

The woman smiled and regarded him under long eyelashes. 'Unfortunately, we cannot hear you if you were to speak, my child—one of the limitations of this technology. Hence, I could not communicate with you the first time we met in that forest. Olbi felt his heartbeat—or a rush where his heart should have been.

It dawned on him; he had seen the woman before. She was one of the blue Spirits in the forest, the one that showed him Alrin Sandol's grave, the one that watched as he buried Boji.

'You have questions, and so do we,' she said. The woman spun around and nodded to the mirrors behind her. 'Listen carefully because we need your help. You and your people are vitally important to the future of us all.' As she spoke, the mirror behind her shimmered, warping and rippling. For a moment, Olbi saw his reflection distorted, twisting and stretching. Then, one more figure appeared through the reflection of his awed face, wearing the same clothing as the woman.

'In your veins runs a gene we believed long gone,' the woman said.

A man stepped forward now, piercing Olbi with blue eyes. Olbi recognised him too—the first Spirit he had seen in the forests stood before him. He looked older, white hair sitting wiry on his chin.

'Long ago,' he said, 'our society collapsed, torn apart by … differences. We can no longer travel to the stars as we once did. You have that ability, in your blood. You and your people have the power to reunite the worlds and bring the Injai back.' His voice echoed around the chamber.

Olbi stared at them, taking the words in. Confusion coursed through his head. How could he bring back the Injai?

❈

310

The woman stepped forward. 'It is paramount you do not trust the one you call Reeva,' she said, her eyes pleading with his as she weaved her hands together as if in prayer.

Olbi's eyes flickered back to her when he heard Reeva's name. The image of her body dropping to the floor was fresh in his mind.

'She has manipulated your world for her benefit and killed many to achieve her goals,' she continued. 'You saw the dead body I led you to. Reeva has systematically killed those in her way or who rival her power. Not just the recent arrivals to your world but throughout your history. She is not Injai—she is an abomination born of deceit. Her kind walked among us for a time, and we have watched her use your people for her gain over a millennium.' The woman stepped closer.

'Reeva is not like us. She has gone by many names: Glymm Jursaine, Cayden Adira, Reeva, and Anukka Oaga are all the same. We know you have no reason to trust us. Just know that Reeva has controlled your history in one body or another, prevented you from reaching your potential and hid you from us for sixteen hundred years. We are your family, son.'

Olbi listened to the Injai as she stepped forward again.

'We had an empire that spanned eighteen worlds, but what was built over millennia was lost. Your planet was hidden away, a bastion for humanity. We have searched the stars, trying to recover the remnants of that society. Arbonar is our best and last chance.'

Olbi's mind swam.

The woman paused. Seconds passed, only silence. Olbi stared at the two people in front of him. They looked back at him with reverence. He sensed their frustration that he was unable to respond, but what did they expect of him? He didn't understand how to help them when he couldn't speak. He was powerless.

Olbi looked around again. The room seemed smaller now as if it was shrinking. He blinked and started to see white lights dancing in his vision.

'We are losing the connection. It's draining too much power from his end,' the man said frantically to the mirrored walls. Olbi looked up. Slowly, the Injai were being erased from his vision as light spread across the room, blinding him.

'We do not have much time.' The woman's voice was fast and panicked. 'You must find the Aetherian codex; it was last seen on Anatara. With that, you can reconnect us all. You and your people are our last chance. We will be there for you always, child, please help ...'

The white light consumed the woman's face. Olbi felt it surge and engulf him once more. He blacked out as he felt a pull, like a strong whirlpool swallowing him, sucking him under the surface of a river.

****

'Olbi, can you hear me? Olbi!'

A voice called out to him in the darkness.

'Olbi, please! Spirits protect you. Wake up, you stupid boy,' Liran pleaded. He couldn't respond, no matter how much he tried.

'Maven, is he breathing?'

'Move, Ayon, give him space. He is burning up. Yes, he is breathing. Remove his robe,' Liran ordered.

Olbi tried to call out, but still no sound left him. His throat was parched. He started to feel warmth in his chest. The heat grew until his head jolted, like an electric current had coursed through his brain. He gasped, sucking in icy air.

He was back in the room lined with cables. The threads weaved across the ceiling in random patterns. He was lying on the floor by the column's base, the holograms and lights had vanished, giving the room a muted stillness. Sweat built on his brow, threatening to streak down his face. Liran's features materialised in his vision, her deep eyes radiating apprehension.

'Liran,' Olbi croaked, 'how long have I been gone?'

Liran laughed, and tears rolled down her cheeks as she embraced him. Her hand fell on his cheek.

For once, he didn't flinch.

'Thank the Spirits, Olbi … you silly boy, we thought you were dead.' Liran lifted him into a sitting position and handed him a water bladder. He drank deeply, savouring the cool water as it stung his cracked lips.

'Where is Ayon?' he said, looking for the Scion.

'I am here, Olbi,' Ayon said from behind.

Olbi spun around, woozy, his vision swimming as he reacquainted himself with his body. The back of his head throbbed violently.

Ayon was facing the other way. Something was bundled up in his arms.

Liran cleared her throat. 'Olbi, what happened? One minute, you were in front of the pillar, and the next, you were consumed by light and collapsed onto the floor. You hit your head so hard on the metal we thought you had knocked yourself dead,' she said, her worry still lingering.

Olbi rubbed the bump growing on the back of his skull. 'I do not know. I met someone … I think. Or I dreamt it. I wasn't *here*.' He could still hear the woman's voice in his mind. The voice telling him to help them, to help the Injai come back.

'You met someone?' Liran asked.

Ayon was still silent but turned to face Olbi. He looked down into his hands to a bundle of material. Ayon's face glistened as an errant tear ran down his cheek.

'Ayon, what is—' Olbi started.

Ayon looked up. A glint in Ayon's hand caught Olbi's eye. It was his robe. And Ayon had seen the pin that the Prime One had given him.

30

ZILLAH

It happened in a flash. Reeva's lifeless body crumpled to the stone before anyone could breathe, her eyes fixed on Sloane, burning with cold, unyielding defiance. No time for Zillah or Joja to react—Sloane was already gone, vanishing into the shadows of the central passageway.

'Damn it,' Joja said, her firearm in her hands. She would not have been able to do much without risking a firing match with Sloane.

Joja offered Zillah a hand and lifted her off the ground. Zillah felt bruising and pain spread to her hips.

'Do we go after him?' Joja asked.

Zillah, for once, was speechless. The situation had unravelled before her, and the thought of chasing Sloane into an unknown corridor was chilling. She looked at Reeva's body. It spooked her. Sloane had just killed an Injai? What would possess him to do something so rash? Zillah gathered her thoughts. She had almost died. Sloane would have killed her, she knew this.

The corridor was quiet, too quiet.

'Where are the others?' she said, scanning the corridors. Each glowed with a different colour.

Joja shrugged. 'They must have run off. I don't blame them—we haven't been the portrait of civility since arriving. How we regain their trust is beyond me.'

Joja was right, but Zillah was wary that maybe the criticism was geared towards her leadership.

The mission to establish a good rapport with the Rahsu was doomed from the start. Convincing them they descended from the same race would not detract nor soften the blow caused by the death and destruction they brought to Arbonar.

Quartab Command would reprimand her—she knew this too. The only hope she had was to explain the situation, from the accidental destruction and death of the local population and her crew to the radio silence and lack of broadcasting footage that was to be used to document the mission. That would be nothing compared to the political fallout back home when she explained Sloane's actions. Something like this could quickly unravel the shaky peace that existed.

All this was moot, however, if the Unity continued to sink. So far, nothing in this facility looked like it could assist in retrieving the craft.

'Just to think, we are in a functioning Injai facility. Nothing like this has ever been found,' Joja said. 'Yet here we are, wondering if we will ever return home and if the years of struggle to search for this place have come at too high a price. Our history is here, everything we are stems from the people who built this.' Her words resonated with a twinge of sadness as she brushed a hand across the wall, almost bouncing on her toes with impatience as she paced the outstretched shadows of the hall.

Zillah sighed and forced herself into action, her fatigue not apparent to her until placing weight on her legs.

'Let's look for Liran and the boys. I doubt they snuck off to the right, so let's check the left tunnel,' Zillah said, peering into the green lights as if expecting to see the others immediately.

'They could have turned tail and run back out,' Joja said.

'True. I guess that is the risk we must take. Keep your gun within reach. We don't want Sloane to sneak up on us.'

Joja nodded and reasserted a stringent grip on her gun.

They descended into the tunnel. The lights at the entrance bathed it in various colours, but with every step, the green won out, and soon, the tunnel was saturated in its hue. Locked doors and offshoot tunnels branched from the central passageway. Some were dark, others were riddled in cobwebs,

long forgotten and disused. They followed the path until they reached a bulkhead door that refused to open.

'Dead end. Fuck, I was worried that this might be the case,' Zillah said, looking around for a panel.

'What would be the case?' Joja asked.

'That you would need a link to the Injai. Perhaps it detects the presence of something or, in our case, the absence of someone.' Zillah ran her fingers over the cool metal. 'I bet the boy can get in.'

'The Prime Scion?' Joja asked as she leaned against the wall.

'Well, perhaps both boys. Olbi did something strange with the fruits in the forest,' Zillah said, moving to one of the side doors.

Joja glanced up from her tablet—Zillah only now noticing she was using it—with a raised eyebrow. '"Did something strange"?'

'Yes, he touched it, and it glowed. A magnificent light emitted from the fruit. He appeared quite shocked, actually.'

'I thought there were laws against touching the fruits?' Joja said.

Zillah mumbled her agreement. 'Do you believe they are batteries?' she asked.

Joja nodded. 'I have been thinking about why we never detected them,' she said. Zillah cocked her eyebrow as Joja continued to flick through her tablet.

'We never detected them because they are hybrid creations. The garjee leaves act as solar panels that grow organic fruit,' Joja explained as Zillah peered at the door's lock mechanism. Joja continued, 'So, as the trees process the sun's power, it is transformed, stored in the fruits as boundless energy. The Manna Altar must be where the garjee is fed into a power grid that keeps this facility running. Think about it: it's pure, sustainable solar energy. The Injai created a power source that grows and never runs out. They were truly far more advanced than us.'

❧

316

'Joja, we would still have detected them if they unleash radiation surges and glow like they do?'

Joja nodded, and Zillah saw her mind ticking.

'The eclipse!' Joja said suddenly.

Zillah thought the doctor was losing her mind.

'Don't you see, Captain? The Rahsu feed the fruits into the altar during an eclipse. An eclipse that blocks Anatara from view. Two moons and Oaga, the gas giant, block us from detecting the radiation and surges in electricity. The same surge of electricity that keeps knocking out our satellites and knocked us out of orbit.

'Think about it. Their whole religion is based on these fruits. Someone created a belief system on this planet to sustain this facility and to keep it hidden from anyone on Anatara who may have detected such advanced systems. It's ingenious! The Rahsu thrive, feeding this facility, and someone has ensured that generations keep feeding the beast, so to speak.'

'You mean Reeva?' Zillah asked.

'Of course! It also explains why she knows about Anatara. This facility is Injai, I bet there is a wealth of knowledge about Anatara here, more than QC could have ever known.

'Captain, this is it. This is what all the struggle has been for—all the funding, the technological research and historical studies, it was all to find this place.'

Zillah nodded. Joja was right, it all made sense. Zillah approached another door shooting off from the main tunnel. She touched it to see if it would budge. Suddenly, there was a surge in the lights above them, and the tunnels went dark.

'What did you do?' Joja said, alarmed.

'Nothing.' Although Zillah was not sure of that. She removed her hand from the door. A few seconds passed, and half the green lights above them flickered back on. The large bulkhead door grumbled and began to slide open.

'Whatever you did, it worked,' Joja said, putting her tablet away and grabbing her gun.

'I don't think it was anything *I* did. It was almost like there was a power surge in the facility.'

Zillah peered beyond the bulkhead as it continued to open. The green lights flickered on as they moved into the large room beyond.

The space appeared like a larger version of Unity's bridge. Panels with glass screens lined parallel sides of the room, and at the far end, they saw their reflections in a glass window that enveloped a wall and looked out into another large chamber. At the centre of the room was a circular console encased in white stone with holograms and touchpads sitting dusty on its circumference.

'Whoa!' Joja exclaimed, strolling in, her face beaming.

Zillah agreed with the sentiment. The room resembled a command centre, but they still needed an inclination of what this place was. She approached the main panel. As she neared, a holographic image rose from the stone slab and filled the circular space.

Zillah's eyes widened—she was looking at schematics, a map of the entire facility. Before she could take in its immensity, the map seamlessly zoomed out to encompass the waterfalls and meadows outside. They continued shrinking until the map comprised the entirety of Arbonar, floating as a sphere.

The planet's myriad of forests were scattered across the map in intricate patterns. Lush and thick, they sprawled across the surface. Where forests didn't grow, great oceans and lakes dotted the planet in a mosaic of pristine nature.

'What do you suppose these are?' Joja asked, pointing at the sphere.

Zillah followed Joja's finger to a perfect circle in the centre of the forest they had walked through.

As soon as Joja gestured, the map changed, and the forest grew, covering the whole panel. Zillah could now discern individual trees dotted with garjee fruits that rimmed the perfectly circular cavity.

'Fascinating!' Joja exclaimed as they studied the map. Zillah glanced sideways at Joja; the doctor's face was focused. Zillah leaned in and saw a live animation of water tumbling over the precipice into the depths.

'This is where I saw Olbi touching the fruit,' she pointed. Again, the map changed. This time, the image expanded. It was a diagram of a connected system of tunnels running from the facility to random areas across the planet's surface. Text appeared alongside the shifting holograms and on the panels in front of them.

'Can you understand any of it?' Zillah said. She recognised some words here and there, but the language was reminiscent of ancient texts found in Injai ruins on Anatara.

'You bet I can. It's part of the reason I was the strongest candidate from the Tobanian delegation,' Joja said, a smug smile appearing at the corner of her lips for the briefest moment.

Zillah suppressed a grimace.

'Let me see,' Joja said, studying the panels. Her eyes bounced across the screens and occasionally darted to the graphic in front of them.

'Amazing. The Injai were bold, I'll give them that,' Joja said, smiling.

Zillah cleared her throat, seeking Joja's attention.

'Terraforming!' Joja shouted, noting Zillah's impatience. 'This facility was the Injai base of operations when the planet was a barren rock.'

Joja then pointed to the tunnels in the lights. 'These tunnels were exhausts, billowing greenhouse gases onto the surface to create an artificial atmosphere. Over the centuries, it turned into the lush planet it is now. Until that time, the Injai lived here, underground, protected from solar radiation and the inhospitable environment. This also explains why Arbonar looks like Anatara. Look here …'

Joja swiped on the panel in front of her. The images on the console of the map faded and were replaced by an array of plants and animals.

'They were all brought here from Anatara—trees, plants, animals, everything, except ...'

'Except what?' Zillah said.

'Except the garjee trees,' Joja said, her brow furrowed.

Zillah watched as the doctor moved her fingers across the panels as if flicking between pages in a book. The display changed with every swipe. A catalogue of information flashed before their eyes, more wealth than any of the ruins on Anatara had ever provided. It was overwhelming, and she relished in the gluttonous trove of knowledge this information could provide Tarea. But how could they take it back? Her heart sank, much like the Unity. There must be something here to—

'Wait. Go back.' Zillah only saw a flash. It couldn't be.

Joja stopped scrolling and returned to previous entries. She slowly flicked back until she arrived at the image that had caught Zillah's eye.

'Stop there,' Zillah said.

Joja stepped back from the panel, staring at the screen.

Reeva's animated face stared at them, haunting Zillah. Knowing that her body was slumped in a tunnel behind them made her skin crawl—one face among many, but undeniably hers. Reeva's cold grey eyes blinked on the screen; her visage seeped in a haze of red as if blotted out. Joja leaned toward the sprawling Injai writing below the Guardian's portrait.

'Third Officer Kartyon Adela, deceased,' Joja said, reading the text. Other faces were blurred in red. All the listed were deceased. Officer Tarjer: deceased. Illin Pawa: deceased. Lou Poffice: deceased. All incredibly human, all faces of those who lived seventeen centuries ago. Yet Zillah felt they could have been anyone who had walked the same streets as her in Aster. Nothing about them appeared foreign or alien. The woman beside Reeva's portrait was rather fetching with long gliding hair. She was smiling, and laugh lines creased her face.

'She was the one that died most recently before Reeva,' Joja said, observing Zillah. 'Her name was Glymm Jursaine.'

'Some of these images are different,' Zillah said. 'Are they all Injai?'

'Check this one, Captain.' Joja was scanning the images below the faces doused in red. Six portraits were missing the hue shrouding the others. Joja devoured the texts under one of the men's images.

'This says that they are still alive,' Joja stammered.

'That's impossible. The Injai were human, like us. There is no way they could live a millennium and a half,' Zillah said. She felt a knot in her stomach as she spoke.

It is possible.

Reeva had been proof of that. As if reading her mind, Joja exchanged an expression that suggested it was possible.

'Captain, I think they might still be in the facility somewhere. There is no mention of whether they ever left or if this place was affected by war or the Injai's demise. Perhaps Reeva was not alone?'

Zillah felt a chill on her neck. The facility was alive. 'There is much we don't know, Doctor. The mere thought of Injai still inhabiting this facility is not a circumstance we foresaw. We don't want to cause any further incident if that is the case,' she said, feeling uncomfortable. 'We must find a way off Arbonar before committing further. I have a bad feeling about the mission, and if we can't raise Unity, all this will be for naught.' Zillah's mind raced with possibilities, each one more unsettling than the last. She was trespassing in the domain of an advanced race, and the weight of that realisation settled heavily on her. A sudden wave of vulnerability washed over her, leaving her keenly aware of just how exposed they were.

'Leave! Already?' Joja exclaimed, her eyes were wide, and her mouth hung open. 'We can't leave. Everything we sought to find is here. This is what the mission was about—returning home is inconsequential. What matters is what we can learn about the Injai, Captain.'

❖

Zillah wanted to express her trepidation regarding their chances of returning to Anatara as she watched a rare scowl flicker across Joja's brow. However, speculation would not aid in their pursuit. Still, she agreed with Joja that this facility was a treasure trove of information about the Injai. About their past.

In the back of her mind was a niggling feeling that information in this facility would drastically alter the political dynamic of Anatara. In Tarean's hands, she could secure a future steered from Aster. Tarea could be the superpower. No doubt Sloane had similar thoughts of triumph for Jaree. And what of Tobania?

Joja was looking over the monitors beside her, mumbling into her tablet about terraforming. Her eyes were alive, like a child in a toy store. Tobanians had a history of looking inward. They never wanted war unless provoked and then always in defence.

But Zillah questioned if that would fundamentally change. Suppose this facility was able to propel Tobania to become a global threat. Hophnam scientists were renowned the world over. Suddenly, Zillah regarded Joja with alarm. Perhaps she shouldn't rely on the doctor too much.

Zillah's tablet beeped, startling her out of a thought train of hypotheticals, each more dire than the last. Another war terrified her, but her politically conscious mind sensed it was inevitable. She grabbed the tablet from her pocket as Joja wandered off to a line of consoles at the back of the room. Each one flashed an array of colours for reasons unknown.

Zillah skimmed the screen and spotted an icon over the communications file—an encrypted message. Zillah's heart skipped. Zaila had programmed a back door program into her device for messages. The team in QC had detected this anomaly; however, Zaila and some other officials had avoided detection by concocting a story that it was a simple glitch in the system, as Zillah's tablet was the primary device networking to the others. She was captain, after all.

✣

Zillah was always impressed with her sister's quick thinking and ability to concoct believable scenarios. Her mind worked at double speed compared to anyone else Zillah knew. Zaila should have been the one to captain the Unity; things would have worked out better, and the crew might have still been alive.

When the prompt sprang up, Zillah clicked the message icon and entered her security code: *CaptainTickles*. She silently chuckled and quickly thought about her sister's odd sense of humour. Tickles, her sister's cat, hated Zillah. She had never warmed to her despite how much she loved the cat.

Zillah scanned her sister's message. It was as if she knew what Zillah had been thinking. She reread the message twice to check that she had not misinterpreted the meaning, but the short communique was blunt and to the point.

UNITY BROKEN - THE EASTERN HEAD FALLS AND THE SWORD LASHES - THE AGENT WILL FOLLOW

Zillah looked over to Joja and wondered if she should tell the doctor that the Jareean President had fallen to the zealous military that once ruled the Eastern Head. Jaree had fallen into its old ways, and its brief experiment with democratic rule had seemingly ended after only a few short years.

As for 'Unity broken' and the reference to 'the agent', she did not need a message from QC to tell her what had transpired on Arbonar. Unity was broken the second the committee had chosen the delegates for this mission. Having the former Jareean war agent—Gideon Sloane—as head of the military contingent harbingered Unity's failure. Zillah hoped she could contain Sloane's ambitions with accountability in front of the world. That's why she chose Alrin Sandol for the mission.

She stared at the transmission, her thoughts racing. She could not risk responding and having it picked up by any technician at QC. No, she would keep this information to herself until Sloane was taken care of, and only then would she subtly include her response into the official communique to command. She knew what she must do. Though the message's briefness ate at her, Tarea would be on high alert. War was imminent if not already triggered.

'Joja, let's retreat, find Liran and the boys, and return to Xylona. From there, we negotiate a peace offering.'

Peace. The Rahsu had every right to lock them away.

Joja smirked at Zillah. The captain sensed giddiness in the young doctor's eyes.

'I have found brisk passage to Xylona. Fancy going for a quick flight?'

'What have you found?'

Joja pressed the controls of the central console. 'Just some ancient Injai flying cars, nothing too fancy.'

An image floated as a hologram before them, displaying a craft somewhere between a spaceship and a train carriage.

'Will they fly?' Zillah said, scepticism streaking through her voice. She was not willing to get too excited. The Tobanian appeared ready to risk their lives in a contraption she knew nothing about.

'Well, if my theory is correct, then yes, they will fly. But we need Ayon or Olbi with us,' Joja said as the small transport vessel disappeared from the console. The image was replaced by a schematic of a smaller facility in a mountainside before it shimmered away.

'Will they get us off the planet?' Zillah asked.

'Doubtful. They don't appear to be equipped for space travel.'

Typical, that would be too easy, Zillah thought.

'There will be a way off this planet, Captain. We are not without resources, and the two boys might very well be our ticket out of here.'

'We don't know where the others went,' Zillah reminded Joja.

Again, Joja turned to the console with a curling smile, as if expecting Zillah's rebuttal. 'Captain, you surprise me. Do you think this facility would not have surveillance?'

Zillah's gaze followed Joja as she bounced towards another wall where a bank of low monitors sat beneath what appeared to be a large black slab of stone above them. Again, Joja flexed her mettle and deciphered the monitors. Soon, a series of images appeared on the black slab above them. A series of corridors, rooms, and a rather misty view of the outside bridge was projected onto the slab.

Scanning the screens and locating the Rahsu sprinting through a maze of tunnels took no time. From one hall, they rushed into another, seemingly lost.

'Where is that?' Zillah asked.

Joja brought up further information with a few touches of the panel before her. 'Not far from here. We can cut them off if we head down this path.' Joja pointed to a route a few screens down.

Zillah observed the images closely and shook her head—countless rooms filled with artefacts. They would have to wait.

'Let's go,' Zillah urged, turning to leave the room as Joja gasped. Zillah, fearing that Sloane had found them, turned. Joja was staring at a screen with her mouth ajar. Something was moving.

Reeva's body was slumped where she had fallen in the corridor. An array of colours caressed her motionless body, but that was not what shocked them.

Beside Reeva's body stood a man. He was short in stature, and the girth around his abdomen matched his height. A dark receding hairline revealed blemishes and scabs on his skull, and his garb was akin to the uniforms doctors wore in Tarea.

'Where did he come from?' Zillah whispered as if expecting the man to hear her.

Joja appeared not to have heard.

Zillah was captivated by him. He seemed wary and cautious of approaching Reeva's body, scanning the passageways, his beady eyes concentrating on something.

'He is one of the Injai listed as still alive,' Joja remarked as she watched the man step closer towards Reeva. He leaned over and studied the dead guardian slumped unceremoniously against the tunnel wall. Blood seeped through her undergarments, staining her armour where Sloane had shredded it with bullets. The man reached towards the corpse and pulled at a thin chain around Reeva's neck.

'He's stealing her jewellery,' Joja exclaimed.

The chain broke away from Reeva, the force of the pull jerking Reeva's head. It slumped forward. He held the necklace in front of his eyes.

Zillah leaned into the monitor, examining the necklace: a silver pendant shaped like a teardrop.

'It's a garjee fruit,' Joja muttered. Her face was craned up to the image, her nose brushing the screen. 'I think I can zoom in.'

Again, after a few touches, Joja enlarged the man's profile. He was sweating profusely. He dropped the necklace onto his neck, where the pendant rested on his white coat.

'Looks like there is a cap at the top of the pendant, where the stem is—it's a clip.' Joja pointed towards the top of the pendant.

Zillah nodded. 'He doesn't look very well; the poor man is about to drop dead,' she said, watching the man walk off towards the same fork that Zillah and Joja had taken. He was using the wall to steady himself as he strode away.

'He is heading this way, Zillah said. 'Time to get out of here. If Injai are walking through this facility, we better not provoke them.'

Joja nodded and switched off the security camera—the black stone slab went dark.

'Right, Captain, this way to cut off Liran and the boys. They are our ticket out of here,' Joja said.

❦

326

Zillah followed the doctor through a door just as footsteps echoed beyond the bulkhead. The jewellery thief had narrowly missed them.

31

OLBI

'Absolutely not! Look what happened the last time you flew something,' Liran declared—her brows lifted in a mix of surprise and confusion when the captain told them about the Injai machines that could fly them to Xylona.

'We wouldn't be doing the flying. Olbi and Ayon will,' Joja replied.

'How is *that* any better? Again, absolutely not.'

'Keep your voices down, will you?' Ayon said, looking around for the mystery man that was hot on their tail. They were also vigilant for any sign of Sloane, who might be lurking in the halls.

The Anatrians stumbled upon them as Olbi struggled to recollect the way out of the tunnels. Zillah had told them about the flying transport and had suggested they follow her heed.

Olbi wobbled as he tried to stand, the after-effects of being knocked out by the light still lingered. He was still unsure what had happened to him and whether it was real. Yet Liran insisted that they needed to move, to leave the facility.

The Maven appeared to believe his story as he recounted the experience while they strode down the corridors. Olbi began with the moment he touched the glyphs that floated around the pillar. Liran let him speak, but her expressions were heavy with concern and wonder as he described the room and the people that spoke to him. They needed him to find the Aetherian Codex, whatever that was. Somehow, it would help bring the Injai back. But where were they? The only thing Olbi omitted in his retelling was that he had recognised the Injai in his visions. The Spirits of the forest were the Injai. Was it right for him to incriminate himself and Ayon? The Scion had offered only an icy and haunted reaction to his story.

'What makes you think Olbi and Ayon could fly one of these vessels you speak of? They are Rahsu. We know nothing of this technology,' Liran asked Joja as she led them down a wide passageway.

Olbi glanced at Ayon, who appeared weary and had barely spoken since Olbi woke. Olbi felt sick. Ayon had seen the pin.

'What else did you find in this place?' Olbi said before Joja had a chance to respond to Liran.

'We are more than happy to share what we have learned. However, we must get moving—if Sloane sees us, he knows he has the upper hand. Remember, he took my gun,' Zillah said.

'I have my spear,' Olbi countered. It could stop the soldier if he got a good throw in.

'Sloane is not the only one we need to worry about. We think there could be more Injai within the depths of this facility,' Joja said. 'If they are as hostile as Reeva, then we best not cross their paths.'

'Should we fear them?' Liran asked.

Zillah bit her lip. 'If the Injai are alive, they would know about the Rahsu and Anatara, but they have been hiding away. I would say they fear us,' she said.

Joja turned into another corridor. Olbi hoped she knew where she was going because he didn't. The passages blended, only slight changes to sign lettering gave him some confidence they were not going in circles.

'Are you feeling okay?' Olbi asked Ayon as they hurried down a brightly lit tunnel. He was beginning to worry the Scion was upset.

'I'm fine,' Ayon mumbled.

Olbi dropped his head. If it were about the pin, he wished Ayon would tell him. Ayon knew about his plans to become a Monitor. Being thrust into the role of Guardian was not much more of a leap.

As if sensing Ayon's silence, Liran moved up next to them. 'Do not worry, Ayon, we will get you out of here. We will not let anything happen to you.'

Ayon gritted his teeth and scowled at Liran, there was no denying his anger.

'I do not need to be babied. Why does everyone think I need protection? I am a grown man who can handle my own.' He avoided looking at Olbi. 'I thought you—of all people, Maven—would understand that.'

'Of course I do, Ayon,' Liran said, a kind smile touching her lips. 'You know I have never pushed you to do anything you don't want.'

Ayon nodded, his expression softening.

Olbi avoided looking at Ayon. Instead, he watched Joja and Zillah dash left into a larger tunnel. That was it then—Ayon didn't ask Olbi to protect him. His stomach twisted. He was doing it for Ayon's mother and the people of Xylona. A direct request from the Prime One. He understood Ayon's temperament, but Ayon must know that even as a Guardian, Olbi would not stop him from living the way he wanted. Unlike Reeva's pledge, Olbi was sworn to protect the Prime Scion, not to dictate his path.

'Through that door. We are close,' Joja said, pointing to an imposing door at the end of a tunnel. It was wider than all the other sections of the facility.

'This must be a service tunnel for personnel and hauling cargo,' Zillah said, looking up at a series of metal beams that clung to the roof.

Occasionally, there would be thick and dusty chains hanging from large metal hooks or conveyor belts that joined up with the beams at junctions with smaller tunnels. Olbi glanced up at the soulless metal. These caverns of an ancient race were cold and angry.

'I will show you what I mean when I said Olbi and Ayon would be the ones to get us out of here,' Joja announced, stopping in front of the large door. 'Notice it has not opened?'

Olbi trembled. He knew what Joja was alluding to. The last thing he needed was for Ayon, and Liran for that matter, to find out that he had the blood.

'Ayon, could you step forward please?' Joja said with a smile, rocking back and forth on the balls of her feet. Olbi sighed, glad that Joja hadn't called him. Ayon slowly ambled forward towards the door. Suddenly, some mechanism and gears began to rumble. Unseen cogs that had lain dormant began to churn back into operation as the door gave off a shrieking snarl of metal on metal. As the doors parted, a gush of wind from within surged over them. Centuries-old stale and musky air freed itself from its stagnate prison.

'The facility sensors are activated when they detect Injai DNA,' Joja proclaimed, holding her hand to the door.

Liran offered a hollow look of confusion.

'This blood, the blood of the Prime Ones, it's Injai blood. It has a unique signature that I'm yet to determine, but it reacts to the world around it electromagnetically, like Injai technology,' Joja said, her eyes animated and wide.

'And the garjee fruit,' Ayon said solemnly.

Joja nodded.

'So, this is our link to the Injai, then?' Liran said. 'If we are connected as you say, then why do none of you Anatrians share this blood? Would it not run through your blood as well?'

Joja furrowed her brow, and Olbi saw her thinking, working things out. Zillah was the one to respond to the Maven.

'We are only a small sample of the genetic makeup of Anatara's gene pool. There is every chance that the blood runs in segments of our population, much like it does here. You say so yourself, the blood is dying. Perhaps it is a recessive gene. By that, I mean eventually it will be diminished until it becomes extinct,' Zillah said.

Joja nodded.

❖

'Yes, I agree,' the doctor said. 'The Injai collapsed over sixteen hundred years ago. No one knows why. That is a long time for both Anatara and Arbonar to deviate genetically, not only from the Injai, but also from one another. Although it's not long enough to suggest the changes are great, a few tweaks here and there and … well, the further in time away from a genetic mutation, then the greater the difference between our blood and that of pure Injai DNA.'

The piercing creak of metal echoed down the corridor, turning their heads.

'We must go. We don't have the luxury of a biology lesson, Doctor,' Zillah said.

'Why did Joja imply you could open the door as well?' Ayon mumbled to Olbi as the Scion returned to standing at his side. Olbi couldn't look Ayon in the eyes but felt his penetrating gaze. His knees were weak, he wanted to flee. All this change was too much, and the last thing he desired was for Ayon to think he was keeping secrets from him— especially this.

'Can we talk about it when there aren't so many ears around, Prime Scion?'

Ayon turned, scowling. Olbi looked at his feet, his shoes had begun breaking at the sides.

'Quickly, Olbi,' Liran called.

When Olbi lifted his head, he was standing alone. The others had passed beyond the door. A part of him wanted to turn and run.

The room beyond the doors stank of mould and stagnant water. Olbi's eyes adjusted slowly to the low light as yet another cavern materialised. Orange streaks stained the rock walls and glistened as the light shone from the cargo passageway.

The water seeping down into the rock had carved vertical rivulets onto its slimy surface. Algae and grime clung to the walls, the room exuded putrefaction. He scrunched his nose as his feet crossed the metal-grated flooring. Beneath it, he couldn't tell if the cavern kept descending into the planet's depths. Behind them, a noise reverberated against stone. Olbi spun, watching the door close behind them. With one final thud, the door locked, and small dull lights flickered on from small sconces attached to the stone.

Ayon was up ahead, speaking to Joja. Her arms flailed as she pointed in all directions of the cavern, but Olbi noticed she was pointing to three bulky objects shrouded in the centre. In the dim, shadow-filled expanse of the cavern their hulking forms, cloaked in a thick layer of dust, stretched upward, casting long, foreboding silhouettes across the floor. The air around them hung heavy, almost reverent, as if the space itself was holding its breath. Olbi ambled up to Liran, observing a clutch of luminescent mushrooms growing in a crevasse of stone.

'Is everything okay between you and Ayon?' Olbi pried, his voice soft and feeble. Liran was poking the mushrooms with her charcoal stick.

'I am not sure—he seems a bit distant at the moment,' Liran said, sketching the mushrooms.

'Okay, I was just checking if I had done something wrong.'

Liran gave a knowing nod. 'I think Ayon is just processing what happens after today. Among other things.'

Olbi peered over to Ayon, who was laughing at something Joja said. Seeing Ayon laugh when he was being so cold to him sent jolting pain to his heart. The pain must have registered on his face because Liran patted his shoulder.

'Do not fret; he will come around. Ayon is just confused, and his emotions are all over the place. You will see, he cares for you. And given the dangers he faces, the last thing he wants is someone to put their life on the line for him.'

Olbi nodded and took a deep breath.

'So, when will you tell him you have Prime blood?'

Olbi's heart skipped, but Liran was smiling.

'I am a Maven, not some drunk at the Stonehall, Olbi. No need to deny or confirm your blood or your true feelings for

Ayon to me,' Liran said, closing her book. 'After you touched the pillar back there, I tried touching it, and it didn't work. But it activated when Ayon moved closer to you. It did not take me too long to put two and two together.'

'Will you tell anyone?' Olbi asked.

Liran shook her head. 'It is not my place. How long have you known?'

'A few days. Since the garjee forest, I touched—'

Liran gave him a stern look but then laughed. 'Tut-tut, it is against the law to touch the fruits.' There was no judgment in her tone. 'I do not think it will matter much anymore.' Liran looked over to the others who approached the shrouded shadows.

'Why is that?' Olbi asked as they strolled over to join the others.

'Because life will never be the same. We must learn how to adapt to the changes that are coming. This is only the beginning of a brave new future, Olbi, and I feel that you and Ayon will play a big part in shaping the Rahsu's fate.'

Olbi's stomach churned.

The thrum of rhythmic vibrations built into a steady rumble where the others stood. Suddenly, a flash erupted from the shadows. One of the dark and dusty monsters had begun glowing and emitted a purring noise. A doorway appeared at its side—Ayon had activated one of the Injai vessels.

Of all the things that he had seen and experienced, seeing this was beyond anything Olbi had ever expected. The craft was long and rectangular and stood upon rippling light. It was hovering a foot above the ground. They would be returning to Xylona in an Injai vessel.

His hair stood on end as another light appeared at the far end of the cavern. At first, it was a pinprick, but soon it bathed the whole cavern. Blinding light stung his eyes as Liran shielded hers from the glare. The rumble of tumbling rocks echoed from the cave mouth. Metal screeched, blasting Olbi's ears, as two massive bulkhead doors melted into the rock on either side of the opening. Beyond it, a curtain of falling water thundered downwards. They were behind the waterfall. A churning maelstrom of mist and cool air billowed towards Olbi.

'Let's go!' Zillah yelled, beckoning Olbi and Liran towards the door cut into the metal capsule. It shone as water droplets from the swirling mist painted its silvery mass.

'One last thing, Olbi'—Liran touched him on the shoulder and sighed—

'You should tell Ayon. But it is up to you whether you wish to challenge him for the Prime Seat.'

'I do not want to challenge him. I do not want any part of it,' Olbi said fiercely.

Liran nodded but did not smile. Olbi resented that people would regard and treat him differently if they knew.

'Good, we need you both to stick together. A fracturing of the Rahsu right now could be disastrous. There will be those who will pressure you to claim that chair. Most of those forces will be from outside Xylona. I believe you know of whom I speak.'

'Hydorans,' Olbi whispered.

Liran nodded again.

Olbi had the urge to ask if Liran knew more about his mother. Somehow, Liran always knew more than she let on.

****

Though Ayon exuded fear, a determination burned behind his eyes as he sat at a console at the head of the Injai ship. Zillah hovered over him, explaining things that Olbi could not hear. Ayon nodded intently as Joja tapped away at her tablet.

Olbi took a seat at a circular booth with a table in the middle, the cushions were soft and bounced when he sat down. He rubbed the back of his head where he had fallen on the stone. Liran took a seat beside him and rested her feet on the table. She sighed, closing her eyes. Within moments, Olbi swore he could hear her snoring.

The Injai vessel fascinated him. It had room enough to seat twelve people. The internal walls were white like Xylonan stone; however, different flashing colours pulsed from small recesses where things could be stored. He was too tired and overwhelmed to look through the compartments, though this new world fascinated him.

'Okay, I think you have it,' Zillah said loudly, stirring Olbi, who had closed his eyes. The captain continued giving Ayon instructions. 'Shut the side door, and then I think we are ready to test the throttle.'

Ayon's eyes darted around after touching a button. The vessel's door began to close. With a hissing click, it locked into place, and Olbi felt the air in his ears compress as the pressure changed. He pinched his nose to readjust the pressure.

Before Ayon turned back to the controls, he glimpsed Olbi. Olbi surrendered a faint smile, hoping that things would improve between them. When Ayon returned a toothy grin, it sent a flurry of butterflies into his chest.

'You sure this is going to work, Zillah?' Ayon asked.

She gave him a pat on the back. 'I trust you. You have this. The controls are very similar to those of the Unity—we designed our vessels loosely on old schematics recovered from Injai ruins on Anatara.

'Everyone secured?' Zillah then asked, scanning the compartment. Liran's head was drooped against the back of the seat beside him.

'Okay, punch it,' Zillah said.

Olbi felt weightless as the vessel moved upwards, shaking and vibrating violently. Liran shot up, waking from her slumber.

'Was that a quake?' Liran exclaimed, startled.

Olbi grasped the table as the whole vessel shuddered.

'Just the engines getting warmed up. After sixteen hundred years, the system's a bit dusty,' Joja said, reading a panel. Her calmness was reassuring.

In the reflection of the glass, Ayon's eyes widened, he looked terrified.

'It's okay, Ayon. Just remember what I told you. Slow and steady.' Zillah helped guide Ayon's hands to the ship's controls. They lurched forward, and Olbi felt his insides fight the sudden movement. Ayon drove the vessel towards the waterfall ahead of them more quickly than expected.

'Captain, I am picking up a warning signal,' Joja said.

Her voice was calm, but Ayon turned a pallid shade of green.

'Something wrong with the vessel?' Zillah asked.

Joja scanned the information and text at her console. Olbi saw her frantically deciphering the language. A flicker of fear illuminated her face, but Olbi did not need to ask her what was wrong. Outside the window, the light at the end of the chamber should have been getting larger and brighter. Instead, it was shrinking, and the slither of light was retreating.

'The doors are closing,' Olbi said, pointing out the window. The sound of the warning alarm pierced Olbi's ears as Joja frantically tapped away. She rushed to where Ayon sat behind the helm.

'Push that image,' Joja commanded, pointing to an illustration on the console in front of the nervous pilot. Ayon pressed his finger to the picture. It flashed red as a message popped up.

'Damn, locked out,' Joja said.

She muttered something in a language that Olbi had never heard before.

'You are going to have to floor it, Ayon,' Zillah said. Behind them, Liran stirred.

'Why is it that every time I want to sleep, there is an incessant sound to disrupt me?' the Maven lamented, sitting up with annoyance. Olbi intently watched the narrowing sliver

of light. Even as the ship's speed increased, the light diminished ahead of them. Olbi felt useless sitting there.

'A malfunction?' Zillah called over to Joja. She remained calm and steady.

'No, definitely not,' Joja replied, pointing out the window. 'There is the culprit.'

Olbi looked off to the left where Joja was pointing. In the dim cavern, it took a few moments for his eyes to discern the lights emanating from behind a glass panel cut into the side of the rock. Inside, a small man was glaring at them. Olbi watched the short, rotund man frantically move around the room in the rock. He appeared to be limping.

The man locked eyes on Olbi as their vessel approached. Olbi stared back, his gape penetrating the command deck of their vessel. The man pushed down on a button as they drew level with the window. The man's voice was suddenly all around them.

'I cannot let you leave. Ayon, stop the ship. If you allow the Anatrians to escape, they will destroy us all.' The man's voice was high yet husky, like a child's voice after breathing smoke from a bonfire.

'Do you know that man?' Zillah asked Ayon, narrowing her eyes at the Scion. Ayon shook his head vehemently and showed no sign of slowing the ship.

Olbi studied the man as the distance between the vessel and the glass room shrank. He could see his round face reddening as it became clear that the ship was not stopping. Around his neck hung a golden chain with a pendant clasped to it. Olbi had seen that pendant before.

In one form or another. The Spirit's words crossed his mind.

'It's Reeva,' Olbi exclaimed.

He turned to the rest of the crew. Only Liran looked over to him. 'The man, it is Reeva. The Spirits told me she has controlled our lives in one form or another.'

Liran rubbed her eyes and moved to the window. Olbi locked eyes with the man, the Injai man had heard him. Through different coloured eyes, he saw the same hatred, the same resentment that Reeva had for him.

'We are not going to make it,' Ayon yelled. Olbi tore his eyes away from the man and back to their destination. The ship was moving too slowly and the metal bulkhead doors were still distant. Olbi could walk faster than this, Ayon was being too careful, and it would get them all killed. Fear and trepidation registered in the Scion's eyes.

'We will have to fight our way out if we don't make it. Olbi, help me search for any weapons,' Zillah said.

She left Ayon's side and began rifling through one of the compartments.

'Stop the ship, Ayon,' the man called again more frantically. He then began to address Olbi with an angry desperation in his voice. 'Olbi, stop Ayon or turn on the Anatrians. They are dangerous and will unleash untold disasters for our people. Tarak, Alvar. Everyone you love will suffer. Listen to me and I will make you the most powerful Rahsu that has ever lived. You will rule the Rahsu. I know who you are, I know what you are.'

It was a man's voice, but Olbi heard Reeva's cadence flowing through the cavern. Olbi glanced over to the table, where his spear was placed. Was Reeva right? Were Zillah and Joja trying to escape for their benefit so they could return and invade the Rahsu? Or should he join them and find the artefact the Injai Spirits had tasked him to find? He didn't want to rule—becoming the Prime One was not his desire.

He only had moments to decide. The alarm blared in his ears, raising his anxiety. He knew what he must do. He watched Ayon, who was trembling in fear. He remembered the oath he swore to Claudya, he was a sworn Guardian. His first decision should be Ayon's safety. If he stayed, would the man let them live? Or maybe Sloane would find them? Liran had never trusted Reeva yet seemed to trust Zillah and Joja. He knew what he must do, even if it risked exposing himself.

'Ayon, out of the chair,' Olbi barked, marching towards him.

'Are you mad?' Liran yelled at him, leaping out of her chair. 'Olbi, we must escape.'

Zillah and Joja stared at Olbi as well. Joja wore a hurt and pained expression, but Zillah remained stone-faced. Ayon faced Olbi, he was ashen with fear, defending his firm grip on the ship's controls. His knuckles matched the colour of his face.

'Move, Ayon. I will fly the ship,' Olbi said.

Ayon let go of the joystick immediately.

'But—' was all Ayon could say as he relinquished the chair. Olbi would explain himself later. Right then, he had to fulfil his duty protecting Ayon and, in doing so, protecting them all from Reeva.

He clasped the joystick and felt a surge of power run through his body. It felt right, it felt good.

Zillah's face relaxed as she sat beside him and started to explain the movements. It did not matter, he had watched Ayon, and he knew what to do. Behind him, Ayon stared at Olbi with his mouth agape as Liran put her arm around the Scion.

Olbi pulled back on the controls. The ship lurched forward. There was still time. Olbi caught the last glimpse of the man in the glass, and as he did, the man raised his arms and fired a weapon. The glass between them shattered, and Olbi felt a blast connecting with the ship's hull.

'Move, move, move!' Zillah yelled.

One more blast hit the side of the ship and somewhere a sound like the town bell bellowed continuously.

'The ship doesn't have any protection,' Zillah stated.

Another harrowing blast rocked the ship. Olbi slipped, smacking his face on the controls as the impact hit the engines.

The forward motion caused the vessel to stutter, and Liran and Ayon fell forward, hitting the floor.

'He's aiming at our rear thrusters,' Joja's voice was barely audible over the noise of the alarms. The darkness grew as the gap between the doors shrank further.

It was now or never.

As the blasts pounded the ship, Olbi grabbed the controls and pulled them back to full throttle. His body fought with the force of the thrust. Ayon and Liran slid across the ship's floor, hitting the chair and table. The door approached, and beyond it, the light. The dazzling waterfall came fast. The doors were closing slowly. It would be a tight fit.

'It's too narrow, we are going to crash,' Joja screamed, but Olbi gritted his teeth.

Reeva's blasts shot past the ship, fizzles of red lightning hitting the cavern's walls.

'Hold on,' Olbi yelled. He felt a surge in his chest, the adrenaline coursed in his veins as they approached the closing door. Olbi straightened, readjusting the direction at the right moment and pushed the ship through the narrow gap in the doorway. The shrieking of metal on metal screamed in his ears, but the damage was superficial. The ship flew through the water curtains of the cascades, and suddenly, they saw the meadows below in the mist.

Joja laughed at his side. 'You are a maniac, Olbi. I love it,' she said, slapping him on the shoulder.

In the reflection of the glass, Olbi could see Ayon's face. There was no doubt about it, Olbi saw the knowing look in those eyes. Ayon now knew he was not the last of the blood.

❖

32

OLBI

Xylona approached as a uniform grid of white squares on the horizon as Olbi charted a westerly course. The green hues of fields and forests spread all around as he flew through the skies of Arbonar. The feeling of freedom and adventure swelled deep within him.

'It is so beautiful,' Liran said, despite the colour in her complexion retreating. The world was zipping by so quickly.

Liran had recovered from being flung around the ship during their escape but would be tender for some time.

Olbi agreed with her as Arbonar took on a new meaning in his mind. Their world was peeled back, revealing a lush, immense globe. There were no demons or *Forbidden Zones*; instead, Olbi looked upon streams and rivers he had never seen. Far-off mountains and a domineering mesa beckoned on the horizon, ripe for exploration.

'You're a natural Olbi. I think there might be a future in this for you.' Zillah uncharacteristically smiled at him.

Olbi beamed. He loved it. And he felt at home in the pilot's seat. Maybe this could be something he did in the future, if Ayon did not need him anymore. The only thing that crossed his mind that caused him any concern was how to land and where.

As if reading his mind, Joja started feeding instructions into his ear and ran through the landing process. He pictured the faces of Xylonans as the flying machine approached the town. Would they fear it, like they had the star that crashed during the Manna Rites?

The landing was easy, somehow. He devoured Joja's instructions as the ship gently touched down on the road to the north of the village.

The sun beat down on them from high in the sky, and Olbi relished the sun's warmth again. The corridors of the facility had been chilling and cruel.

Townspeople carting freshly cut wood down the road on wagons paused in their tracks, eyes focused on the foreign behemoth blocking the route into Xylona. When they spotted Ayon emerging, they gasped.

Almost a week had passed since the Outsiders' arrival, and repairs to Xylona were ongoing. The villagers glanced towards the ship in wonder as the five returning travellers stepped down the platform to the ground. The villagers approached Ayon and gave him the salute of the Primes, their faces ashen when he returned the gesture. Olbi could tell something was wrong by how the farmers avoided their gaze. One man was on the verge of tears as Liran approached him.

'What has happened?' Liran asked, weariness etching her tired face. The man said nothing as he lowered his head, but his subtle glances towards Ayon spoke volumes.

'Is my mother well?' Ayon questioned.

The mood was sombre. The man wept, clinging to his cart. Ayon slumped forward. Zillah and Joja were the last to approach the cart. Rage burned in one of the women's eyes as Zillah stepped forward.

'The Prime One lives, but Syrona declares her days are numbered,' she said, choking on her words.

Ayon turned and sprinted towards the arches leading into Xylona.

'Ayon, wait,' Olbi yelled. He felt a hand on his shoulder. Liran gave him a gentle squeeze.

'Let him go, Olbi,' she said. 'He will need us soon, but now he needs to be with her.'

****

Olbi lifted his head from the end of his father's bed. He had awakened from a dreamless sleep that left him groggy.

'Olbi, the healer needs to check my legs,' Tarak said as Olbi stirred. His eyes laboured to open. Tarak glimpsed down at him. The healer was standing there, too, her elderly face blank, waiting for Olbi to wake.

'Sorry,' Olbi mumbled sheepishly as he shuffled off the warm blankets.

The hall was quieter today with many of the injured now gone. Most of the populace had recovered and were back at work repairing Xylona. The disciple assumed the seat Olbi had occupied, lifting the blankets and removing the bandages on Tarak's legs. Intense purple bruises covered both Tarak's legs, and where the splinter had punctured his abdomen, yellow splotches from medicines stained his skin. Olbi winced.

'I guess I need to find a new livelihood. I fear my days as a trader are behind me,' Tarak said as the healer reapplied a thick paste to the cuts and bruises on his body. His father grinned, but Olbi could see sadness brewing behind the smile.

'I have been thinking, Olbi,' Tarak said, looking away from the damage to his body, 'about what you told me of your journey.'

The healer moved on to another patient leaving Olbi alone with his father.

'I think you should talk to Faiyor. Tell them what you have seen, what can be found in the Forbidden Zone. The Rahsu have a right to know, and Faiyor most of all.' Tarak coughed and grimaced, agony painted itself prominently across his face.

'Father, I will, but please do not pain yourself. Rest now. All will be well, you will see.' Olbi took his father's hand and gently caressed it.

It had been three days since Olbi had returned from the Forbidden Zone. The rumour mill had been running wild, and only hints of what transpired on their travels had come to light.

Reeva's absence was conspicuous in town. There had been no word on Sloane's whereabouts, or the man Olbi knew to be Reeva. The focus had understandably been on Claudya.

❖

The Prime One had collapsed after working tirelessly to repair a market stall the day before they arrived back in town. Xylonans thought she had worked herself to the bone and collapsed from exhaustion, but those who knew, understood otherwise. Olbi hadn't seen Ayon since, but once the bells tolled that morning for a full hour, he knew Claudya had joined the Spirits. The townspeople's sorrow and tears swept through the streets, and a heavy fog of uncertainty descended over the town.

Anguish was the new normal for Xylona, ever since the falling star. Ayon was now the Prime One. Olbi paced the hall, wondering what this meant for the future of the Rahsu. He knew Ayon would be trapped—the very thing Ayon dreaded. They had both tasted a new life, but with the arrival of the Anatrians, the future of Arbonar was muddied.

Olbi gazed through the window, listening to the gentle snores of Tarak behind him. He had drifted off moments after the soothing paste had been applied to his injuries. Olbi smelt the sweet, burning bouquet of the paste wafting around the hall.

Through the window, Olbi watched the sun rise over the square as people began meandering through the streets, speaking in docile voices. The damage had not yet been cleared, and many buildings had been boarded shut, but there was a sense of returning normality. People needed to get on with their lives, they had things to do, and preparations were already underway for Ayon's ascent.

Delegates from across Arbonar would be arriving in Xylona to witness the blood that still belonged to Claudya's line. They would swear allegiance and bestow Xylona with gifts. Olbi knew it was now his duty to present himself to the Prime House, whether or not Ayon wanted that.

Behind him, Tarak's snores grew fiercer. A young girl in a bed beside them huffed at Tarak with contempt. She turned on her bed and smothered her ears with a pillow.

Olbi let his father rest and wandered towards the Prime House, towards his new fate. His feet felt heavy as they dragged through the stone of the lanes into the garden cloister.

'You look glum today, Olbi.' Two people sat on a stone bench, looking over at him and smiling. Joja waved him over to her. He almost didn't recognise her and Zillah seated in the garden adorned in traditional Rahsu garb.

Joja stood up and twirled. 'What do you think? If we are stuck here, I thought we better fit in,' she said, beaming and patting down the yar wool shawl that adorned her shoulders. Zillah looked less conspicuous as she wore her Anatrian captain's suit under a bright red scarf wrapped around her neck.

'You both look great,' he replied.

Joja laughed and punched his shoulder playfully.

'So, if you say you are trapped, does that mean your ship is gone?'

Joja nodded.

'Ayon took us there yesterday. Although it would have been faster walking with the speed he flies,' Joja quipped. 'The Unity is still there but has sunk at least ten metres into the bog.'

Olbi gasped, but Joja brushed him away.

'The new Prime One has offered us refuge,' she said.

'Are you ready to see the Prime One?' Zillah asked as she stood.

Joja had a beaming smile on her face, she looked like she was ready to burst with excitement. Even Zillah seemed to be hiding a smile behind her ordinarily serious face.

'What is going on?' Olbi said as he studied them.

'You will just have to wait and see,' Joja smirked, grabbing his arm and pulling him toward the Prime House.

Olbi hated surprises. He also hated when everyone knew what was happening and he didn't. They climbed the steps from the Great Hall towards the doors to Claudya's room on the first floor of the Prime House. Only it wasn't Claudya's room anymore, it was Ayon's, and reality kicked in.

Monitors were everywhere in the halls of the house, scuttering about in a chaotic frenzy. Some wore worried faces, and some seemed genuinely buoyant. Olbi was even more confused as they reached the end of the corridor. Two guards stood out the front, their halberds blocking the door. The taps of laboured footsteps approached from behind them.

'That is unnecessary, gentleman. We have been over this.' Phran passed them and stared down the guards. 'Things have changed. I do not think the new Prime One will have much patience for tradition and has even expressed a desire to forego the so-called pomp.' He sounded annoyed but stood firm until the guards exchanged glances and moved their weapons that blocked the door.

'You may proceed, the Prime One is expecting you,' Phran said, his arms straining to push the heavy wooden door. There was no joy in his voice. Olbi was feeling uncomfortable and nervous to see Ayon for the first time since Claudya's passing.

The room was quiet compared to the hubbub of the hallways. Only two Monitors moved around the large bedroom. Olbi had been here once before when he'd visited during his lessons. It looked different now—much of the red draping that adorned the walls was gone. They had displayed the Lyfera sigil with the garjee fruit trimmed into the borders.

Now, the walls looked naked, stripped of their power and respect. Were they changing the drawings because Ayon wanted new ones? That did not sound right. Olbi scanned the room, though Ayon was nowhere to be seen. Instead, the voice of a woman behind a modesty screen spoke.

'Phran, another thing we will eliminate is these heavy yar wool coats in summer. I do not care if it's tradition. Nobody ever liked it, and we all smell worse than yar shit already.'

Olbi glanced at Phran, who tightened his jaw.

'Yes, Prime One.' His voice was automatic, but he paused and looked like he had swallowed something unflattering when he said it.

Olbi was confused. Where was Ayon? He turned and looked at Joja and Zillah. Joja was giggling. The woman moved from behind the screen, and Olbi audibly gasped.

Liran looked so different, dressed in royal robes. A Monitor fussed with her cuffs as sweat built on her forehead. She looked up, her eyes connecting with Olbi's confused face. She smiled.

'I guess you have not told him yet, then?' Liran said, looking from Zillah to Joja.

'What is going on?' Olbi demanded.

Liran took a step back. His voice was angrier than it should have been.

'Where is Ayon?'

'Olbi, everything is going to be okay. Things will not be the same, and some adjustments are coming, but the Rahsu will survive.' Liran ushered them to a table in the corner of the room, away from the Monitors. Olbi took a seat, still confused.

'You have the blood?' Olbi asked when Liran took a seat. She appeared well-rested and in better health than she had in a long time. She shook her head.

'No Olbi, I do not.'

'Then how can you be the Prime One? How will you conduct the Manna Rites, only Ayon and—'

He stopped before implicating himself, aware Monitors may be listening.

Joja leaned in, resting her elbows on the wooden table. 'Olbi, remember the garjee fruit is a battery. They store energy for running the Injai facility.' Joja looked around and lowered her voice. 'There is nothing divine about them. Reeva deceived the Rahsu. The truth is you do not need to offer garjee any longer. What you need is a leader that will govern for you, not a faceless Injai,' Joja said, smiling.

Olbi was still baffled and Zillah could see that.

'But why you, Maven?' Olbi stammered.

Liran leaned back and raised a finger, stood up and strode to a bookcase. 'A good question, Olbi,' she said, wandering back while flicking through a tome plucked from the shelf. 'You see, in the history of the Primes, there have been occasions when a Prime One has died and in the interim period—when a Consanguine Court has been called, or as the seat moved from one town to the next—the Maven steps up as the leader.'

Olbi nodded but Joja almost leapt up in her seat.

'That name!' Joja said, pointing to the book that Liran placed before them. Olbi regarded the book.

'G Jursaine,' Joja announced, 'that was the name of the Injai that died before Reeva, I saw her name.'

Liran laughed, which surprised everyone.

'What is so funny Mav—Prime One,' Olbi said. It sounded strange to call Liran that.

Liran sighed, but still smiling handed Olbi the book.

'I once asked Reeva if she had read this book,' Liran said, 'if we are to believe your story, Olbi, then Reeva was the one who wrote this nearly one hundred years ago.'

Olbi stared at the tattered book, as if somehow Reeva was alive within it, listening to them.

'How can that be? It does not seem real, yet I know it to be true.' Olbi mumbled, shaking his head.

Joja again offered her knowledge. 'Although I'm unsure of the science behind it, somehow Reeva—if that is her name—was able to inhabit the bodies of the Injai. The truth is we may never know what Reeva is or looks like.'

Olbi felt a sudden chill enter the room as if a haunting presence had arrived.

'We discovered much in the facility, Olbi,' Zillah said, 'yet we have barely scratched the surface. The garjee fruit was created to hide you from us. An undetectable power source responsible for turning a barren rocky planet into a lush paradise.'

'The scriptures weren't a complete falsehood, Olbi,' Liran said, grabbing his hand. 'Long ago, the garjee powered the planet, breathing life into the world. If the fruit ceased being harvested, then the machines keeping Arbonar safe would have stopped. If that happened, then the atmosphere would have been torn from the planet. The air would disappear and the world would have died. In a way, the Primes have kept Arbonar and the Rahsu alive.' Liran squeezed his hand.

'That's right,' Joja said, nodding. 'Who knows how long *she* has been controlling the narrative of your lives. The Manna Rites were Reeva's doing, but let's not assume she is the villain here. What she has done may have ensured your way of life continued and that Arbonar remained habitable.

'Perhaps that is why the Rahsu never expanded across the planet. It must have been quite difficult to keep a population from growing beyond her control for the last millennia and a half. In a way, the garjee forests are a form of geo-fencing, to keep the Rahsu contained. Suffice to say, I think it would be foolish to assume we have seen the last of her, or Sloane for that matter.'

Olbi shook his head. He didn't care about Reeva nor Sloane, or the scriptures. There was only one person on his mind.

'Olbi'—Zillah stared deeply into his eyes—'if what I witnessed in the forest is an indication of what power the Injai have, then you are a precious commodity. Both you and Ayon have an unblemished link to the Injai. Now, we here at this table suggest you keep this a secret. It is one of the things I have omitted from my reports for our mission.' Zillah finished and smiled at Olbi.

'I do not wish to challenge Liran if that is what you are thinking—' Olbi said.

'No, we know that' Joja said. 'It is just … well, if our leaders and commanders on Anatara knew of this …' Joja drifted off, but Olbi didn't need to hear it to know that there would be consequences.

❖

'What of Ayon?' Olbi asked, slumping in his chair, not knowing what to think. His head ached and knowing Ayon was safe and well was at the front of his mind. 'Where is he? Why have I not seen him in days?'

Liran sighed heavily, her breath making the candle on the table dance on its wick. 'Mourning. We all are mourning, but he is taking it hard. He does not want anyone around, but I think he needs you.' Liran looked down, saddened, and shifted in her seat.

Phran walked back into the room accompanied by Faiyor and Monitors holding stacks of books. Liran stood up, excusing herself, but Olbi cleared his throat. He needed Liran to know what he knew in his heart.

'Liran, the girl in your fresco, the girl in your sketch, I think it was Reeva, her true form.'

Liran didn't blink. She stood like a statue in the gardens outside, staring at him with unyielding eyes until she spun and glided across the room to Phran.

'Liran is turning the room into a public library for the Rahsu,' Zillah said to Olbi as they watched Phran's face drop at something Liran said.

'She wants the Rahsu to learn about their true past and to let everyone learn whatever they wish,' Joja said.

They rose from the table and Zillah led them out of the room. As Olbi moved through the Prime House, he could feel the energy of change surging through the place. This time would be a defining point in the history of the Rahsu. He hoped they were ready to protect themselves when the time came.

Zillah and Joja walked him to the garden cloister. It was midday, and the sun burned brightly above him. Several townspeople enjoyed the gardens, and Joja and Zillah seemed at ease. The townspeople barely gave them a second look. Gone was the fear and trepidation about their presence.

'What will you do now? Are you sure that the Unity will not be able to fly back to Anatara?' Olbi asked.

Zillah looked up at the sky—no clouds appeared, and the moons were lazily pale above them. Olbi thought her eyes looked like they were searching for something. Perhaps her home world was out of reach without repairing the damage inflicted on the crashed ship.

'I don't know about Zillah, but I plan on helping the Rahsu rebuild. Then I will assist Liran in discovering more about the Injai and the facility. There is a lifetime of information there,' Joja said, waving at Olbi and bouncing the way she had when they first met. Olbi smiled and turned to Zillah.

'I will help too, Olbi, with the rebuild and restructuring. Liran has advised me that my diplomatic knowledge could prove useful when the delegates from other Rahsu villages convene soon. They will be shocked and might not understand why the Manna Rites will no longer be necessary—no doubt they will take more convincing than Xylonans. As for the Unity, I will trek back and see what can be salvaged, but I don't hold out much hope.' Olbi nodded as she bowed her head and started back to the Prime House.

Olbi felt alone for the first time in a while. He had grown used to having people around him. His first instinct had been to grab his spear, which he had left in the Stonehall. His regular bed had been taken by people still waiting to repair their house, so Alvar had stored all his things in the cellar.

However, Olbi's thoughts quickly turned to Ayon. What was he considered now? If he had given up his birthright as the next Prime, what was Olbi's responsibility when fulfilling the role of his protector? He knew his feelings for Ayon ran deeper than mere dedication to duty and upholding his word. Profound feelings had developed, and he did not understand what they meant.

Standing in the garden, he watched a flock of birds fly overhead, their songs filling his ears and fading into the distance. They were flying towards the Great Lake. Maybe it was time to go fishing there like he had always wanted. Perhaps Ayon would wish to join him and continue exploring the world like they had always wanted. The idea moved butterflies in his stomach. An adventure, alone, just the two of them. Maybe it would help Ayon move on and help him with his new life. But first, he would need to find Ayon.

He had the feeling he knew where he would find the former Scion.

33

LIRAN

Phran was driving Liran to the edge. Every proposal she made was met with a new objection, the Head Monitor clinging stubbornly to the notion that the old ways—the deeply entrenched traditions—must be preserved at all costs. Still, Liran had managed to push through some shifts, hoping they would chip away at the rigid belief that a Prime One must possess the bloodline. But she wasn't foolish. The Rahsu would not all welcome the upheaval. Liran braced herself for the inevitable backlash, knowing that this fight for change would bring more than resistance—it would stir something darker, something that had been waiting, dormant, beneath their way of life. Claudya's death would bring about a renewed push for Ayon to sire children, and as for Olbi, if anyone revealed he had the blood, then there would be those who would turn that to their advantage. She smiled as she walked away from Olbi and the Outsiders and towards Phran and Faiyor.

The poetry of two people with the bloodline finding each other and forming a companionship was too beautiful. She wasn't blind. She had never seen Ayon care for someone as deeply as he did for Olbi. She hoped Olbi would be courageous enough to open his heart to the love they both desperately deserved. The Rahsu did not fear their love, but they did fear the unknown. If this was the path Ayon and Olbi would walk, then unseen forces would work against them.

'Faiyor, thank you for agreeing to meet with me. How fairs Tarak?' Liran asked as she took Faiyor's hand. Faiyor bowed to the new leader.

'Prime One, burn bright,' Faiyor said, a slim smile touching the corner of their lips. 'Tarak is well, he is a tough one and will get through this.'

Liran was relieved, not only for Tarak but for Olbi, who, out of the corner of her eye, was leaving the chamber with the Anatrians.

'Prime One, what is it you called me here for?'

'It will take some getting used to being called that, Faiyor. Please, I would still like you to call me Liran.'

Faiyor nodded, bowing.

'Down to business then,' Liran said, gesturing for Phran and the Monitors to leave. Phran wore an indignant expression but nevertheless clicked his fingers, and the other Monitors quickly moved from the room.

Faiyor and Cotsh had been helping around Xylona since the departure for the Forbidden Zone. With Faiyor's help, many of the wounded were remedied, and as for Cotsh, his toil at the mill ensured it was back in production, supplying Xylona with enough food to stave off famine. These were people she wanted around to rebuild Xylona in the wake of the preceding events, and to count as friends who could be vital allies in the days to come.

'Firstly, thank you for your dedication to Xylona's rebuild. We owe you a great debt.' Faiyor nodded. 'Please pass on my gratitude to Cotsh as well. I understand he readies himself for Hydoran.'

'The Hydorans will take convincing Pri— Liran. The idea that the Manna Rites and the lineage have ended will not bode well for Xylona if Hydoran does not accept your leadership. However, I believe Cotsh can guarantee a shipment of supplies quickly to assist with recovery.'

Liran rubbed her temples. The weight of a paradigm shift within the structure of the Rahsu was unknown.

'I suspect Hydoran may call their own Consanguine and exclude Xylona in defiance of the downfall of the Lyfera dynasty. Aldrowens will likely favour Hydoran efforts to re-

establish the Prime seat, and as for Kanowna and Japheles interests, well, that remains to be seen.'

Faiyor spoke true. Liran knew this.

'Might I suggest that you find your replacement, Liran? I fear you will need all the help you can get.'

'My replacement?' Liran said, surprised.

'The next Maven, Prime One,' Faiyor said.

Liran felt sick. She had entirely forgotten that Xylona was without a Maven. The image of Euyan's self-entitled grin flashed in her eyes, making her shudder.

Liran sighed heavily and ambled towards a bench by the window. Her thoughts danced nervously as she gazed across the vegetable gardens below where hands toiled, basking under the healing sunlight.

Already, she missed Claudya. Liran hadn't allowed herself time to mourn for her friend since Joja announced the Manna Rites were a farce told to the Rahsu. She pictured Claudya's smiling face and allowed herself a moment to weep. She hoped Claudya would be proud.

Being the Prime One was a title she never coveted, but now that she held it, she desired to live up to her predecessor's legacy. As for Ayon, she promised Claudya in her last hours to watch over him. Although he relinquished the Prime seat to Liran, Ayon was a born leader, filled with compassion and love for his people.

Faiyor said nothing but instead poured a goblet of water and placed it in front of Liran.

'Thank you, Faiyor. I apologise, it's been a week and well to be frank, the arrival of the Outsiders and becoming Prime One just came at a terrible time for me.'

Faiyor raised a brow, but Liran quickly chuckled.

'I jest, Faiyor. When you have lost everything, sometimes humour is all that can mask the pain.' Faiyor would understand soon enough. Liran mulled over what she intended to ask Faiyor since learning the name. It had been eating at her, gnawing at her quest to understand what happened *that* day.

Liran took a swig of water, regretting it didn't contain zirge.

She inhaled a heavy breath. 'Faiyor, last year I lost my son. I lost my only child, and for over a year, I have not known why. I believe you know of whom I speak.'

Faiyor placed a finger over their mouth. 'Spirits be damned,' Faiyor muttered under their breath. Liran continued slowly, fighting the emotion that stirred within like a treacherous ocean.

'Hayda was brought to me on the back of a cart, Faiyor. My only son. His pupils had been burned away, and the veins in his face were blackened and bulging like worms beneath his skin. The townspeople tell me a trader found him. Hayda had emerged screaming on the road south of Kanowna.'

Faiyor stumbled and found a seat, running their hands through their hair.

'Please, Faiyor, tell me honestly. What happened that day you found Hayda?'

Faiyor's head hung limp. When they spoke, it was with a quiver. 'I heard screams,' Faiyor croaked. 'I was camping alone by the road and cooking a rabbit over a fire.' Faiyor's gaze had clouded over as if in a trance relieving the memories. 'I remember scanning the forest, searching for the source of the screams. It was nearing nightfall, and the forest played tricks with my eyes, but I soon spotted a shadow bumbling through the undergrowth with outstretched arms. I brandished my sword, believing it to be a demon, as I was close to the Forbidden Zone. But when the shadow emerged from the murk of the forest, I saw it was a blind man speaking incoherently.' Liran flinched, gasping. Faiyor glanced up at her.

'Please continue, Faiyor, I must know.'

'I ran over to the man as he tripped on the roots of a garjee. He writhed around in the dirt, speaking of spirits. I asked him his name, but he couldn't hear me. He screamed again, his blind eyes staring into the trees. I looked up and saw an apparition cloaked in blue light. Your son screamed that the Spirits had tried to consume him. That they tried to inhabit his body.'

Liran clutched at her robes, unable to breathe. This wasn't the first time she had heard such stories, recalling the night of the Outsiders' arrival and the woman who had grasped Olbi. She saw the fear in his eyes that night: Olbi had seen the Spirits.

'Liran, I tried. I tried to help, but he was speaking in tongues. That's when I saw a second figure emerge from the forest farther down the road. She was looking for Hayda, carrying a blade, screaming his name.'

Liran didn't need to know who Faiyor spoke of as they began hyperventilating. Retelling the story was inflicting trauma on them both.

'Liran, it was Reeva. Reeva killed your son.' Faiyor broke down in tears as a burning resolve clenched Liran's heart.

OLBI

Along the road to Hydoran, an hour's journey north of Xylona, the route threaded a cut in a bluff. The jagged rocky outcrops here were the first quarries of Xylona and were some thousand years old, or so the townspeople believed. These days, the white stone of the ridge stood out like towering walls rising above the green carpet of trees.

The chalky alabaster stone served Xylonan Primes, providing a place to rest in a chamber carved into the side of the cliff face. Olbi wondered if there was a connection to the Injai. Much like the way the Injai structures had been built into cliffs, so too had a similar place been chosen for their Primes.

Olbi had never visited the quarries. There was no need, especially since there were no streams nearby to fish.

As meadows and farms fell behind him, Olbi walked into the forest. These were not garjee trees, but memories of his journey were fresh on his mind. The same birds he saw in Xylona continued to fly over his head, passing north as if to keep him company.

In his mind, he played over what he intended to say to Ayon. He questioned why he thought heading to the crypts was a good notion. Maybe Ayon did not want to travel and explore with him now he was no longer the Scion. Had Olbi read too much into their friendship? With each step, he thought of another rationale as to why he should turn back and instead retreat to the garjee and hunt or fish to help Xylonans who had lost everything. Olbi voiced his thoughts to himself as he walked towards the white stone.

'Muttering to yourself again?' a familiar voice called. 'This is why people think you are weird.'

Ayon sat on a smooth boulder with his legs folded. He held one of the Outsiders' tablets. Behind the rock, tucked behind the exposed roots of a tree that had long since died, the jagged entrance to the chamber of the Primes waited. In there, Claudya's body—as well as the past Primes of Xylona—would be resting. Each would be wrapped in a yar wool shroud, and a stone tablet would be placed over the cavity in the wall with their runes etched into it.

Olbi scowled at Ayon and then remembered he was grieving, so he softened his glare. Ayon caught the change and sighed.

'Please, not you too, Olbi. My mother and I had known for years that her time was brief.' Ayon slid off the smooth rock and landed in front of Olbi. White powder from the stone streaked along his pants in chalky lines. Ayon did not attempt to dust it off.

'When I was younger, my mother told me that she was a sickly child. The healers did not think the Spirits touched her. Many anticipated her death. Some said that her heartbeat was irregular, whatever that meant.' Ayon paced on the grass, his bare feet dirty and red. Olbi listened quietly.

'"Every moment is a gift, Ayon. Remember that," my mother forever told me. When she gave birth, she worried that I would suffer the same health problems as she did. When it became apparent that I would live and carry the blood, she did everything she could to ensure I was ready to lead.' Ayon smiled lightly and sat in the grass. He placed the tablet by his side.

Olbi looked down at the man whom he vowed to protect. Ayon looked back up at Olbi, the sun making him squint. He patted the grass, beckoning Olbi to sit down.

Olbi hesitated, peering into Ayon's dark eyes. He felt a flutter. Ayon appeared oddly relaxed as if a tremendous weight had been lifted from him. In a way, Olbi knew that to be true.

'Sit down, Olbi. I have something for you,' Ayon said.

❦

The grass felt soft as Olbi complied and sat next to Ayon. 'Ayon, I have something I want to say,' he said, folding his legs.

Ayon placed the tablet on the grass and turned to him, making Olbi feel nervous. He needed to come clean but wondered if now was the right time. His chest tightened as he speculated on Ayon's response.

'Ayon,' Olbi whispered, 'I did not know I had the blood until the forests. I didn't know how to tell you and grew worried you would think I wanted the Prime seat for myself. I do not want it. I have never wanted anything but to protect the Primes, to protect you from those who wish you harm.'

Olbi dropped his gaze, staring at a small flower at his feet. Suddenly, he felt Ayon's hand on his chin, lifting his face to look up.

'Olbi, I know, and I hold no animosity. If you had wanted the seat, I would have given it to you freely, but I know you would never want it. Your secret is safe with me. No one must know you have the blood. Plus, Liran is the only one that I trust to see the Rahsu through this time of transition.'

Relief spread throughout Olbi's body. He smiled gingerly at Ayon, who was now reaching into his pocket.

'I made you something,' Ayon said, bringing out a closed fist. 'Hold out your hand.'

Olbi held out his palm, not breaking contact with the eyes he cherished.

'Tayaun—the man that makes toys—showed me how to do this once. He was my teacher for a time,' Ayon explained.

Olbi felt something wooden being placed into his palm. It was small but felt soft to the touch. He looked down into his hand at a wooden carving of a four-legged animal with a big head and scratching's on its back, creating the illusion that the sculpture had fur.

'Now you will be able to take Boji with you wherever you go. Which leads me to the next thing I want to show you.'

A swell of emotions filled Olbi as his lips trembled. He was speechless as he stared at the effigy of Boji resting in his hand.

'Joja showed me how to use one of the tablets and connect to the dancing stars in the sky,' Ayon started, picking up the tablet and handing it to Olbi. Olbi looked at the images displayed on the screen: it was an intricate, coloured map of a large lake with hundreds of slim, snaky islands. Olbi looked up and stared at Ayon as a smile formed on his face.

'This is on the far side of Arbonar. Look, you can zoom in,' Ayon said, putting his finger on a small button. Olbi could see dozens of rivers, lakes, forests and vast mountain ranges. His eyes lit up. He looked up and locked eyes with Ayon, who beamed.

'So which isle should we explore first?' Ayon erupted.

Olbi did not know how to respond, but he had never seen Ayon so cheerful. Olbi laughed.

'You mean you still want to explore, even after everything that has happened?' Olbi said, his eyes darting to the front of the Prime crypt. He felt uncomfortable.

Suddenly, Ayon grabbed Olbi by the hand, brushing his fingers gently back and forth over Olbi's. Olbi looked down and swallowed, his cheeks turned red, his belly doing summersaults.

'Olbi, we need to reveal the secrets of the Injai. Together, we can bring them back, like they told you. We can help protect the Rahsu and reconnect the stars. Will you run away with me? Not as my guardian but as my companion.' Ayon looked into his eyes, searching for doubt.

Olbi's heart thumped as Ayon leaned forward.

Did he say companion? Olbi thought.

'Please, Olbi, the world does not need the Manna Rites anymore. The bloodline can die with us.' Olbi gulped as Ayon lifted his hand and placed it on Olbi's cheek. Ayon bit his lip and leaned closer.

Olbi smelt Ayon's perfume, and he felt a sudden rush of warmth through his body as Ayon's lips connected with his. Every nerve in his body was on fire. Ayon's hand caressed the back of his head, sending pleasure to Olbi's extremities. Ayon let go and looked deep into Olbi's eyes, with a wide smirk.

'I've been wanting to do that since your fifteenth birthday when we first met in the kitchens,' Ayon said, letting out a breath.

Olbi was speechless.

He looked up as more birds squawked above, crossing the sky, flying further north towards the Great Lake. Towards unknown parts of Arbonar. Ayon wanted to see what was out there, and Olbi wanted to help him realise those dreams.

'We may need to find a way to Anatara, that is where the Aetherian Codex is,' Olbi said, looking up at the blue sky above. The task seemed impossible. 'I also want to meet my mother, to learn from her. Maybe she knows more about the blood.'

Ayon nodded. 'We can do this, Olbi. Together we will find a way.'

'Let's go then,' Olbi said with a big smile.

Ayon squeezed Olbi's hand and leapt at him, clinging to him in a warm embrace. They lay wrapped together in the grass until the dancing stars crossed the dusk.

Olbi felt at peace, just him and his forever Prime One.

EPILOGUE

GIDEON SLOANE

Blood seeped through Gideon's uniform.

The wound radiated intense shards of pain down his legs where the bitch had stabbed him. When he had knocked Zillah to the floor in the tunnel, the wound reopened. He should have fired the gun on her, too, but no, the Injai needed to be neutralised first.

He limped down the tunnel, away from the others, leaving a path of bloodstains in his wake. Despite the pain, he took satisfaction in watching Reeva drop to the floor and his eagerness to report to his superiors urged him forward. Gideon would be delighted to report the Injai facility was fully operational, and on top of that, Reeva's demise meant that the Injai were not invincible.
He could kill them and remove them as an obstacle to what he sought.

The flashing lights and the pain formed a disorientating haze as he stumbled through a series of doors and hatches. How much blood had he lost? After an hour, he fell onto the floor, his cheeks connecting with cold stone. He opened his eyes and, through the blur, saw vents passing into the next room. Cool air gushed at his face.

With agonising exertion, he dragged himself across the floor, crawling slowly, leaving crimson streaks of blood. Rage fuelled him as well as the knowledge that right now on Anatara, and at Quartab Command, Jarrean soldiers were taking control of the Unity mission. He wished he was there, walking in and executing all those officers who remarked he shouldn't be on the mission.

The vent was tight, but Gideon moved through it quickly, pushing himself out at the end. Through the darkness, his eyes misjudged the drop to a platform beneath him. The three-metre fall through the air shocked him. He slammed into the metal landing with the cracking of bones—winding him—the clang of his impact echoed through the large chamber.

Gideon screamed.

The pain was excruciating. His left arm had shattered beneath his elbow. The only thing that answered his screams was the echoes of his exclamation against the unseen ends of an immense subterranean cavern. The pinging and rush of bat wings jetted around him.

He propped himself up. His muscles spasmed and convulsed as they fought the movement.

'Fuck,' he uttered through gritted teeth. The taste of blood slathered his tongue.

He grabbed his pill bottle with his good arm and heard the solitary capsule bounce in its plastic chamber. He opened the canister and chomped down on the bitter pill. It wouldn't stop the bleeding or reset his bones, but it was better than nothing to fight off infection.

Gideon closed his eyes and imagined Zillah's face when she learned Aster was under attack. It was to be the first target, a target he requested. He wouldn't forget her opposition to his selection for the mission. It filled him with a knowing satisfaction every time he had to obey one of her orders. Despite the discomfort it elicited, he chuckled into the void.

Gideon took a brief pause, inhaling deeply as the medication coursed through his veins, thinning his blood. As he reopened his eyes and surveyed the room he had landed in, a hearty laugh escaped him. Although it took a moment for his vision to adjust to the dimness, the colossal hulls shrouded in shadows confirmed he had found his prize. They were precisely where they had instructed him to go.

Operation Dormant Bird accomplished.

The eight beasts sat suspended in the largest cavern of the Injai facility. The last bastion of the resistance in the dying days of the Injai war. Weapons the last Injai never got to use and that now would serve Jaree. Gideon greedily soaked in the

❧

satisfaction that these immense weapons would dominate any enemy of Jaree and lead to their capitulation. Gideon couldn't take his eyes off the behemoths. They stretched for hundreds of metres, lying dormant in their millennia-old sarcophagus.

He reached for his tablet and brought up communications, turning on the record button. Gideon licked his cracked and flaking lips before speaking.

'Command, this is Commodore Gideon Sloane. I can confirm that all eight Injai battleships are present and accounted for. Send the scout mission as soon as Quartab is seized,' Gideon said before pausing.

He had lost a lot of blood and felt weak. He put back his fingers, pressing the record button. 'Tell General Jakkus that today begins the start of Jareean dominion over all Anatara and Arbonar. Tarea and Tobania will pay for their impudence,' Gideon declared before the pain became too much. He keeled over as the pinging validation from his tablet sounded around him.

Gideon successfully sent the message.

Acknowledgements

What a journey these last two years of writing have been! What started as a New Year's resolution turned into a world that I have fallen in love with.

Although writing is mostly a solitary experience, I couldn't have written this story without the help of so many people and resources.

Firstly, thanks to you. Yes, you. The one staring at these words. Thank you for picking up this book, downloading it, or even conveying it through interpretive dance. However you are consuming it, you have made my day. No, you have made my millennium.

Secondly, I would like to thank my book club, A Novel Idea: The Word Appreciation Society. Not only did they agree to be my guinea pigs, but they also pushed me to expand my mind by delving into an eclectic mismatch of genres. Thanks for being the first to read it, critique it, love it, yearn for it, and encouraging me to stick with writing. Reader, if you are not part of a book club, join one, do it now. I have discovered stories and worlds I never would have if not for being forced to. The scorn of a fellow book club member is a powerful remedy for procrastination.

I would also like to thank the following people who provided me with support, ideas, and genuine interest as I crafted the world of Arbonar:

James Savage, for his gamifying Excel spreadsheet which made word counts a challenge. You believed in me in the early days. You are a wonderful human and cynical bitch.

Crispin Roberts, for keeping me on my toes and letting me run ideas by him. I have missed those deep philosophical journeys we took together.

My brother, Tobias, your cheerleading pep talks were one of a kind. I always appreciate your support, and I look forward to writing more about Tobania in the future.

❖

Tina MacDonald, for starting an underground market of draft copies to get people hooked on the book. The number of times someone said they enjoyed the book before publication was truly staggering. If I ever need to set up a black-market book bazaar, you'll be the ringleader of that operation without a doubt.

Now, I was not a writer before this book. Sure, I have written a few travel blogs and witty Facebook posts, but there is so much thought and process that goes into writing a book. So even though they don't know who I am, I would like to thank the following YouTube channels that helped and motivated me to craft the best book I possibly could: Fellow Western Australian and fantasy writer Jed Herne, Brandon McNulty for his easy-to-follow YouTube content, Brandon Sanderson for his in-depth online lectures, and Jenna Moreci for her humorous insight into the world of writing.

Permit me to also mention the podcasts that I listened to. I didn't have any formal schooling around creative writing but delved deep into a rabbit hole of online content. Jim Thayer with his podcast *The Essential Guide to Writing a Novel*—I could listen to his stories and the antics of his mischievous cat, Jack, for days. And *Writing Excuses*, for their short episodes on all aspects of writing. One day I hope to join a writer's cruise with them, how very swank that would be.

To my coworkers who asked me questions about my book in the lunchroom where I wrote during my precious moments of free time. I know I was being a bore, knee deep in the edits, not engaging in the raucous gossip and chatter of the workplace. I am sure I gave you all the material to bolster my reputation as 'that boring gay'.

My editor, Liam Selby, you poor man, thanks for helping turn my random thoughts into coherent sentences. I appreciate all the advice and support and will get that sequel to you soon.

My first beta reader, Angela. You began as a stranger on Goodreads on the other side of this far-flung world, but not only did you help strengthen my novel, you restored my faith in humanity.

The staff of Cherry and Grapes in West Perth: Aron, Bee, and Christian. You kept me caffeinated and made sure I had a comfortable spot to park my bum and write.

Finally, thank you to my darling partner, James. Without you letting me lock myself away in the library, Olbi, Liran, and Zillah would never have been born. You were incredibly supportive, and I feel so loved and nurtured. Oh, and I really am sorry about Boji … I hope you are not still mad at me for that.

ABOUT THE AUTHOR

Wesley is a Science Fiction author from Western Australia, whose unique upbringing in the remote outback, often under some of the darkest night skies, shaped his fascination with humanity's place in the cosmos. A Political Science graduate from Edith Cowan University, he was home-schooled and lived much of his early life in a tent in regional Western Australia. When not crafting stories, Wesley can be found walking in nature for weeks at a time or sharing the quirky fact that, at 36, he still has two baby teeth.
He lives in Boorloo/Perth with his fiancé James and their little doggo, Oscar.

www.wesleycroft.com